Dravincia

By Blake Severson

Book One of The Dimensional Wars Series

To my Mom, the toughest woman I know. Keep fighting and don't give up, just as you have taught us.

Chapter 1

A Fool's Bravery

Arthur yawned as he leaned back in his office chair. While his job paid well, it sure could be annoying. Engineering had never given him any glory or fame, but he still enjoyed it. Someone had to make sure that the buildings stayed standing. It wouldn't do to have an eccentric rich guy's mansion collapse because his aesthetic wishes didn't include supporting columns and walls.

"I swear that clock is broken and not moving. It's been 4:30 for over an hour," he sighed, "Hey James, you have any plans for this evening?"

"Just sitting at home with the wife and kids. Might try to watch a little TV when the kids go to bed. You have any plans, Arthur?" James asked.

"Not really, do you want to go to the bar and get a drink tonight?"

"On a weeknight? My wife would kill me. She doesn't want to have to deal with the kids by herself this evening."

"Fine, if you don't want to live a little, I can't make you."

"Not all of us can live the carefree life of a single man. When are you going to find you a good woman to settle down with?"

"I've had a few women try, but none of them felt like the right one to keep around."

"Well, maybe one day, you can find a nice woman and settle down," James stated. "I'm sure it would thrill your Mom and Dad to have another woman around the family. When was the last time you talked to Eve and John, anyway?"

Evelyn and Johnathan Sorrenson were not technically his mother and father, biologically at least, but they were in every other sense. He had been with them for as long as he could remember. They had adopted him when he was about two years old.

"I called them a few days ago to check in. Mom gets upset if I don't check in at least that often. I'm sure I'll end up talking to her tonight."

Arthur's mom and dad lived in Phoenix, AZ. His mom was a legal assistant at a lawyer's office, and his dad worked as a general contractor. Arthur moved to Austin, Texas ten years ago, but would still go home and visit on holidays when he wasn't busy with a project. Other than his parents, Arthur didn't have any strong ties to Phoenix. He had one serious relationship that had crashed and burned. When that happened, Arthur moved away and started over. It allowed him to get his degree in engineering in Austin, and then he started working at his current job.

"Oh, finally time to wrap it up! I'll see you tomorrow," Arthur called to him as he saw the time on the clock.

Arthur grabbed his sketch pad off the desk and tossed it into his bag. He walked to the parking lot and ran his hand along the fender of his dark blue 1967 Chevrolet Camaro. The white racing stripes on the car really made it pop and drew attention. He had collected it partially restored a few years ago and had put the extra work into finishing it. Having extra money to work on a project like this was one benefit to his bachelor style life.

Luckily, the office wasn't in the middle of downtown, so he wasn't forced to slog his way through traffic. Within twenty minutes, he pulled into the driveway of the small house he had to himself. It was considered a small farmhouse that had two bedrooms and two bathrooms, but the city had grown into this area already, so there wasn't much open land around it. At least he wasn't trapped in an overcrowded neighborhood. The white house with dark gray shingles didn't stand out and was dull. It fit him perfectly fine how it was.

He walked into the house and to the office. His bag fell to the desk unceremoniously. A trip to the kitchen was his next step, but the refrigerator revealed nothing but some drinks and sandwich items. He couldn't remember the last time he cooked something at the house. He made himself a quick sandwich and sat down in the recliner to watch some television.

His phone came out and he swiped his thumb across the screen to wake it up. Scrolling through the options, he selected his mom's number and hit the call button. His mom picked up after only two rings.

"How's my baby doing today?" his mom asked.

"Doing fine. Nothing new going on in my day today. How are you and Dad doing?"

"Just working, as usual. I have a big case I'm assisting with at the firm. Your dad is working on that house for the Baker family still. They were able to get the roof completed today, so progress is coming along ahead of schedule."

"Well, that's good news. Is the old man taking care of himself? I know you told him to try and let some of the workers take on more of the load, but I know he never listens." Arthur said with concern.

"Your hard-headed father never listens. Work will be the death of him one day. I did hear one other tidbit of information today, though. Joanne is getting married." She said cautiously.

That one sentence hit him like a rock from a slingshot. He felt queasy all of a sudden. Joanne was his one serious relationship that came to an abrupt end when high school was over. He initially left Phoenix to get away from Joanne after their relationship had crashed and burned, but those feelings never completely faded.

"That's fantastic news! I'm happy she found someone," he said, almost a bit too forced.

"Any new women in your life I should know about?" she asked.

"No, Mom, you can stop asking me that, though. I don't go out that often. Work has been busy lately. I might decide to look for a woman when work slows down again, but it isn't a priority. I'm fine by myself."

"I know, I know," she responded. "I just don't like you being alone out there."

"I'll be perfectly fine. I haven't had a girlfriend for years, and it hasn't bothered me," Arthur told her.

His thoughts went to the girl he met at the bar last week and the fun they had. She smelled of lavender, and her smooth skin was tantalizing. They had a great night and had never even bothered to exchange numbers. The world moved on after the encounter.

"Well, I love you, and I hope you can come and visit us before too long."

"I'll see what I can arrange. Love you guys. Tell Dad I said hi."

"Will do."

Arthur looked at his phone and tapped the red end call button and put it back in his pocket. His mom never failed to ask about a woman in his life. She had been hounding him for years to settle down with a nice woman and start a family of his own. It just never seemed to be a priority to him. If a good woman came along, he would be thrilled, but he never really went out searching for one. He relaxed at home and watched some TV or sometimes played a video game, instead of wasting his time in bars and clubs.

The thought of watching TV fled his mind and his thoughts turned toward a nice, hot shower. Rising from the chair, his course took him in the direction of the bathroom. He never really enjoyed going to bed dirty unless it was for the right reason, of course. His clothes dropped to the floor, and he bent over to grab them. They were casually tossed in the laundry basket as he passed it and continued to the bathroom. The bland slate tile in the bathroom described most of the house. It was all simple, with no modern design tones anywhere in this place. Nothing was outdated, but it also wasn't a contemporary style decor. It was all neutral colors with a bare minimum style and no decorations to speak of.

    He turned on the water and went to the
mirror to inspect himself while waiting for
the shower water to warm up. Naturally, he had
to flex a bit here and there and check the
different parts of his body. Typical guy
behavior, he guessed. He was unassuming with
dirty blond hair cut short on the top with
sides shaved almost to the skin with a gradual
fade. His eyes were always a little odd to
him, though. They were a dark brown, but he
could swear from time to time they would flare
with a bit of red. It must be his overactive
imagination. He was right at six feet tall and
sat around two hundred and ten pounds. His
lifestyle had led him to be a little out of
shape. The gym was calling for his attention,
but he did a marvelous job of drowning it out.
His broad shoulders and torso always drew
attention away from his expanding midsection,
though.

    He finished adjusting the water after it
warmed up and hopped in. A quick scrub down
later, and he was out and dried off. He walked
over to his room and checked out his rather
bland queen size bed with bland solid black
sheets and a black and blue comforter. There
were no signs of a woman's touch anywhere in
this house. A t-shirt and some mesh basketball
shorts were pulled out of his dresser to
lounge around in.

Walking back to the living room, he heard some commotion outside. It sounded like a man yelling, but it was hard to make out. He peered out the front window and looked down the street. A man and a woman were standing next to each other, and it was clear the man was yelling at her. Her look told him she was either nervous or scared of the man. Arthur wasn't big on confrontation, but he'd be damned if he sat by and let a guy treat a woman like that for any reason. He grabbed his tennis shoes and slid them on as he walked outside.

It was early fall, so still slightly warm here in Texas. His limited clothing wasn't an issue. The breeze that blew against his skin was almost the same temperature as the house he had left. Next week would be a different story, according to the weatherman. As he got closer, he could hear part of the conversation.

"You thought I wouldn't find out you were sneaking over here, Dana? You must think I'm a fool!" the man yelled.

"I couldn't bring myself to tell you, Roger. I've been miserable with you and all of your yelling. Nothing is ever good enough for you. I cook, clean, and take care of the kids, all while still working at the local supermarket, but I just can't live up to the standards you want." Dana said with tears in her eyes.

"Well, if he is so much better than me, you can just stay with him." He huffed. "I don't want to see you back in my house again."

"Excuse me? I'm sure that's OUR house, and I can come back in it if I damn well please."

"If you don't want your ass beaten, I suggest you don't return."

"Oh, so now you are threatening me? Shouldn't surprise me, you are nothing but an abusive piece of shit anyway, and you wonder why I would be with another man. If you insist on me leaving, I'll make sure I get the house and the kids. It would be a good payment for the crap I have had to deal with from you." She sneered.

Roger exploded with rage at that point and backhanded her hard across the face.

"As usual, nothing but an abusive prick trying to compensate for his utter lack of a dick. You wonder why I would cheat on you? I just like to feel something during sex." She told him as blood dribbled from the corner of her lip.

The fury built in the man's eyes and he reared his leg back to kick her. Arthur took off at a run toward Roger.

"Don't you dare touch her again!" Arthur yelled, right before Roger kicked her. She lay on the ground, looking at her husband in defiance, holding her cheek. He turned and looked at Arthur.

"Mind your own fucking business, or you can join her on the ground." He replied.

That pissed Arthur off to no end.

"If you touch her again, you will be the one joining her. I have already called the cops, and they are on their way." He bluffed. He was sure he wouldn't know if that was true or not.

"You did what?" he yelled at Arthur. Arthur watched as Roger took a step toward him and then was surprised to see a fist flying for his head. The attack wasn't a complete surprise since he had just seen him hit a defenseless woman, but he still wasn't expecting him to react that quickly. Regardless, Arthur kept his senses and ducked under the hand. Arthur sent his right fist up and into Roger's jaw. The force of the blow stunned both of them for a moment and Arthur grimaced at the pain in his fist from the contact.

The man took a small step backward to regain his balance, and his head had twisted a bit with the punch, but it didn't seem to affect him too much. The man was obviously more familiar with physical violence than Arthur. Arthur wasn't trained in hand to hand fighting in any way, but his size, coupled with his naturally giant fists, was a lot of weight to toss at someone.

The pathetic excuse for a man looked back at Arthur and had an evil gleam in his eye. This time Roger took a swing for his midsection, and Arthur wasn't quick enough to get out of the way. The punch landed on his ribs on the left side of his body, and he immediately lost all the air he had in him. Doubling over and feeling like a fish out of water, Arthur tried to gulp some air back in but was not having any luck. Arthur lifted his head to see a foot headed his direction. The impact sent him backward, and he sprawled onto the concrete. The fall jarred Arthur's awareness back to the overall picture here, and he sucked in a sharp breath that burned as it came back into his lungs.

Arthur kicked out while on the ground and hit the guy's ankle. He let out a sharp yell and started to fall but caught himself with one hand. Arthur's kick had done nothing but infuriate him. He rolled to the side and got back into a crouching position.

"Get out of here and go somewhere safe while you can!" Arthur yelled at Dana. She had just about made it back to her feet while the fight was unfolding and looked up at Arthur with tears in her eyes and gave him a quick nod before dashing off toward the closest house. *I sure hope that is her lover's house so she can get help.*

"Oh no, you don't," Roger said as he pulled a pistol from the back of his waist and pointed it at Dana. *Was this guy out of his mind? Surely he wouldn't shoot this woman over an altercation in the street?* Arthur made it to a knee and dove at Roger's midsection, and they both went tumbling. During the fall, Arthur heard the sharp crack as the gun went off. Luckily, it didn't seem to hit anything. It was hard to tell with them tangled up on the ground, but he could still hear Dana running. That gave him hope she was uninjured.

He reached for the gun in Roger's hands to wrestle it away from him, and their hands both locked firmly on it. They were in a never-ending struggle to pull one way and the other. Arthur was struggling with all of his might but this man was slowly overpowering him. His forehead started to sweat as he noticed the barrel of the gun gradually turning to face him.

"Well, if you're going to be Mr. Hero and butt into business that doesn't concern you, then you shall reap the consequences. It looks like I have nothing left to lose anyway." He said with that evil gleam in his eyes.

Arthur heard another loud crack, felt a horrible pain on the left side of his chest, and all of his strength was immediately sapped from his body. He lay there on the ground, slowly growing cold with no energy to even move. Arthur could see the guy was on his feet and was staring at him.

"You can tell whatever God you pray to that Roger sent your wanna be hero ass to meet him," Roger said. He dashed off down the street and out of sight.

As Arthur lay there, his life started to flash before his eyes. He could remember the birthdays, the Christmas celebrations with his parents, even Joanna. He felt tears coming to his eyes over all the missed opportunities. *If only I could change things.* He thought as the world faded to black.

Chapter 2

A Second Chance

Arthur awoke in a solid white chair. *This is odd. I'm pretty sure I died,* Arthur thought to himself. That thought was interrupted by the view of his surroundings. An infinite stretch of pure white greeted his vision. He couldn't describe it in any other way. There didn't appear to be anything resembling walls as far as the eye could see. The bleakness of his surroundings was startling but the feeling quickly left. He was seated in a chair of solid white that blended in well with the surroundings. He reached down and touched his chest only to find everything was intact. There was no blood or damage of any kind.

"It can be a little disorienting, can't it?" A musical voice said.

"Um, yeah, and speaking of, where am I? Who are you? Where are you?" Arthur asked.

"Typical human, always impatient with endless streams of questions, although I guess it isn't unexpected in this odd scenario. Your first question is both difficult and easy to answer. I have you suspended between worlds in a dimensional space of my choosing. It isn't as simple as that, but that explanation should suffice. As for me, I'm called Lianna, and I'm a Goddess." Lianna said.

"A Goddess? Is this some sort of elaborate prank? I don't know of any Goddesses, especially not in any of our religions. I know there were Goddesses in some older religions, but I don't recall the name Lianna being used for any of them."

"Regardless of whether or not you know my name, it doesn't change your predicament. If you haven't figured it out yet, you are for all intents and purposes, dead."

Arthur's jaw almost hit the floor. This couldn't be right. *If I was dead, how could I be here breathing and talking to this floating voice…? Well, maybe that was a little of a red flag, but still. I remember the argument and the gunshot, lying on the ground, and wishing I could change things. That's all I can remember.*

"I would imagine this comes as a bit of a shock to you. Let me come join you, and we can have a civilized discussion about why I brought you here." She intoned.

Arthur spotted a flurry of sparkles ahead of him and to the right. Out of the shining mass walked the most beautiful woman he had ever laid eyes on. She stood close to six feet tall with perfectly flat strawberry blond hair that flowed to her lower back. The last foot of her hair gently curled into bouncing rings. Her body was in perfect proportions with all the curves in the right places. She walked with a majestic grace that would make a runway model weep as she moved toward where he was sitting. She had a perfectly smooth face with skin the color of pale moonlight, but most striking of all were her eyes. They reflected the purest gold color he had ever seen. The irises were solid gold that seemed to sparkle from time to time, but that could have just been his imagination.

She motioned to the side, and another pure white chair, identical to the one Arthur was sitting on, rose from the ground. It rose from the ground as if made by liquid and solidified, not five feet in front of him. She walked up to the seat and deliberately turned to look at Arthur as she slowly sat down in the chair. The pure sight of it made his breath catch in his throat.

"There, that's much better, don't you agree?" she said.

Arthur just sat there with his mouth hanging open. Her sheer presence made it almost impossible to respond. She was so beautiful that it didn't matter what part of her he gazed at. He would find himself stuck staring until he finally moved his sight somewhere else on her body, and the process repeated.

"I believe the phrase on your world goes, 'If you don't close your mouth, you will end up catching flies,' but I could be mistaken. The general idea is the same, though." She giggled.
Arthur felt his cheeks become hot and snapped his mouth shut. He finally got a little composure to himself and displayed a shy smile at her.

"I understand my visage can be distracting, especially to mortals such as yourself, but I need to have a serious conversation with you about your situation."

That caught his attention. "If I'm dead, as you stated, I'm not sure what I can do to help," He replied, finally able to get words out.

"Ha, you silly boy, it isn't what you can do for me but what I can do for you. I have a bit of a business proposal for you. You have some unique factors about yourself that allow me to interfere with your situation. Namely, your parentage and the circumstances of your death." She said with a gleam in her eyes.

"My parentage? I never knew my birth parents and my adoptive parents mentioned no details about them if they ever even knew any. What would my parentage have to do with a situation like this? This seems like a situation on a biblical level, not that I was ever overly religious."

"I'm aware of that, but since I'm not a deity of your world, that doesn't affect my actions."

"How would you be able to take action for my death then if you have no influence in my world? Not to cause any offense, but it seems to me there are at least some rules set down based on your earlier statement."

"Well, I can say I'm pleased you are smart enough to at least grasp that much based on the little conversation we have had so far. To answer that question is easy, and I was hoping you would put it together yourself based on the two conditions I told you."
He thought about what she said. The only two things she mentioned were his parentage and how he died. He imagined getting shot by some random stranger didn't have anything to do with it, so that only left the ancestry.

"Well, the only thing that would make sense is something to do with my parents, but I can't for the life of me figure out how." He said.

"I'll give you that much since you never knew of other planes of existence. The quickest explanation is that your parents were not from Earth originally, and in fact, were born on a plane I have at least partial reign of."

"Wait... so my parents are aliens from another planet? Is that what you mean by another plane?" He asked.

"No, it isn't. I mean your parents are from another plane. It's difficult to understand. The planes are similar to what humans on Earth referred to as dimensions in their theories. I have no direct reign over the plane that Earth is part of, but since your parents were from my plane, it gives me a chance to at least check in on you. The circumstances of your death allow me to extend an offer to you. Since you sacrificed your life to help save another, I've been given a chance for divine interference and allowed to give you a choice."

"While I appreciate the sentiment, I only did it because of a natural reaction and not out of any sense of heroism."

"I understand that, and it is part of why this offer is possible. You did it out of instinct and not trying to earn any favor or renown. The offer is both simple and complicated, though. I will offer you life, with some stipulations and conditions of my own. First and foremost is there is a time frame for your service to me, which will require you to serve my interests for five years. Once you have completed these five years, your life is yours to do with as you wish." She intoned.

"As long as you don't expect me to become some kind of assassin or a mass murderer, I think that would be fair. What would be the next stipulation?"

"The next part isn't so much of a stipulation as it is a warning. You are not allowed to betray me on our agreed-upon deal. If you try this, our deal is forfeit, and so is your life. This includes trying to partner with other deities without my consent to work with them."

"So, be loyal then, got it. Anything else?" Arthur asked.

"There is so much more, but alas, I'm limited in what I can tell you. This world will differ greatly from what you're used to on Earth, and yet much will be the same. The easiest way to summarize it would be to say that this world is what would happen if you took Earth and mixed it with one of the role-playing games that are commonly played there." She said with a grin.

"In what way? Are people going to run around with yellow exclamation marks over their heads, randomly run into objects, or get stuck on odd terrain from time to time?" He asked with a smirk.

"The plane of existence you are going to will track your progress like an RPG. There are skill levels for almost anything you do over there. For instance, skinning, mining, leatherworking, and so on. This also applies to combat and magic skills too."

"Hold on a minute. There's magic there as well? As in real swords and sorcery type of magic from fantasy novels and games?" He said in surprise.

"Yes, but it doesn't work exactly like the magic you know of. There are many ways magic is described in those fantasy novels and video games you refer to, and each differs from one another. You will get the hang of it quickly, I'm sure." She intoned.

"So, you're sending me to this plane for what purpose?"

"I'm glad you asked. As I stated earlier, I don't intend this to be anything distasteful, although there will undoubtedly be some unpleasant things by the end of your time there. I simply want you to help those you find and help make that world a better place. I wish for you to harbor goodwill among the citizens and eventually try to convert them to my worship. You will understand why this is important, the longer you stay there. The world itself is corrupt, and you will have to be cautious with some of those you help, but I have faith that you can do this."

"All of that said, there are a few little pointers I want to give you before I send you on your way. We are almost out of the allotted time, so I'll make this fast. The first thing is that I'll put you in a small wooded forest when you first arrive. I'll outfit you with some basic items to get you started, but that's the best I can do. You must spend time in this forest getting used to the new way this world works. It's also important that you take some time to gain some levels and skills because I will place you in the world at level 1. There's no way I can get around that, and honestly, you'll seem very odd to anyone there as a full-grown adult at level 1."

"Wait, there are levels in that plane as well?" Arthur asked.

"Of course, I told you it's like one of your RPG games." She huffed. "Now, don't interrupt me again. If I have any time to spare, I'll answer a few questions. Where was I? Oh right, progress your skills quickly and preferably before you leave the forest. Hunt the small animals and things to gain the experience needed to level up. You have played enough RPGs over your life to understand most of the things you need to know for this. Above all, do not leave the forest until you have gained a few levels. Most people in that plane will be level five by their teens, and most of that's just playing around or learning skills around the house to help out."

"You have one incredible advantage that others don't have. You know about the advanced civilization on Earth and many of its quirks. I have to stress this because it will be essential for you. This world is real, don't get sucked into thinking of it like one of your games on Earth. You can die, you can be wounded, stabbed, you can lose a limb, and anything else you can imagine that would happen to you on Earth. Just because it has some game-style elements doesn't mean it is that different. The thing I truly need you to remember is that because it is real, you can change anything in it. The normal restrictions you saw on video games do not apply here. There are no skills or items that aren't able to be discovered or made. The world rewards ingenuity and will seamlessly integrate new skills if you develop them. This will be your greatest strength if you can make it work for you." She explained.

"So consider mechanics like I'm playing a game, but remember that consequences are genuine, got it," he stated flatly.

"In a nutshell, yes. There are many things I wish I could go into more detail about, but our time is almost up, and I have to get you on your way. Do you have any final questions for me?"

"I think I have a firm grasp on everything you said. I would ask, though, what will happen on Earth with my parents and everything."

She smiled at him sadly. "They will get the news from the local police force, arrange the funeral, and everything will proceed as it would for any other funeral. I'm sorry there isn't anything I can do in that regard. Since you have accepted my offer, I'll compel the young lady you helped to come forward and testify to the events. This will ensure she can help police catch the person who killed you. I'll also make sure the story of your heroism makes it to your adopted parents, so they understand why they lost you. I wish I could do more, but, as I said before, I have limitations."

"That will do then." he sighed in resignation, "I don't want to see them hurt over this, but at least they can have a little comfort knowing it was because I was trying to help someone. Maybe that can help ease their burden."

"All right then, it looks like it is time to go. I will drop you in a forest that's in a remote area. This will give you time to acclimate yourself to the world a bit."

They both stood up from their chairs, and she walked up close enough to where they were almost touching. One last thought came to Arthur when she got closer.

"What is the name of the world, anyway? Might be important to know?" He asked.

"Dravincia," she replied and then forcefully shoved him backward. He stumbled and fell into blackness.

Chapter 3

New Beginnings

Arthur woke and quickly checked his surroundings. He immediately noticed the fresh smell of cedar around him. He slowly pushed himself up to his feet and started to inspect his surroundings. The Goddess Lianna must have been telling the truth. He was obviously in a forest. Some trees towered over him, while others were a size similar to those around his old home. He idly wondered how those survived with the larger ones blocking out so much of the sun.

There wasn't much visible underbrush around him. A soft layer of grass blanketed the ground below his feet, but it was easy to spot the numerous game trails worn through the forest, showing bare dirt.

"Well, I guess it's time to get started. The real question is where I should start," he said to himself. "I guess I can start with what the Goddess suggested and try to find some local wildlife to hunt."

A small bag lying next to him caught his attention. He picked it up, and to his surprise, it had a bit of weight to it. He carefully reached in and felt a sharp pain on the edge on one of his fingers.

"Ouch, damn it!" he exclaimed as the bag fell from his hands. Clanking noises emanated from the pack as it hit the ground. *Well, let's try this another way.*

He reached down and picked up the bag again. This time he held it lower to the ground and turned it upside down to empty the contents. A small collection of items fell out, and he immediately noticed the culprit that caused the slight bleeding on his finger. A small dagger lay on the ground amidst the collection of items. He vaguely remembered Lianna telling him she would provide him with some things to get him started.

He picked up the ugly dagger to examine it. There was no real ornamentation or decoration of any kind. It was sharp and functional, but that was the extent of it. He studied it carefully, trying to find any issues with it and noticed something flash in the corner of his vision. He jerked his head quickly in the direction he thought he saw the flash and found nothing but trees. A few moments scanning the tree line revealed nothing moving. He chalked it up to his imagination and turned back to look at the dagger.

After a few seconds of looking at it again, he saw the flash in his vision. Instead of turning his head to look in the direction, he thought about focusing on the disturbance mentally. To his surprise, what he saw was a floating, semi-transparent window next to the dagger itself. Not only that, but the window had writing in it. He carefully looked through what it said.

Item: Simple Iron Dagger	**Attack:** 3-5
	Durability: 35/35
	Rarity: Common
	Quality: Well Crafted

	Weight: 0.8 kg
	Slot: Main Hand/Off Hand
	Traits: A simple dagger made of iron.

"Holy shit!" he exclaimed as he looked at the window. The game style aspects of this world were already starting to show themselves. The question was, do other items here all have the same style of description boxes? He wondered if creatures and people had the same. "Really? Had to be kilograms, huh? Couldn't be good old-fashioned American pounds?" He said out loud to himself. "Even other universes shun our system."

A leather sheath was lying on the ground near where the dagger had been. It would figure the blade would have a sheath but be bare in the bag so it could cut him. Someone had a sick sense of humor.

His attention shifted to some of the other items in a pile. The next thing he picked up was a small metal box that he couldn't quite tell what it was. After looking at it for a few seconds, the ever-helpful window popped open to assist him.

Item: Tinderbox	**Durability**: 50/50
	Rarity: Common
	Quality: Well Crafted
	Weight: 0.3 kg

	Traits: Contains a small piece of flint, firesteel, and tinder for lighting fires.

"Well, that should come in handy." He mused as he read over the description. With some practice, he was confident he could figure out how to make it work. Using flint and steel to start a fire hadn't been a task he had tried before. The basic idea was easy to grasp, though. He then grabbed the next item, which appeared to be a waterskin.

Item: Simple Leather Waterskin	**Durability**: 50/50 **Rarity**: Common **Quality**: Well Crafted **Weight**: 2.0 kg **Traits**: Treated leather to hold liquids and sewn into a pouch. **Status**: Filled (40/40)

It was good that the item would tell him the contents. He wasn't sure how those numbers were measured, but it would be useful. The next thing he grabbed was a bundle of arrows. He pulled one out of the bunch and gave it a quick assessment.

Item: Simple Iron Arrow	**Damage Modifier**: +1 **Durability**: 15/15

	Rarity: Common
	Quality: Well Crafted
	Weight: 0.6 kg
	Slot: Ammunition
	Traits: Iron tipped arrow with feather fletching.

Those would be helpful, but he was a bit confused. They didn't have a damage amount on them, only a modifier. Then it clicked with him. The modifier must increase the damage stats on the bow. The bundle appeared to have thirty arrows in it. The thing was, he couldn't use them without a bow, and one didn't fall out of the bag when he dumped out the contents.

He swept his vision around him. There was a tree ten feet from him and leaning against it; he saw a bow. He walked over and picked it up.

Item: Simple Ash Bow	Attack: 5-7
	Durability: 40/40
	Rarity: Common
	Quality: Well Crafted
	Weight: 1.5 kg
	Slot: Main Hand/Off Hand

	Draw Weight: 20 kg
	Traits: Bow made of ash wood.

    Well, that at least solves that dilemma. Now that Arthur had both a bow and arrows, it should make hunting game easier. As long as there are no large predator style animals such as wolves or bears, he should be perfectly fine.

  He walked back over to the last two items on the ground. Both were small pouches tied tight with a string. He opened one and peeked inside. He found strips of dried meat in the bag and took it out to look one over.

Item: Dried Venison	**Durability**: 5/5
	Rarity: Common
	Weight: 0.2 kg
	Traits: Deer meat dried and ready to eat.

  This was a welcome sight and gave him some time to get acclimated here before he had to stress over food. He put the piece of dried meat back into the bag and cinched the string tight on it. He opened the final container and took a peek inside. It was filled with a white crystalline substance that smelled vaguely familiar. He took a few granules of it and put it on his tongue. He quickly discovered it was salt. Salt was a necessity in the world. He'd be able to put it to good use cooking and curing meats and hides if he could ever get the hang of the hunting out here.

As he gathered his items, he noticed
something he had not before. He saw he was
dressed in different clothing than he was
familiar with. He should have seen earlier,
but he had been so captivated with the sights
and then the bag of goodies he didn't pay
enough attention. Looking down, he saw that he
wore a pair of standard trousers with a small
brown leather belt. The pants themselves were
a brown color that was almost a light tan. He
was wearing a white shirt with what he assumed
was a green tunic over it. Arthur guessed he
was wearing a tunic, based on the historical
pictures he'd seen online.

"Well, I guess I need to blend in with the
locals once I find them. Can't show up in a
cotton t-shirt and basketball shorts." He said
to no one in particular. *I'll have to stop
talking out loud*, he thought to himself.
Someone would eventually come along and hear
him talking to himself and think there was
something wrong with him.

He picked up the two small pouches
containing the dried venison and salt and tied
each of them to the short leather belt holding
the waist of his new pants up. He also
attached the dagger sheath to his belt with
the dagger now firmly protected in it. He
picked up the bag that the items had been in
and dropped the tinderbox back into it. He
noticed it had a wide strap attached to it, as
well. He didn't know if this was common or if
Lianna threw him a bone, but he wouldn't
question good fortune.

He slung the bag over one shoulder, knowing
it would come in handy for hauling stuff
through this forest. Since it fit over his
shoulder, he could also use it as a makeshift
quiver and stuff the arrows back into it while
keeping the feathered end sticking up for a
more natural reach. The bag was deep enough
that the bolts didn't quite stick out from the
top, but it was better than trying to carry
them around with him. He separated a few of
the arrows from the bundle to let them sit
loosely in the bag if he needed to grab them.

Finally, he hefted the bow and took off
walking. He decided it would suit him best to
follow one of the well-traveled game trails
and see if he could find water. It shouldn't
be difficult to run across a small stream
here.

As he traveled along the path, he marveled
at the simplicity of nature here. The sounds
of the birds in the trees were soothing along
with the rustling of the leaves from the
frequent breezes it made for a rather calm
trip. He noticed a handful of bushes as he
walked, and some of them even had small
berries on them, he considered stopping to
pick a few but quickly changed his mind. There
was no guarantee that the fruit here would be
the same ones he was familiar with on earth,
and even if they were, there was also no
guarantee he could trust them on this plane.
The last thing he needed was to eat a berry
that said it was a blackberry only to find out
they are poisonous on this plane. He would
have to avoid the fruits until he could
identify some safe ones here.

He continued for what felt like hours, but
in all reality was probably only an hour and
stumbled across a small stream. The clean
water flowed through a small clearing and was
an enticing scene. He walked closer and saw
the bottom of the stream was layered in fine
gravel with larger rocks in the pathway from
time to time. Small fish swam throughout that
couldn't have been much more than a perch of
some kind.

He checked the water in his waterskin, and
it was still close to full. He had only taken
a few drinks of it, but honestly, the water
inside wasn't the freshest tasting to start.
He dumped out the water he had and refilled it
with the crisp, clean water from the stream —
no sense in drinking older, slightly stale,
water when he didn't need to.

He looked up from where he crouched down and
saw some movement near a small bush across the
stream from him. He sealed the water skin and
placed it in his bag. He picked up the bow he
had laid on the ground near him so he could
fill up the water skin and slowly fetched an
arrow from the bag over his shoulder.

He wasn't sure what was in the brush, but he
was determined to attempt to take it down
either way.

He pulled the bow up and knocked the arrow,
ensuring that the fletching was arranged
correctly to avoid damage. He was passably
familiar with the bow from deer hunting a few
times, but that had always been a compound
bow. This would be slightly more challenging,
but he hoped by shooting at full draw, he'd be
able to compensate for any small issues he
might have.

He pulled the arrow back until the tension felt right and held it. He watched the small bush that continued to dance from time to time but never in any serious manner. His arms started to ache after only a handful of seconds, and the strain was slowly proving a little much. He wasn't in bad shape but holding an arrow taut for so long used muscles many people didn't regularly use, and it was wearing on him.

When he thought he couldn't hold it any longer, a small brown rabbit hopped out of the bush and slowly started taking short hops toward the stream. He was sure the rabbit hadn't spotted him because it didn't appear spooked at all. He took a quick sight on the animal and let the arrow fly. The arrow flew true, but his aim was not as good as he hoped. The rabbit was twenty yards away, but his inexperience showed, and the arrow took the rabbit in the back leg and pinned it to the dirt. The squealing noises that came from the rabbit hurt him to hear. He didn't want the animal to suffer. He took off in a quick dash closing the distance and pulled the dagger out of his waistband. With a fast motion, he brought the knife down into the neck of the rabbit, almost decapitating it with the large blade, and the rabbit fell silent.

He heard a small chime, but he couldn't quite pinpoint where it was coming from or what it meant. He decided to ignore it for now, and he could contemplate it later.

He removed his dagger and inspected the
damage. He'd ruined a bit of meat in some
spots due to bruising when it was shot and
stabbed, but a decent amount was still in good
order. He carefully skinned out the entire
animal to ensure he wasted nothing. If it were
like most role-playing games, he could use
almost everything from it.

When he made the last cut to separate the
skin, he heard that chiming noise again from
earlier. He was beginning to think he was
going a little crazy, but he still saw nothing
around him. He picked up the skin and looked
at it. A window popped up next to it.

Item: Uncured Rabbit Hide	**Durability:** 5/5 **Rarity:** Common **Quality:** Poor **Weight:** 0.1 kg **Traits:** A normal rabbit hide that has not been cured for use.

His thoughts were correct. The world would
automatically identify items as he gathered
them. He wondered if it would have identified
the rabbit at all. It had appeared so fast,
and his shot had immediately followed. He
hadn't taken the time to look at it for very
long. He'd have to try that out next time he
saw something.

He laid out the hide, fur side down, and proceeded to clean off the bits of dirt and leaves he saw. He took a small handful of salt and roughly rubbed it into the raw side of the hide and allowed it to sit in the sunshine through a break in the trees.

He walked over to the carcass that he had set down on a rock and picked it up. He made a small cut down the center of its stomach and pulled the organs out of it. Arthur took the guts to the edge of the clearing so he could adequately discard them so they wouldn't bring any scavengers near him. He stooped over the water and thoroughly washed the rabbit. After cleaning the carcass, Arthur looked at it carefully. The window he had come to expect quickly popped into existence.

Item: Raw Rabbit Meat	**Durability:** 5/5 **Rarity:** Common **Quality:** Poor **Weight:** 0.3 kg **Portion:** Whole **Traits:** Raw rabbit meat that has not been cooked.

Well, that was a new attribute. Arthur imagined if the body were cut in half, it would be a half portion. He couldn't be sure, though. It could mean that the rabbit was equal to one full portion meal, but he had a feeling this just referred to its quantity. It would be easier to cook whole on a stick than trying to test his theory by cutting it in half.

He decided that this little clearing would make a good camp with a steady supply of water that was present. He found a spot near a large tree on the edge of the clearing farthest from the stream and started to stack up small pieces of wood. He'd never started a fire with tinder, but he had burnt plenty of brush piles back home during his earlier years. He knew that the way you stacked the wood was essential for getting the wood to light properly.

He arranged the wood in the way he thought would be best to light a fire. He placed a small amount of the tinder under the pile and stuck the flint on the fire-steel to spark. After a few strikes, he got the tinder to smolder, and after blowing on it for a few seconds, the tinder caught fire. He was so excited that he realized too late that the flame sputtered out less than a minute later.

He examined the pile and discovered his stacking skills must not have been as good as he thought. That and he was used to cheating by soaking a little gasoline on the wood first to get things going. The tinder had burned well, but as fast as it had burned, it caught nothing else on fire. It was time to try it again.

He stacked the wood a little different, and this time he kept a decent pile of small wood scraps and dry leaves to the side. This time, as soon as he got a flame, he carefully added some dried leaves to get the fire burning bigger and then stacked on some smaller wood scraps and twigs he had set to the side to build a more stable fire. A few minutes later, after careful tending and stacking, he had a good flame going and was rather proud of himself. It was a lot more difficult doing this than he had imagined it would be.

Yet again, he heard that odd chime sound. It just made no sense to him. Why would he be hearing chiming noises? There was nothing anywhere near him so he couldn't imagine where it was coming from.

Putting that in the back of his mind, he set up a small cooking rack. He found two forked branches and stuck them into the ground until they were sturdy on either side of the fire. He then found a straight and sturdy stick that would cross between them. He took the rabbit carcass and inserted the newly found spit through the center of it and rested it over the fire.

He sat there, enjoying the beauty of his surroundings. The weather here was lovely. He would guess it probably hovered around the seventy-degree mark with a touch of a fresh breeze here and there. The sun was still high in the sky, but based on where it sat, he doubted the temperature would rise much more than it was now.

He occasionally reached over and rotated the spit a bit with the rabbit on it. He didn't want to burn it inadvertently. He knew he had the dried rations in his bag, but there was no point in wasting something he might need later on. Collecting anything he could to help him survive now would give him a head start on his progress here.

He slowly turned the rabbit every few minutes and let it cook for half an hour. He was watching grease from the fatty parts slowly run down the rabbit meat. He would have loved to have a bit of seasoning to toss on it, but he saved the salt he had in case he needed to cure any more hides. Typically hides could be sold to local markets as a decent way to make money.

He removed the spit from over the fire and tenderly poked at some of the thicker portions of meat. As expected, it appeared cooked perfectly. He looked at the cooked rabbit and willed the window up for it.

Item: Roasted Rabbit Meat	**Durability:** 5/5 **Rarity:** Common **Quality:** Fair **Weight:** 0.3 kg **Portion:** Whole **Traits:** Rabbit meat that has been roasted over a fire.

     This time he heard that unmistakable
chime again, only immediately after, he heard
a resounding trumpet blast of duh-dun-a-dun.
What the holy hell was that? He thought to
himself.

Chapter 4

Self-Discovery

A feeling of power rushed through him immediately following the trumpet sounds. That sound itched at the back of his mind, though. Instinctively, he knew that he was the only one that could hear those sounds when they happened. When you hear the noise around you, it's typically possible to pinpoint a general area of where it came from. These sounds were different. They seemed to originate inside his mind.

Why do these sounds seem familiar? Arthur thought to himself. He knew something based this world on RPG mechanics since Lianna had told him as much. She also told him to make sure he leveled up. That was when it hit him. The trumpet blast sounded like a notification for something. It only stood to reason that if he could level up, he should be able to see his statistic display. He focused inward and imagined seeing his stats.

```
Name: Arthur
Level: 2
Age: 26
Race: Human
HP: 100/100
MP: 100/100
Stamina: 100/100
```

Strength: 3 **Agility:** 2 **Intellect:** 2 **Wisdom:** 1 **Endurance:** 3 **Charisma:** 2 **Luck:** 4	**Experience:** 25/750 (5 stat points available)
	Skills (25% boost to any skill for level up) **Combat Skills:** **Archery:** 1 (25/500) **Small Blades:** 1 (25/500) **Professions:** **Cooking:** 1 (25/500) **Firemaking:** 1 (25/500) **Skinning:** 1 (25/500)

Arthur wasn't sure if the screen was a good or bad thing as he looked over those stats. The thing he noticed that was odd was the age it listed him as since Arthur was thirty-three before coming to this world. That was a mystery for later. The stats were a welcome sight but didn't answer where the sounds came from. The trumpet sound had to be him leveling up since he was barely into level 2, but he needed to figure out the rest. He approached this a little different and instead focused on seeing a log.

Rabbit (Level 1) has died.
You have gained 25 experience for killing Rabbit (Level 1).
Congratulations, you have learned Small Blades for a 100 experience bonus. Be careful with that. It's sharp!
You have gained 25 experience in Small Blades for killing Rabbit (Level 1).
Congratulations, you have learned Archery for a 100 experience bonus. Stab it in the face, from a distance.

You have gained 25 experience in Archery for killing Rabbit (Level 1).

Congratulations, you have learned Skinning for a 100 experience bonus. Ew, it feels slimy.

You have gained 25 experience in Skinning for skinning Rabbit (Level 1).

Congratulations, you have learned Firemaking for a 100 experience bonus. Don't burn yourself on that.

You have gained 25 experience in Firemaking for making Basic Fire.

Congratulations, you have learned Cooking for a 100 experience bonus. A little blackened but edible.

You have gained 25 experience in Cooking for cooking Raw Rabbit Meat.

Congratulations, you have progressed to Level 2. Stay firm on your path!

Well, it appeared this world highly encouraged you to learn many skills. The critical questions were, did you only receive experience when initially learning them, or did they grant bonus experience as you hit certain levels? It will be interesting to see as he progressed. It was clear that he had some stat points he needed to sort out. Those would always come in handy.

He assigned 2 to Agility since that should help his Archery skill, 2 to Endurance since that should bump up his HP a bit, and for the fun of it, he tossed 1 into Charisma. This brought him to 4 Agility, 5 Endurance, and 3 Charisma. The Intellect and Wisdom wouldn't be useful since he didn't have magic, at least not yet. While Strength was always excellent, Agility seemed to serve him better. These adjustments also brought his HP up to 120 and his Stamina up to 120. That was a welcome change. From the looks of it when he put the first point into Endurance, not much had happened, but the second point pushed both up by 20. He assumed it had something to do with the 5-point mark but couldn't be sure how. He would hold on to the 25% boost to a skill until later. It was wasting it to spend it on this low of a level of skill.

With the self-reflection completed, he figured it was time to double down on the grind. The question was where to start. It was clear that leveling itself would take a significant amount of time since the kill experience for the animal he finished was rather low, but what else could he do?

He walked over to the skin he had laid out in the sun, and it looked different from what he remembered. As soon as the window popped open, he realized why.

Item: Cured Rabbit Hide	**Durability:** 5/5 **Rarity:** Common **Quality:** Poor **Weight:** 0.1 kg

	Traits: A normal rabbit hide that has been cured for use

That seemed to work faster than he was accustomed to. Hopefully, that would give him a bit of an experience boost. He pulled open his character status sheet again.

Name: Arthur **Level**: 2 **Age**: 26 **Race**: Human **HP**: 120/120 **MP**: 100/100 **Stamina**: 120/120	
Strength: 3 **Agility**: 4 **Intellect**: 2 **Wisdom**: 1 **Endurance**: 5 **Charisma**: 3 **Luck**: 4	**Experience**: 25/750 **Skills** (25% boost to any skill for level up) **Combat Skills**: **Archery**: 1 (25/500) **Small Blades**: 1 (25/500) **Professions**: **Cooking**: 1 (25/500) **Firemaking**: 1 (25/500) **Skinning**: 1 (100/500)

It looked like curing the hide gave much more experience than just skinning it. Arthur would have to check with other skills as well to see if building on that skill awarded more experience per step. It was time to get to work. He rolled the cured skin up and placed it in his bag. He piled two more massive logs onto the fire to let them smolder and keep the coals burning.

He grabbed his bag and slung it over his shoulder while picking up his bow and took off toward the edge of the clearing. Walking through the trees, he kept on the lookout for absolutely anything. He wasn't opposed to sitting in the forest and shooting birds if he thought it would help him level. He wouldn't mind finding more animals with fur for the skinning experience as well as the money those hides were likely to bring.

He walked around the trunk of an unusually large tree and froze in place. There was a boar that looked to weigh around seventy-five pounds grazing near some trees ahead of him. He knew they could be aggressive, and although he was small, the tusks he had on him could do some damage if he got too close. Not only that, but both their skulls and the hide near their front shoulders were extremely tough and durable. Placing an arrow just right to kill it might be a challenge.

He wanted to test out his theory of looking at its stats, though. With a bit of concentration, Arthur could get a status window to show up for the boar.

Name: Boar	
Level: 3	
Type: Creature	
Rarity: Common	
HP: ???/???	
Stamina: ???/???	
Strength: ?	Experience: N/A
Agility: ?	Skills
Endurance: ?	Combat Skills:
	Charge: ? (???/???)
	Gore: ? (???/???)

He assumed having some information was better than none. It was good to know its level, and it somewhat surprised him to see the skills it had listed. He had no way to know how developed the boar's abilities were, but at least it let him get a glimpse of what to expect it to try if it attacked. Nothing out of the ordinary for a boar in all fairness. It was also only one level higher than him, so it should be reasonably straightforward to take down.

He went for the kill and slowly brought his bow up and placed the arrow on the string. He steadily pulled back the line. Looking down the shaft, he picked the point he wanted to hit. He had aimed for the heart, directly behind the front shoulder. That should prove the best chance of killing it without too much hassle. A head-shot would only work if he could shoot it directly in the eye to avoid the thick bone on its face. With his skill level so low in Archery, there was no way he was taking that chance.

He took a steadying breath and released the string. The arrow launched directly at the target, and to his dismay, it hit a little further back than he had intended. Instead of a shot right behind its front shoulder, it hit closer to the gut of the beast. The boar squealed and jumped forward for a moment with the arrow still sticking out of its side. It came to a stop again and looked around until it spotted Arthur. He could almost see the fury in its eyes when it spotted him. It turned in his direction and charged right at him.

It was at that point he finally noticed he had been standing there like an idiot staring at the boar instead of getting another projectile ready. *Leave it up to me to screw up something simple.* He thought to himself. He tried to fumble through his bag and find another arrow quickly. After a bit of fighting trying to get an arrow free of the large sack, he realized it was now too late as the boar was almost right on top of him.

Right before it reached him, he quickly jumped to his left to avoid its charge, but much to his dismay, it still clipped his right leg a bit with its substantial body and sent him sprawling to the ground. Most of his items even stayed in his bag, but a couple of arrows had fallen out. He scrambled quickly to get back to his feet as the boar slowed his charge and turned back toward him. He didn't seem to have as much speed as he returned and wasn't running with his head down this time. Instead, he was staring straight at him with his hateful glare.

Instead of running into him, he stopped close to him and swung his head at him with his sharp tusks. He jumped backward, but the boar was so quick that one of his teeth caught the shin of Arthur's left leg and caused a shallow cut. This would inevitably end badly if he didn't try something else. Arthur could see it now. *Sent here for a second chance and killed by a level 3 boar. How embarrassing would that be?* With the beast already on top of him, there was no time to fit another arrow onto the bow. Facing this massive beast with his small dagger was laughable.

He did the only thing he could think of
and ran to his left. The thud of its footfalls
echoed behind him, and he knew there was no
way he could outrun this monster in a straight
footrace, especially if it charged him again.
Instead, he started weaving around the trees
to keep it off balance and to make it lose
some momentum-changing directions.

Rounding one tree, Arthur caught his foot
on a root and went sprawling into the dirt. He
struggled to regain his feet while hearing the
stomping of the boar closing in on him.
Reaching his feet, he started off again, but
before he made it three steps, the boar
crashed into him and caused a significant cut
on his right leg as he fell.

The boar continued past and started to
circle back toward him again. Arthur regained
his feet while trying to ignore the pain of
the new bleeding gash on his leg and took off
again, weaving through the trees.

After about a minute, he was feeling
somewhat winded and drained. He also noticed
he was slowing down a bit. He recalled a
stamina stat on the character sheet and
decided he must be running low. He thought
about the stat, and the stat number appeared
on the edge of his vision.

Stamina: 15/120

That confirmed his thoughts on the issue.
He had to do something quickly, or he would
run out of stamina and be screwed. He had a
small cut and got hit a bit by its charge, so
Arthur also pulled up a partial stat window to
check the vital stats.

HP: 45/120

It was plain he had taken some damage. The worst part was he knew that the hits he got on him were not very solid except the last one, so he guessed the damage was much lower than it could be. He started looking around, trying to see what else he could do. It was obvious, based on how long they had run so far, that this monster would not reset like a video game and just give up and walk back to where it was.

He glimpsed a slightly lower branch up ahead that looked low enough for him to reach and sufficiently sturdy for it to hold him. He only hoped and prayed this would work. He dropped the arrow he had been holding, knowing he couldn't get it nocked in time and slung the bow onto his shoulder. When he was close enough to the branch, he jumped with everything he had and grabbed the branch. He pulled and slowly lifted himself up and onto the branch. Luckily the boar wasn't large enough to reach him even from this relatively low perch he had found.

The boar stared at him from the ground, so he decided it was a good time to finish this. He steadied himself on the branch and pulled his bow off his shoulder. He grabbed an arrow from his bag and sighted it on the boar. When he let fly, it hit closer to the heart but higher along its spine this time. The boar squealed this time but wasn't moving as fast. The thing was resilient, so Arthur fetched one more arrow, sighted on the boar, and shot. This time, the boar went down from the shaft and lay there unmoving.

He sat on the branch sucking air from the long run. He leaned back near the trunk of the tree to relax for a few minutes and let his heart slow down. The adrenaline of the situation started to wear off, and some exhaustion was creeping in. It was clear now how badly that encounter could have gone even though it had appeared to be simple. Once his breathing had slowed, and he was a little more in control of his emotions, he lowered himself from the tree limb.

He walked over to the boar and gave it a fearsome glare for a while until he was sure it wasn't breathing anymore. He reflected on the encounter he just had with this wild beast and yearned to learn more about it. With that thought in his mind, he visualized a combat log for the encounter, and luckily it responded to his wishes.

You have dealt 14 HP damage to Boar (Level 3) with Simple Iron Arrow.

Boar (Level 3) has dealt 15 HP damage to you with Charge (Glancing Blow).

Boar (Level 3) has dealt 20 HP damage to you with Gore (Glancing Blow).

Boar (Level 3) has dealt 40 HP damage to you with Charge.

You have dealt 28 HP damage to Boar (Level 3) with Simple Iron Arrow (Critical).

You have dealt 8 HP damage to Boar (Level 3) with Simple Iron Arrow.

Boar (Level 3) has died.

You have gained 100 experience for killing Boar (Level 3).

You have gained 100 experience in Archery for killing Boar (Level 3).

Arthur was thankful to see it on the ground and was elated at the kill itself. It was odd how the damage didn't appear to line up with his weapons damage statistics, though. There must be special modifiers he didn't know about yet. He would discover that as time went on or he could ask someone when he thought he had a high enough level to venture on.

Arthur spent the next five days roaming the area around his camp by the stream. He never ventured farther than half a day away to ensure he could make it back to his camp by nightfall. This allowed him to rack up many more kills and more experience. Overall, he could get his level up to five and improve many of his skills.

Name: Arthur **Level:** 5 **Age:** 26 **Race:** Human **HP:** 120/120 **MP:** 100/100 **Stamina:** 120/120	
Strength: 3 **Agility:** 4 **Intellect:** 2 **Wisdom:** 1 **Endurance:** 5 **Charisma:** 3 **Luck:** 4	**Experience:** 350/1900 (15 stat points available) **Skills** (100% boost to any skill for level up) **Combat Skills:** **Archery:** 3 (700/1000) **Small Blades:** 2 (150/750) **Professions:** **Cooking:** 2 (400/750) **Firemaking:** 2 (700/750)

Arthur hated nothing more than being so indecisive. Instinctively, he knew that sitting on all those stat points was a complete and utter waste, but it was hard to tell what would be the best use for them. If he was honest with himself, he didn't want to focus on a pure archery class and would have preferred to be a caster of some kind. What person on Earth didn't dream of being some all-powerful magician at one point in their lives? The problem was that it was hard to justify using those points for stats that he may not have a use for in the foreseeable future.

It was also holding him back a little on progressing with faster kills, he was sure. The plus side was that it awarded him five points per level to play with. This seemed a little steep compared to some other games he used to play, back on Earth, but who was he to judge this world? He also discovered some new attributes to his skills. The initial level when he learned them had given him a boost to experience, but so far, he had received no more as he leveled them up. What he discovered is that they had given him additional perks when he had leveled them. He went back over the notifications he had seen.

Congratulations, you have progressed to Level 2 in Archery. You are granted a 2% bonus to accuracy. The arrow that flies is the best kind.

Congratulations, you have progressed to Level 3 in Archery. You are granted a 4% bonus to accuracy. How did you miss? It was three feet in front of you!

Congratulations, you have progressed to Level 2 in Small Blades. Your attack speed has increased by 2%. Watch what you poke in the back.

Congratulations, you have progressed to Level 2 in Cooking. Dishes you cook gain a 3% bonus to effectiveness. Still not very edible but getting there.

Congratulations, you have progressed to Level 2 in Firemaking. You have a 3% better chance of successfully lighting a fire. Well, we may make a caveman out of you yet.

Congratulations, you have progressed to Level 2 in Skinning. You have a 4% chance for any furs you skin to be of a 1 level higher quality than your skill would typically allow. Just throw some salt on it I'm sure it will be fine.

Congratulations, you have progressed to Level 3 in Skinning. You have an 8% chance for any furs you skin to be of a 1 level higher quality than your skill would normally allow. Clean the blood off first!

After some trial and error, Arthur also streamlined some of his notifications, so he only got the information he needed to see. While before he had to actively will any information, he needed to come up, Arthur could now customize what he saw and when. He had experimented with showing actual damage from the combat log while fighting a few of the animals he had hunted and quickly discovered that this method worked pretty well. The skill gains and other notifications felt natural to him as they flowed into him. It didn't distract him during a fight, and it seemed that he just knew the information. It didn't take up any of his vision or anything, so it never affected his combat.

It was time for Arthur to make his way out of this forest and find some inhabitants of the world. With the amount of meat and skins he had gained, it was time for him to find somewhere to offload the goods and stockpile some necessities. He should at least be high enough level not to look overly suspicious.

He had also almost run out of arrows now. Many of them had broken during his hunting, and while the iron heads were usually intact and it was simple to get replacement shafts, the issue came when trying to find suitable fletching and an adhesive for it. Since he was down to only ten, he did not feel very comfortable staying in the forest for much longer. Adding in the fact that he wasn't sure how much travel it would require to leave the woods and find a town for supplies, he decided now was the time to go.

Before he left, he wanted to get the stats out of the way, though. After careful thinking, he had decided he was hampering himself pretty severely, and in all honesty, if he could get five points per level, it wouldn't take him long to accrue more points for further stats later. With fifteen points to play with, he went with 5 points into Strength to bring it up to a respectable 8. It wasn't overly critical now, but he was sure it would help him lug more weight if nothing else. He had felt his muscles grow stronger when he selected that option. When he looked at his stats after this, he noticed that both his Stamina and his HP had jumped up 20 points. Another mystery he couldn't figure out right now but would have to look into it.

Next, he dropped 4 points into Agility, bringing him up to 8. Since he was currently focusing on Small Blades and Archery, that skill would greatly benefit them. He noticed that every point he invested from 5 and on in Agility made him feel a little faster. He couldn't quite explain it, but he felt like he could move and run quicker.

He also put 3 more into Endurance to bring it to 8 as well. Having more health and Stamina was always a good thing. This added another 60 to each of those stats, so Arthur assumed he was getting 20 HP and 20 Stamina for every point of Endurance he invested in. He also dropped 2 points into Charisma to make it an excellent 5 since he would have to interact with other people before long, and he even invested 1 into Luck to hit 5 with it.

The low numbers for Intellect and Wisdom made him feel bad, but he could always make it up later if he ever found any skills needing those stats. He was happy with his current setup, though. He felt a little lighter on his feet, and his bag, now loaded with all of his supplies and the many numerous hides he had cured, felt much lighter than it had before. Also, seeing he now had higher health and stamina made him feel more secure.

He topped off his water skin and ensured everything was packed. He grabbed his bow that had been leaning on a nearby tree and bid farewell to the only home he had known in this world. He was off to see the world.

Chapter 5

Alem's Crossing

Arthur worked his way through the forest in a northeastern direction, as far as he could tell. He kept walking through the day and would stop to camp at night. Carrying all of his belongings, Arthur hadn't been able to travel without making a considerable amount of noise, so this had allowed no hunting. He had enough cured food in his bag to last him a long time on the road, so it was unnecessary, anyway. He occasionally passed by small creeks and streams and would refill his waterskin when necessary.

Midmorning of the fourth day, he finally broke through the tree line and looked out over an open field. The view before him was bleak. It was an area that should have been picturesque. Long, rolling hills that should have been covered in tall, swaying grass should be everywhere the eye could see. This landscape looked barren, to be honest. He could see something on the horizon along with a hard-packed dirt round that might be a town but was hard to tell.

The forest had seemed beautiful when he
was out in it, but he had noticed that the
closer he got to the edge, the sicklier the
trees had looked. What in the world could have
happened to this land to make it look this
bad? It looked like the land had just given up
and laid down to wait and die. Nothing seemed
to grow anywhere.

With a resigned sigh, Arthur decided he
could do nothing but move forward. He took off
toward what he assumed was a town. As Arthur
got closer, he noticed there was plowed land
for planting around the village, but it didn't
appear to be growing much of anything. Most of
the fields lay empty. As he got even closer,
he also noticed that the town was a semi-small
affair with what appeared to be eighteen
houses of varying design and repair, and one
modest-sized building that he assumed was an
inn based on the posts out front to tie
animals too. That building also had a stable
next to it, so it seemed to be the most
logical conclusion.

Arthur didn't see anywhere that looked like it was a shop, so he visited the inn. He knew it wasn't uncommon for an inn to act as a merchant shop for essential goods in small towns. As he approached the inn, he noticed a few people milling around some of the houses. Most of them were wearing clothes that looked threadbare, and they also appeared somewhat malnourished. A few looked like they hadn't had a bath in months. Arthur had even forced himself to wash off in the chilly stream before he left his small glade. The smell he had accumulated was driving him crazy. Learning to live with some dirt and grime had been annoying to him the first few days after he arrived. You sure took daily hot showers for granted until you didn't have them anymore.

Many of the villagers gave him cursory looks and quickly continued on their way. None of them even had the courtesy to say hello or give him a nod in greeting. This was turning into a dismal state of affairs.

He walked into the inn and noticed that there wasn't a single customer in the building. It was close to the middle of the day, so Arthur had thought there might at least be a couple of people here enjoying some lunch. The man behind the bar let his gaze lazily sweep toward Arthur as he entered. The man had seen better days. He was almost as threadbare looking as some people Arthur had noticed outside. The bar itself was at least relatively clean. The most concerning problem here was the man looked far too malnourished. It was hard to trust a cook who was that skinny. The bigger and more joyous looking guys and gals cooked the best food. You could tell because they ate it abundantly to get their figure. Arthur wasn't sure he would trust this sad-looking man to make a dish for his dog if he had one.

Arthur walked up to the man at the counter, and the man eyed him suspiciously. He looked over Arthur's shoulder at the bag he was carrying and got an odd look to his face.

"Greetings," Arthur said.

"Hello? What brings you to Alem's Crossing?" The innkeeper replied.

"I was looking for somewhere in the town I could sell some of my goods. I have some furs and excess meat I would part with." Arthur said with a smile.

"What do you mean, excess meat? I don't believe such a thing exists anymore," The innkeeper said in a deadpan tone.

Something was seriously off here, and he couldn't imagine what it could be. Arthur wasn't familiar enough with absolutely anything in this world to even guess at the woes of these people. He needed some information on the current state of affairs, but he had to be careful doing it.

"I'm from a place much farther away on the other side of the forest southwest of here, so I'm not sure what you are referring to," Arthur told him cautiously.

The innkeeper gave him a long look before sighing.

"I didn't think anyone could even pass through the Forest of Nodara safely, but I guess it could be possible. Let's say I believe you, just to simplify things; there isn't much I can do to help you, unfortunately. I'm sure you noticed the sad state of affairs outside when you entered the village?" He asked.

"I noticed the place looked a little worse for wear. What has happened here to make things so bad?" Arthur asked in return.

"You must truly be from the other side of that large forest if you don't know. The local lord has crushed everyone here and in the lord's domain. He keeps taking more from us until we can barely survive. Therefore, I said I couldn't help you. I honestly don't have any coin to provide you with." He stated matter of factually. "The only reason we haven't all starved to death is that we live in the farthest corner of the lord's domain, and he doesn't send his enforcers out this way very often, but when he does, they strip everything. There isn't a thing we can do to stop them even if we wanted to."

"Well, if you have no coin, do you have
any items you would part with for trade? I
would hate to see good meat go to waste."
Arthur smiled.

"As I said, they took everything. I would
tell you to continue to another city along the
road, but I have a feeling things would be
just as bad there, if not worse. The closer
you get to the lord's seat of power, the worse
things get. You have to travel through his
entire territory just to get to another place.
We are walled in by almost impassable
mountains on all sides except the forest you
came through. Many who try to navigate through
there either end up wandering right back out
to here or never return."

"I have an idea then, based on what you
have told me, I have no desire to trek through
the countryside just to get caught in worse
places, so what if I trade you the meat and
some furs I have for rooms and food? I know
you have little to offer, but if I'm going to
stick around here for a bit, this place would
be great for me to stay at." Arthur said
happily.

"Well, I suppose I could agree to that.
There shouldn't be any problem from any of the
lord's men for some time since they were here
recently, so it should be relatively quiet for
you."

"That won't do," Arthur responded. "I'm a
bit of an adventurer and am looking for some
tasks to help improve my skills. Do you or
anyone nearby know of anything around here
that needs to be dealt with? An infestation of
creatures somewhere? An odd location that
needs investigating? I don't expect big
rewards or anything just looking for ways to
increase my power a bit."

The innkeeper gave Arthur an odd look. "You don't look like a member of the Adventurer's Guild, but who am I to question. I didn't think they allowed anyone your low of level myself, but we rarely ever see one of their types around here. The lord runs them out quickly if he finds them in his lands."

"I'm not a member of the Adventurer's Guild," Arthur responded quickly. He didn't want him mistaking his ignorance for a false claim on something. That was a quick way to get himself into trouble.

"I'm working on my skills, though, and may one day entertain the idea of joining them," Arthur explained.

"I know there are a few people around the village who could use some good, honest help but don't expect a big reward for any of it. They are as destitute as or worse than I am. You could try Dalia down the road. She lives three houses down on the right. She has been looking for someone to help clear out a problem." He told Arthur.

"Thank you for the advice." Arthur pulled out five of the smaller hides he had cured and laid them on the counter. He then pulled out five of the larger muscles he had taken off of the boar who'd caused him so much trouble and laid them on the counter. While the innkeeper looked pleased when he saw the furs, Arthur was almost sure the man would burst into tears when he saw the meat he laid on the table. It was clear the people had eaten little.

"If things are truly so bad, why does no one try to hunt any of the forests near here?" Arthur asked.

"Oh, we have had plenty who tried, but, as I told you before, they either wander right back out of the forest or don't return. We also have nothing to our names. There are only a couple of villagers here capable of using a bow in the first place, and they sold their bows since they couldn't find anything in the forest. We have one ranger who does her best to help keep the village from falling apart, but she is wary of traveling too far by herself with the disappearances. The enforcers came through and took almost every bit of our planting stock, leaving us with almost nothing to plant. I fear the village won't survive much longer. Each time these enforcers show up, they take more than last time, and I'm not sure the village can survive after this round." He stated dejectedly.

"Well, would these furs and this meat be acceptable for, say a fortnight? I could provide more meat every few days as well for dinner." Arthur asked.

The innkeeper looked Arthur over, nodded at him, and extended his hand. Arthur took it, and he gave a firm handshake. Immediately after the handshake, he saw a notification pop up.

Congratulations, you have learned Barter for a 100 experience bonus. Money runs the world.

You have gained 1300 experience in Barter for this transaction.

Congratulations, you have progressed to Level 2 in Barter. All trading agreements will favor you with 1% more value to your goods. Rub those coins together.

Congratulations, you have progressed to Level 3 in Barter. All trading agreements will favor you with 2% more value to your goods. My precious.

Arthur realized he must have had good favor on his side of that bargain to get enough experience for it to jump straight to level 3.

"I think I'll take some of my items to my room and then go check with Dalia, as you suggested," Arthur told the innkeeper.

The innkeeper nodded, reached under his counter, and removed a key he handed to Arthur.

"Here is the key to your room. The doors and windows are sturdy, and the lock is in good repair, so anything you wish to leave behind should be safe. You can have the door at the end of the hall." He told Arthur.

"I appreciate it," Arthur said as he grabbed the key and moved up the stairs. The room that the innkeeper had referenced was spacious enough for his needs. It was roughly the size of an average-sized motel room back on Earth. This room only had a small bed with a lumpy-looking mattress, but it appeared to be clean. There was a small chest at the foot of the bed for storing personal items

He placed the remaining skins and about half of the salted meat he had gained into the chest. That was enough weight to make him feel a little better walking around. He wouldn't put all of his food in there in case he ended up on a quest that would take him from the village. He closed the chest and locked it. He tossed the key into his bag, hoping he didn't end up losing it amongst his other possessions. Shouldering the bag, he walked back out of the room and locked the door behind him.

Arthur took off down the stairs and headed outside. The innkeeper was nowhere to be seen, but that didn't concern him — no need for the man to be out here with no other customers. From the sound of it, he hadn't had many customers in a while. Once on the packed dirt road, he started toward Dalia's house. Half of the buildings here looked like they were on the verge of collapsing. The occasional patchwork of stray boards could be seen nailed at odd angles. It was obvious someone that didn't have much skill in construction made the repairs.

He made it to Dalia's house and walked up to the door. He had raised his hand to knock on the door when it flew open wildly, and a somewhat frizzy-haired woman stepped forward. She was a small thing that stood around five and a half feet tall with fiery red hair. She had a light patchwork of freckles on her cheeks, but that didn't detract from her good looks, even if she was a little dirty.

She brought her hands to her hips and glared at Arthur.

"What do you want?" she asked in a less than friendly tone.

"I just came from the inn, and the innkeeper told me you might need the help of someone interested in a bit of adventuring," Arthur said. She began to answer him, but he wanted to head off part of this conversation before it started. "Don't worry, I understand at least some of the hardship here and am not expecting much of a reward or money in return. I merely wish to help while I'm here in the village."

She looked at him with her mouth open and slowly closed it. She stared at him for a few moments and then opened her mouth again to start speaking.

"Well, if you put it that way, I guess I can't refuse, can I? There is something I need, but that's a completely different matter." She said to him with a shy smile and a wink. "That's not related to what you came here about, though. I could use your help with a small issue. In the forest directly south of the village, there is a ruined manor house. The house itself is roughly a mile into the forest. The manor was once a holding in my family before ill-fortune struck us generations ago. Some items in the house could help improve my status in the world if I had access to them. If you retrieved them for me, I would be ever so grateful, and I'm sure we could come to terms with an appropriate reward."

She put a little extra emphasis on an appropriate reward, so he had a general idea of what she proposed might be part of that reward. After looking at her and talking to her, he didn't disagree with the notion.

"That seems easy enough, but what is the catch?" Arthur asked.

"Well, the forest itself can be dangerous, and I don't have the skills to protect myself. The main problem is the manor is supposedly overrun with some type of creatures, but I know not what." She replied.

Arthur knew that the vague response probably meant there was something relatively nasty waiting there for this quest. He also saw a small notification icon flashing in the top right of his vision. He checked it to find a message waiting.

You have been offered the quest:

Patents of Nobility I	
Requirements: Level 5 Rewards: 1000 experience, 1 silver coin, unknown rewards also possible.	Description: Dalia has asked you to infiltrate her family's decrepit manor and recover items that could help prove her status among the gentry.

That much experience was nothing to turn your nose up at. Arthur considered the request and decided that the threat should be negligible since it was only level 5. It might also be useful to be on her side in case she could raise her status. It was becoming apparent that Arthur would probably be stuck in this small village for a while, or at least until he got a little stronger. If she turned out to be nobility, as the quest title suggested, this could be a great opportunity.

"I'd be happy to assist you with this," Arthur replied with a smile, which earned him a smile in return from her. "I guess I'll head out now to take care of this matter for you. I have everything I should need already with me, and there should be plenty of daylight left to make the trip."

Arthur turned to head toward the door when he felt a firm swat on his right ass cheek. He looked over his shoulder to see a coy smile plastered on her face and with one more wink; She turned and slowly walked further back into the house, swaying her hips a bit the whole way. Arthur sighed and had to smile to himself. She was a feisty one, and he liked women who knew exactly what they wanted and weren't afraid to go for it.

Arthur walked back onto the dirt road, and as soon as he passed the edge of the house, he turned south. Since there were no other directions, he assumed there would be some kind of trail he would stumble upon after he reached the forest. With no further details on the location, this was all he had to go by. There were a couple of small farm plots in this direction, but nothing that would hamper his travel. As with the other fields, he saw when entering the village, there wasn't much planted in these fields. They looked more like small personal gardens than an actual farm plot. Arthur idly wondered how that would be sustainable to this lord's domain without the excess crops he would require in tribute. This should eventually cause the entire kingdom to collapse.

There were also no walls of any kind around the village, other than those skirting a couple of farming plots, so it was a easy walk to make it back to the forest. This forest wrapped around the southern side of the village itself and continued even farther west in the direction he had formerly come from. The edge of the forest in this direction was only about a mile away, so the trip was leisurely.

Arthur noticed the same sad and sickly look of some trees near the edge of the forest, but once he pushed in a few hundred yards, everything started perking up again. While walking, he noticed there wasn't much noise in the forest, and it was quiet. He hadn't truly paid much attention to his trek toward the village, but now that he thought back on it, he didn't recall hearing much of anything roaming around within a couple of miles of the forest edge. This had that same eerily quiet feeling. There wasn't even so much as a simple bird call anywhere near.

Arthur was eager to get to this old manor house to investigate but was a little wary of what he might find there. It was evident that Arthur would have a fight on his hands. After about three-quarters of a mile, he spotted a clearing ahead of him. Arthur slowed his pace to approach it cautiously. If he were going to a quest zone with potentially dangerous creatures, he wouldn't rush in headfirst regardless of the quest level.

Arthur slowly crept forward and tried to keep concealed from the clearing itself as much as possible. He reached the edge of the tree line before entering the opening and froze. He slowly surveyed the area. The large manor was easily spotted, being a two-story affair almost directly in the center of the clearing. It looked like it used to be either a yellow or white color on the outside. It was difficult to tell if it once was white but turned to yellow over the years, or if it started yellow and faded a bit.

The northern side of the house had a decent fenced off section that Arthur guessed had been a modest garden for the home. The grass was unkempt had grown up around the home and was up to Arthur's thigh. At a glance, Arthur saw nothing near the house. He waited and observed the house. After five minutes of waiting, he had started toward the house, but right before he took that first step, he saw something moving in the grass near the outside of the fence to the old garden.

He watched the same spot and noticed that whatever was moving, the grass was too short to see in the thick grass. He kept catching glimpses of black amongst the green but could never get a good enough view of what it was. Taking a random shot into the foliage would be foolish so he started looking around the clearing. Two other places were seen that had grass swaying in suspicious ways, showing something else was present. None of the spots he had seen the grass moving had veered too far from where they had started, though.

Arthur finally decided that sitting there and staring at the same spots was not getting him anywhere, so he decided the best course of action was to ready his bow and slowly crept toward the closest disturbance. When he got within ten yards, the grass went from its occasional swaying to a quick jerk and then froze. Before Arthur knew it, the grass started rustling again, only this time it headed in his direction. At the five-yard mark, Arthur finally caught a glimpse of what he was facing off against.

"What the hell is that?" He yelled.

Chapter 6

The Manor

You *have got to be fucking kidding me? Someone must be playing some great cosmic joke. What kind of asshole would pin me in a fight against giant rats of all things?*

"There is no way in hell I'm dealing with this crap." He exclaimed as those thoughts rolled through his head.

Regular rats are bad enough, but giant rats the size of a large house cat? Nope, so done for the day. Arthur wasn't afraid of rats, but no one in their right mind liked them. Almost everyone has dealt with mice and rats at some point in their life and even if they're not scared of them, the idea of touching one, even on a trap, usually gives people the creeps. They are typically such filthy little creatures. No one wants to take chances.

Despite all of his misgivings, it was apparent he didn't have any choice in this matter as the creature was already barreling at him. The rat had already reached him by the time he was ready to fire. He didn't even have time to aim before the rat leaped into the air at him. Without a target lined up, he just pointed in the general direction and fired the arrow.

While the arrow didn't have a solid hit, it hit the front left shoulder of the rat for a glancing blow and had enough force behind it to push it off of its course. Instead of flying straight into Arthur's face, it whipped by him on his left. He followed it with his eyes as it passed, and this time enough of it was visible to see some of the creature's information.

Name: Giant Rat	
Level: 5	
Type: Creature	
Rarity: Common	
HP: ???/???	
Stamina: ???/???	
Strength: ?	Experience: N/A
Agility: ?	Skills
Endurance: ?	Combat Skills:
	Scratch: ? (???/???)
	Leaping Bite: ? (???/???)

Arthur wished he could see more details about the creatures he found but had no way of knowing if that was possible or not. Maybe when he got back into the village, he could ask a few questions and learn some more about how this world worked. Doing this without drawing too much attention to his complete lack of knowledge would be the trick.

He worked to focus on the problem at hand instead of letting his mind wander. The rat that had leaped past him had now turned around and was facing him again. This time it wasn't in a mad dash at him, but it was close enough where it didn't need to be. The main problem in the scenario was how to deal with it.

The rat was already too close for him to have the time to fit another arrow to the string. The only other option was the small dagger he had, but, quite honestly, the thought of getting that close to this nasty creature to kill it with a knife sent shivers down his spine. The dagger blade itself was around nine inches long, but that thing had huge teeth on it as well.

He decided there was no helping it, though. He just wasn't well equipped for this scenario and would have to push through it. He dropped his bow next to him and pulled the dagger out of its sheath. He thought about picking the bow back up to use as a club to push the rat around when needed but didn't want to take the chance of breaking his only ranged weapon.

Instead of using logic, he went for it by instinct. The rat ran toward him again and jumped once more. This time Arthur was expecting it and took a step to his left and slashed down as hard as he could against the rat's side. The blade dug in deep behind the shoulder, and blood sprayed out of the new wound.

It must have hit something significant because the rat collapsed shortly after landing. The rat tried to regain its feet once but just fell back to the ground, and this time stopped moving for good. Arthur looked at it for a few moments and was sure it wasn't getting up again, but it didn't take long for him to hear some scurrying to his right. He looked over just in time to see one of the other rats that he had forgotten about dashing through the tall grass in his direction. At least he assumed it was another rat since it moved similarly, and he hadn't seen it yet.

This second rat was already too close even to attempt to pick his bow up and get a shot off, so he braced himself for it to come leaping toward him. This time, the rat did something different. Instead of getting a running leap at him, it ran straight for his feet and started trying to claw his legs. Arthur jumped backward, but the little furry rodent was relentless and kept pursuing him.

Arthur was sure he looked like an absolute fool hopping around trying to avoid a giant rat, but at the time, it was irrelevant. He kept trying to take quick swings at it but worried about missing the rat and hitting himself. He would need to try a different approach. He waited for the rat to get close to his foot again after his last dodge, and this time, instead of jumping away again, he kicked it as hard as he could with his right leg. The rat flew back almost ten feet before landing in a bit of a heap.

The rat got back up, and it also changed tactics. The rat took off in a dash toward Arthur and tried the Leaping Bite attack like the last one he fought. He was hoping for this to happen and tried the same strategy he had last time. He sidestepped the leap and brought his dagger down hard toward the side of the creature — unfortunately, this time, he had misjudged the attack and swung just a bit too late. Instead of hitting the rat on its side, he only managed to cut its tail off. The rat landed and hissed in displeasure.

Now he was at a loss for what to do. The only thing he could think of doing was take the chance to stab at it and hope he didn't hit himself or leave himself wide open for a counterattack if he missed. He also knew there was one other rat somewhere and didn't know if it had made its way toward him yet or not. He took the chance, and when the rat closed in the next time, he stabbed straight down at it. His luck must have been working in his favor because he connected directly into the back on the rat's neck, and the creature went limp. A chime sounded, and he ignored it.

The final rat was in sight, but it was still forty yards away and didn't appear to be in a hurry to come at him. He dashed the couple steps to his bow and picked it up. Grabbing an arrow from his bag, he put it to the string and sighted on the area where the final rat was. With the grass as tall as it was, he was having a hard time determining exactly where the rat was. He knew the general area, but just firing blindly into tall grass seemed like a waste.

He baited the rat a bit. He released the tension on the bow and crouched down to conceal himself a little. He grabbed a nearby rock and threw it to the right of the rat in front of him. This accomplished what he had hoped. The rat took off in the rock's direction, and this gave Arthur the chance to spot it as it moved through the tall grass. Wanting to get the ranged attack on this animal instead of having to fight it off with his short dagger, he aimed for the front of the moving grass and judged the depth of the shot into the green blades. He aimed at a slightly less dense patch of grass in front of the moving rat. Hoping the less crowded grass would allow for a better shot, he waited for the rat to reach his chosen spot and let the arrow fly.

Arthur heard the rat squeal and was delighted he had hit the half-hidden creature. The grass was rustling, but nothing was leaving the area it had landed. Arthur dropped his bow again and drew the knife on his belt. He stalked forward while remaining crouched toward the disturbance in the grass. When he was five feet away, he could see the rat had been hit with the arrow in its back leg and had pinned it to the ground. The rat was struggling to pull itself off of the shaft while clawing at the ground to get free.

Arthur was happy it wasn't facing him. This allowed him to take a quick jump and plunge the dagger directly into the side of the rat, and it stopped moving. He heard a chime again but ignored it. Arthur finally let out a heavy sigh and stood up. He grimaced at the ugly creature in disgust.

Honestly, why do rats this size even exist? Such filthy creatures, Arthur thought to himself.

He looked around the clearing at the three spots with the dead rats. The thought of dealing with any more of these creatures was making his skin crawl — much less wandering through small hallways and confined spaces in a building. Hopefully, the manor wouldn't have many of these nasty things in it. He was already here and really couldn't turn back now, though. He walked over to the rat that had its tail removed and chuckled a bit. The thought of that amused him. He glanced over and looked at the rat tail in the grass near it. He was turning to look back toward the manor when a box popped up.

Item: Giant Rat Tail	**Durability:** 5/5
	Rarity: Common
	Quality: Fair
	Weight: 0.2 kg
	Traits: Tail from a Giant Rat.

Well, shit, this stupid tail must be used for something since it registered as a standard item. Since it was still showing as a common rarity, it must not be out of the ordinary. Arthur was tired of having little to no information on things like this, though.

What good are these boxes if they couldn't tell you anything useful? Arthur thought.

As much as he hated it, he decided he might as well gather the tails from all three rats. He wasn't about to go digging around in these beady-eyed things looking for other useful parts, though. He quickly collected the three tails and placed them in his bag. He found the arrows he had used and cleaned them off on the grass. He also wiped his dagger off on the grass and placed it back in its sheath. He grabbed his bow and moved forward toward the house. On his way, he walked near the small enclosure near the manor and was delighted to see there was an old garden, but even better, it was growing a few things wild now. He would have to check through the garden a little more thoroughly on his way out to see if anything could be useful.

He made it to the front door and noticed it was rotted and looked to be barely hanging on by its hinges. It would take a miracle for any paper to still be intact in this place, but he was sure the quest wouldn't have popped up if there wasn't something he could use to complete it. For all he knew, this world could just be screwing with him.

He gave the door a slight nudge with his foot, and it creaked open loudly. Arthur was sure he was about to be that idiot that everyone watched at a movie theater yelling, "Don't go in there," "It's haunted," "You're going to die," but there wasn't much use for it. Arthur got his bow nocked and ready just in case.

Immediately through the door was a large, open room with an expansive staircase in the center. The staircase was one of those gaudy affairs with an extensive bottom section that branched apart to form a "Y" style leading to the upper floor. There were doors to his right and left and one on each side of the staircase. The entire room must have been forty feet across and looked like a lot of wasted space. Now the trick was deciding where to start.

After thinking about it for a bit, he decided to start on the top floor. The reasoning behind this was simple. If he started on the floor, he was on now; then, there was a chance a monster could attack him from an upper level and box him somewhere. This would be especially dangerous if the second floor were rotted through anywhere, and the beast could jump on him from the top floor. The same logic applied if this place had a basement. Start from the top and work your way down. Maybe it was a habit he picked up from learning how to clean properly? He mused to himself.

He proceeded to the stairs and slowly made his way forward. The necessity of testing his weight on each foot for the stability of the floor slowed his progress considerably. His progress was slow and painstaking, but he made his way to the top of the stairs and discovered that both sections of the stairs ended on the same landing on the second floor. This was further proof it was just for looks and not that way for any functional reason. He crept forward down a hallway on the right of him and came across a door.

Not knowing what to expect, he slowly nudged the door with his foot, and it glided open. Looking through the doorway, he saw nothing of interest. The few pieces of furniture were rotten and falling apart. The bed frame was in three different parts, and all of them were leaning at odd angles. There were some random piles of trash lying around the room that Arthur wasn't going to mess with. He turned his gaze back on the hall and continued down it.

The next-door he came across was on his left, and he tried the same process as last time. This time when he nudged the door, the door didn't move. He reached over and grabbed the handle, and it snapped off due to decay. He decided if it were that weak, he would force the door open. He braced himself directly against the door and gave one solid push. He heard the door cracking, and before he could stop himself, he foolishly fell through the door and into the room.

To his immense relief, he didn't see anything moving in the room. *That was all he needed, to fall helpless into a place and have a monster bite his face off before he could get himself oriented.* It was clear that the door was in much worse shape than he had estimated. He got to his feet and started making his way around the room. There didn't seem to be any good reason this room would have been locked, although it was hard to tell if it was a lock on the door or just the rot wedging it shut.

He made a slow pass around the room and found much the same as the last. Arthur walked up to the one small table that was somewhat intact. Peeking inside the drawer it contained, he did find one item of interest.

Item: Silver Hair Pin	**Durability**: 25/25 **Rarity**: Common **Quality**: Well Crafted **Weight**: 0.05 kg **Slot**: Accessory **Traits**: A decorative silver hairpin.

  Hmm, that item actually could be worn, but it didn't have any unique properties, so Arthur didn't bother equipping it. He was sure with it being silver; it could sell for a reasonable price. Arthur tossed it into his bag and continued his trip around the room. When he made it back to the door, he walked back out into the hall and continued forward. The next room was on the left, and after a quick look, it appeared to be a washroom and possibly what would pass for a restroom in this land. Nothing looked of interest, so he moved to the last room in this hall. When he came near it, he heard faint rustling noises coming from the other side. He got his bow back up and ready.

     This time he had his arrow pulled back
and ready to release when he nudged the door
open. When the door opened, he saw another
giant rat scurrying around the far side of the
room. It was walking along the back wall and
appeared to be investigating everything it
came across. Without a thought, Arthur
released his arrow, and with a satisfying
crunch, followed by a dull thunk, the arrow
passed straight through the rat's eye and into
the floor, causing the shaft to stand up and
quiver. He walked over to the rat and
collected its tail as well and tossed it into
his bag.
     A quick inspection of this room turned up
nothing, so he collected the arrow from the
rat. The tip seemed to be in good shape and
still pretty sharp, so back in the bag, it
went. Once again, in the hall, he had to
backtrack to the staircase. Once back at the
stairs, he had two options. He could either
take the hallway to his right, which would
lead him directly away from the entry door, or
he could walk straight ahead to the entrance
on the other side. He decided to save the
middle for last and walked to the other side.
     This hallway appeared to also have four
rooms with two on each side. Creeping down the
hall, he came to the first on the left and
slowly opened the door. It turned out to be
another place of nothing but rotten furniture.
The remaining rooms in the corridor were also
empty. Oddly enough, when he got to the last
room, he again heard a noise on the other side
of the door. Readying his bow, he opened the
door again.

As soon as it swung open, Arthur looked in quickly and saw absolutely nothing. He stuck his head through the doorway cautiously and looked in each direction and saw nothing that could have made the noise. It was at this point he could see the window frame on the left side of the room and noticed a tree had grown right up to the window. The wind appeared to have been blowing it against the window and causing a scratching noise. Relieved, Arthur let the tension go from the bow. He started walking around the room, and when he got to the back of the corner, his footing gave way a bit. Luckily he hadn't shifted all of his weight yet and was able to backpedal quickly, but a small section of the floor crumbled away, revealing rafters and the room below.

It appeared nothing was moving in the room below him, which he was thankful for. He glanced around the room and saw nothing worth searching and worked his way to the central hallway. When he reached the central hall, he started down it. This one seemed to be a similar length to the other two, but there was only one door on each side. That struck him as a little odd, but he went with it anyway.

The first door that came up was the one on his right. He gave the door a small push, and it swung open without an issue. Peering inside, he realized why there was only one door in this long hallway. This room appeared to be a guest room of some sort. The first room looked to be a common area or a sitting room, and beyond it was a door on each side of the back wall. If his guess were right, those would be guest quarters. This place reminded him of the dorm rooms he had in his technical school for the U.S. Navy.

A glance around the front room showed nothing of interest was there unless he was planning on starting a fire. He moved and methodically checked the other two places in the back as well. Nothing was in either of them except for a few rotting bed frames and collapsed desks. He would have to give up on this side of the house and try the other. He walked back to the hallway and opened the other door. The sitting room was identical to the other side and just as barren. The room on the left had an odd sound coming from it that sounded like scratching again, so Arthur quickly checked the right before dealing with it.

Finding the right side empty, he nocked an arrow and pulled it back to prepare to fire. Pushing the door open showed another rat scavenging around a broken bed. He let loose the arrow and, once again, was given the satisfaction of a clean kill through the head. He guessed his archery wasn't as rusty as he thought it was. He walked up to the rat to collect another tail and froze. What lay on the discarded bed was enough to give him pause and disturbed him a bit.

Chapter 7

The Haunted Mansion

Arthur froze. On the bed was the skeleton of what appeared to be a small person. He didn't exactly have experience with skeletons, but this one couldn't have belonged to someone older than ten. He couldn't imagine what could have happened here for someone to have left a child this young on their own to die in this room. Shortly after that thought, he saw the bloodstain on the chest of the tattered clothing attached to the skeleton. It looked like someone may have killed this person. That thought just made him angry.

He walked up to the skeleton to get a closer look and, to his surprise, found a small blade stuck in the ribcage of the remains. He picked it up and checked it.

Item: Ornate Jeweled Dagger	Attack: 1-2 Durability: 15/35 Rarity: Common Quality: Well Crafted Weight: 1.0 kg

	Slot: Main Hand/Off Hand **Traits**: A decorative dagger inlaid with jewels.

The dagger didn't look very useful, to be honest. The blade was dull, but it was obviously used to kill this child. There were even still bloodstains on the hilt. His anger seethed in him for this injustice. He wished he could do something about it, and just as that thought came, so did a notification.

Justice for the Slain I	
Requirements: Level 5 Rewards: 800 experience	Description: You have found the skeleton of a murdered child in the abandoned manor. Find someone that can provide details about this murder to help find the culprit.

His anger cooled a bit, seeing he had found another quest and better yet this quest was for precisely what he already wanted to do. With this quest, he kept the dagger because it could provide clues to the murderer. He also noticed that the box the notification was in wasn't blue like the last one had been but green. He wasn't sure what that meant, but he was suspecting the quests had rarities just like items did.

He dropped this dagger into his bag and looked around some more. Nothing he saw piqued his interest, so he decided that the tour of the upstairs was complete. He worked his way out of the room and back down the stairs to the main entrance. Now was the time to decide again. He figured the best option was to do it the same way as before, so he started with the door immediately to the right when walking through the front door.

This was a hallway similar to the one upstairs, but it had eight rooms in it, and the doors were closer together. As Arthur made his way through each of them, he quickly realized why. The rooms were much smaller. If he had to guess, he would say they belonged to the people who kept the manor running, such as the cooks, gardeners, valets, and the like. They looked serviceable enough if you took away the years of rot. There was nothing of interest in this hallway, so he continued back to the main entrance.

He then checked the door on the left of the entryway. This door was a large double door. When he entered this room, it was a vast, open affair. It appeared to be a formal ballroom. There was a large dining table in the center of it, but Arthur thought this room might have a different purpose as well. The floor in here was a smooth wooden floor instead of the rougher wood and rare stone he had seen in the rest of the house. If his guess was right, they probably hosted parties and dances here. The room had a large window toward the front of the house and on the side. The wall on his right had a single door on it he proceeded to.

He opened this door and entered into what appeared to be a sitting room of some kind. Probably a study considering the bookshelves lining the walls. Most of what was on them looked brown and moldy. The books that he could make out looked like they might turn to dust if touched. Something about the room seemed off, though. All the places on the other side of the building seemed to all be pretty uniform. Unless the space behind this one that branched off of the corridor near the stairs was also overly broad, then this room was not the correct size.

This thought immediately kicked off Arthur's suspicion. He had seen enough crime-solving mysteries to begin to expect the age-old hidden room trick. The real problem was, would the usual cliches hold? This world could be very different in its approach. He started searching the bookshelves on the back wall. There really couldn't be much of anything on the left or right walls. One would go directly outside and the other toward the adjacent hallway. They also looked to be the right distance away from the door compared to the previous room. It was the depth of the room that appeared off.

He carefully searched each bookshelf until he was in front of the one almost directly behind the remnants of an old rotten desk sitting in the middle of the room. He could swear there was a visible crack in the wall behind it that looked like one solid and straight seam. The wall itself was made of paneled wood, which was in oddly good condition, but all the end grains of the wood lined up at this same spot. It would have been odd for them not to have been blended here otherwise.

Arthur decided to use brute force on this section and pull it right off of the wall. The cabinet was well attached, and he had to struggle and pull hard. He heard a creak and what sounded like a faint pop, and then the resistance disappeared, and he stumbled back. Looking at the shelf, he realized it was still firmly attached to the wall, but the wall itself had opened. Looking around the backside of the wall, he saw this section of the wall was mounted on metal hinges and that a small metal lock appeared to have broken when he had pulled on the bookshelf.

Peeking into the room, he was in for a bit of a shock. The room itself was pretty well preserved. He wasn't sure how, but the furniture here was still in serviceable order. To his surprise on the wall on the left was a sword hanging from a wooden wall mount. He walked to this first since it was the most obvious place to start. Picking up the sword, he was both surprised and disappointed.

Item: Unknown Steel Longsword	**Attack**: ? **Durability**: 55/75 **Rarity**: Uncommon **Quality**: Well Crafted **Weight**: 1.5 kg **Slot**: Main Hand/Off Hand

	Traits: An unknown magical longsword. Either use a skill to identify this item or find someone who can identify it for you to discover its potential.

It was great to finally have a sword but not much use if he didn't know what it could do. Trying to take a few swings with it felt off as well. Every time he did, it felt like the sword was trying to slip from his grasp. He held onto it until he could find a use for it. He found the scabbard to it leaning against the back wall in the corner. He sheathed the sword and belted it around his waist.

He checked out the books next. He browsed through book after book and noticed a few that looked like odd writing at first, but then after looking for a bit, he could read them with no issues. Most appeared to be ordinary books on government and family history. Nothing he could see being important enough to hide in a secret room, but then four books over he found something intriguing. A book title had caught his eye.

Item: Skillbook: Identify Magic	**Durability**: 45/55 **Rarity**: Uncommon **Quality**: Well Crafted **Weight**: 0.5 kg

	Traits: A Skillbook that will teach the Identify Magic skill. This skill allows the user to identify magical item's characteristics.

Arthur couldn't believe it. Could he have been lucky enough to find a skill book this early in the world? Not only that but for Identify? Just the thing he truly needed for his new sword. He grabbed the book off the shelf and opened it. As soon as he looked at the open book, a notification appeared.

You have opened Skillbook: Identify Magic. Do you wish to consume this book to learn this ability? Yes/No.

Was it going to be that easy? He didn't actually need to read it but only absorb the knowledge? He immediately thought of YES, but nothing happened. Odd, how was he supposed to select things in this world. Maybe there needed to be a bit of a safety measure in this. What would happen if you found something exciting and quickly decided to use it before being one hundred percent sure it was what you wanted? Maybe he needed to confirm it dually.

Arthur focused on the word, yes, in the notification and then softly said "Yes" out loud. The letters on the page started to cause a small vortex above the book, and the pages began flipping on their own, faster and faster, making the vortex grow larger. The tiny storm absorbed the contents of the book and entered his eyes as a flowing stream of text. He could see the letters as they flew in, but they registered only as nonsense. That didn't bother him because his mind was working in overdrive, absorbing the book itself. After the vortex had disappeared, the book slammed shut and crumbled to dust in his hands. He heard a chime.

He ignored the chime; he was getting used to those and knew they typically meant he learned a skill. He would check on them later. He also remembered hearing one when he was fighting the rats outside. He wasn't sure what that one was for, but this time he was pretty sure the reason was he had learned Identify Magic.

Arthur pulled the longsword out of its sheath and used Identify Magic on it. The skill seemed natural now that he had absorbed the details of its use.

Item: Steel Longsword of Minor Beastslaying	**Attack:** 14-18
	Durability: 55/75
	Rarity: Uncommon
	Quality: Well Crafted
	Weight: 1.5 kg
	Slot: Main Hand/Off Hand

	Traits: Longsword enchanted with the skill Beastslaying ● Beastslaying: Deals +3 damage against beasts.

     Well, that was one hell of an upgrade. While he didn't have any training with a sword, swinging it around after he had identified it felt much more natural. If nothing else, he should be able to use it without hurting himself. He put the sword back in its sheath and continued scouring the bookshelf.

     He was coming close to the end of the books and was about ready to give up when one more book caught his eye.

Item: Skillbook: Scan	**Durability**: 25/30 **Rarity**: Common **Quality**: Good **Weight**: 0.5 kg **Traits**: A Skillbook that will teach the Scan skill. This skill allows the user to identify information about people and creatures.

It was a great skill to have, but it was odd that the book was listed as a low rarity item. Arthur didn't imagine it was that easy to create Skillbooks much less to bother making one of common rarity. Either way, he opened this one up, and it followed the same pattern as the last. The vortex appeared with the swirl of letters and was all absorbed straight into his eyes. Once again, he instinctively knew how to use the skill, and the book crumbled to dust.

There was nothing seen on the adjacent wall, so he moved to the desk. The desk was a sturdy and functional design with two drawers on each side of the sitting area. Checking the two on the right contained some random papers which didn't appear of interest. Opening the top drawer on the left side revealed a neat document with official-looking calligraphy and wax seals. Upon touching it, he received a prompt.

Patents of Nobility I	
Requirements: Level 5 Rewards: 1000 experience, 1 silver coin, unknown rewards also possible.	Description: Dalia has asked you to infiltrate her family's decrepit manor and recover items that could help prove her status among the gentry.
You have successfully fulfilled the required objectives. Do you wish to complete this quest now? Yes/No	

That was odd. It asked Arthur if he
wanted to complete the quest, which wasn't
abnormal. The strange part was he hadn't
delivered it to Dalia yet. Looking carefully
at the description, though, it only said he
had to find it, not return it. He focused on
Yes. He heard the beautiful sound of trumpets
from gaining a level, and another window
popped into his view.

Patents of Nobility II	
Requirements: Level 5 Rewards: 800 experience, 5 silver coins, unknown rewards also possible.	Description: You have recovered the patent of nobility from the decrepit manor. You now have the option of claiming the title of nobility for yourself or honoring your original agreement with Dalia and returning it to her.
Do you wish to accept this quest? Yes/No	

He quickly selected Yes again. With the
quest prompts cleared, he could finally study
the document itself.

Item: Patent of Nobility (Flamekissed)	**Durability**: 58/60 **Rarity**: Rare **Quality**: Exceptional **Weight**: 0.01 kg

	Traits: A sealed and certified document used to proclaim nobility for the Flamekissed family.

Tucking the document into his bag, he held off on reviewing the notifications and alerts while still in here. Once he got out of here and closer to the village, he could sort through all of them.

That last quest prompt was intriguing, though. Looking at the description, it seemed Arthur changed his outlook in life. It essentially meant he could claim the title himself, probably through deceit, instead of handing the patent over. The prospect of it was intriguing, and Dalia had done nothing for him.

With that being said, he wasn't sure he wanted that kind of attention this early. On the one hand, it could help him garner some favor and hopefully push his rather vague guidelines from the Goddess Lianna, but on the other, it could paint a target on his back way earlier than he was prepared for. Based on how bad the situation is in this small village, he wasn't sure he wanted that kind of attention on him yet. Arthur thought it might be more beneficial for him to turn it over to Dalia and keep close to her for the power draw he might need. She was somewhat open about her intentions for a reward.

Coming back to himself, he decided it was time to keep moving. Before he left, though, he tried the last drawer in the desk. Looking in the bottom drawer on the left, it was empty except for a small golden ring with a red ruby in it. Picking up the ring, he saw what it was.

Item: Delilah's Cursed Ruby Ring	**Durability**: 28/30 **Rarity**: Uncommon **Quality**: Well Crafted **Weight**: 0.2 kg **Slot**: Finger **Traits**: A cursed ring that once belonged to the mistress Delilah of the manor house. This ring can not be worn without extreme penalties due to its cursed status. ● All primary attributes -5

That was terrible news. The odd thing was that the color of the notification didn't match the standard shade of green as the uncommon quality magic items he had found earlier. Instead, it matched the color of the quest prompt for the murder of the small child. Getting a bad feeling about this, he continued to examine the ring for a few moments and heard a shrill scream coming from the main entrance. The sound sent a chill up his spine and gave him goosebumps at the same time. He could feel an oppressive air around the place now. It was a sense of fear and dread settling onto him.

He tried and set the ring back in the drawer, hoping this would go away. To his disappointment, that oppressive feeling didn't go away, so he picked the ring back up and put it in his bag. He decided it was time to face whatever hell he had woke up in the central area. There wasn't any other way he could have exited, short of jumping out of a second-story window. While tempting, he decided against it. He crept back through the dining room and approached the entryway. The sight he saw on the other side of the door made his blood run cold.

Standing in the entryway, well floating really, was what appeared to be a ghost. This wasn't one of those ghost hunter television show type ghosts with vague signs of things moving in the dark while running around with poor quality cameras. This was a full glory, spectral white creature floating half a foot off the floor. It looked like a human woman, but any features were hard to tell with it being partly translucent.

Can't tell hair color when the whole thing looks a pale white color, Arthur thought to himself.

He looked at it, and the box he expected popped up.

Name: Specter of Delilah	
Level: 5	
Type: Spirit	
Rarity: Uncommon	
HP: ???/???	
MP: ???/???	
Stamina: ???/???	
Strength: ?	Experience: N/A
Agility: ?	Skills
Intellect: ?	Combat Skills:
Wisdom: ?	
Endurance: ?	Sonic Wail: ? (???/???)
Charisma: ?	Soul Swipe: ? (???/???)
Luck: ?	

Well damn, Arthur thought. As usual, there wasn't much information, but what he saw concerned him. This one had the full range of characteristics and also had MP, which meant it might have command of some type of magic. It was also listed as a spirit type, and he hadn't encountered one of those yet. The lack of information was rather annoying. If he knew a bit more about where its weaknesses may lie, it could help him. It was at that moment he smiled because he had remembered his new skill.

Arthur focused on the spirit and activated his Scan ability. The result he got back was better.

Name: Specter of Delilah
Level: 5

Type: Spirit	
Rarity: Uncommon	
HP: 140/140	
MP: 100/100	
Stamina: 60/60	
Strength: 6	Experience: N/A
Agility: 3	Skills
Intellect: 7	Combat Skills:
Wisdom: 5	
Endurance: 3	Sonic Wail: ? (???/???)
Charisma: 1	Soul Swipe: ? (???/???)
Luck: 1	

He was sure the more he used the skill, the more information he could get from it. It might even show hidden things about people or creatures in the future. All of that aside, though, it gave him more to go on. The amount of HP this monster had was a little higher than he wanted to deal with, but he could make it happen. The trick would be actually damaging it. Arthur had a suspicion this thing would be like most RPG style games he had seen before. Ghosts usually couldn't be damaged by standard weapons and items. He was hoping his new sword could destroy it.

As much as he didn't want to deal with a ghost, he figured it was time to make his move. He slowly opened the door and started creeping toward the spirit. He didn't make it over three steps before the ghost turned and looked directly at him. The woman's eyes glowed a bright blue with an appearance that looked like they were flames licking upward on her face.

"Oh shit," Arthur mumbled under his breath.

The specter shrieked at him and then loudly said, "How dare you enter my house without permission? You disturb my son and me in our own house!"

That statement set him back a bit. If he could take this ghost's meaning directly, then that meant the murdered child upstairs is the son of this woman. That led to a host of questions he didn't have the time to answer.

"I'll forcibly remove your corpse from this house after I kill you." The ghost proclaimed.

The apparition darted in his direction, and Arthur quickly dropped his bow. The weapon would be useless in this fight and would only end up tangling him up when he tried to dodge. He pulled his new sword up just in time to block the creatures swing. The skeletal hand bounced back from the flat of the blade, not touching him, but the impact was slightly jarring. The speed of the shade was allowing it to knock Arthur off balance. He took a huge step to his right and brought the sword back between them again. For the next swing, he was better braced, and it didn't move him or knock him off balance.

The big problem quickly became apparent to Arthur. This spirit could attack him fast enough that he couldn't get a swing in or risk opening himself up. He had hoped the creature's low agility would be his key to killing it, but the spirit, being incorporeal and having no real resistance to air or gravitational forces, made it able to retain speed with lower agility.

He took five more blows in rapid
succession and focused on his health in the
same way he did in the fight with the boar. A
small box quickly popped up to give him the
information.

HP: 225/230
Mana: 100/100
Stamina 225/230

He immediately noticed his health had
fallen a bit but figured that had to do with
the blow that knocked him off balance. The
stamina drain surprised him, though. He could
only imagine that blocking the attacks was
draining his stamina. That meant he couldn't
just wait and do nothing. He doubted this
creature would get tired, so he needed to make
a move. After considering the situation for a
moment, he changed tactics.
Arthur needed to knock the ghost off
balance while maintaining his guard, and he
could only think of one effective way to do
it. He had read about the technique many times
being a fan of fantasy novels but never tried
it in real life. What he needed to do was
parry the monster. Parrying was pretty simple-
sounding, but most people didn't understand
the mechanics behind it. It required the
person to catch the edge of the blade at just
the right angle to redirect the force. On top
of that, the person parrying needed to apply a
small amount of power immediately following
the attack to push them into the off-balance
state while maintaining this angle.

    Every time he had read books, they always
just glanced over the details of the maneuver
and never really stressed the difficulty of
doing it correctly. Sure, you could
effortlessly block the attack with an angled
blade to glance the strike, but if you didn't
successfully apply the force to knock them off
their swing a little, then you didn't
correctly accomplish a full parry.
    With this thought in mind, Arthur tried
it on the next swing. He saw the strike coming
on his left and held the blade in a downward
angle across his body. He had the hilt in his
right hand slightly above shoulder level, and
the blade angled down toward his left hip. The
strike hit, and the sword collapsed back
toward him, causing the edge of the blade to
inflict a small cut on his left arm. The
impact had knocked the blade backward, and he
couldn't slide the force effectively.
    Luckily, the damage it caused was
minimal, and he was still able to block the
blow. He decided he would have to brace the
blade with his left hand on the flat during
the creature's next swing. He wanted to wait
until the spirit swung with the right again.
He didn't trust his ability to switch his
sword to the other hand in the middle of a
fight. When the spirit made her move, he
caught the attack on the edge of the sword and
gave the blade a slight twist and pushed the
hand down and across, causing it to slide
farther than the spirit wished. This allowed
him the chance to take a solid swing right at
the creature's chest. The blade came around in
an arc and connected directly with the side of
the ribcage.

Arthur wanted to jump and holler in triumph at his success. That feeling lasted all of about half a second when he realized it didn't appear to damage the monster at all. He used Scan at that moment to see what he had accomplished.

<table>
<tr><td colspan="2">Name: Specter of Delilah
Level: 5
Type: Spirit
Rarity: Uncommon
HP: 130/140
MP: 100/100
Stamina: 60/60</td></tr>
<tr><td>Strength: 6</td><td>Experience: N/A</td></tr>
<tr><td>Agility: 3
Intellect: 7
Wisdom: 5
Endurance: 3
Charisma: 1
Luck: 1</td><td>Skills
Combat Skills:

Sonic Wail: ? (???/???)
Soul Swipe: ? (???/???)</td></tr>
</table>

Well, that felt like a complete waste of effort. There was no way he'd be able to last long enough to kill it with so little health being taken away. He would run out of stamina before then. Arthur was quickly approaching a state of panic. There wasn't a way he could wear this thing down in time. His thoughts had drawn his attention away from the fight temporarily, and the creature landed a hard blow across his left shoulder, and Arthur fell to the ground. His bag had swung with the impact, and he ended up dropping it on the ground. He quickly scrambled back to his feet and got his blade back up to guard. This constant blocking would never end the fight in any way other than his defeat.

Arthur needed to move around more to
avoid having to block as often. He took off in
a dash to his left, trying to gain some
distance from the creature. When he had
reached the wall in that direction, he turned
to face the spirit. It was quickly approaching
him and not far behind. Arthur grinned and
thought now was a good time to change things
up a bit. He dashed at the spirit and quickly
dove to its left. As Arthur passed by, he
extended his sword, and it slashed across the
shoulder of the creature but yet again
appeared to do almost no damage. Arthur wasn't
sure what else he could do. Looking toward his
bag, he saw the small jeweled dagger that was
used to kill the child. Only now, the knife
glowed with some unseen power. Could this be
his ticket to freedom? Did the blade itself
want revenge for the wrong it was forced to
commit? He couldn't dwell on it at the moment,
but he had a strange feeling that he needed to
get that dagger quick.

He tried another parry as he had before,
but this time he needed to use a little more
force. It should give him the time he needed
to get the dagger. He readied himself for the
attack that was coming, and when the spirit
connected with his blade, he pushed with much
more force and sent the ghost backward a bit.
Oddly, it almost looked like the ghost had
stumbled, although, with its floating, he
wasn't sure how that could happen.

Arthur quickly dashed to the bag and
grasped the knife by the hilt, picking it up.
It was indeed glowing as he thought it had
been. The sight of the dagger in his hand
caused the spirit to screech in a fury.

"How dare you disturb my precious boy! I only did what I had to do to protect him. I couldn't take the beatings his father inflicted on us both, and I had to save him from them. I'll make you pay for disturbing him in his sleep." The ghost said. The fire in its eyes shifted from a deep blue to a dull orange, and Arthur knew things just went from bad to worse.

He had to end this quickly but needed an opening to use the dagger. It would require him to get closer, but that would be hard to do without making himself a large target. A parry was possible but would be hard to do with timing and the knife itself. Arthur decided to put his faith in speed and the blade. Instead of trying to parry, he waited for the ghost to swing with its left hand this time.

When the ghost committed to the swing, Arthur swung backhand with his sword straight for the arm and, at the same time, stepped forward and plunged the dagger directly into the chest of the specter. The creature froze instantly and looked at Arthur in shock. White cracks began to form and spread from the blade, like spider webs. A glowing white light shone from the cracks as they spread to cover the entire body.

"I had to do it to save him. I had to do it to save him. He was my little boy. It was my job to save him from the pain. He is no longer in any pain." The ghost kept mumbling as the cracks spread. The creature finally looked to Arthur, and to his shock, it appeared to smile at him with a look of relief before promptly bursting into tiny fragments of translucent light. It also surprised Arthur to see a small chain fall to the ground that had a key attached to it. Another quiet chime followed.

Chapter 8

Gifts From An Admirer

Arthur looked at the key that had fallen and saw a box pop up.

Item: Delilah's Key	**Durability**: 35/40 **Rarity**: Uncommon **Quality**: Well Crafted **Weight**: 0.2 kg **Traits**: This key will open Delilah's Treasure.

Arthur looked it over carefully but saw nothing that might give him a hint of where this treasure might be. He didn't remember seeing anything else in the house he hadn't been able to open.

Shortly after that thought, he had a notification appear.

Justice for the Slain I

Requirements: Level 5 Rewards: 800 experience	Description: You have found the skeleton of a murdered child in the abandoned manor. Find someone that can provide details about this murder to help find the culprit.
You have successfully fulfilled the required objectives. Do you wish to complete this quest now? Yes/No	

He selected Yes, and immediately after another notification came up.

Justice for the Slain II	
Requirements: Level 6 Rewards: 400 experience	Description: Delilah's ghost has been laid to rest, but what would drive a woman to murder her children? Find someone who can provide information for this quest.
Do you wish to accept this quest? Yes/No	

Another *Yes* selection, and he determined he had been in this house long enough and wanted out. He put the necklace over his head that held the key and gathered up his bow and bag. The jeweled dagger had exploded with the specter so he couldn't recover any of it.

He walked to the front door and proceeded back outside. Luckily for him, the sun was still up. It was an immense relief to feel the sun on his face after the gloomy manor house. He saw nothing moving in the grass and assumed all the rats were genuinely dealt with. He started walking in the village's direction and stopped. Looking back over his shoulder, he remembered the garden. When he first saw it, he thought it would be an excellent opportunity to check things out since there appeared to be some plants growing wild. With the sad state of food in the village, it would be a boon for him to find anything.

He thought the short delay would be worth it and walked to the small fenced-off area. He walked through a hole in one area of the fence and into the central part of the garden. Tall grasses had invaded much of the garden, but he saw many plants growing a variety of things. He bent down near one plant near him and was sure he recognized the item growing on it. He pulled one of the green vegetables off of the small bush and was pleased he had indeed recognized it.

Item: Jalapeño	**Durability:** 20/20 **Rarity:** Common **Weight:** 0.1 kg **Traits:** This small vegetable appears spicy.

Arthur heard another small chime that he
ignored for now. He would need a thorough bit
of introspection on his way back to the
village.

This jalapeño would give a spicy flavor
to anything that it was cooked with. Arthur
searched around the immediate area and ended
up finding forty jalapeños. From here, he
wandered a little farther back into the
garden. The knee-high grass made it difficult
to spot the hidden vegetable plants buried
within. He kept walking by small weeds spaced
all over the place, but they didn't grow
nearly as tall. After he walked by a handful
of them, he stopped and looked at one more
closely.

Once he got down lower and studied the
plant, he thought he recognized it. If it was
what he thought it was, then he had never
grown them himself because the soil where he
lived was hard. Root type vegetables couldn't
flourish very well in harder soil. He reached
down near the base of the plant and pulled
carefully. Out of the ground popped a long
orange vegetable that he was very familiar
with. To his delight, they had been what he
suspected. To think he had almost passed over
these beauties.

Item: Carrot	**Durability:** 20/20 **Rarity:** Common **Weight:** 0.3 kg **Traits:** This orange root can be prepared multiple ways or eaten raw.

After some careful searching for their
small leafy stems, he found thirty carrots
that he dumped into his bag. Luckily, the bag
was a rather large affair, but if he kept
piling much more in here, it would get too
heavy and uncomfortable to carry.

From here, he made his way to the last
section in the back of the garden. There was a
small building in the rear he had assumed held
the gardening tools at one point. Arthur
walked toward the shed and stopped when he
noticed one final grouping of plants he
recognized. This one was a large, green, and
leafy one, but unlike the jalapeño plants,
this one had nothing growing on it. Mainly
because this was another root plant and not
only that it was his absolute favorite, he
dashed over to the first plant and slowly
started pulling it out of the ground. Once he
had the main stem out, a few of his prizes
fell from the roots.

Item: Potato	**Durability:** 20/20 **Rarity:** Common **Weight:** 0.3 kg **Traits:** A root vegetable with a variety of uses.

    Cha-Ching! Arthur had hit the jackpot.
Back on Earth, potatoes had been one of his
absolute favorite foods, and he loved to eat
them in almost any way you could cook them.
Scalloped, fried, baked, mashed, you name it,
and Arthur was all over it. He dug in the dirt
around where he had pulled the plant up,
knowing the potatoes would grow farther out
than directly under the plant. He found five
more plants to bring his total to fifty. Not a
bad haul for a food run.
    Before he left, he checked in the shed.
He walked up to the building and opened the
door. The rotten tool handles and pieces lying
around caused a musty smell. There were also
rusted chunks of metal that were once useful
tools scattered around the bottom of the shed.
Everything around looked to be in horrible
condition. He walked around and saw a small
tool chest in the back. Peeking in, he noticed
nothing inside the chest and continued looking
around. Not paying attention, he tripped over
the small chest in the back, but he caught
himself before falling.
    Looking in the chest's direction, it
surprised him to see something metallic
shining under the box. He walked back over and
kicked the remnants of the tool chest out of
the way. Hidden underneath was a small metal
box. It was around one square foot and a few
inches deep. Looking at the metal box, he saw
it was hinged with two-barrel hinges, and to
his surprise, the other side had a small lock.

He got excited when he realized he probably had the key for this box. He walked back out of the small shed to get some better light and pulled the necklace over his head. He put the key in the lock and turned, hearing the satisfying click. He was a little giddy in anticipation, and as soon as he opened the box, he saw a letter sitting on top with something else under it. He inspected the message first.

Arthur studied it for a moment having trouble making out what it said, and then suddenly, it seemed like the words came into focus, and he could read it without an issue.

My Dearest Arthur,

I do hope you enjoy the contents of this box I have left for you. I'm limited in what I can do to assist you, but I have found I can place items in locations in hopes that someone may find them. To this end, I have given you something I believe you will be eternally grateful for and will probably make you more than a little excited.

Continue your excellent work for me, and I'll continue to find ways of rewarding you.

Your Loving Goddess,
Lianna

Arthur's mouth began to water at the prospect of what she may have left for him. He slowly picked up the letter. Beneath was something he could never have imagined.

Item:	**Durability:** 110/110
Tome of Elemental Earth Control	**Rarity:** Epic

	Quality: Exquisite **Weight:** 0.8 kg **Traits:** This book can grant the user the knowledge to control the power of elemental earth. Control learned from this book can be applied to teaching you the Earth Magic skill.

After Arthur picked his jaw up off of the floor, he jumped up and hollered, "Hell, Yea! I'm gonna learn magic, bitches!" This was beyond anything he could have imagined. The fact that Lianna had left it in his path meant she had directly interfered with placing it here. It was clear this item was far too rare and valuable to have ever been the real reward offered for killing the spirit. He was eternally grateful she had given him this exceptional gift. Now he would have to work toward fulfilling his promise to assist her cause in this world.

As much as he wanted to learn this immediately, he was unsure how much daylight he had left and needed to make it back to the clearing around the village before it got dark. He waited until he reached the safety of the village before using the book. The other books had absorbed quickly, but this book was a much more sophisticated version and may require more time. He couldn't risk standing defenseless in this clearing as night crept up if that was the case.

The shadows were already starting to lengthen, so he assumed there wasn't a lot of time left before dark. He stuffed the book into his bulging sack and started back toward the village. He decided now would be the perfect time to pull up his stat sheet and see where he stood.

Name: Arthur **Level:** 6 **Age:** 26 **Race:** Human **HP:** 230/230 **MP:** 100/100 **Stamina:** 230/230	
Strength: 8 **Agility:** 8 **Intellect:** 2 **Wisdom:** 1 **Endurance:** 8 **Charisma:** 5 **Luck:** 5	**Experience:** 1800/2500 (You have 5 available skill points)
	Skills (100% boost to any skill for level up) **Combat Skills:** **Archery:** 3 (975/1000) **Block:** 1 (130/500) **Detect Hidden:** 1 (50/500) **Identify:** 1 (75/500) **Parry:** 1 (100/500) **Scan:** 1 (50/500) **Small Blades:** 2 (500/750) **Stealth:** 1 (150/500) **Swords:** 1 (50/500) **Unarmed:** 1 (25/500) **Professions:** **Barter:** 3 (50/1000) **Cooking:** 2 (400/750)

	Farming: 4 (200/1400)
	Firemaking: 2 (700/750)
	Herbalism: 3 (200/1000)
	Skinning: 3 (400/1000)

He had a decent amount of new skills listed. As he walked through the forest, he focused on pulling up the stats of his endeavors. A massive wall of notifications and a never-ending list of damages, bleeds, debuffs, and more immediately assaulted him. It was becoming apparent this world loved to be thorough. Arthur cleared it up a little and removed the bleed damages and notifications about inflicting these bleeds. He also hid all the dodges, parries, and blocks. Taking it a step farther, he collapsed the fights with the rats together since he didn't care to see all of their damages and mainly wanted to focus on the battle with the spirit. All the experience and level gains were dropped in together as well.

Giant Rat (Level 5) has died (x5).
You have gained 250 experience for killing Giant Rat (Level 5) (x5).
You have gained 275 experience in Archery for killing Giant Rat (Level 5) (x4).
You have gained 200 experience in Small Blades for killing Giant Rat (Level 5) (x3).
Congratulations, you have learned Unarmed for a 100 experience bonus.
You have gained 25 experience in Unarmed for killing Giant Rat (2) (Level 5).
Congratulations, you have learned Stealth for a 100 experience bonus.
You have gained 150 experience in Stealth for killing Giant Rat (Level 5) (x3).

Congratulations, you have learned the ability Identify for a 100 experience boost.

You have gained 75 experience in Identify for Identifying Steel Longsword of Minor Beastslaying.

Congratulations, you have learned the ability Scan for a 100 experience boost.

Congratulations, you have completed the quest Patents of Nobility I for 1000 experience.

Congratulations, you have advanced to Level 6. You're slowly getting somewhere.

Specter of Delilah (Level 5)

You have gained 50 experience in Scan for successful use against Specter of Delilah (Level 5).

Your attempt at Stealth failed against Specter of Delilah (Level 5).

You have suffered 5 HP damage and staggered due to partial Block and lost 5 additional Stamina.

You have suffered 5 HP damage from your own Steel Longsword of Minor Beastslaying (Glancing) due to an improper Parry and lost an additional 5 Stamina.

You have dealt 24 damage to Specter of Delilah (Level 5) with Steel Longsword of Minor Beastslaying (-14 damage due to 60% resistance to physical)

You have suffered 20 HP damage from Soul Swipe (Level 1) from Specter of Delilah (Level 5).

You have dealt 24 damage to Specter of Delilah (Level 5) with Steel Longsword of Minor Beastslaying (-14 damage due to 60% resistance to physical)

You have dealt 130 HP damage to Specter of Delilah (Level 5) with Ornate Jeweled Dagger (Enspelled) (Critical Strike) (Doom of Delilah).

Spirit of Delilah (Level 5) has died.

You have gained 150 experience for killing Specter of Delilah (Level 5).

Congratulations, you have learned the ability Block for a 100 experience boost.

Congratulations, you have learned the ability Parry for a 100 experience boost.

Congratulations, you have learned Dual Wield for a 100 experience bonus.

You have gained 100 experience in Dual Wield during your encounter with Specter of Delilah (Level 5).

You have gained 130 experience in Block during your encounter with Specter of Delilah (Level 5).

You have gained 100 experience in Parry during your encounter with Specter of Delilah (Level 5).

You have gained 150 experience in Small Blades for killing Specter of Delilah (Level 5).

You have gained 50 experience in Swords for killing Specter of Delilah (Level 5).

Congratulations, you have learned Herbalism for a 100 experience bonus.

Congratulations, you have learned Farming for a 100 experience bonus.

You have gained 1,450 total experience in Herbalism.

Congratulations, you have progressed to Levels 2 and 3 in Herbalism. Increases the chance of identifying a plant by 6%. Are you sure those aren't weeds?

You have gained 2,400 total experience in Farming.

Congratulations, you have progressed to Levels 2, 3, and 4 in Farming. Increases possible yield of gathered items by 4%. Still playing in the dirt, huh?

Congratulations, you have learned Detect Hidden, a subskill of Stealth for a 100 experience bonus.

You have gained 50 experience in Detect Hidden.

Wow, that was pure information overload, Arthur thought to himself. There had to be a better way to do that. Some of that information would have been useful to him had he been able to harness it during his fight. Knowing for sure a creature had a physical resistance would have been nice. He knew he could keep his small status available whenever he wished, so there should be no reason he wouldn't be able to do the same with his combat information.

He was pleased with all the new skills he had acquired, though. He knew all of his other skills had unique traits to them and wanted to know what his traits were for the new skills. He tried thinking about the information differently and was pleased when the new skills showed up in a neat list with their attributes listed next to them.

Block – Each level increases the maximum damage you can block by 4% per attack.

Parry – Each level increases the chance to stagger opponents by 3% on parry.

Stealth- Each level decreases sounds you make while moving in stealth by 2% and reduces the chance you will be spotted in shadows by 2%.

Detect Hidden - Each level increases the chance of finding hidden items by 3%.

Swords - Swing speed with swords increased by 3%.

Unarmed - Each level increases damage done unarmed by 4%.

Farming - Each level increases the possible yield of gathered items by 4%.

Herbalism - Each level increases the chance of identifying a plant by 3%.

All in all, not a bad set of skills, Arthur reflected. There were still far too many things to consider in all of that information. As before, he was still confused about why the damages didn't always match up with what he thought they should be based on his weapons potential. He tried to focus on the damage values themselves hoping it would reveal more details, but nothing happened.

One thing he thought was interesting is that you seemed to get more experience for skills upon a critical strike with that skill during that specific encounter. At least that was the only typical pattern he could see on some fights where one skill got more than it did on a similar previous encounter. There were just far too many things he needed to know, and he would have to find someone he could trust, at least a little, to turn to and help him.

His contemplating had burned more time than he thought. Before he knew it, he was exiting the forest and back in the clearing around Alem's Crossing. He sucked in a deep breath, relieved to be back near the village if nothing else. Arthur had no trouble being alone and sometimes preferred it, but there was no substitute for the occasional conversation. He got within a hundred yards of the outskirts of the small village and veered toward the inn. He knew he had the patent to deliver to Dalia if that's what he decided to do, but wanted to go to the inn first.

He wanted to use the Skillbook there in the relative safety of his room, and then he needed to get cleaned up and eat before going to see Dalia. He had a feeling that might be prudent if her promise carried the weight it had seemed to before. He entered the inn and smiled at the innkeeper. He looked around slightly confused since the place was quite empty except for two people nursing small cups in the back corner of the room.

This might have been common during the middle of the day, but with the sun almost set, this place should be much livelier. He walked over to the bar and got the innkeeper's attention. He opened his mouth to speak and then froze and shut his mouth. He shook his head and looked at the innkeeper.

"This is rather horrible to admit, but I just realized that I never got your name when I was here last time. I feel terrible about that and am glad my parents are not here to scold me for my lack of manners. My name is Arthur." He said while extending his hand.

The innkeeper smiled jovially and took his hand. "My name is Daniel," the innkeeper replied. "I wasn't sure if you were just rude, forgetful, or used to odd customs, to be honest."

"I'm afraid it seems I'm a little of all three. Why's this place so empty? Is it because of the shortages?" Arthur asked.

"That would be most of the problem. Why come to an inn when no one has much to eat, even the inn, for that matter? Even if I had something, few have anything to pay for that food with." He said downtrodden.

"Daniel, I know I'm a stranger here, but I would like to help. I've been sent here by my Goddess to assist this little village in any way I can, and I want to help you turn this place around. Would you be interested in helping me in my endeavor?" Arthur asked.

Daniel gave Arthur an odd look before saying, "I'm not sure we should rile up the gods for any reason. They can be more trouble than they are worth, and most that worship them live near the larger cities."

"I understand the skepticism," Arthur started, "but I can assure you I have nothing but the best intentions. I want to turn this place around before any of the local lord's men come back to terrorize the place. With the aid of my Goddess, it should be possible."

"What Goddess do you pay homage to Arthur?" Daniel asked.

"The Goddess Lianna is the one I serve. She has been nothing but kind and has provided me with guidance while I have been traveling." Arthur said.

"I'm not familiar with that name. I guess I can agree to help as long as you don't ask too much of me. I don't want to get involved with any of the religious fanatics near the larger cities and draw their attention here. Relying on a relatively unknown goddess shouldn't cause any harm." He told Arthur with a smile.

"That's fantastic news. Now I have a couple of quick questions for you. What do I need to do to arrange a bath here, and what are you cooking for dinner?" Arthur asked with a smile.

He looked at Arthur and grinned. "For the bath, we have a small room on the bottom floor below the stairs. It has a large wooden washtub. I can prepare some hot water for you to bathe in if you give me roughly twenty minutes. As for dinner, I'm cooking some of the pork that you so graciously handed over for us. Not much that I can do about something to go with it, but it should be good either way."

Arthur looked at the man and asked: "Can we walk to the kitchen and talk real quick, out of the way of prying eyes?"

He gave Arthur an odd look and beckoned him back around the counter. They walked back into the kitchen. The place was much cleaner than Arthur would have thought. Most of the surfaces were wooden and polished to a subtle glow. There was hardly any dust seen anywhere. A large kettle hung over a fire pit in the corner of the room. Arthur walked to the empty table in the center of the room and eyed Daniel.

"I found some things while in the forest that will help, but I need you to determine what would be the best course to take with them. You are more familiar with the struggles of this place and would know what is best." Arthur said.

Arthur reached into his bag and started emptying the vegetables he had found onto the counter. The more he stacked up there, the bigger the innkeeper's eyes got. When finished unpacking all the pieces, Arthur turned and looked at the innkeeper. The man had tears in his eyes as he looked at the food in front of him. His gaze drifted from one vegetable to another until finally returning to Arthur.

"How?" Was the only word he could manage to get out.

"I was in the forest trying to fix the problem that Dalia needed help with. While out there, I stumbled on an old, run-down, mansion home and it had an overgrown garden near it. Luckily for me, these plants had been growing wild when I found them." Arthur intoned.

"It appears this Goddess of yours truly is a miracle worker. While this isn't an overly large amount of food, it's a great start. As I mentioned before, the lord's men have taken almost everything, and unfortunately, that also means they have taken almost everything we could use to replant more food. I know this is the food you found, but I would like to suggest a few things." He said graciously.

Arthur nodded at the man to continue.

"I would suggest we use most of the potatoes for replanting. These potatoes are big enough, with some eyes still on them, to cut into three pieces and use as seed potatoes. As long as there are enough eyes left on each one, we can plant them when the skin hardens over the cut part. This will allow us to grow many more potatoes." The innkeeper said happily. He noticed Arthur's downcast look pretty quick, though.

"Is there a problem with that, Arthur?" he asked.

Arthur looked at him and said, "No, I agree with your assessment, and it would probably be best that they were used for that purpose. I'm merely upset because they're one of my most favorite foods, and I was looking forward to eating some."

Daniel laughed boisterously and said, "No fear, Arthur. We can use some of these smaller potatoes for us to eat the next couple of days. You would be lucky to even get two seed potatoes out of each, so we might as well eat them instead. As for the jalapeños, I'd like to get about half of them immediately cut to be dried out. This allows me to get numerous seeds for planting and can also help me preserve some for cooking spices. The rest I can use fresh, as needed, for now. If you can keep bringing little snippets of food, then it will go a long way."

"I'll see what I can do to keep the place supplied," Arthur said.

"The carrots themselves can also be used beneficially. If I left the top of the carrot intact and lay them in a small basin of shallow water, they would sprout more greens from the top. The greens themselves are edible and nutritious. They can't regrow the carrots, unfortunately, but I can let some carrot plants completely go to bloom and harvest seeds from them." Daniel told him.

"That sounds great. My main concern now would be the lord's men. I know you said they don't come by very often, but I assume it isn't a long enough span for these things to grow before they return? On top of that, if you dish out food in the inn in abundance, you will draw the attention of every villager here, and I imagine they would fight over the scraps than play the long game and try to solve this problem." Arthur retorted.

"Those are both valid concerns. As for the inn itself, I'll still keep up outward appearances as usual. I've been known to sneak a small bowl of food to the truly needy. Mainly those that have children relying on them, but I do that in the evenings and try to keep it quiet so as not to start a rush. I won't stop doing that." He said with a steely glare.

"I would never ask that of an honest man like yourself. Maybe my Goddess truly wanted us to meet." Arthur mused.

"As for the lord's men, they rarely show up, but four times a year. Since they were just here, it's probably a little over 100 days until they arrive again. That should give the plants enough time for at least one round of harvest. I know a private farm toward the edge of the village that has a man living there I can trust with the task. Can't plant them anywhere near the village for fear of the people trying to steal and eat the plants before they have had time to mature." He said casually.

Did he just say over one hundred days? Arthur thought. If they came by four times a year, then that should be much less than every one hundred days. Then it clicked with him. That's why he was younger than he thought he should have been. He looked at Daniel and asked, "How many days are in a year here?"

Daniel looked at him and said, "Four hundred and fifty, like everywhere else on this land."

Arthur laughed and said, "Just making sure."

Yep, that explained it. Arthur bet that if he took the number of days he had lived on earth and divided them by four hundred and fifty instead of three hundred and sixty-five, he would end up with his current age.

"Well, Daniel, I'm heading to the room for a bit to give you a chance to get some water ready, and then I'll head down to bathe. Once I get a bath and some food, I need to make an important house call on a certain lady." Arthur said with a mischievous grin.

Daniel gave him a wink, and he took off up the stairs. He opened his door and sat down on the edge of the bed. Now it was time to explore his new book.

Chapter 9

Just Rewards

Arthur pulled the tome out of his bag with a bit of nervous excitement. Sitting on the edge of the bed was very comfortable after being on his feet most of the day. It was good to take a deep breath and relax for a moment, but he knew he wouldn't be able to put this off. Not only was the anticipation of using the book killing him but also his nervousness. It was never a good idea to casually carry around super rare items of unknown value. The faster he could use the tome, the less he would have to worry about the chance of it being stolen.

He opened the tome and was greeted by the message he was expecting.

You have opened Tome of Elemental Earth Control. Do you wish to consume this book to learn this ability? Yes/No.

He selected YES and was again assaulted by a fantastic light show. This time, after the vortex appeared and started absorbing the letters, sparks of lighting could be seen flashing around the storm. It looked like a tiny thunderstorm contained inside of a tornado that was eating words out of a book. When the tome reached the end, it slammed shut. This book also shimmered and turned to dust, but the powder itself even swirled into the vortex.

Bracing himself, Arthur waited for the assault of knowledge and didn't have to wait long. The storm released a gout of words directly into his face that seeped into his mouth, eyes, and nose. Flashes of experiences went through his head. He watched as multiple people performed different feats of earth magic, from raising walls to smoothing and breaking soil for cultivation. He only caught brief flashes of each, but it showed him the true scope of earth magic and what it could be used for.

Suddenly, the images vanished, and he was sitting in his room again in the inn. He looked around and saw nothing out of place. The sun was almost completely gone from the sky, and only a dull bit of orange lit the horizon, so it couldn't have been long since he opened the book. He couldn't explain how, but he now knew how to control earth with magic. Instinctively, he knew the method would not work for the other elements, though. He couldn't explain that either, but he was happy to understand one if nothing else. Hopefully, he could unlock some other schools of magic in the future.

The odd thing was that although he knew how to control the earth, he didn't receive any information about spells, nor had he learned any. Usually, learning magic in an RPG was heralded by learning a spell of some type first. That, or when magic was awakened, it might grant the knowledge of some elemental spells. Now that he had magical skills, he had one thing he needed to do immediately. He quickly threw three of his points into Intellect and two into Wisdom to assist with his new skill.

His next level might prove troublesome for him to decide on how to allocate points, though. He would need to see the actual benefits of his earth magic to determine how he would need to assign them later on. Now that he could go either way, it would need to be carefully thought out. Before now, he was working under the assumption he wouldn't need those stats since he had no magic that could use them.

It was time for him to get downstairs and get cleaned up, though. One day in this village wasn't going to provide him with all the answers he needed. Now he had a business partner, though, so he hoped he could have him help with some of his lack of knowledge. He left his bow in the room and unloaded the arrows to lighten his bag. It was considerably lighter without those veggies and bolts in it. He noticed a bit of dirt collecting in the bottom and resolved to clean the bag out later. He wasn't able to get all the vegetables he had brought back completely clean since there wasn't any water close to the house that he had passed.

He opened his door and walked downstairs.
He looked at Daniel standing by the bar, and
the innkeeper waved him over.

"I thought I was going to have to come to
check on you for a moment there. I thought you
would be down closer to fifteen minutes, not
over half an hour later."

*Had it taken that long to absorb the
information from the book?* Arthur guessed it
must have. He was relieved he had waited until
he got here for it. That could have turned out
bad if he sat in a forest clearing,
defenseless, for half an hour.

"I was trying to organize my stuff and do
a bit of cleaning on some items. Bath ready?"
Arthur asked.

"Yeah, I finished getting the water
dumped in about ten minutes ago. It probably
cooled off by now but should still be warm.
Dinner probably has another half hour until
it's done, so take your time and relax."

"Thanks, Daniel. I'll see to that bath
now." Arthur said as he walked toward the room
below the stairs that contained the tub.

Entering the room, he still saw a bit of
steam coming off of the water and felt immense
satisfaction. The room was small enough that
it radiated heat, similar to a sauna. He took
off the sword belt and placed it and his
dagger on a low stool in the room's corner.
Once those two items were down, he dropped the
bag next to him and then couldn't get out of
his clothes fast enough.

    The clothes were nothing special, and he
wished he had the time to wash and dry them
out before going to see Dalia, but there was
no way they would dry in time. He also didn't
have another set of clothes to wear while they
were drying. His current clothing had splashes
of rat blood on different places and some dust
and decay from the old mansion that needed
cleaning. The idea of walking around in the
early evening with soggy clothes did not
appeal to him, though.
    He lowered himself into the tub and let
out a long sigh. The water was still nice and
warm, and the heat felt terrific. He hadn't
realized how tired and sore he was until
settling down in the tub. He laid back and
rested his head on the side of the wooden tub.
It was short enough for the back of his head
to rest almost entirely on the top of the rim.
    He laid there and enjoyed his time
soaking in the tub. He couldn't tell how long
he relaxed there, but he also gave up caring.
After an undetermined amount of time, he found
a small bar of what he guessed was soap, next
to the tub. It had a slightly rough and sandy
texture to it and had no scent at all, but it
did the job perfectly fine. He lathered up
some soap in his hands and used it to get his
hair clean and rinsed off.

He hopped out of the bath, feeling renewed and refreshed. He dried off with a large piece of rough cloth hanging on the wall. He dusted his clothes off, rinsed some of the filthy spots on them, and put them back on. He picked up his stuff and wandered back into the main room. The cooler air hit him like a brick wall as soon as he exited the steamy washroom and took his breath away. The feeling passed quickly as he adjusted to the new temperature.

He walked over to the bar, took a seat, and waved Daniel over.

"Ready for dinner? Everything's done cooking and ready to eat." Daniel informed him.

"Sounds great. I'll eat here at the bar if you don't mind."

He shook his head and told him, "No problem at all. I'll be back in a moment with your meal." He walked into the back and returned with a plate of food. On it was a good portion of meat that looked like it had been roasted, and it had a layer of gravy on it that made his mouth water. Next to it sat a small potato that was smashed flat and toasted in a skillet. The sight of it made him want to cry tears of joy. Next to it were some slices of carrot that were cooked to perfect tenderness.

"This looks amazing, Daniel!" Arthur told him.

"I'm glad you approve. Since you just got here and were generous with your food, I wanted to make you a good-sized meal. I would suggest we not have this large of a meal every evening though. The supplies won't stretch very long when used in that manner." He told Arthur with a knowing nod.

"I won't argue with that logic. I plan on doing more hunting in the forest around here to gather some meat, but that's never a guarantee. To be honest, I'd like to get more Archery experience. Coming up pretty close to another level. If only I could find someone that could teach me some abilities or subskills in Archery, that would be great." Arthur remarked casually.

Daniel looked at Arthur with a face that made Arthur think he had said something profoundly stupid, so he asked. "What?"

"Well, I have heard you can learn some subskills from trainers and other people, but I would assume you would use your talent tree as most others do." He stated offhandedly.

Arthur choked on a piece of the potato he was eating for a moment and then cleared his throat. "What do you mean, talent trees?"

"I know you are from far off, but I would have assumed growing up, you would have learned many of these things already. How can you have made it to your age without knowing these basic aspects?" He eyed Arthur suspiciously.

Arthur had to scramble to come up with a feasible excuse for this situation. He blurted out the first thing that came to mind.

"I grew up as an orphan. Some of the local adults helped keep an eye on me from time to time, but I never had the chance to fully learn much about the ways of the world. I was mostly forgotten. It was part of the reason I could just pick up and leave. Most of what I learned all came from books."

He adopted a sad look on his face while Arthur spoke.

"I'm sorry to hear that, Arthur. No one should ever have to go without a family to help them, but I'll do whatever I can to assist you in these things as they come up. Since you didn't understand what I meant by talent trees, I'll explain them. Any skills you can gain have a unique talent tree unto themselves. Each talent in these trees gives different bonuses to that skill. Some bonuses may be increased power, decrease mana requirements, stamina usage, or even teach new subskills."

Arthur's eyes grew, the more Daniel went on. This was on another level entirely to customize his skills on top of leveling them.

"The talents also vary from person to person. One person's talent tree in Archery, for instance, may not have the same available talents in its tree as yours will. Because of this, it's hard to tell what will be available to you. The trees are also in a hierarchical format, so you can't see some later talents in the branches until you have used talent points on the previous talent. For each level starting at level five of skill, you're granted one talent point to distribute in your skill for unique bonuses."

"That's great news. Now to work toward leveling some skills more and digging through their talent trees." Arthur said.

"Out of curiosity, do you know anything about magic?" Arthur asked.

"Few people know a lot of details about magic. It's a largely guarded skill and difficult to acquire. Those who can acquire it only do so using great wealth or by serving their days in one of the dedicated mage guilds. I know that people who wield their forces can be of immense use, though. Their services can be costly, though, so they're not commonly found outside of the major cities." He replied offhandedly.

"Do you know anything about the spells they use in particular?"

"Not from first-hand knowledge. I have heard that many of them learn spells from fellow mages, but there is also a rumor that spells can be created or discovered. That could all be nothing more than gossip though, as I have never spoken to a mage for more than a few seconds before." He said while eyeing Arthur. "Those are some rather specific questions. Anything I need to know of?"

"No, I was merely curious is all. On my side of the world, I had never seen a mage. I can't remember ever hearing much about one other than fanciful gossip and never saw one." Arthur replied quickly.

"Well, I can't fault a man for curiosity. Have any plans for the evening?" He asked Arthur with a knowing look.

"I have a house call that I expect to be rather eventful as soon as I finish this fantastic meal," Arthur said with a grin.

"Be careful with yourself, and don't let that crazy she-devil do you any harm." He laughed jovially.

Arthur finished up his meal and stood up.

"That was great, Daniel, but I've got to go see a man about a horse, or in this case, a woman." Arthur waved to Daniel, picked up his bag, and walked out the door.

Once outside, he felt the cool breeze on his skin, and it put a pep in his step. Feeling energized with the beautiful weather and the excellent food, he started down the road toward Dalia's house. He noticed the streets were empty, and most of the homes along them were closed uptight.

He stepped off to the side of the road and was curious about his new Earth Magic. Now that he could wield magic, he just had to try it out. *Honestly, what person wouldn't want to?*

He focused on a patch of bare earth near his feet and stretched his right hand out to it. Within moments he saw the ground start to move, and it practically flowed with his will. He pulled up on the flow, and a small mound began to rise from the ground. He pulled some more and noticed he was getting a little tired. He looked at his mana bar and saw it was continually dropping while he was using three mana every second of his manipulation.

He stopped controlling the earth, and it froze in the small hill he had last made it into. His mana usage stopped, but in the short time he had been using his magic, he had already burned through thirty-six mana. He wasn't sure just how useful this magic would be if it burned mana continuously at that rate. He also didn't see any increase in his Earth Magic experience.

Deciding he would work with it later, he resumed his trip to Dalia's. When he made it to her house, he walked up to the door. Raising his hand to knock, she once again opened the door right before his hand met the door. She was standing in front of him in a tight-fitting dress that accented her curves. It appeared she had cleaned up and even took the time to smooth out her hair. It now flowed and shone with an intense red color. Her eyes had a deep hunger in them as she looked at him.

"Do you have something for me, Arthur? I haven't forgotten your promise of help and would love to get you your deserved reward if you have what I want." She said and ran her tongue over her lips.

He gulped and asked if he could enter to allow them to talk.

She led him inside, and they sat at a sturdy and serviceable table, in what he assumed was the dining area.

"I would like to discuss some of the details of our arrangement first, Dalia." He said.

She frowned at him but nodded for him to continue.

"What was your family name?" he asked her.

She gave him an odd look and answered, "Flamekissed, I'm told it stemmed from our hereditary red hair."

"Do you know anything about a Delilah?" Arthur asked.

Her face grew serious. "She was a distant relative of mine. It isn't common knowledge, but my family has passed down part of her tragic tale. She was the wife of an abusive husband. She had three children, two boys, and one girl. One night, after one of her husband's abuses, she snapped and went mad. She ended up killing one of her sons in her madness, and the other two children escaped the house."

"No one was ever sure what truly happened to her, but no one ever saw her again. A few people reported hearing her in the house talking for years following the child's death, but before long, no one dared venture out there anymore." She explained. "The abusive husband also fled the home but was later found dead by bandits along the road. No one made a fuss about it because they knew his reputation. Some adults in the community helped raise the children. The son died in a fight with an invading goblin tribe many generations ago, but the daughter is where my bloodline stems from."

Arthur had a message pop up in his view.

Justice for the Slain II	
Requirements: Level 6 Rewards: 400 experience	Description: Delilah's ghost has been laid to rest, but what would drive a woman to murder her children? Find someone who can provide information for this quest.
You have successfully fulfilled the required objectives. Do you wish to complete this quest now? Yes/No	

Arthur smiled to himself and selected YES.

"That's a specific topic to discuss with me and something almost no one knows. How would you even think to ask these questions unless... Were you successful? Did you make it into the house and return?" She asked with an excited tone in her voice.

"I have one more question for you before I answer yours. What are your intentions if you are to prove your family heritage?"

She smiled coyly at Arthur and replied: "Why, are you looking to wed minor nobility for a better lot in life?"

"No, I was considering a business deal," Arthur replied with a smile.

She pouted at him but said, "Well, you're no fun. To answer your question, I plan on gaining my title and trying to establish a small hold over the local village here. The people here have had a rough life and have had no solid leadership in a while."

"I think we might be able to work something out then. I want to propose a deal for you. If I can get you the proof you need, I would like your backing for me within the community. I also have plans to help this village. My Goddess wishes for me to help."

Dalia flashed a sour look on her face at the mention of a goddess.

"Don't worry. This isn't a Goddess I believe is common in the land or any of the major cities, so it shouldn't draw any undue attention to this place. The Goddess I follow is Lianna, and I would like to dedicate our work to the betterment of the village to her. If you agree to help me in this endeavor, I'll do everything in my power to restore your nobility and also help support you with the village, now and in the future."

She looked at Arthur for a long while and then nodded.

"I believe I can agree with that." She said.

"Well then, Miss Dalia, I do believe it is time for you to become a noble again." He reached into his bag and removed the Patent of Nobility. He handed it to her and saw a hint of tears in her eyes. She looked it over quickly and then jumped at him with her arms spread wide. She wrapped him in a fierce hug and kissed him hard. Her breasts pressed against his chest, and he quickly started to feel hot and flushed. Another message popped up in front of him.

Patents of Nobility II	
Requirements: Level 5 Rewards: 800 experience, 5 silver coins, unknown rewards also possible.	Description: You have recovered the patent of nobility from the decrepit manor. You have decided to entrust the patent to Dalia and grant her the titles to her family name.
You have successfully fulfilled the required objectives. Do you wish to complete this quest now? Yes/No	

He selected YES and heard trumpets blasting. He looked down at Dalia in his arms.

She separated from him and looked at him in the eye. "I recall promising you a reward, and I have the perfect idea for what that reward shall be."

She stood up and grabbed Arthur's hand. He stood up with her, and she led him toward the back of the house toward what he assumed was the bedroom. They got to the room, and she didn't even pause as her shirt magically disappeared. At least it felt like magic, as fast as she got rid of it.

The view of her body was fantastic. She had a well-proportioned set of perky tits. They were by no means huge but not tiny things either. Her figure was also alluring. Just looking at her, anyone could see she was a beautiful young woman, but the clothes that everyone wore here didn't do anyone any favors. Her body was so much better than he had imagined it to be. The large and ill-fitting clothing hid too much of her physique. Once that flesh was exposed, Arthur completely forgot about anything but this woman.

He took his top off and threw it across the room. It appeared to Arthur that she was impressed with what she saw as well. The clothing didn't do him any favors either. Since coming here, his physique had slimmed a bit around the midsection and looked more muscular than flabby. His broad shoulders were already well-muscled, and she took an appreciative look.

He walked forward and grabbed her firmly
around the waist. She melted into his arms as
he kissed her. Her passion was apparent, and
the rest of their clothes disappeared quickly.
They fell onto the bed in a tangle, and Arthur
thought this was going to be a fantastic
reward.

Chapter 10

A Strange Dream

Arthur felt like he was floating. He couldn't quite describe the feeling. Something between a dream and feeling tipsy from alcohol. He looked all around him, and it appeared he was floating in a gray nothingness. Everywhere he looked, it seemed to be an infinite stretch of gray.

"Hello?" he said out loud. "Anyone around here? Where am I?"

This was supremely odd. Arthur recalled a memorable encounter with Dalia and her beautiful breasts. She also had a tantalizing moan in her pleasure that made him even more aroused, but he was sure they had fallen asleep. If this was a dream, it was both odd and surreal.

Arthur continued to look around but couldn't find anything, so he settled on just reflecting on things that had happened. He recalled the manor fight and the ghost. Those disgusting giant rats still gave him small shivers when he thought of them. The boar chase in the forest got his pulse moving a little quicker. In the end, he settled on his parents. He wasn't sure why, but more than likely, it was because he missed them. He hoped they were doing okay without him around. He doubted it would be easy losing their son, even if he was adopted. They had never treated him as anything other than a biological son.

As he continued to think about his parents, he noticed a window in the gray expanse. He willed himself to float to it, and to his surprise, the scene inside was not something he ever thought he would see.

"Everything will be fine, dear." Said Arthur's Father, Johnathan. "I'm sure it is just the stress from us missing Arthur. You will be good as new before long."

"I don't know, Hun. I keep getting random body aches and am just tired. More tired than usual. The doctor expressed some concerns and wanted me to come back next week to get a checkup and have some blood work done. I worry it could be something more serious." Arthur's Mom, Evelyn said.

"Eve, don't talk like this. We have both been struggling a bit since we lost Arthur, but I have faith we will make it. I know it's hard not hearing from him, but we'll see him again one day."

Evelyn sighed. "All of this at once is just too much to deal with. I still haven't been able to get past losing Arthur. I'm happy that he saved that woman, and he did the right thing, but I wish we wouldn't have lost him in the process. Luckily, the trial for the man that murdered him ended quickly, and he received the death sentence he deserved. Now he won't be able to harm anyone else."

"Now, on top of that, I have to deal with whatever this health problem is too? It just seems like we can't catch a break. I've always said bad things come in threes, so now it just feels like we are waiting for the final piece to fall, only to make things worse."

"We will get through this together like we always have. We've made it through many tough times together before and can do it again. I don't doubt that." Johnathan said, wiping a tear from her face. "Our friends have been very supportive of us and check in on us often."

"I know, but they can't bring him back John, no matter what they say or do, they can't bring him back to me." She cried and pressed her face into his neck.

"I miss him too." He said as he held her. "We have that appointment next week so we can find out more about all of this then. The doctor can do the few tests he needs, and then we can put this whole mess to bed as a bad coincidence. Probably an odd virus or something that you keep catching and never has a chance to fully resolve."

"I truly hope that's all that it is." She said.

The picture faded, and soon he was looking into a vast ocean of gray again. He felt tears on his face and wished he could have held his mother at that moment. She was his rock back in life. His Dad had always been tough and was there for him if he needed help with something or just to hang out and go fishing, but his Mom always helped him through tough emotional things. Dads rarely had that kind of relationship with their boys. Maybe with their daughters, but not their sons.

He had always found it amusing that daughters and sons usually went to the opposite side of the parents for emotional comfort when they could. He would bet that emotional support was a higher percentage on the mom side of every family, but that was honestly to be expected.

He hadn't been thinking about the situation long before the grayness disappeared.

Arthur shot upright and looked around. From the look of things, he was back in Dalia's house. It had been pretty late when he arrived last night, and there wasn't a lot of light around at the time, so Arthur hadn't got a good look at the house. Looking around it now, in the morning sun, he could see that it was similar to the rest of the village — a patchwork of different styles of building and repairs layered over top of each other. A lot of places looked on the verge of collapse but had random boards attached, trying to hold them from different angles.

Thinking about it, he hadn't been around the entire village yet, but he wondered where they got their building supplies from. The villagers didn't like the forest and seemed to be afraid of it. He had seen no kind of lumber mill that he could remember, so where would they get the supplies for repairs? He also hadn't met a carpenter here either, granted he had only talked to a few people so far.

That train of thought faded, and his mind was drawn back to his strange dream. It had seemed so real. Being able to see his parents made him feel a little better, but it looked like he was trying to make up a future conversation for them. That was quite concerning. It just showed how the mind could wander and come up with many odd things.

He put the thoughts of that out of his head and continued to look around. To his delight, the beautiful form of Dalia was still in bed with him, and one of her breasts was currently exposed. It was a delightful sight to wake up to in the morning. His lower region seemed to agree, as well. That and the fact he had to pee. Sadly, he was sure the urge to pee was causing most of that.

He debated on nuzzling up to her and stealing some kisses or going out back to relieve himself when she stirred and looked up at him. He smiled at her, and she smiled right back. Bending down, he gently kissed her on the neck a few times and then a deeper kiss on the lips. Arthur's hand drifted down slowly and cupped her exposed breast while rubbing the nipple with his thumb. She reached down below, and discovering his predicament, raised an eyebrow at him.

"Happy to see me this morning, I see." She said to him.

"Anyone would have to be a fool not to admire the view no matter the time of day," Arthur responded. He wasn't about to tell her that much of it was him having to pee. He would suffer through it like a champ and pee afterward.

From there, everything quickly escalated into a hot and steamy sex session that left both parties panting on the bed and heart rates going wild. Arthur couldn't take it anymore and had to go out back to relieve a different kind of pressure. Walking back in, he discovered she was already partially dressed and decided it was time for him to do so as well.

"So what's this grand plan of yours?" she asked while putting her shirt back on.

"Honestly, I'm still working on what could best help the village. Being new here, I'm not familiar with all the people here and what the main concerns are. I still need to get out and meet more of the people to get a general idea. I know that the place is partially starving because of the Lord's men and, no offense, but most of the buildings look to be on the verge of falling."

"You're not wrong there. The Lord's group of criminals keeps most of the villages either starving or right on the verge. People try to hide things from time to time, but it never works. They do extensive searches of everything until they find it. As for the houses, you're also not wrong. We don't have a carpenter in the village, nor do we have a sawmill, so all the lumber used here was supplied from a neighboring town. Once in a while, we will have a tinker traveling through here with a caravan of lumber, which can make some quick repairs for people just to keep things standing, but people usually have no coin for such things." Dalia said offhandedly.

"That would explain all the overlapping wood and quick looking repairs that are patching this place together. I wouldn't be surprised if one stray spark sent this entire place to ash."

"You would probably be correct. The problem is no one here can do much about it. We have a local smith who can make a few things, but just like everyone else, he rarely has any supplies and can't afford much of anything. Tools are almost unheard of, besides a few for planting, but without seed stock, that's also a worthless endeavor. I honestly don't understand how the cities and the Lord himself even survive. They keep taking what little food we have and never leaving seeds to plant with, so each time it is less and less food. They must suffer from at least some shortage, although I doubt it affects them personally. I'd hate to see the state of some of the larger cities."

"Why does no one do anything about it? You can't keep surviving like this? Everyone will starve and die before long. The land itself looks horrible being so barren. Is there no recourse?"

"No one can do anything to the Lord Golgara. He controls the only armed force in the region, although most of it consists of his little force of bandits he has, that act like they are an army. No one here has anything to fight back with either. The few that had weapons were slowly forced to sell them off to survive. With no one willing to brave the woods, we haven't been able to gather wood to make bows. It seems everyone who ventures there never returns for some reason or another. Everyone but you, of course." She smiled at Arthur.

"Is there no one this Golgara has to answer to that can be petitioned?" Arthur asked.

"I guess you could petition the King here, but the few who have tried have mysteriously been found dead every time. I can't imagine the King doesn't know, though, and if he does, he's done nothing to stop it. Although I have never met him, I would guess he operates similarly." She sighed.

"Well damn, I can help supplement supplies in the village in the forest, but there's no way I can hunt and forage for the entire village. The food problem is the worst problem at the moment and the number one issue to solve. If I can get that fixed, we might be able to convince some of the other villagers to assist with other projects. It would be nice to team up with the smith and get a rudimentary sawmill running to start harvesting some lumber nearby. If we could start improving housing in addition to the food issue, that would greatly swing the population in our favor. The bad thing is that we have limited time. I'll need to find some people in the village to assist me soon because we have a limited time to get this place defensible and back on track before Golgara's men return for another raid."

"Look at you with your big ideas. If you can work to get this village into better shape, I can work on getting my nobility recognized and then having my title transfer to the village under my family name. This would ensure that no one could demand anything from the village without my approval short of Golgara himself. That might give us a delay when the next group of his thieves comes through. We will need to be able to defend the place, though." She said with a look of concentration on her face.

"You're pretty sexy when you concentrate that hard," Arthur told her as he swatted her lightly on the ass.

"You have work to do, sir, no more playing around. I better see some progress in this village if you wish to sample the wares again." She said with a coy smile.

"I'll endeavor to get right on that, my lady," Arthur said with a mock bow. "I do hope to see you around later."

"I'll consider it." She replied with a smile.

Arthur turned and walked out the door. Right before he closed the door, he blew her a kiss with a wink, and she gave an exasperated sigh. He walked out into the morning sunlight. It was already mid-morning with their late-night fun, sleeping in, and then another round of morning action.

Arthur headed back to the Inn and checked in with Daniel. He would know if anything was going on around here. A few minutes later, Arthur was walking back into the empty inn. Seeing Daniel in his usual spot over by the bar, he waved at him in greeting and sat down at the bar in front of him.

"Have yourself a good evening, Arthur?" Daniel said with a grin on his face.

"You could say that. You could also say it was a good morning, too." He said with a chuckle.

"I was able to get those potatoes cut up and have them drying in pieces for seed stock. I've also put the carrot tops in water to start their process of growing the greens. Have any plans for today?" Daniel asked.

"I know the basics of what needs to get done, and just so you're aware, I have recruited Dalia into our mission. She now has her patents of nobility and is going to work on getting the paperwork filed, and her position approved over the village. That should help give us as a bit of a buffer against Golgara's men and may also delay them next time they show up demanding to rob the place." Arthur told him.

"Well, that's a good start, but she alone won't be able to do anything about it. If there were enough people here that could stand with her and bully them away with a show of force, it might work, but no one here has any type of weapons to make themselves threatening. Most of them have no skills that would go with it either." He said.

"From my conversation with Dalia, there are some things that we can do to help, but this is something that will take more than just myself. Unfortunately, it will also require going into the forest, and no one seems willing to do that."

"I might know someone who can help, but what exactly do you envision here? As you know, our most pressing issue is food. Weapons are useless if we don't have it, and no one could fight while starving." He retorted.

"I'm aware of this. By using the forest, we should be able to gather other plants and hunt some meat to supplement supplies. It also gives us the chance to harvest different varieties of wood that will come in handy, making bows and arrows. If we can equip more people with those, it will give us a fighting chance against the bandits and also provide us with more people I can teach to hunt and help the food stores even more. There are many benefits to living next to the forest if you can get the people here to brave going in and survive it. I think if I can take someone with me, we can start working toward this goal. I also know of some techniques to help the blacksmith, although I'm told he is short on supplies. I need to stop by and talk with him." Arthur said thoughtfully.

"Well, lucky for you, Rowan is just who I was going to refer you to. He might be willing to help, and he also happens to be the village blacksmith. There's one other who may also help, but I'll have to talk to her. She's been the one to help keep us afloat and somewhat fed, but she has been struggling with it lately." Daniel said jovially.

"I guess there's no point sitting around then. Which way to his house?" Arthur asked.

"Take the road that branches off to the North that's part of the intersection outside the inn. His building is the last one on the left." Daniel informed Arthur.

"That sounds great. I'll come back by later for dinner. I'll be too busy, so I'll probably skip lunch." Arthur said.

He walked up the stairs and gathered his arrows to put back in his bag. He also grabbed his bow before he left the room. He went back down the stairs and proceeded out of the door with a wave to Daniel.

Arthur proceeded down the road toward Dalia's and took a left to head north as he was directed. He got to the end and saw another little rundown house that appeared to be on the verge of falling; only this one had a small and sturdy looking shop built next to it. Luckily enough, the bottom part of it appeared to be made of earth and stone, so it didn't weather quite as bad. The roof wasn't in the best of shape, but nothing in this place was.

Arthur walked into the building and saw a
man sitting in the corner, looking downcast
and a little lost. Arthur had seen that look
in people before. It usually signaled someone
on the verge of just giving up. The man had a
barrel-chested build and probably topped out a
little over six feet, although that was a bit
hard to determine with him sitting down. He
had a square and chiseled jaw and features
that some might describe as handsome. His face
still had a bit of a boyish cast to it, and
his bright blue eyes and golden blonde hair
were a stark contrast to the rest of him. He
looked a little gaunt, but that was common in
this village. Arthur walked toward the man
and waved.

    "Hi, my name is Arthur, would you happen to
be Rowan?" Arthur asked.

    The man looked up quickly, obviously
surprised to see someone in the building other
than him.

    "I'm Rowan. Is there something I can do for
you, stranger?" Rowan asked.

    "I'm here at the behest of Daniel over at
the inn. I'm new to here, but we've undertaken
a little mission of our own to get this place
back on its feet. I'm only telling you this
because he referred me to you, and I don't
believe he would have if you weren't
trustworthy." Arthur said coolly.

    Rowan perked up a bit at that, and fire
sparked alive in his eyes.

"It wouldn't surprise me that the rascal is up to something. I don't know you, but if you truly wish to help, I would love to help. Things have been dire here for a while, and it is almost to the breaking point for many people. Honestly, I have been thinking long and hard lately about just packing up and moving on to somewhere else. The only thing holding me back is I know we are practically prisoners in Golgara's land and can't get out. Anywhere in this land is bound to be a nightmare." He replied.

"Well, I have some ideas on how to change that. I see you have a decent building here, so I can assume you know your business. Looking around, I see your tools are in serviceable shape, and it's clear you run a well-maintained shop. Daniel, Dalia, and I have come together for this undertaking and each plan to contribute to the effort. The problem is that most of what is necessary to get this place moving again has to be obtained in the forest, and it seems anyone from here that have tried rarely makes it back. I need someone with me, though, to help gather some things we may need." Arthur said.

Rowan gave him an odd look and then glanced around his shop. He took a slow look around the area and then settled back onto Arthur.

"I'll help you. Without help, this place will drive itself into ruin in no time. I had considered offering to help Vana on her efforts to supply the village, but she's had little luck herself lately. If we can turn the village around, that will help, but what's preventing Golgara's men from coming back through like the plague they are?" he asked.

"Well, that's also on the agenda. Tell me a bit about your skills. For instance, are you familiar with making charcoal or coke?" Arthur asked him.

"I'm familiar with making charcoal and occasionally do. I'm not sure what you are referring to with coke, though? In the forge, I typically use coal or charcoal. I keep a large amount of it in the storage shed out back, and since I rarely have any metals I can use, I don't use it often." He told Arthur.

"Well, that's good news. I have some ideas for what we can do, but we should get to the forest for the supplies we need. Do you have any experience with a bow?"

"Not really. Being a smith, I'm more familiar with handheld weapons. I keep a large hatchet here in the shop for protection and have my hammers, but they are for forging and not a battle." He replied.

"That will work out, all right. I can try to teach you a bit of archery because we will need to scour the forest looking for food and hunting for meat. I also want us to gather what we will need to produce bows for the villagers to help train a small army of hunters that can double as village protection against Golgara's thugs. We may also get lucky and find some sources of metal out there that we can take advantage of for your work." Arthur informed him.

"That sounds like you have the beginning of a plan. What is coke that you mentioned, though?" he asked.

"Oh, it is a refined version of coal. It's made in a very similar way to making charcoal from wood you just do almost the same process to coal. It produces chunks of coke that burn hotter and cleaner than coal and help you achieve melting temperatures with iron that help filter impurities and raise the carbon content of the metal." Arthur said offhandedly.

"I understood most of that but not sure what you mean by carbon. Either way, it sounds like something I need to work on. It could come in handy in the endeavor. Anything specific I need to bring with me?" he asked.

"You'll need your hatchet and something to help carry things with. I have my bag, but I sincerely hope we can find much more. Even finding one decent size deer would help tremendously and wouldn't be difficult for us to cart back. I also don't want to waste anything on any animal we kill." Arthur told him.

"I think I have just what we need. It's a small hand cart that's lightweight but is strong and can support heavy loads. Let me grab it." Rowan said.

He walked around the side of the building and wheeled around a cart that looked similar to a wheelbarrow. It had a flat and sturdy wooden frame that was vaguely shaped like a triangle. At the wide end, it sported two long poles that stretched back to hold on to, and on the point was mounted a wheel to help push it along. With two short legs on the wide end of it, it worked practically identical to wheelbarrows he had seen before. The small cart would work for what they needed.

"That'll work perfectly," Arthur told him.

Rowan smiled and dropped it down where he
was standing. He jogged back to the forge and
returned with his hatchet attached to his
belt. He ran back to the cart and picked it
up.

"Ready to go?" he asked. Arthur could see
the excitement in his eyes. Giving the man a
purpose had brought life back into him, which
Arthur was grateful to see.

"Off we go," replied Arthur.

They took off back down the road toward the
center of the village and then veered in a
southeastern direction toward the forest line.
Arthur had come from the southwestern side and
had been to the south when he investigated the
manor. He could see one of the mountainous
cliffs to the southeast that Daniel had
mentioned walled them in a ways past the
border of the forest and wanted to investigate
in that direction.

They reached the border to the forest, and
he looked to Rowan.

"You ready for this adventure?" Arthur
asked with a smile.

Rowan had a nervous look to him, but then
his face hardened with determination, and he
looked at Arthur.

"Let's go." He replied.

They both squared off and started their way
into the forest.

Chapter 11

Forest Excursion

Arthur entered the forest with Rowan close behind him, pushing the cart. They kept a wary eye on their surroundings as they walked. Arthur had his bow in hand with an arrow ready but not pulled back, and his beastslaying sword was buckled to his waist. They slowly crept through the forest, trying to be quiet to avoid spooking anything.

They kept an eye out for other things as well. Arthur was interested in finding any trails for animals they may come across, but he also needed to find some good wood for bows and arrows. They had to keep an eye out for useful plants as they went. Being able to find more plants would be very helpful in the long run. They continued past the mile mark into the forest, and it seemed to come alive as it did every other time he entered. Something seemed to press into the edge of the woods that stopped everything from entering.

They searched as they went, and Arthur was happy to stumble upon a small cluster of plants he recognized. They were thick, green stems that came out of the ground and had thin leaves out in opposite directions that looked like giant blades of grass. This was another of those items he had to dig for but knew it would be worth it. After a few minutes of digging, he looked at his prize.

Item: Head of Garlic	**Durability:** 20/20 **Rarity:** Common **Weight:** 0.1 kg **Traits:** This head of garlic contains multiple cloves. It would make a good component for seasoning dishes.

Arthur heard the chime and let the notification wash over him and absorbed the information.

You have gained 1000 experience in Herbalism for identifying a Garlic Plant (x10).

Congratulations, you have reached level 4 in Herbalism. You now have 9% more chance of successfully identifying an herb.

Arthur was happy to find something but wished it was directly edible. Wouldn't do much good to harvest spices if you had nothing to use them on. He didn't dwell on it and instead gathered all he found. Luckily, these could be split and replanted with ease if needed. Once he picked them all, he let the notifications add up for himself.

You have gained 500 experience in Farming for successfully harvesting Head of Garlic (x10).

After they pulled up the garlic and got it into Arthur's bag, they headed out again. It excited Arthur when they ran across a pine tree that was damaged. He walked over to it and took a careful look at the damaged area. The tree had released some of its sap to repair the area, and it had hardened. He pulled out his dagger and set to work. He needed to harvest as much of this as was possible for the plan he had. When he got the first piece off, he looked at it.

Item: Ball of Pine Sap	**Durability**: 10/10 **Rarity**: Common **Weight**: 0.01 kg **Slot**: Crafting Ingredient **Traits**: Pine sap is a commonly occurring substance produced by pine trees. There may be uses for this substance.

Excited that the world recognized part of his intent, he set to work. The damaged area was considerably large. When he finished, he checked his log for the update.

You have gained 600 experience in Herbalism for harvesting a Ball of Pine Sap (x60).

    One more thing that Arthur could check
off his list. Rowan gave him an odd look when
he finished.

    "Why were you digging into that tree,
anyway? It didn't look like you had gained
anything useful." He said.

    "It may not look like it, but that's
vital to one of my ideas. I need that sap to
make a resin used as a glue. It will help make
bows and arrows." Arthur told him.

    "Well, I'm no bowyer, but I guess it
sounds reasonable. Each craft is a little
protective of its secrets, so it's no surprise
I hadn't heard of it." Rowan responded.

    "That's understandable, I guess. To make
a common resin, you only need three things.
You need the sap, some charcoal, and either
poop from a plant-eating animal or beeswax.
Those two options make two different resins.
The resin with the poop will be more brittle,
while the resin with the beeswax will be more
malleable. I want to find a honey bee hive to
try to collect some beeswax. It'd be the best
candidate for laminating bows since it's more
flexible. If we can find a good sturdy yew
wood, though, we wouldn't need to laminate
anything. It's still useful for attaching the
arrowheads and the fletching, regardless."
Arthur informed him.

    "Thanks for the information. I'm glad you
know what you are looking for. I would have
never spotted the garlic you found earlier. I
knew what it was as soon as you harvested it,
but I didn't know what the plant itself looked
like by sight." He told Arthur.

"I spent a lot of spare time doing some gardening myself, so I'm familiar with most of the common plants and some less common ones." Arthur let him know. "Let's keep moving and see what else we can find."

They took off again, and after a few hundred yards, Arthur pulled up to a stop. He looked at the ground and noticed some deer poop in the middle of the game trail. The small pellets still had steam coming off of them, which told him it was close. He signaled to Rowan to stay as quiet as possible and to follow at a distance. He didn't want the cart to creak and risk spooking the deer away.

He crept along slowly, trying to maintain silence. His attempt wasn't terrible, but his low level in Stealth was showing with the occasional crunch of leaves and cracking of twigs. He followed the trail for a few hundred yards and came across a small pond under a large tree. The large puddle was a deep blueish-green color, and the edge was covered in smooth stones. It looked like a mixture of natural and man-made, but it was hard to tell for sure. He saw two other items that excited him, though. One was the deer that was standing by the pool and drinking from the water. The other was the large tree next to the pond. The tree looked like a web of smaller trees intertwined together, and then the tops started bending down and out away from it like spider webs. It was precisely what Arthur needed because it was a yew tree.

Arthur smoothly pulled up the bow, drew it back, and sighted on the deer. He decided it was time for a shot to the head to preserve as much meat as possible. Hoping the arrow was up to the task, Arthur took his customary slow and steady breath and then released it. He felt a slight twinge as he released and knew he had jerked a hair at the end. It wasn't enough to avoid the deer, but it was enough to drive his aim off and hit the animal in the neck, directly behind its head, instead of the head itself.

You have dealt 75 damage to Deer (Level 6) with Simple Iron Arrow (Sneak Attack) (Critical Strike) (Mortal Strike).

The animal fell and started thrashing. Blood was leaking out of the wound quickly, so he was sure he had hit a major artery. He didn't want the creature to suffer, though, so he pulled out his sword and chopped into its neck right at the base of the skull. The blade bit in and stopped after it penetrated halfway through the vertebrae. The creature stopped thrashing and went silent.

You have dealt 15 damage to Deer (Level 6) with Steel Longsword of Minor Beastslaying.

He heard the chimes and let the combat information roll over him and took it in again.

Deer (Level 6) has died.
You have gained 60 experience in Stealth for successful use against Deer (Level 6).
You have gained 90 experience in Archery for killing Deer (Level 6).

Congratulations, you have progressed to Level 4 in Archery. You are granted a 6% bonus to accuracy.

You have gained 35 experience in Swords for killing Deer (Level 6).

You have gained 75 experience for killing Deer (Level 6).

Arthur watched as Rowan came up behind him and waved him over. Gaining another level in Archery was thrilling. Hopefully, that would help him with the bad shots he was suffering from. He was also happy with the results of his notifications. They appeared to be working as he intended and rolled over him as the event happened. It didn't even distract him. Rowan caught up to him and had a massive grin on his face when he saw the dead deer.

"We need to get this thing field dressed and on the cart so we can keep moving. It would be nice to kill at least one more animal before we leave the forest. We should chop some of the lower hanging limbs from that tree by the water. That yew will be a good candidate for some bows." Arthur told Rowan.

"If you want to get started on your glorious kill, I can run over and select some better-looking wood and get to chopping. I have the hatchet, anyway." Rowan said.

"Sounds good to me. If you can cut a dozen good pieces of the wood that are each close to five feet in length, that'd be great." Arthur told him.

He nodded and headed toward the tree. While he handled that, Arthur walked over to the deer and started the slow process of gutting it. The blade quickly cut into the belly and sliced up through the ribcage and into the neck. He then continued skinning back down until he made it to the asshole of the animal. The best way to clean one effectively was to skin to the bottom, as he did, and then take the blade and cut around the asshole so it could be pulled out with the guts. He completed the task and ripped the guts out of the interior bit by bit, trying to ensure he didn't accidentally rupture any of the organs that held the smellier items in them. He got the guts out without too much trouble. He dragged the deer carcass a little closer to the pool and splashed some water into the cavity to help wash most of the excess blood and hair out. He then rinsed his hands off as best as he could to clean off the blood.

He dragged the deer closer to the cart that Rowan had left near him and eyed the carcass. It shouldn't be too much trouble for him to load the animal by himself. He lifted the front of the deer and set it on the cart and followed that with the ass end of the animal as he slid it onto the cart. He walked around the cart, grabbed the handles, and moved to where Rowan was going to town on the tree. It looked like he was using the opportunity to blow off some steam, but Arthur would never begrudge the man for that.

By the time Arthur got over to Rowan, he had already finished getting seven of the pieces Arthur had requested. He looked at one to see what it stated.

Item: Yew Log	**Durability:** 50/50 **Rarity:** Uncommon **Weight:** 2.0 kg **Traits:** Yew logs are commonly prized for their uses in making bows.

It was nice to find something that wasn't a common ingredient for once. While Rowan finished chopping the last of the logs, Arthur started loading the chunks of wood onto the cart and packed them around the deer where needed.

They continued forward and made it less than a mile before they heard a shrill cry followed by a bunch of odd noises that neither of them could identify. They gave each other a nod and hurried toward the noise. As they got closer, the sound got louder. They slowed as they approached to get a better look. The sight that greeted them was something neither had expected.

They peeked out between two trees and saw five rather ugly, green creatures, who had backed a person against a tree and had them cornered. The creatures were hideous, standing around four feet tall with mottled green skin, and long, sharp teeth sticking out at all angles from their mouths. Their skin looked rough and bumpy in most places, and their joints were large and knobby.

The creatures themselves weren't what drew their attention, though. The person they had trapped did. She was not like anyone Arthur had ever seen. Her skin was a dark purple hue, she stood a little over six feet tall, and she had a slender build which reminded Arthur of some long-distance runners back during track in school. Tall and lean, with well-defined muscle, pretty much described her look from head to toe. She had dull gray hair that looked almost silver, and she appeared to be frightened. She was holding a small dagger, swiping it toward any of the creatures that got too close.

Arthur did a quick scan of one of the monsters to see what they were dealing with.

Name: Goblin	
Level: 6	
Type: Creature (Sentient)	
Rarity: Common	
HP: 120/120	
Stamina: 120/120	
Strength: 4	Experience: N/A
Agility: 6	Skills
Intellect: 1	Combat Skills:
Wisdom: 1	
Endurance: 2	Ferocious Bite: ?
Charisma: 1	(???/???)
Luck: 2	

You have gained 75 experience in Scan for successful use against Goblin (Level 6).

Well, that explained the ugly. Arthur thought to himself. He looked to Rowan, who had fear in his eyes.

"You can stay back and not get involved
in this fight. I will see what I can do to
help the young lady with her goblin problem.
You may want to backtrack a bit to avoid any
confrontation." Arthur whispered to Rowan.

Rowan just gave Arthur a fearful look and
nodded almost imperceptibly. He slowly started
backing up toward where they had come from.
This would not be an easy fight. There were
five of them, and he was only one person. He
didn't imagine the woman would be of much
help, and he had already sent Rowan away.

He would have to go for the surprise
attack and try to take as many out as quickly
as possible with well-placed arrow shots when
he started firing. Luckily, they were all
facing the girl and not paying attention to
anything around them. They were also making a
large amount of noise so that it would add to
the confusion. Arthur was a good sixty yards
from them, causing the shots to be a little
tricky until they started to close the
distance. He was getting ready to take his
first shot when he froze. Remembering that he
had leveled Archery to level 4, he could
unlock the Talent Tree for it at level five
and may get a useful skill out of that. Arthur
used some of his saved skill progress from
leveling and bumped the Archery skill up to 5.

*Congratulations, you have progressed to
Level 5 in Archery. You are granted an 8%
bonus to accuracy.*

He quickly checked the skill, and when
concentrating upon it, another box appeared.

You have 2 unused Talent Points.

Talent	Description
Tier 1	
Aim Shot (0/1)	This ability allows the user to slow down the moments while being able to see farther and more accurately, to pick the perfect shot. Cost: 25 Stamina
Steady Fire (0/5)	This ability allows the user to fire faster. Each level adds 4% to rate of fire. Maximum of 20%.
Arrow Straightening. (0/1)	This ability allows the user to use a small amount of mana to ensure arrows are perfectly straight and true. Cost: 5 Mana

Arthur scanned over the options and was in awe. It would be fantastic if only he could have all of them. It was slightly confusing that it said he had 2 Talent Points, though. Daniel told him you only get 1 Talent Point per level, starting at five, but he wasn't going to look a gift horse in the mouth. He made a quick decision and put one point into Aim Shot.

Congratulations, you have learned Aim Shot, a Subskill of Archery, for a 100 experience bonus.

He was happy with that purchase. But now, where to spend the other point? He looked back at the chart and noticed it had changed.

You have 1 unused Talent Point.

Talent	Description
Tier 1	
Aim Shot (1/1)	*This ability allows the user to slow down the moments while being able to see farther and more accurately, to pick the perfect shot.* *Cost: 25 Stamina*
Steady Fire (0/5)	*This ability allows the user to fire faster. Each level adds 4% to the rate of fire. Maximum of 20%.*
Arrow Straightening (0/1)	*This ability allows the user to use a small amount of mana to ensure arrows are perfectly straight and true.* *Cost: 5 Mana*
Tier 2	
Sustained Focus (0/4)	*This ability decreases the Stamina cost of using Aim Shot by 5 per level, maximum of 20 Stamina reduction.*

Sharpened Arrowheads (0/5)	*This ability increases the likelihood that critical strikes will also cause mortal damage. Each level increases this chance by 5% for a maximum of 25%.*

Arthur was happy to see that his purchase had revealed more talents in the next tier. He hadn't been sure if the different lines were level based or if they were based on what had been unlocked, but it was clear now. With the current scenario, he decided to put his second point in Steady Fire. He needed the extra speed to kill these things before they got to him. He didn't bother rechecking the tree to see if anything new showed up because he had a woman to save and no more points he could use.

Arthur lifted the bow and drew back his arrow while activating his Aim Shot, and his view zoomed in as he looked down the shaft. The sight made him feel five feet from the monster, which was a little disorienting, but he got a hold of the sensation. Aiming directly for the creature's back, where its heart should be, he released the arrow. He scrambled to grab another projectile as quickly as possible. He had just snatched it and was pulling it from his bag when he heard the first goblin howl. The others looked to him and had a confused stare on their faces.

You have dealt 80 damage to Goblin (1) (Level 6) with Aim Shot (Sneak Attack) (Critical Strike) (Mortal Strike) for 25 Stamina.

Their fellow goblin stumbled around and began coughing up blood. The goblins surrounding the injured one couldn't see the arrow in its back from how they were positioned, though. The goblin collapsed onto his side, still coughing up blood. Arthur got his next shaft up onto the string and activated Aim Shot again. His vision flew forward, and he aimed at the next goblin to the right of the one he had just hit. Releasing, Arthur watched the arrow fly while scrambling for another shaft. This shot wasn't perfect, but it hit relatively close to where he had aimed. Instead of impacting where he wanted, it had hit a little closer to the spine in the lower middle of the back.

You have dealt 80 damage to Goblin (2) (Level 6) with Aim Shot (Sneak Attack) (Critical Strike) (Mortal Strike) for 25 Stamina.

It howled in anguish and hunched over. The other goblins saw the arrow this time. The goblins looked around and quickly spotted Arthur as he fitted his next shaft to the string.

He pulled this one up as well and noticed the goblins were charging for him at a dead sprint. He activated Aim Shot once again, and this time could distinctly see that not only was his vision zoomed in, but they also moved at a much slower pace. The skill was not exaggerating that it slowed down the surroundings when in use. He chose the next goblin in line and fired directly into its heart. The creature pitched face first in the dirt and stopped moving.

He reached for another arrow and pulled it from his bag. He got the shaft to the string, but before he could raise it to aim, the two remaining goblins were on top of him. He dropped the bow and pulled his sword clear of its scabbard just in time to block a blow intended for his head.

The goblin had swung a nasty looking wooden club that was studded with sharp pieces of metal. The other goblin had a small dagger in hand. Arthur reached down and quickly grabbed his blade from its sheath and held it in his left hand while maintaining a grip on his sword in his right.

The small dagger was the next best thing since he didn't have a shield. He only hoped it wouldn't come back to bite him later. The goblin with the dagger was dancing around but not getting any closer while Arthur was facing off with the club-wielding one. Arthur was thankful for that, but at the moment, he couldn't sit around and wait long.

He waited for the next swing from the club, and it came down in a massive overhand strike. He caught it on his sword and pushed the weapon farther up while taking a step forward and thrusting the dagger directly into the bottom of the goblin's jaw and up through its head. The creature collapsed before he could pull the knife back out, and it took the blade down with it.

You have dealt 120 damage to Goblin (4) (Level 6) with Simple Iron Dagger (Brain Rupture).

Goblin (4)(Level 6) has died.

You have gained 75 experience in Block for killing Goblin (4) (Level 6).

You have gained 75 experience in Swords for killing Goblin (4) (Level 6).

You have gained 75 experience in Small Blades for killing Goblin (4) (Level 6).

You have gained 75 experience in Dual Wield for killing Goblin (4) (Level 6).

You have gained 125 experience for slaying Goblin (4) (Level 6).

Goblin (1) (Level 6) has died.

You have gained 80 experience in Stealth for successful use against Goblin (1) (Level 6).

You have gained 75 experience in both Archery and the Subskill Aim shot for killing Goblin (1) (Level 6).

He turned to face the other goblin only to find it was already right on top of him. It swung the dagger at him, and he was able to get the sword up and deflect part of the hit but not fast enough to block all of it. The edge of the blade dug into his left shoulder but wasn't a terrible injury.

Goblin (5) (Level 6) has dealt 20 damage to you with Rusty Iron Dagger (Glancing Blow).

The initial hit barely registered to Arthur, due to the adrenaline raging in him, but it started to ache shortly after the goblin pulled back. He took a glance at his status.

HP: 210/230
Mana: 100/100
Stamina 150/230

He was pleased that he was holding up pretty well so far. The surprise attack that helped him drop some of them quickly had given him the upper hand so far, but he wasn't sure what would be the best method for taking out the last goblin. He wasn't keen on being stabbed himself, and honestly, he wasn't a skilled swordsman.

The goblin rushed back in with a flurry of strikes, and Arthur struggled to keep up. Since he didn't have his dagger to help block, he was only using the sword, and the little creature's speed was faster than he could move. The goblin was alternating between clawing him with its freehand and slashing with the rusty dagger it was holding. Arthur did his best to block the attacks but was trying to focus on the blade and ignoring the freehand. This allowed a few more hits to land.

Goblin (5) (Level 6) has dealt 5 damage to you with Melee.
Goblin (5) (Level 6) has dealt 5 damage to you with Melee.

Goblin (5) (Level 6) has dealt 5 damage to you with Melee.
Goblin (5) (Level 6) has dealt 20 damage to you with Rusty Iron Dagger (Glancing Blow).

The quickness of the goblin was keeping him from being able to retaliate. He was searching for ideas when the decision was taken out of his hands. A hatchet suddenly sprouted from the top of the Goblin's head, and it fell to the ground, dead.

Goblin (2) (Level 6) has died.
You have gained 80 experience in Stealth for successful use against Goblin (2) (Level 6).
You have gained 75 experience in both Archery and the Subskill Aim shot for killing Goblin (2) (Level 6).
You have gained 125 experience for slaying Goblin (2) (Level 6).
You have gained 125 experience for the death of Goblin (5) (Level 6).

Standing behind the goblin, with a grim look of determination, was Rowan. He looked at the goblin and then at Arthur. He smiled at Arthur and shrugged. "I couldn't let you have all the fun."

"You arrived just in time. I was debating on what to do about it, and you took care of the problem for me. I'm gonna go check on our damsel in distress over there." Arthur told him. He had taken two steps when Rowan grabbed his arm and turned Arthur toward him.

"Are you sure about that? It might not be a good idea to be conversing with her kind. I don't mind helping her, because goblins are disgusting, but I'm not sure we should approach her." He told Arthur.

"Why would I not talk to her? She's drop-dead gorgeous and needed help. I'd like to see how she got caught out here by goblins, to begin with. How about you search each of the goblins and take everything off of them that could be useful? Anything they had, like the dagger the last goblin was using, could be used, smelted down, and reforged if needed. Probably worth salvaging the metal out of the other one's club as well. Just sort through everything they have and gather it up while I talk to her." Arthur suggested.

"Alright." Rowan said, "I'm not a big fan of talking to her, but I'll trust your judgment on the matter. I'll start working my way through the goblin bodies."

Rowan turned to the nearest body and knelt down to start his work while Arthur turned back toward the woman and started walking.

Chapter 12

Meeting with an Elf

Arthur strolled toward the lady that was still backed up to the tree with her dagger still in hand. She had a few scrapes and cuts on her, but nothing that looked serious. He raised his hands with his palms facing her to show he had nothing in his hands. Now that the fight was over and he was getting closer, he could see more details of the woman.

She had smooth features and a slender build, as he noticed before. Her eyes were almond-shaped and slightly larger than he would expect but not unattractive. Her thin eyebrows were furrowed, although he suspected that was due to the situation and her not knowing him. She had high and sharp cheekbones that almost looked alien but did not take away from her striking good looks. Her breasts were slightly small but sat on her frame well. Her hair was a gunmetal gray, and her eye color was the most exciting part of all. It was a bright lavender color.

Arthur used Scan as he approached.

You have gained 125 experience in Scan for successful use against Allendria (Level 10).

Name: Allendria	
Level: 10	
Age: ??	
Race: Elf (Dark)	
HP: 100/160	
MP: 0/100	
Stamina: 10/160	
Strength: ?	**Experience**: ???
Agility: ?	**Skills**
Intellect: ?	
Wisdom: ?	???
Endurance: ?	
Charisma: ?	
Luck: ?	

Arthur was surprised at the lack of information. He quickly dismissed it as his low level in the ability, though. He guessed people not classified as creatures probably required a higher level to glean information from.

Arthur came to a stop five feet from the woman and looked at her.

"Hello, my name is Arthur. Is there anything I can do to help you now that the goblins have been defeated?" he asked.

She gave him a look that flashed with a bit of fury and took him off guard.

"I'm thankful for the help, but what do you want from me?" she asked him.

"My friend and I were merely traveling in the forest hunting when we heard your scream. We felt it necessary to help. No one deserves to be at the mercy of those nasty creatures. I desire nothing from you, but I'm intrigued by you. I have never seen one of the dark elf kindreds before. Is your beauty a normal trait shared by your race?" he asked nonchalantly.

She blushed slightly, and then the steely look flashed back over her face again.

"I don't want any trouble with your kind. The goblins only surprised me in too large of numbers for me to counter effectively."

That was an odd thing for her to say. Was there some kind of tension between dark elves and humans? That might explain some of Rowan's hesitance on him speaking with her.

"I merely wish to make sure you need no further assistance, although I was hoping you might tell me why you were out here alone. I noticed you also have some cuts and that you're bleeding in a few spots. Do you need help in cleaning the wounds?" Arthur asked.

Her voice changed a little the next time she spoke.

"Please give me the strength to make it through this human's lies and get out of here." She mumbled.

"I told you the truth. I have no wish to harm you and only want to help." Arthur said, but he also noticed a slight change to his voice as well. He couldn't place what it was, though. As soon as he saw the look on her face, he forgot all about it.

She ran at him and grabbed him by the front of the shirt.

"How do you know the Tongue of the Fallen?" she screamed at him.

"What are you talking about? What is this Tongue of the Fallen you are referring to?"

She cocked her head at him and looked at him closely. Arthur imagined the incredulous look on his face helped ease her fury a little because she backed up and took a deep breath.

"I'm not sure how you don't realize this, but you spoke a different language, as did I. When I mumbled about the lies, I was speaking the language of the Dark Elves, the language referred to as the Tongue of the Fallen. Somehow, not only did you understand it, but you subconsciously respond to me in the same language even though you claim to know nothing of it. Either you are lying about your associations, which I find as unlikely based on your reaction, or you have some special abilities with languages." She said with a thoughtful look.

Arthur looked at her dumbfounded. "You are serious? I spoke a different language, then? I didn't mean any disrespect or anything. I didn't mean to anger you and was honestly only hoping to help. I'm not very familiar with many of the customs around here and have never met a Dark Elf myself, so if I offered any insult, I apologize."

Her tone changed again when she replied, "Well, it is surprising to find another with knowledge of our language, but there are no laws in our culture, that I'm aware of, preventing others from knowing it. Usually, other people cannot understand it even when we attempt to teach it. I also don't detect any magical device on you that could assist in translation, although I can tell you have a magical affinity with at least one element. I have to say it's refreshing to meet a polite and civilized human."

"Thank you for the compliment, but I can honestly say I don't understand all of what is happening. Do you mind filling me in on what you mean? Why would there be animosity between humans and dark elves? Again, I'm not from around here, so this is the first I have heard of this." Right after he said that something clicked with him, though. "Wait, how can you tell I have a magic affinity with an element?"

She let out a quick laugh that was beautiful and musical. "Well, I'll tell you that I can detect your magic. Elves, in general, are quite sensitive to magic, and the fact that I have an affinity in magic as well makes it even easier for me to detect yours. I'm not advanced enough in my magical ability to determine exactly what element or elements you can control, but I can tell you can control at least one."

"I guess that's good to know. I have little knowledge about magic and haven't used mine much at all since I can't seem to figure it out. I know we just met and all, but would you be willing to help me with a little magical training? If you're busy or don't have the time, I understand." Arthur responded.

She gave Arthur a thoughtful look and stood in silence for a few moments.

"This is unusual for a human to cavort with one of my kind, much less to ask for help. Since you have treated me fairly and with no prejudice, I'll agree to accompany and assist you with your training if you agree to do something for me first." She said.

"I suppose that would be fair to gain the help of a fabulous looking dark elf for the price of a task," Arthur said as he winked at her. "What is this task you need to be done?".

She blushed, which was somewhat hard to
tell with the dark complexion she had, but it
was still visible if you looked just right.

"It's rather simple, but with the danger
we just faced, I could use some help. Before
those creatures found me, I was camped in a
small cave in the mountain not far from here.
I heard them as I was returning to the cave
and didn't have enough time to grab my few
belongings before I fled. If you could assist
me in recovering these items, I'll accompany
you back to where you're staying and assist
you with the training of your magical skills."

Aiding Allendria	
Requirements: Level 6 Rewards: Gain a companion	Description: After saving Allendria at the hands of goblins, she has asked you to help recover the few possessions she had before her fleeing their pursuit. Assist her in finding and retrieving the items.
Note: Companions will only accompany you until the terms of your agreements have been met or until your goals and feelings no longer align. Do you wish to Accept this Quest? Yes/No	

Arthur grinned and acknowledged the quest
acceptance. "Of course, I'll assist you with
that. That's more than fair. Let's finish
sorting out this mess with the bodies, and we
can try to find this cave you stayed in before
heading back to the village. I wasn't planning
on us being out here much longer anyway with
the amount of stuff we had gathered."

Arthur turned and walked back toward Rowan. He could hear Allendria following behind him and smirked at the idea of this beautiful woman becoming his magic teacher. Hopefully, there wouldn't be any issues with her being in the village with him. The amount of abject disdain he had seen from Rowan, for what appeared to be no reason, baffled him.

As he got closer, he noticed that Rowan had finished his work with the goblins. They were all lined up in a neat row, and it appeared they had been stripped of any possession worth note. There were still scraps of clothing on some of them, but nothing that looked like he would ever want it to touch his body. Rowan himself had a small pile of items off to the side and looked like he was sorting through it.

When Arthur got close, Rowan looked up at him. The man gave him a quick smile and then a quick look of shock and fear crossed his face when he saw Allendria approaching Arthur. Arthur decided he needed to head this off quickly.

"Rowan, I'd like for you to meet Allendria. She will be accompanying us for a while. I agreed to help her find some of her belongings she lost while fleeing these creatures, and then she has agreed to help me with an issue of my own once we return to the village." Arthur said with a smile. "Allendria, this is Rowan, the local blacksmith, and my traveling companion." Arthur waved his hand toward Rowan.

Allendria and Rowan both stared at each other for a few moments with looks of apprehension on their faces before he saw a determination in Rowan's eyes. He stood up, walked over to her, and extended his hand out to her. "Pleasure to meet you, Allendria."

She gave a lopsided smile, and after a moment's hesitation, reached out her hand to shake his.

"It's a pleasure to meet you as well, Rowan, although I'll say this is one of the first times I have ever used the human style greeting of shaking hands. I'm familiar with many of your customs, but the lack of communication between our races has never given me much chance to practice." She said with a slightly humorous note in her voice.

"Great! Now that we are all acquainted with each other, what did you find, Rowan?" Arthur asked.

Rowan looked back to Arthur. "Not much of value, to be honest. There were a few scraps of cloth that were somewhat serviceable, after extensive washing, of course. There were also a few weapons that aren't worth much of anything as they are, but with the shortage of metal in the village, they can be reforged into something useful. No other belongings of any note were on any of them." He summarized.

"Alright then, let's load the few things
worth keeping on the cart and get moving. We
need to help Allendria find her belongings
quickly so we can get back to the village. We
want to have plenty of time left to get some
of this stuff cleaned up and worked on. We
also don't want this meat sitting out very
long today before we can get it cleaned and
stored. Luckily, it isn't hot under cover of
the trees here, so that's helping us right
now." Arthur told them.

They both nodded and set to work, putting
the few items in the cart. Arthur saw no
reason to bother with the bodies of the
goblins now. The creatures of the forest would
pick the bones clean, and whatever was left
would return to the soil over time. The cart
was loaded rather quickly since there weren't
more than a few things to put on it, and they
started in the general direction Allendria had
indicated.

Allendria wasn't entirely sure where the
cave she had slept in was since she had been
in a mad dash when escaping, but said she
would recognize the area when close. She spent
a decent amount of time looking for what she
thought was a safe place to sleep. This
allowed her to be familiar with the area close
to the cave, but during the flight from the
creatures, she wasn't able to keep up with her
surroundings.

During the trip, Rowan motioned to Arthur
to join him by the cart while Allendria was
leading the way. Arthur fell back to walk side
by side with him as they continued to follow
her.

"Are you sure this is a good idea,
Arthur?" he asked.

"I don't know if it's a good idea, but I also don't see any harm in it. Allendria needed help, so we helped her and are finishing the job. We're out here to look around for any useful resources anyway, so walking toward her cave only gives us more of a chance to find any additional resources we may need. I also have a deal with her to assist me back in the village." Arthur stated.

"That might be another problem. I wasn't joking when I said our peoples don't have the best relationship. They may be somewhat hostile around her. I don't know if anyone would outright attack her since she's a woman, but I also doubt she'll feel very welcome in a village of humans." He said, sounding downcast.

"We can cross that bridge when we get to it. And for what it's worth, I appreciate you swallowing those prejudices and being cordial during your introduction. I saw the struggle play out on your face. I know it's hard to get past ingrained hatred."

Rowan gave Arthur a lopsided grin. "I have no personal problem with dark elves myself and have never run ill of one before either. I only know of the things that have been repeated around me to fall back on. I'm not sure if others will do the same, though. We also know almost nothing about this woman. Why's she out in the middle of the forest on her own, anyway? It just seems like nothing but trouble."

"There are things we don't know, but I could argue almost the same thing about you. I honestly don't know you very well personally, other than our interactions today. I'll monitor her for anything suspicious, but I think she could be beneficial to us helping get the village back in order." Arthur told him.

Rowan winked at him. "I'm sure you'll keep your eye on her. Not that I could blame you with how beautiful she is."

Arthur laughed. "I agree with that, as well. Let's get this little trip finished up. We have a lot of things to take care of when we get back. All these supplies will need to be sorted out and worked on. The meat will have to all be quartered and salted. I'm sure we can get Daniel to assist with some of this. The hides will need to be scraped and prepared for use, and the other herbs and things we have found will need to be stored. Daniel will handle most of the food items, and as soon as we get a decent amount of stock together, I want us to get a plan together to provide some food to the villagers."

"This will take more people than just Daniel, you, and myself, but if we can get the foundation started, and get the people back on their feet, I think we have a better chance of getting the place back in order. We can start by finding some other necessary craftsmen, if there are any others in this place, to start bringing into the fold. Enticing them with some of our food and supplies to work with should get most of them to help as we need. First and foremost, I want to make sure we have something in place to check that the women and children are provided for no matter what."

"Once everything is back in order, and everyone is contributing, this won't be an issue anymore, but the women and children will have to be fed quietly, so we don't start a mad rush of people trying to get food without working for it. I know Daniel has already tried to help some of the women and children on his own, so I think with what we bring in today, it will help him greatly." Arthur continued.

"While I don't mean to offend, and I appreciate what you are trying to do for the village, what's your purpose in this? As far as I know, you don't know anyone here and are from an unknown land. You didn't know about the local problems or the lords until you arrived, and now you are trying to face off against these people and help out a whole group of strangers. The situation just makes no sense." Rowan said.

"A fair question, to be honest, the main reason is that I'm essentially on a divine mission here from a Goddess to assist this land in fixing some of its problems. I'm also unable to return to my previous home, so I need to make this home a good one. If I am living here for the foreseeable future, I need to make it a place worth staying." Arthur answered.

"If that's the case, then let's make the village something worthwhile again. I came to the village right around the time the decline started, and I remember the stories of how great the place used to be and remember seeing some evidence to support that before everything started falling apart from neglect and abuse by Lord Golgara. If we can find more people to help us on our hunting trips, it would be useful. This forest has always been dangerous, and there were rumors that people kept disappearing because of the Dark Elves and the goblins when they ventured in here. That's why almost no one will brave it." Rowan told him.

"We'll have to work on it, but I look forward to seeing the results," Arthur told him. They continued in silence for a few more moments until Arthur turned to Rowan and motioned that he was headed up front to speak with Allendria. Rowan gave him a quick smile, followed by a wink as Arthur left. Arthur sped up slightly so he could get out in front of Rowan and the cart and catch up to Allendria. He noticed she was scanning the area in front of her constantly in what he could only imagine was her trying to find something she recognized.

"Find anything familiar yet?" Arthur asked her.

She gave him a frustrated glare followed by a sigh, "Nothing yet, but I'm sure we are at least headed in the correct direction. Although it appears I may have signed on for a little more than I had thought. From the sounds of things, you are trying to bring a village back from the ashes, and I'm not quite sure if that's metaphorical or not."

Arthur chuckled. "Honestly, it may be a bit of both. The village is pretty run down, but most of the trouble is the local lord. He has a band of cronies he sends out every few months to strip the poor people of pretty much everything. Because of this, they haven't been able to support the village very well. There was almost no food before the lord's men stole most of it, so they don't even have what they need to plant more. Combined with the horrible state of repair on many of the buildings, the place isn't far away from being a ghost town."

"I have started the recovery process and have been able to get a few locals involved with helping in the endeavor. The village only has one hunter that's skilled enough to brave the forest, and the rest of the villagers are too terrified to enter it. It's often said in the village that any that enter are usually never seen again. While that's certainly possible, especially for the ones with little skill, I'm not sure how true that is. I guess from your statement, you must have heard the conversation. I guess the hearing ability of the elves isn't overly exaggerated."

"We do have excellent hearing, honestly. Although I haven't quite decided how much of your eyes, I want on me yet." She said with a smirk.

Arthur's cheeks flushed in embarrassment, but he quickly recovered and gave her a lopsided grin. "Sorry about that, just guy talk."

"Uh-huh, next time, you better remember how good my hearing is instead. Rowan's concerns about the woods are not unfounded, though. It isn't uncommon for some of my people to kill people they see as invaders if they get too close to our patrols. The goblins patrol as well, but we haven't been patrolling much with our internal struggles. Many of our kind don't share this prejudice, but there are a few groups. I'll honor my agreement, though, and do what I can to help you. How far along are you in magical studies? What basic spells do you have as a foundation to work off of? I'm not by any means close to a master, but elves tend to have a better understanding and connection to the magical forces, so we usually have a breadth of knowledge."

Arthur looked downcast from her statement, and she studied his face carefully. Her gaze stared into what felt like his soul until he relented with an answer for her.

"To be honest, I know practically nothing about my magic. I know absolutely no spells of any kind, nor do I know how you learn one. The only thing I've done so far was manipulating the earth a bit, but it didn't seem very useful at the time and just seemed to steadily drain mana with no real reward." Arthur told her sheepishly.

"How in the name of the Immortal Ones do you have magic but absolutely no understanding of it? It isn't something you can normally just discover without a teacher of some kind." She asked exasperated.

"Well, I was fortunate enough to find a magical tome that granted me earth magic. While it taught me the skill, it didn't teach me how to use it nor any spells with it." Arthur told her.

    Allendria's eyes got so full he thought
they might pop out of her beautiful face. "You
found a tome that granted the skill of earth
magic? A magical tome has not been seen in
over 50 years. There haven't been, but a
handful discovered in 300 years. You must have
some incredible luck to find one of those.
That increases the difficulty of my job,
though."

    "I'm sorry for being so much trouble, but
at least now you can understand why I needed
so much help," Arthur told her sincerely.

    "You're at least correct in that regard.
I assume I can skip over some of the more
boring details and history of magic and start
with some fundamentals. You'll need to become
more familiar with how magic works and ways to
take advantage of it. It appears we're in for
a long discussion." She said with a sigh.

Chapter 13

Magical Instruction

"Your magic has a specific feeling to it, or at least it should. Earth magic is usually described as a thrumming or low drumbeat type of feeling inside your senses when trying to control it." Allendria told him.

"Now that you mention it, that was the feeling I had when manipulating the earth the way I did. I wasn't very aware of the sensation myself, but now that you mention it, I can distinctly remember that feeling." Arthur told her.

"Well, each branch of magic has a different feel to it. I can control two different magics, I'm considered a bit of an oddity myself, to be honest, because I have learned the opposing magics of water and fire. Typically, magic users will attempt to learn complementing magics before incorporating a third. My Fire Magic feels like a pleasant warmth on a bright summer day when I use it while my water feels like standing in a cool, running stream. The key thing to any of the magic is imagination. Magic isn't limited by anything but your imagination. The spells I referred to before are just building blocks. Many times when someone is taught a magic skill, the person instructing them also teaches them a basic spell or two to get them used to the way the magic is controlled."

Arthur nodded in understanding at this. So far, it seemed pretty straightforward.

"Once you have the basic knowledge of this and have some practice, mages can develop their spells. I'm not sure if you have ever noticed, but this world rewards ingenuity. Unique ideas are usually rewarded greatly, and therefore why imagination is so important. For instance, I know one common spell taught to earth mages is to make a small earthen wall. It's typically only about one foot tall and three foot wide, but it can be constantly built upon with the same spell. The main benefit of creating or discovering a spell is that it becomes a known spell at that point and, once known, can be cast with ease as long as you have the specified mana cost. Mastering a spell is also important. The more times you cast a specific spell, the more your mastery level of it raises. Mastery levels grant bonuses for the spells when you attain them. It could decrease the base cost of that spell, and in cases of a spell such as Earthen Wall, it could also increase the standard size of the affected area. For instance, that same spell at mastery level two may create a wall that's two-foot-tall and four foot wide." She went on.

"Wait, you mean I can just do anything with my mana that produces a specific effect, and this can make a spell for me? Why didn't it do anything when I was manipulating earth before?" Arthur asked.

"Did you ever try to do anything with a specific goal in mind? You need to have a specific goal, and it has to be of measurable use to be classified as a successful spell completion." She told him.

"Well, I guess not. I remember just shaping the ground in different ways, but I never tried to cause any meaningful change with a specific outcome," Arthur told her sheepishly.

"I would suggest you try to get the earth wall spell unlocked first. It may not seem like much, but it can be very versatile, especially to someone trying to help a struggling village survive. Being able to build earthen walls quickly can help construction projects as well as defense. I'll warn you that discovering or creating a spell will be a challenge. As you noted before, your mana will drain as quickly as it did when you were manipulating the ground. It will do the same when you attempt to discover the spell. It's prevalent for creating spells to require an extensive amount of mana, but the key benefit is that once discovered, their mana cost becomes a set amount and is usually much more efficient. Couple that with mastery, and it gets even more so. To start, you will need to envision the exact wall you wish to make. For the discovery, I would suggest you try to make one that's one foot tall, one foot wide, and three feet long. This is the typical basis for the earthen wall spell. Why don't we take a break for a few minutes, and you can try?" she asked.

Arthur nodded his head and waved Rowan over to him. "Let's stop here for a few minutes and get a quick snack and a drink. I'm gonna try something with Allendria." Arthur told him.

"I'm sure you are," Rowan said with a sly grin. "Try to make sure she doesn't beat you bloody for it." He told Arthur.

Arthur ignored him, and he and Allendria moved a little ways away from Rowan. Arthur wasn't very concerned with Rowan finding out about his magic, but he didn't need the distraction of the guy gawking and prodding him with questions while attempting to concentrate.

Arthur stretched his hand to the bare spot of ground in front of them and called forth that familiar thrum he had felt before. He concentrated hard on the place and visualized what he wanted to see.

The ground started swirling and rising. It looked like a sloppy mud puddle with kids splashing around in it and creating rising waves of earth. It rose until it had reached the one-foot mark and then started to expand. He could feel sweat beginning to drip down his face as he managed to get the area to a small one-foot square block. A glance at his mana showed he still had one-hundred mana left, so he focused on the block and began to expand the length of one side to try to stretch it out to the three-foot requirement Allendria had mentioned.

He then noticed that the strain became much worse. He watched the small little section of earth start to expand, but when it reached the two-foot mark, the force of will was getting to him. Not only that, but he checked his mana reserves and saw they had dropped drastically. He had gone from one-hundred mana to sixty. The initial block had only cost around twenty mana to make, but expanding that block one foot took twice that. Gritting his teeth and pushing through the effort caused sweat to cover his body, but he was determined not to get distracted.

He saw the wall slowly expand, and there was a flash in his vision. He wasn't sure how, but he could tell that it meant he was almost out of mana. Determined to finish, he pushed through while ignoring the flash. He kept watching the small section of the ground slowly expand until he saw it reach the size it needed to be and heard a quiet chime accompanied by a red flash in his vision. He noticed his mana status had a flashing red twenty on it and realized it took him precisely one hundred mana to complete this. That would be tedious if he could only make such small stretches of a wall for such a high cost, especially with his low mana pool and regeneration rate. He looked to his notification and was slightly startled.

Congratulations, you have discovered the Earth Magic Spell: Earthen Wall. You have gained 250 experience in Earth Magic for discovering a known spell.
You have gained 60 experience in Earth Magic for successfully casting Earthen Wall.

Spell: Earthen Wall	
Requirements: Earth Magic Mana Cost: 20 MP Cast Time: 2 seconds	Description: Creates a wall of earth that's 1' x 1' x 3'.
Mastery Level: 1	

Allendria wasn't exaggerating, Arthur thought to himself. It had drained every bit of his mana to discover that, but the final spell ended up only costing a base of twenty mana. On top of that, she had told him the mana cost could get better with mastery. Arthur turned toward Allendria, who'd been carefully watching him. He was breathing very heavily as he looked her in the eye. As they looked at each other, a slow smile started to creep on each of their faces, and then suddenly, both burst into laughter.

"Well, that was exhilarating!" Arthur exclaimed.

"I'm rather impressed. I have rarely ever heard of anyone successfully creating a spell on the first attempt. Usually, it takes a few failures before they can finally figure out the best way to manipulate the element to what they want. The best part for you, though, is it gives you something to build your magic skill. Now that you understand how to create spells, the sky is the limit for you when it comes to your earth magic. I also know you are unfamiliar with anything in magic, as you have stated multiple times, so I want to make sure I tell you that any spell learned can be initiated by visualizing the effect and the area and willing it to happen. Now that you have officially learned it, the effect will start as soon as you will it and will take the designated time for casting shown while using the designated mana amount from your mana pool." She told him.

"I guess I'll have to work on developing some better spells over time then. Earthen Wall makes for great primitive defenses but would cost a lot of mana and a tremendous amount of time to make it useful. I wish it could be reliable for building buildings with, that could be a good way to help the villagers with their run-down houses, but an earthen wall couldn't support the weight for buildings properly. I'd need the walls made of stone." Arthur said dejectedly.

Allendria smiled at him in a placating manner, "That is possible. I'm not an earth mage myself, but while studying at my home, we were informed of the many uses for each style of magic. I know an earth mage can transmute an earthen wall into a stone wall, and I recall it having something to do with aligning the crystalline structures necessary to make it happen, but alas, I was not an earth mage and had not earned the chance to learn it. I would suggest you find a good source of solid stone and examine it with your magic, and once you have an idea of how it looks to your magic, you could try to realign the structure of one of your earthen walls to match. I have seen magic-users create stone walls directly without making an earthen one first, but they were advanced in their craft."

"It's good to know I have something to look forward to then. Do you know the extent of what I can do with earth magic?" Arthur asked.

"I know earth magic can control any stone or dirt. So, it can also move most things connected to the ground, such as trees or plants, and can move metals and sift them from the ground. But it can't be used to shape or mold metals in any way due to the hardness of the metal. As I stated before, though, much of it evolves with your magic level and your imagination." She said.

"From here, I would suggest we get moving again. It would be good to recover my items and return to a village for safety. It's still early enough now not to be a worry, but there's no point in taking chances. You can use this time to let your mana regenerate. I also encourage you to keep casting that spell to level your skill and increase its mastery."

"Sounds like a plan to me. Let's get a quick drink and keep moving." Arthur told her.

Arthur waved at Rowan and let him know it was time to get moving. Rowan grabbed the cart, and they continued on their way again. They kept moving through the trees in the general direction Allendria was leading them. After another half hour of walking, she came to a stop.

"We're close, and I now recognize the area. The cave I was in is in that general direction." She said as she pointed her finger toward the East.

After walking around for a while, Arthur could see cliff sides through the trees. He also noticed that his mana had fully recovered. The last time Arthur had used it, he was too distracted with what needed to be done next that he paid no attention to how fast it recovered. This time he could judge he had a reasonable mana regen rate of 5 mana every minute. Figuring it was foolish to waste mana regen for no reason, he cast his Earthen Wall spell again.

He looked to an area beside him and then froze. He realized he didn't understand how to cast a learned spell, either. There must be a quicker way to do it instead of the way he learned it. He decided to wing it and held his hand out in the general direction he wanted to cast the spell and just said, "Earthen Wall." He looked around in bewilderment when nothing happened. When he looked toward Allendria and Rowan, they looked at him with confusion.

Rowan looked like he had no clue what was going on while Allendria looked like she was trying to keep from either breaking out in laughter or crying desperately. Honestly, it might have been a bit of both.

"You're a bit special, aren't you?" Allendria asked him with a chuckle. "I assume from the little performance there you were trying to cast your learned spell?"

"I was trying, but as you can see, nothing happened. Care to enlighten me on the correct way to do it?" Arthur asked while looking at his feet. He was sure his embarrassed flush was as bright as the noonday sun.

Allendria let out a soft sigh. "You'd think you would learn to ask before making a fool of yourself, but then again, I'm new to traveling with humans. To cast a spell you have learned, you envision the effect of the spell on your specified area. For instance, to cast your wall, picture the completed wall to the correct dimensions wherever you wish it to be. When you have this image in place, you simply will it to happen. When you initiate this process, the cast sequence will automatically start and will take the specified time for the spell. Depending on the spell, it can be interrupted by another, and the spell will fail mid cast. I gave you the basic idea of this when we last spoke, but I guess I needed to explain that fully."

"Thank you, Allendria. I'll try to remember to ask first next time," Arthur told her.

He turned to the area he had been looking at for his previous attempt and this time envisioned a foot tall, foot thick, and three-foot-long stretch of wall. He noticed while doing this, the image came quickly and appeared to be to the exact dimensions needed even though he had been horrible with estimating measurements before. He willed the wall into being, and his body took over as Allendria had told him. His arms started flowing in a quick set of weaves and circles before finishing 2 seconds later.

Arthur looked on in wonder as the wall he envisioned quickly rose from the ground into shape in less than a second. He was elated now that he could see the results of real magic he had cast.

Arthur reflected over his fight with the goblins and subsequent magic use in wonder. The experience gained from killing the goblins seemed to be much higher than animals of equal levels. Arthur assumed it had something to do with them being sentient creatures.

Looking at it, he also noticed a startling fact, the goblins they had been fighting lived past when they collapsed and appeared to die. He had seen this in the logs before but never quite noticed the importance of this. Dealing a blow that would kill most people or animals would disable them until they lost their HP from bleeds unless it struck either the heart or brain. It wasn't as noticeable since he had blocked most of the knockdown and bleed notifications from showing.

Arthur decided it was an excellent time to look at his character sheet and see the recent changes.

Name: Arthur	
Level: 7	
Age: 26	
Race: Human	
HP: 230/230	
MP: 80/120	
Stamina: 230/230	
Strength: 8	**Experience:** 1350/3200
Agility: 8	(5 stat points
Intellect: 5	available)
Wisdom: 3	**Skills** (50% boost to
Endurance: 8	any skill for level up)
Charisma: 5	**Combat Skills:**

Luck: 5	
	Archery: 5 (315/1900)
	- **Aim Shot:** 1 (225/500)
	Block: 1 (180/500)
	Parry: 1 (100/500)
	Small Blades: 2 (575/750)
	Stealth: 1 (370/500)
	- **Detect Hidden:** 1 (50/500)
	Swords: 1 (135/500)
	Unarmed: 1 (25/500)
	Magic:
	Earth Magic: 1 (360/500)
	- **Earthen Wall** (1)
	Professions:
	Barter: 3 (100/1000)
	Cooking: 2 (400/750)
	Farming: 4 (650/1400)
	Firemaking: 2 (700/750)
	Herbalism: 4 (560/1400)
	Skinning: 3 (500/1000)

Well, hot damn he had leveled up and didn't remember it. Thinking back on it, he realized it was back when he had turned in the quest with Dalia. He vaguely remembered hearing the trumpets, but he had his attention on other things at the time. Now was as good a time as any to allocate a few points.

Since he fully understood more about the benefits of using his magic, he desperately wanted to beef up his stats to support it. To start, he threw a point into Intellect to see what it did. He wanted to know if it had a similar effect as it did when he reached five intellect. He was happy with what he saw. His Intellect had indeed gone up to 6, and his mana had risen another twenty points also, bringing it to 140 total. Although elated at the extra mana, especially since it meant he could discover some more advanced spells, he wasn't sure why he had gotten it. He assumed it must have been a common occurrence for stats every point after five.

Trying it once again, he added another point to Intellect, bringing it to 7. Arthur was thrilled to see his maximum mana raise to 160. It was good to know that Intellect gave him 20 mana per point. It appeared to only happen after 5 points, though. To test this theory, he threw 2 points into Wisdom to bring it up to 5. Not only did his Wisdom raise, but he gained another 10 MP to his maximum pool. He found that this augmented his mana regen by an additional 3 per minute on top of his default 5 per minute.

He was doubly excited now. Wisdom seemed a great boon if it would increase his regen and his mana pool. Intellect also increased his maximum mana by 20 per point, so it was always a good option. He was also sure that Intellect affected the power of his spells. At least it usually did in the games he had played.

    With these new details in mind, he decided now may be a good time to shift some of his focus. Currently, he was more of a ranged archer style build, but after a taste of magic, and an understanding that the sky may be the limit, he decided now was the perfect time to shift his stats toward a caster style of play. With him trying to help the village, he knew deep down that his magic would be instrumental. With this in mind, he put his last point into Intellect to bring it to 8.

    "Allendria, any idea how far we may have to go?" Arthur asked.

    "I believe we are about ten minutes away." She told him.

    "Sounds good. I'll cast a few more Earthen Wall spells while we travel. Going to start grinding some magic experience." Arthur said.

    "Please do, you need to always work on improving your skills." She told him.

    Arthur went into a bit of autopilot while daydreaming about the possibilities of his new magic while following Allendria and randomly casting Earthen Wall. He wanted to ensure he had a bit of mana left when they got there in case of an emergency.

Chapter 14

Allendria's Request

They continued and followed Allendria through the winding trees and knew they were getting close when they could see the cliff face getting larger in their view. From a distance, Arthur had thought this cliff was only fifty or sixty feet tall, but as they kept getting closer, he quickly realized he was wrong. From where they were, it looked closer to two-hundred feet high.

Arthur had cast his Earthen Wall spell four more times up to this point and cast another five as they kept walking.

You have gained 540 experience in Earth Magic for successfully casting Earthen Wall (x9).

Congratulations, you have reached level 2 in Earth Magic. Increases the effect of your earth magic spells by 3%. More playing in the dirt? Wasn't farming enough?

With his regen, he could still get close to 100 mana by the time they reached a small cave in the cliff.

Allendria approached it carefully while continually scanning the trees around. Arthur assumed she was worried that some goblins might still be in the area. They were able to reach the cave without any issues and quickly ducked inside. Arthur discovered that his early assessment was incorrect. It looked like a small cave from the outside, but on the inside, it was spacious. The opening for it was narrow and was barely big enough for their cart to fit, but once inside, it quickly opened up for them to travel. The cavern itself looked to be about one hundred feet wide and half again as long.

The most puzzling part was that some of it appeared to have been carved out and wasn't naturally forming. Smooth cuts covered much of the edges of the cavern toward the back. Everything, past the twenty-foot mark from the entrance, looked to be worked. The cave itself had nothing of interest in it except for a small cloth bag in the back corner. Allendria took off for the bag as soon as she saw it.

Arthur took Allendria's previous advice and inspected the stonework here. She had told him he could use his magic in many ways, and one he vaguely remembered was detecting metals. He decided now was a good chance to check this out. He was now up to around 110 MP, so he had plenty to experiment a little.

Arthur stepped to the back wall and placed his hand on one spot on the wall. Allendria had told him to examine the structure of the stone and compare it to the construction of the earthen wall he could create and use that comparison to advance the spell. He was sure that being able to analyze this stone would be the starting point for his detection spell.

He closed his eyes and 'felt' with his power into the stone. His awareness slowly moved into the rock, and he could see the granular structure of the stone and its mineral composition. The stone itself appeared to be a variation of granite, although he was no expert to know precisely what variety. Now that he'd been able to determine this, he tried the detection spell he wanted. Since he had already used some mana in the initial investigation, he might as well continue instead of wasting that mana. Not sure how to proceed, he quickly pushed his awareness of the stone directly away from him in a cone type pattern.

As he envisioned this and pushed his will into it, he felt as though he could see through the stone in the direction he had willed. It was a slow-moving process, and it felt like he was crawling through at a snail's pace. He could feel his consciousness expanding into the stone, but it was more like a spectral ghost slowly floating through the wall. He expected to get information on the rock as his magic moved, but so far, it just felt like trudging through a muddy swamp. He didn't receive any information from his spell. He felt his mana bottoming out again and grit his teeth to keep pushing his awareness forward.

The magic finished, and a flood of information came back to him. He instinctively knew everything that had been in the rock in front of him for one hundred yards. He now understood why he had gotten none of this information when performing the spell. It sent out the magic that would crawl and identify everything in its path and then would compile all the details and deliver it back to the caster in one fell swoop.

Congratulations, you have discovered the Earth Magic Spell: Magical Prospecting. You have gained 250 experience in Earth Magic for discovering a known spell.
You have gained 100 experience in Earth Magic for successfully casting Magical Prospecting.
Congratulations, you have reached level 3 in Earth Magic. Increases the effect of your earth magic spells by 6%. What's next, pottery?

Spell: Magical Prospecting	
Requirements: Earth Magic Mana Cost: 35 MP Cast Time: 5 seconds	Description: Sends out a pulse of magic that can identify any earthen elements in a cone for 30 yards. The details return to the caster upon completion.
Mastery Level: 1	

Arthur looked toward Allendria with a big smile plastered on his face. He saw her reverently pulling a bracelet from the small bag and kept quiet for now. Arthur walked over to talk to Rowan.

"You wouldn't happen to have anything with you that could dig through rock, would you?" Arthur asked in hushed tones.

Rowan gave him a sidelong glance, "I guess that depends on the reason. Just for fun, no. For something important, I would probably make an exception." he told him.

"Well, my new spell just told me that there is an iron ore vein about two yards in that wall," Arthur told him with a vague wave at the wall.

Rowan eyed him curiously. "I suppose I could use the backside of my axe to break into the stone. I can't guarantee it will work, but for iron, I'll try. We desperately need it." he told Arthur.

"Give it a shot."

Rowan walked over to the wall and flipped the axe around backward while taking a firm grasp on it. He reared back and swung into the stone. Chips of rock and dust flew from the wall as Rowan continued to pound. His physical prowess from swinging a hammer at the smithy helped him keep a steady pace of swinging the axe.

Dodging stone chips as they flew, Arthur walked around the cave while Rowan worked. He didn't want to get in the way and get hit by him. Rowan was doing an admirable job of slowly widening his original hole while continuing to push deeper. Arthur wasn't positive, but he believed Rowan must have the mining skill. It would make a bit of sense with his profession of blacksmithing.

Arthur randomly glanced at Allendria as he was walking around. She was murmuring to the bracelet she had pulled out. Arthur wasn't about to interrupt whatever she was doing. He assumed it was some religious ceremony for her people. Allendria finally rose, put the bracelet back in the bag, and secured the bag to her waist. He decided to talk to her while Rowan was busy swinging an axe at a wall like a madman.

"I hope everything of yours was still here?" Arthur said.

"Yes, it was. Thank you for your assistance in the matter. My apologies for taking so much time when we got here. I know you have other things to do too." She said only to notice the loud smashing sound in the room from Rowan's methodical swings slamming into the wall. She gave him an odd look and turned back to Arthur. "He knows there are better tools for that, right? He's bound to cut himself with the sharp side of that axe."

Arthur chuckled. "Yes, he's aware of better tools, but as we've discussed, there are limits on what we have. While you were busy, I took your advice and was able to connect with the stone and get a feel for it. From there, I discovered Magical Prospecting and found an iron vein about two yards into the wall. Since we have no other tools and desperately need iron to make more, this was the best solution we could come up with."

"Well, I would say that you could assist with this, but I'm sure your mana's depleted since you discovered your new spell."

"It's been around ten minutes since then, so I'm back up to around 80 mana. The regen isn't terrible."

Allendria's eyes looked like they were about to bulge out of her head. "How in the world do you already have that much mana? Surely you didn't use all your stats in Wisdom?"

"What do you mean? I only have five total points in Wisdom." Arthur told her.

Her eyes narrowed at him. "So how did you regenerate 80 mana in 10 minutes, then?"

Arthur started feeling slightly uncomfortable, "Well, I have the base regen of 5 mana per minute, and then when I put the 5th point in it gave me an additional three mana per minute, so I sit at eight mana per minute."

She looked like she was about to burst a blood vessel. "Are you kidding me? How in the hell do you have that much regen? You know what, never mind. I've only just met you, but it seems that every other thing you do is incredibly odd. You've decided to go on some crusade to save a bunch of random people. You seem to have random bits of knowledge about many things, but none of the skills to accompany that knowledge and you seem to have distinctly different rules regarding your stats."

Arthur was taken aback by her response. "What do you mean by, I have different rules with my stats?"

"Well, for starters, mana regen is typically nowhere near that high. For instance, I have a base regen of three mana per minute, and I only gain one mana per minute for every two points of Wisdom. Humans are typically different and, by default, usually only have two mana per minute regen and get an additional point for every three wisdom points spent. There are a few exceptions with some very special mages over the years, but yours is by far the highest I have ever heard. Especially gaining three mana per minute with every point of Wisdom. You have the potential to be an outstanding mage if you work for it." She told him.

Arthur wasn't sure how to feel about that. Obviously, it was great to know that he had such potential with magic. The gears in his head started turning toward all the possibilities. With this information, Arthur thought a magical build would be the way to go, but something gave him pause. If he was different in this, what else might be different as well? He could have an entirely different set of rules to his leveling than other people. It might make it difficult to get advice, and if the wrong people were to learn of his differences, they might try to get rid of him because of them. He could potentially see how this information could be hazardous to his health. Rivals were always easier to deal with before they could consolidate their power. It made him think of the skill points he got in archery. He had gained two points at level five and had thought it was odd because Daniel had mentioned it was one point per level. Was this going to be another thing about him that was different?

"Honestly, I'm not sure how that happened, but it's what my notifications tell me, and it appears to regen at that rate. I'll say I'm not disappointed by my luck in this matter, though." Arthur said with a small grin.

Allendria took one last look into his eyes, "Arthur, you must never tell another person about this. I know you may not understand why, but some people in this world would have you killed outright just for the threat you may pose to them one day. I know you didn't understand the implications of this, but I appreciate you being open with me about this, anyway."

She looked toward Rowan, still swinging away at the wall. She turned back to Arthur and grinned. "Care to make Rowan angry with you? In a couple more minutes, I think I can help guide you to creating the spell you need to get the ore out of the stone. By then, you should have a sufficient supply of mana."

Arthur looked over at the man, who was now sweating profusely and was still a few yards short of being to the ore and smiled. Oh, man, was he going to be pissed!

Allendria and Arthur waited a few minutes and then approached Rowan.

"Rowan," Arthur shouted at him. "Take a break and let me see what I can do about this. You look like you could use a drink."

"No offense Arthur but I'm not sure you could swing my axe without severely harming yourself." He told Arthur.

"Oh, I completely agree that I'm more likely to hurt myself with your axe trying to do that. But no worries. I'm gonna attempt some magic on it instead while you take a break."

Rowan grunted and walked over to their cart to grab one of their skins of water. He sat against the wagon and took a long drink of the refreshing water while eyeing Arthur. Arthur walked over to the wall where Rowan had been swinging away and then looked to Allendria.

"So, now what?" He asked.

"Well, you'll start the way you did on prospecting, but this will change a little. You need to get a feel for the stone itself, but this time you need to expand your reach into the area you wish to influence as a whole. Typically, a good starting size for this spell is about five feet square. It's usually good enough to learn the spell at its base rank."

"How in the world am I supposed to control five square feet of stone at once when it took all of my will and concentration to raise a wall of dirt that's one foot, by one foot, by three-foot?"

"This spell doesn't require you to shift anything directly. The amount of area you can influence is reliant on your magic level and your spell mastery levels, but the difficulty of spells also changes with the way they work. Controlling anything and making it flow or create always takes more effort than just destroying something or changing its properties. With the wall, you have to physically create the structure in a space where nothing but air existed before. Due to this, it requires more effort to force the natural world to accept this change. For this spell, you'll destroy the stone in the area. Well, technically, you'll be transforming the stone in this area, but either way, it's taking place in the same space." She told him.

"Alright, you haven't steered me wrong yet, so let's get to work." He said.

Arthur felt out with his magical senses and pushed his awareness into the stone as he did last time. Instead of sending out a pulsing wave, though, this time, he allowed his sense to 'expand' and get a better understanding of the area. It was an odd sensation, but Arthur compared it to looking at something with squinted eyes for a long time and then slowly starting to open them to encompass more and more of it. He got to the full five-foot square she had mentioned and was thrilled that he still had a sufficient amount of mana left. He had only used about twenty mana in this step.

"Alright, now comes the difficult part of the process," Allendria whispered next to his ear. "You need to force your will on this area and start to vibrate the stone inside your influence very quickly. Be sure that none of these vibrations escape the influence of your spell area, though, or you could cause problems elsewhere."

The sound of her voice that close to his ear sent chills down his spine. He could barely feel her warm breath on his ear as she spoke, and the sheer thrill of it almost broke him out of his concentration. He grasped on her words, though, and focused.

He knew that just trying to shake this area with his power wouldn't work and would probably only cause a cave in. Instead, he used force to accomplish his goals. He made waves of power that continually rolled through the area from all sides at once to constantly batter the rock in the contained area. He started this process and could see dirt and dust beginning to fall on the outside, so he kept at it. He slowly increased the speed of the waves and the frequency of when they started and was seeing a drastic shift in the wall. Parts of it were beginning to crumble. He kept at this, and soon the pressure vanished, and his spell finished. He saw the stone in front of him in a perfect square crumble into gravel and start flowing back his direction as it collapsed on itself like a kid pouring sand into a pile.

Congratulations, you have discovered the Earth Magic Spell: Transform Stone: Gravel. You have gained 250 experience in Earth Magic for discovering a known spell.

You have gained 150 experience in Earth Magic for successfully casting Transform Stone: Gravel.

Congratulations, you have learned the Subskill Magical Mining for a 100 experience bonus.

Congratulations, you have learned Mining for a 100 experience bonus.

You have gained 150 experience in Mining and Magical Mining for finding Raw Iron Ore (x6).

Spell: Transform Stone: Gravel

Requirements: Earth Magic Mana Cost: 50 MP Cast Time: 5 seconds	Description: Causes all stone in a 5-foot square area to be reduced to gravel.
Mastery Level: 1	

Arthur took a step back to avoid all of it getting on him and turned to Allendria. "I can't thank you enough, Allendria. I know we have an agreement in place for you to assist, but I feel like you're going above and beyond to help me. I know you could take our agreement very literally and be very selective in what you show me, but you've been nothing but helpful, and I appreciate that."

Allendria had the grace to blush with that statement, which was humorous to see on a purple-skinned face, but Arthur thought it made her look even more beautiful than she already was.

"As I said before, I have had minimal contact with humans, but in the society of Dark Elves, we are very straightforward. I was wary of this arrangement at first, but I think it may end up being a great benefit in the long run. You have some amazing potential in you, and I'm sure you have the capacity for many other schools of magic, as well. Who knows, maybe if you impress me enough, I may teach you my fire magic." She said with a wink and started to walk off.

Rowan stomped up to Arthur after he had seen what he had done and yelled at him, "Are you fucking kidding me, Arthur? You had me here sweating my ass off swinging a damn axe at a wall to mine for this iron, and you could have just made the damn thing fall apart the whole time? I should hit you square in the nose and be done with it."

"Whoa Rowan, I honestly didn't know I could do this until Allendria told me a couple of minutes ago. She was the one that guided and showed me how to do this. Now that I know it's possible, it should make this process much easier, and you can put your axe away." Arthur soothed.

Arthur reflected on the spell. The spell didn't destroy, as she had suggested, but transformed the stone. That explained why the stone started running out of the wall and looked like someone dumping out sand. The gravel would need to be swept out of their way, but that would be easy. Arthur walked back to the cart, found the old rusty dagger from one of the goblins, and used it along his feet to move the gravel out of his way. Once most of it was out of the way, and he had a clear view of the back wall, he was happy with what he saw. Rowan had managed to get them a couple of feet into the wall with his axes, but now that Arthur had taken out another five-foot, he could see the edge of the iron vein. A few small pieces of the iron had fallen out and were resting on some gravel. Arthur picked up one of them that was about the size of his fist to check it out.

Item: Raw Iron Ore	**Durability:** 20/20
	Rarity: Common
	Weight: 1.5 kg
	Traits: A chunk of unrefined iron ore.

Well, this was fantastic and just what they needed. It appeared Arthur's spell had the added benefit of breaking up most of the standard stone that was attached to the iron ore as well. That would save a lot of time for Rowan when he started refining the metal. Now that he knew this spell could take care of this for him, he gathered the few pieces that had fallen out and handed them to Rowan. Rowan beamed upon seeing the ore, and there was a bit of glee reflected in his eyes.

"We can stay here and relax a little longer while I let my mana recover so I can do that spell again. It'll be much quicker than trying to mine it with incorrect tools. Discovering that spell sapped my mana, and I'm almost completely out again." Arthur said.

Rowan nodded, and they walked over to the cart and sat down. Arthur got him a drink and just relaxed with his back against the side of the cart's wheel. It felt good to take a load off and get off his feet for a bit.

"Allendria, why don't you come to sit with us? Feels good to take a break and get off the feet for a short while. I'm waiting for some mana to recover so I can cast the spell again. Another two spells should be enough to get through the main portion of this iron vein." Arthur said.

She rolled her eyes at him and walked over to join them. Arthur supposed all women must be the same no matter what world or what race they ended up being. Some mannerisms were universal. They sat there in companionable silence and all just relaxed. Arthur had his eyes closed and was enjoying the relative cool in the cavern.

They waited about twenty minutes just enjoying the break when Arthur decided it was time to get up and get back to work. His mana pool was back up to a respectable number of 160, not quite full but nowhere near empty. He went back to the wall and focused on the next section and cast the spell. His hand reached out and touched the stone, and he could feel the waves of energy running through the rock even though he didn't directly cast them himself consciously. Five seconds later, another five-foot square section turned to gravel and starting to pour out of the tunnel he was creating.

You have gained 150 experience in Earth Magic for successfully casting Transform Stone: Gravel.
You have gained 550 experience in Mining and Magical Mining for finding Raw Iron Ore (x22).
Congratulations, you have reached level 2 in Mining. You have a 3% increased chance to find rare materials while mining. Whistle while you work!
Congratulations, you have reached level 2 in Magical Mining. Increases the chance that items found will be a higher rarity of 3%. Kind of cheating, isn't it?

He went back to work with the rusted dagger and pushed the gravel out of the entrance. While he did this, he gathered all the pieces of iron and handed them out to Rowan so he could store them in the cart. He finished getting the metal sorted out of the gravel and moved to the next section of the wall.

You have gained 150 experience in Earth Magic for successfully casting Transform Stone: Gravel.

You have gained 600 experience in Mining and Magical Mining for finding Raw Iron Ore (x24).

Congratulations, you have reached level 3 in Mining. You have a 6% increased chance to find rare materials while mining. Dig for gold!

Congratulations, you have reached level 3 in Magical Mining. Increases the chance that items found will be a higher rarity by 6%. Still pretty sure it's cheating.

When he finished sorting through the final section he had destroyed, he decided enough was enough.

He walked out of the small tunnel he had created in the wall and walked to an adjacent area and triggered his prospecting spell again.

You have gained 100 experience in Earth Magic for successfully casting Magical Prospecting.

This time he found a few other pockets of iron ore, but most were deeper. He had no intention of doing anything with them at the moment, but it was good to know there'd be a chance to come back and get more iron when needed.

Arthur was pleased to gain not only a new skill but also a Subskill. To top that off, he also advanced a level in Earth Magic.

"Rowan, is all that ore loaded and secure?" Arthur asked.

"All packed down and ready to go. I almost feel giddy with the chance to get back to the village and get to work for once. The shortage of iron has severely limited my usefulness in the village. Now I can start working on things needed to improve the place with you. The question will be, what we need to work on and in what order. We should consult with Daniel about this as well." Rowan responded.

"I agree, we might have to bring Dalia into the conversation since she is officially part of the endeavor now. Either way, the few things we found today should be a good start, but we can't afford to delay any longer. We need to get back to the village as quickly as possible. That deer's carcass will begin to turn if we don't get it boned out and at least salted down."

"I guess this means I finally get to see the little village I'll be staying in for a bit," Allendria said with a little more cheer than Arthur expected.

They all headed back out with Rowan pushing the wheeled cart again. They made good time on their way back to the village and didn't run into any other issues. Arthur spotted a few different plants on the trip that were useful and gathered them to take with them.

You have gained 1500 experience in Herbalism for identifying a Wild Onion (x15).

Congratulations, you have reached level 5 in Herbalism. You now have a 12% higher chance of identifying an herb successfully. At least your eyes work.

You have gained 750 experience in Farming for successfully harvesting Wild Onion (x15).

Congratulations, you have reached level 5 in Farming. You now have a chance for up to 20% increased yield from plants. You are on your way to a green thumb.

Leveling both of these to five gave him the itch to check out their talent trees. He started with Herbalism.

You have 2 unused Talent Points.

Talent	Description
Tier 1	
Green View (0/5)	*This ability allows the user to see plants you have previously identified with a soft glow when within 50 feet of them.*
Rarity Upgrade (0/5)	*This ability increases the chance that the herbs you gather will increase in rarity. Note: this won't change the plant itself, just the rarity of that specific type of plant.*
Regrowth (0/5)	*This ability allows you to commune with nature and spend some of your mana to improve the growing speed and yield of surrounding plants by 20% per point.* *Cost 30 Mana*

Well, those were some exciting benefits. Level 1 of Green View was an absolute no-brainer. That skill would help ensure he didn't miss herbs that he passed when traveling. His second point would be tricky. He could put another point into Green View and see what the benefit there could be, but he thought Regrowth might be the better option. He hoped that he could use the ability to improve their fledgling garden that Daniel was working on getting ready. That skill would probably pay off more than any of the others. He put the initial point into Green View, and the skill tree changed again. He checked the new tier of options.

You have 1 unused Talent Point.

Talent	Description
Tier 2	
Nature's Knowledge (0/1)	*This ability allows you to sense when usable plants are nearby. This ability works on plants you haven't discovered yet, as well.*
Will of the Land (0/1)	*This ability allows you to improve the fertility of any specified area of land in exchange for mana. This ability affects an area that's 100 square feet.* *Cost: 50 Mana* *Cooldown: 12 hours*

The two new skills were intriguing, but he stuck with his previous decision and used the second point for Regrowth. From here, he took a peek at the Farming tree.

You have 2 unused Talent Points.

Talent	Description
Tier 1	
Planting Efficiency (0/5)	*This ability increases the speed of planting, reduces the time required for plants to reach maturity, and increases the yield of the plants by 10%.*
Germination (0/1)	*This ability allows you to harvest seeds from a plant by expending mana, even if the plant has not seeded itself yet. This ability only applies to plants that have been cultivated.* *Cost: 100 Mana*

| Cultivation (0/1) | This ability allows you to take natively wild plants and cultivate them anywhere they would be viable. Note: They still can't survive in conditions that are considered harsh by the plant. This ability also allows for the Germination skill to be used on wild plants. |

Arthur thought this skill tree had some real potential. Being able to speed up the growth of plants would be great, but he didn't see himself having the time to sit around and farm. Helping out when needed was fine, but most of his skill came from harvesting wild plants. He thought the combination of Germination and Cultivation would be fantastic for him since he would be able to essentially domesticate the native plants he found and cause them to seed purposely. This ability would help them get the village back in order and give them seeds to plant instead of the few things he had found.

He selected Germination and saw what Tier 2 options appeared.

Talent	Description
Tier 2	

Water of Life (0/1)	This ability allows you to conjure a small water shower over a 10-foot square area that lasts for 5 minutes. This ability costs mana. Cost: 40 Mana Cooldown: 1 hour
Reap What You Sow (0/5)	Plants harvested by you have a 15% increased chance of providing additional useful items. These may include seeds, higher quality ingredients, and extra items.

Arthur wasn't sure how to proceed here. There were many options available that could be very beneficial. He still wanted to get Cultivation so he could use it in conjunction with Germination to help improve their stores in the village, but both Water of Life and Reap What You Sow also had great benefits. The Water of Life may end up being a necessary option since he had seen no irrigation system around any of the farms. Reap What You Sow would probably help him greatly with as much as he gathered and how often. It was always great to have free stuff. Arthur stuck with his gut, went with his original choice, and put his remaining point into Cultivation. He would get more points at his next level if needed.

They steadily made their way back, and
when they made it to the edge of the forest,
they stopped long enough for Rowan to cover
the cart with canvas to help protect the meat
and plants from the heat of the sun as they
walked across the open area to the village. It
was late afternoon now and getting rather hot.
They approached the village, and Arthur saw a
handful of worried faces around. The village
itself always had a somber feeling, but now it
looked worse than usual. He saw people casting
furtive glances toward the inn and had a bad
feeling something was happening.

They stowed the cart behind the inn, out
of sight, and the three of them walked to the
door. As soon as they entered, Arthur tensed
up. There were four men in there who he didn't
recognize, and they didn't look like they
belonged. Arthur saw Daniel casting nervous
glances his way and sighed to himself. He had
a bad feeling about this.

Chapter 15

The Thief Crew

Arthur inspected the four men seated at the table in front of him. The guy on the left looked like a run-of-the-mill cutthroat. He had shaggy black hair that gathered around his ears. His eyes looked a muddy brown, and he had a gaunt-looking face. His clothing looked like it had been somewhat decent at one point, but years of wear on the road seemed to have taken their toll.

The man sitting on his left had a similar lanky build, but he had dirty blonde hair kept short and close-cropped. His short beard matched his hair and hazel eyes, his nose appeared to have been broken and flattened a few times in fights, and he was constantly fidgeting with a dagger hilt on his belt.

To the man's left was the third member of the group. He had a slightly stockier build but still looked built for speed. The man had long, shoulder-length, brown hair partially tied back. His green eyes seemed to be an odd contrast with his hook nose rounding out the face. He was also missing part of his ear lobe on his left ear.

The final guy to their left, sitting closest to Daniel, appeared to be the leader of the group. This man was much stockier and looked like he was a pure strength build. He was the tallest of the group and seemed to reach right over six feet tall. His broad shoulders would almost lead you to believe he was a blacksmith himself with the strength he exuded. That impression lasted until you saw his dirty teeth and slightly ragged clothing that also appeared to have been a courtier's style of dress at one point, but it was worn down and had faded over the years. He had a dagger strapped on his belt but also had a short sword attached to his other side.

Arthur started to walk toward the bar and hoped they would ignore him when their Leader piped up.

"Would you look at that, Jeremy? Fresh meat in the village and no one even bothered to tell us." He told the first man.

"Fresh may not be the right word, judging by their appearance, but seeing a Dark Elf here is quite a shock. She's a pretty little thing, though. She might be worth a little of my effort to get some quality time with her. Would you be interested in trying her out with me, Alex?" Jeremy said and turned to address the third man at the table.

"I don't know. She seems a little small for my taste, but it might be a bit of fun to hear her squeal. That sound does warm the heart. You want in on the action, Xavier?" Alex asked the second man at the table.

"You could persuade me to join, but I only want to hear her cry and beg. Maybe I'll take her last so I can get what I want without ruining your time with her. You object, boss?" Xavier said as he turned to the leader of the group.

"No, you boys can have your fun with her. I'll not sully myself with her kind. I'll find some local woman who I fancy and take her to bed. Who knows, if she isn't half bad, I may let her eat my dinner scraps as a reward." The leader said casually.

Arthur felt a fury rise in him he had never known before in his life. These men had just brazenly discussed raping Allendria right here in the middle of a public inn. Not only that, but they acted like it was commonplace, and they could do what they wanted. Seeing their brazen disregard for everything and remembering the looks he got from the villagers and Daniel upon his return, he could only assume this was one of the local lord's infamous gangs of enforcers.

Arthur froze in his place as Jeremy stood up and headed in their direction. Jeremy walked up to Allendria, reached out his hand, and caressed her hair. He then moved his hand down toward her breasts.

"Touch her again without her permission, and you'll immediately regret it," Arthur said with anger boiling in him.

Jeremy flinched for a moment and looked in Arthur's direction. "I can see you're new here and don't quite understand how things work. You would do well not to cross us." He said, and his hand continued down, and he squeezed Allendria's breast. Arthur saw her wince a bit and could tell she wanted nothing more than to burn this guy alive, but she wasn't sure what she should do. Arthur took that decision away from her quickly.

Arthur cocked back his arm and swung as hard as he could at Jeremy's jaw. The man had turned his attention to Allendria and was not expecting any action from them. Arthur's punch connected firmly and sent Jeremy sprawling across the floor.

You have dealt 25 damage to Jeremy (Level 10) with Fist (Sneak Attack).

The other three members of the gang sprung to their feet in shock and stared at Arthur.

Jeremy sprung back to his feet and was furious.

"I warned you not to touch her. I won't tolerate you disrespecting my friends." Arthur told him in a much more calm tone than he felt.

"Now, it's you who will regret that you bastard!" Jeremy yelled and sprang forward at Arthur. Jeremy was quick and, had Arthur not been expecting it, he would have caught him entirely off guard. Instead, it was clear Jeremy relied solely on his speed because he was taking the broadest swing Arthur had ever seen. Arthur wasn't sure how Jeremy could hit him without breaking his hand in the process with a punch that out of control. Arthur would not give him a chance. Instead, Arthur waited until he was within arm's reach and took a small step into the man and punched him as hard as he could directly in the stomach.

You have dealt 20 damage to Jeremy (Level 10) with Fist.
You have inflicted Knockdown on Jeremy (Level 10).

This time Jeremy fell to the ground and rolled around, unable to catch his breath.

"Arthur, behind you!" Allendria yelled.

Arthur turned just in time to see Alex and Xavier rushing him. Arthur was getting nervous about the prospect of fighting against two of them until Rowan stepped in from the side and floored Xavier with a tremendous punch right into the side of his head. Xavier crumpled like a sack of potatoes while Alex kept his pace toward Arthur.

Arthur tried to avoid Alex's punch using a sidestep, but the blow still glanced off of his cheek and caused him to stumble for a moment.

Alex (Level 10) has dealt 15 damage to you with Melee attack (Glancing Blow).

Arthur recovered quicker than Alex and sent a sharp left hook into Alex's kidney while he was still off-balance.

You have dealt 20 damage to Alex (Level 10) with Fist. (Critical Hit)

Alex arched his back a bit and cringed before regaining his footing and slamming a fist into Arthur's ribs.

Alex (Level 10) has dealt 15 damage to you with Melee attack.

Arthur attempted to ignore the pain and let loose a swing at Alex's head but missed as the man ducked and came back with another hit to Arthur's ribs.

You have missed an Unarmed swing on Alex (Level 10).
Alex (Level 10) has dealt 15 damage to you with Melee attack.

The second strike hurt infinitely worse than the first and caused Arthur to stumble back a step. Alex didn't stop, though, and stepped forward with two more quick attacks to the ribs and one good hit to Arthur's jaw.

Alex (Level 10) has dealt 15 damage to you with Melee attack.
Alex (Level 10) has dealt 15 damage to you with Melee attack.
Alex (Level 10) has dealt 15 damage to you with Melee attack.

Arthur worried he would be in trouble when, yet again, Rowan showed up and hit the man from the side.

Alex stumbled backward a few steps and looked around. He spotted Jeremy getting to his feet and saw Xavier had stirred and tried to get to his knees. The man looked pretty shaken, and Alex wasn't sure he could stand.

"Alright, fuck this. I won't put up with this crap from some nobodies in a tiny, worthless village like this." Alex yelled as he pulled a dagger from his belt. Arthur also saw Jeremy reach down and grab a small blade out of the top of his boot.

"Be careful now, Alex. If you escalate things, I will not hold back, and there's a high chance some of us won't be leaving this room," Arthur told him.

"Oh, I'm counting on it," Alex responded and leaped for Arthur. Jeremy wasn't far behind charging in their direction.

Arthur took another step back to give him the extra second he needed to get his sword out before Alex closed the distance. Arthur swept his sword across his body to push the incoming dagger thrust out of the path of his body and kicked straight at Alex's leg. Arthur had hoped to hit him right in the kneecap and take his knee out but instead ended up getting a solid hit on the man's thigh.

You have dealt 20 damage to Alex (Level 10) with Kick.

Alex yelled in pain as he stumbled backward, and Arthur stepped forward with a hard overhanded strike. Just before the sword hit the man's shoulder, Jeremy arrived and caught the blade with his dagger and redirected it away from Alex's body. Before Arthur could regain his balance, Jeremy lunged forward, and Arthur felt a searing pain in his left shoulder.

Your attack with Steel Longsword of Minor Beastslaying was parried.
Jeremy (Level 10) has dealt 25 damage to you with Simple Iron Dagger.
You have been inflicted with Minor Bleed.

"Tough luck for you. Now it's time for you to die." Jeremy spat at him as he swung his dagger straight for Arthur's throat. Right before the dagger hit, Jeremy's body spasmed, and the man dropped his knife. He collapsed forward onto the ground, and as he fell, Arthur saw Rowan pulling his axe from the man's back. Arthur looked and saw Alex with rage on his face taking a swing straight for Rowan's throat, and Arthur reacted on instinct. He judged the arc of the blade and took a downward chop directly into the path the man's hand was heading. Before the edge reached Rowan, Alex's arm was cut clean off, and the dagger went flying with the rest of the man's hand.

You have dealt 45 damage to Alex (Level 10) with Steel Longsword of Minor Beastslaying (Critical Hit) (Hand Dismember).

Alex dropped to the ground and screamed as he looked at his missing hand.

"That's enough!" The leader roared as his steely gaze swept around the room, watching as everyone slowed to a stop.

"I don't know who you are or where you came from, but you made a huge mistake here today. You'll quickly come to regret your actions." Said the leader.

"The rest of you worthless fools that are still alive come with me. We're leaving." The leader took a contemptuous look around and walked straight for the door, motioning for his people to follow. The rest of his crew looked around in confused wonderment before finally ducking their heads and shuffling out the door behind him.

You have gained 125 experience in Unarmed for your fight with Alex (Level 10).

You have gained 125 experience in Unarmed for your fight with Jeremy (Level 10).

You have gained 75 experience in Swords for the death of Jeremy (Level 10).

You have gained 75 experience in Swords for the fight with Alex (Level 10).

You have gained 250 experience for the death of Jeremy (Level 10).

Arthur turned and looked at Rowan. "You alright? Anybody hurt?"

"Couple of bumps and bruises but nothing major," said Rowan.

Arthur turned to look at Allendria and was surprised at what he saw. She seemed to have a mixture of impossible emotions on her face. It was a mixture of anger, resentment, and shame all at the same time.

"Are you alright, Allendria?" Arthur asked her.

She seemed to snap out of her bewilderment. "Yes, I shall be fine, just surprised is all."

Arthur looked back at Rowan and was concerned at what he saw. He had told Arthur he would be alright, but the look on his face told a different story. Arthur wasn't sure what was wrong with his new friend, but it had him concerned.

Arthur turned to Daniel. "I was hoping we would have more time before any of those goons showed up to give us any trouble."
Daniel seemed to snap out of his trance. He had been staring at the body of Jeremy, who Rowan killed.

"I can honestly say we weren't expecting to see them back so soon. This gang was not one I'm familiar with. It must be one of the newer bands. Lord Golgara likes to rotate in newer members and dispose of older members consistently. It's common practice for him. It helps make sure none of his goons live long enough to gain the power needed to oppose him."

"Well, Daniel, I'm sorry to say, but I think our plans are gonna have to accelerate. I know we're nowhere near ready to oppose Golgara, but this will end up forcing the issue. I have no doubt these guys are going to disappear and come back with more help."
Arthur stated flatly.

Daniel sighed. "I imagine you're correct. That won't change the unfortunate truth that this village is nowhere near prepared enough to face them."

"I don't doubt your words, Daniel. I haven't even met most of the villagers yet and can tell you that's true. How long do you think we have before they return?" Arthur asked.

Daniel stared at the ceiling in contemplation for a few moments. "That depends on where they have to travel to go get reinforcements. Even if they take a direct trip to the closest city of Seora, it will take them two weeks to get there another two to get back. That's their nearest gang hall. It looks like we have a month's worth of time to prepare."

Arthur breathed a small sigh of relief with that news. They could accomplish much in a month.

Arthur noticed that Daniel's gaze went straight to Allendria and settled on her.

"Daniel, allow me to introduce you to Allendria. We had the fortune of running into her out in the forest today and ended up assisting her in dispatching some goblins. She agreed to accompany us back to the village to help assist me with some training. Would you have an available room she could use?"

Daniel looked increasingly uneasy as Arthur spoke. "Arthur, I understand you're new here, but I'm not sure you understand what this decision could do. Her presence here could cause a lot of trouble with the villagers."

"Daniel, I honestly don't care how people feel about it. I'm here to help the village when they don't even help themselves. So far, I've been the only one other than yourself, Rowan, and the mysterious Vana, even remotely interested in turning this place around. The villagers don't have to like it, but they'll have to get used to her being here for the time being." Arthur told him sternly.

"Alright, Arthur, that's fine. I'll trust your judgment. You haven't led me wrong yet. I'm sure I can find a room for her upstairs. There are plenty available right now. As much as you've done to help this place so far anyway, it's not like I'm out anything. Speaking of your trip to the forest, did you find anything interesting while you were out?" Daniel asked with a gleam in his eye.

"We ran into a few things that would be useful to us. I have a deer carcass out there that we need to get inside and get it cut up before it gets too hot. Don't want the meat to spoil from the heat. The rest of it I can fill you in on, but first, we need to get this mess cleaned up." Arthur said as he gestured to the dead body on the floor.

"Allendria, can you show Daniel out to our cart in the back so he can start getting the deer together and get it inside?" Arthur asked. "I'll work on this gentleman here on the ground."

"Daniel, do you have anywhere we can use as storage? We found a decent supply of different materials, and I'd like to get them stored and out of the way before anybody sees them." Arthur said.

"Of course, I'm sure we can find a
suitable spot we can use. With the lack of
travelers, there's always extra room in the
inn somewhere."

Arthur turned to look at Rowan and saw
that he had taken a seat at one of the nearby
tables. He gave the man a little more time to
himself and bent down to examine the body in
front of him.

Most of the man's gear was utter garbage,
but there were a couple of pieces that caught
Arthur's eye.

Item: Supple Leather Boots of Silence	**Durability**: 55/75 **Rarity**: Uncommon **Quality**: Well Crafted **Weight**: 0.8 kg **Slot**: Feet **Traits**: A pair of soft leather boots. These boots have the following effect: • Reduces chance you will be detected in Stealth by 10%.

Item: Basic Iron Dagger	Attack: 5-7 **Durability**: 40/50 **Rarity**: Common **Quality**: Well Crafted

	Weight: 0.8 kg **Slot**: Main Hand/Off Hand **Traits**: A dagger made of iron.

    Arthur was excited to see the pair of boots. He hadn't gotten the chance to replace any of the gear he had been wearing since he arrived here, and most of it was looking very shabby. His current boots had practically no padding, and it felt like walking around on bare dirt the whole time. Worst of all, they caused him to feel every tiny little rock and pebble on the ground as he walked. Hopefully, these new boots, with some padding in them, would ease some of that.

    More than anything, Arthur just hoped they would fit him. The boots said nothing about size, so it confused him. He removed the shoes off of the dead man's feet and his old boots and slipped on the new boots. Initially, they were too large for his feet by almost a full size. After a moment, the shoes seemed to shrink and contour to his feet until they were comfortable and snug. One thing was sure, though. They were a lot more comfortable than his old boots.

    The dagger was nothing special, but it would be an excellent addition to their arsenal; they were slowly building up. If nothing else, they could always reuse the metal by reforging it into something else.

Blood was pooling on each side of the dead body, so Arthur decided it was time to get it out of here before it made too much of a mess. He grabbed both of the dead man's arms and slowly started dragging him toward the door, but before he made it to the door, he stopped. Arthur couldn't just pull a dead body of one of the Lord's men out the front door. He didn't want to alarm them too much yet. It would take some extra time to get a plan together before springing that on them. Instead, he turned and started pulling the body toward the back door.

Once out the back, he noticed that Daniel had pulled the cart over to the back door. Daniel had planned to unload the cart directly through the back door and into whatever storage location he decided on.

Arthur turned to Daniel, "What should I do with the body? Is there a place somewhere nearby that they usually bury people? Do we have any tools that could help with that?"

"Well, there's a shovel that you can use, but honestly, I don't know where we would even bury that man. He isn't part of the village, so I wouldn't want him buried with the rest of the villagers." Daniel said.

"I may be of some assistance with that," Allendria told him. "I would suggest that we take the body farther out of the village to dispose of it."

"If that's the case, let me help you get that cart unloaded. Once we get all this put in the inn, Daniel can start working on the deer carcass, and Allendria and I can take that body out of the village." Arthur said.

They quickly got to work unloading the cart. The look of amazement on Daniel's face as they removed items from the cart, was priceless. They made sure to set the ore off to the side in a pile of its own. That would have to be loaded back up and taken over to the forge for use. Daniel looked downright giddy with the different things they had unloaded.

"Daniel, you good to start on that deer now while we dispose of the body?" Arthur asked. "I can come to help you when we finish up."

"Not a problem. I'll have it taken care of in no time at all." Daniel said with a grin.

Arthur and Allendria loaded up the cart with the dead body and covered it in a tarp. They slowly pushed the cart out from behind the inn and toward the road. They didn't want to alarm anyone by acting odd, so they took the path out of the village as usual. A few people gave them strange looks, but Arthur was pretty sure it was from seeing a Dark Elf and not from anything they were doing. They finally passed a small hill outside of the village, and Allendria motioned for them to stop.

"This should be far enough out of the village, and that small hill we just went over will block the view of us." She said.

They both unloaded the man and set him on the ground.

"Can you move the cart away from him a little further?" Allendria asked. "Don't want to damage it in the process."

"Sure thing."

Arthur moved the cart to a spot a little over ten yards away. He turned to face Allendria and waited. He had a fair idea of what she was going to do and was excited to see her magic in action finally.

Allendria looked down at the body and seemed to concentrate somewhat hard. The pretty lines on her face were hardening, and creases were appearing on her brow. Arthur saw flames envelop her hands, and then she moved both hands toward the dead man with her palms up. Flames started to flow toward the dead man from her hands. At first, it looked like the heat that radiated off of hot asphalt in the summer, just a distortion. It gradually turned into a steady yellow flame and then morphed into a bright orange as she fed it power. Arthur could see the sweat beading on the woman's brow as she continued to fuel the flames. To Arthur's amazement, the fire changed again. They were almost hot enough to be the pure blue and white combo seen in a cutting torch.

Allendria had started to sway and looked like she might collapse. Arthur had started in her direction so he could catch her if needed. Before he made it there, the flames abruptly died. Allendria looked up with an expression equally pleased and a bit disgusted. Arthur looked toward the spot and saw nothing but ash. The bones disintegrated, as well.

"Are you alright?" Arthur asked.

"I'll be fine. That almost drained me dry. I was able to learn a new spell, though. I've never needed to incinerate anything before, so I was worried that I wouldn't be able to finish the spell before I ran out of mana."

"That's amazing. I know the situation wasn't ideal, but at least you learned a spell."

"It was the least I could do since you and Rowan stood up for me at the inn. I didn't want to use my magic unless necessary, though. It tends to scare people when they see it. Especially those who are not familiar with magic." Allendria told him.

"I suppose I can understand that. It was awesome to watch, but I grew up fascinated by tales of things like that, so seeing it in person was simply breathtaking. That would be amazing to do."

Allendria cocked her head a bit and looked at him. "I swear you become odder the longer I talk with you. You have seen no magic before, have you? Not only that, but none of it bothers you. Typically, those not familiar with magic fear it."

"Well, you don't have to worry about that with me. I imagine I'll be fascinated with magic for a while to come." Arthur told her as he approached. He noticed Allendria's breathing had slowed back to an average pace, and the sweat was quickly disappearing. "I appreciate your help with this, though. Not sure how else we would have easily disposed of the body. We could have buried it in a random place in the forest, but that would cause even more problems. That and I didn't fancy needing to dig a hole, so this worked out great."

"I'm glad I could help, and I just wanted to say thank you. No one has ever stood up for me like that before, and honestly, the last person I ever expected to do it was a human. I'm happy that I came with you so far. Now, if we can get you a bit more knowledge into magic, it would be even better."

"Well, I'm sorry to say I think we just lost a lot of time. I had originally hoped not to see any of the local enforcers for a couple of months, but this has just drastically decreased the time we have. I can still hope they will come back with only a small group hoping to deal with just the three of us. That'll give us a good chance of making it through the fight without too much trouble. I want to prepare for the worst-case scenario, though. I want us to spend the next few weeks strengthening this place so it can withstand an assault from at least thirty."

"You keep saying you want to prepare this place, but from what I can see, the process hasn't even really started, much less is anything done. How do you intend to get anything accomplished here?"

"Well, we can try to come up with a good plan back at the inn with the others, but the gist of it will be to get this village fed, get the buy-in of the villagers, and get to crafting what we need. I think if we can get that started, it will greatly improve our odds and give us a place to start from." Arthur told her confidently.

"Let's get to the inn and get this figured out then," Allendria told him.

Chapter 16

Planning for a Confrontation

Arthur and Allendria returned to the inn and parked the cart in the back. Arthur entered a pandemic scene of comedy. Rowan and Daniel were both in what appeared to be a colorful argument about the butchering of the deer.

"Are you out of your damn mind? You have to cut the muscles away from the bones. I'll keep some bones for stock, but we aren't cutting steaks and chops with these," Daniel said.

"I thought you were an innkeeper? What innkeeper doesn't know the meaning of a good steak? A true steak needs a little bone for flavor. There are some exceptions to that, but not the point. You must be a cut-rate innkeeper who makes stew and roast," retorted Rowan.

"How dare you question my cooking abilities? You haven't been here long enough to judge anything, and the few times you have come in here, we never had much of a selection for me to work with. I'm the one cooking this food, so I'll dictate how it's cut." Huffed Daniel.

Arthur decided enough was enough. "That's enough of this conversation. Let's settle this before it goes any farther. Daniel is the one who will decide how it's cut and prepared since he'll be cooking it." Arthur waved away Rowan's objections when he opened his mouth to talk. "I'm not questioning your judgment or skills, Rowan. I'm sure it's a sound plan, but Daniel also has more experience in stretching food to feed as many as possible. For now, we're trying to feed the most possible with what little we have and not trying to get the best cuts of steaks."

"I promise you as we get more supplies, we can shift focus on the types of meat we prepare. Until then, let's stick with what feeds the most." Arthur said. His eyes swept back and forth between Daniel and Rowan.

"How much is left to complete, Daniel?" Arthur asked.

"We're almost done. We're each working on a front shoulder, and everything else has already been cut up and salted as necessary. Let us finish this real quick, and we can meet in the common room. I sent a message over to Dalia to join us over here." Daniel told him.

"Allendria and I'll wait for you two upfront then," Arthur said as he and Allendria walked forward through the doorway and toward the front of the inn. They continued down the small hall and turned into the main dining room. Arthur was shocked to see that Dalia had already arrived. He supposed it shouldn't be a big surprise since it wasn't a large village and it was a relatively quick trip to her house and back.

"Good evening Dalia, I'd like to introduce you to my friend Allendria," Arthur said as he motioned to Allendria at his side. "Allendria, this is Lady Dalia Flamekissed."

Dalia looked at Allendria, and a palpable tension settled over the room. Arthur could see the hormones swirling in the air between them at their contest of feminine wiles. After a few tense moments of silence, Dalia had the grace to stand and face Allendria. She extended her hand in greeting, "Pleased to meet you, Allendria." She said as she gave Arthur a sidelong glance that told him he needed to explain what was happening.

"A pleasure to meet you as well." Said Allendria as she took Dalia's hand in a quick shake. Arthur swore he saw sparks erupt between the two but chalked it up to the imagination.

"Rowan and I ran across Allendria when we were hunting in the woods. We had to assist her in dispatching a group of goblins that had been chasing her. She's agreed to help me with some training and to assist with our endeavor here, at least temporarily." Arthur told Dalia in a thorough explanation.

"Rowan and Daniel are finishing up in the back, and they'll join us shortly. We can discuss plans from there. I can get you caught up, though. One of Lord Golgara's enforcer crews were in the inn earlier today." Arthur told her.
She nodded with his explanation. He was sure she already knew they were in the village.

"We had a bit of an altercation with them. We ended up killing one bandit and injuring two others. The leader called an abrupt end of the fight and left with the two survivors in tow. We have a sinking feeling he will be making for Seora at full speed and gathering help to return and deal with us. We're currently expecting them to bring enough to face down me, Rowan, and possibly Allendria. Now's the time for us to plan how we want the village to move forward." Arthur told her.

Paleness washed over her face at the news of them killing one of Golgara's men. She composed herself quickly, though, and nodded at Arthur. "I agree with your assessment. I would estimate we have about a month as well for them to arrive back. And that's if they run into no issues and have enough members on hand in Seora to immediately return. That time frame could be anywhere from a few days to even a week more than that, but I wouldn't count on that estimate. I know I agreed to assist you in this endeavor, so it looks like now is the time to go all in."

"Where are you from Allendria? I can say I haven't had the pleasure of meeting a Dark Elf." Dalia asked.

"I hail from a city on the southeastern edge of the forest near here," Allendria responded.

"How did you end up this direction on the wrong side of the forest? I would imagine a trek through the forest isn't safe."

"It was a bit of a last-minute flight from home. There was a change of power, and I didn't want to remain for the aftermath of it. I was sure there'd be a lot of casualties from it." Allendria said as she looked at her feet angrily.

Arthur gazed at Dalia and shook his head as if to ask her to drop those questions.

"I'm sorry to hear that. I recall Arthur mentioning you would be training him. What skills do you have that he was interested enough to bargain for?" Dalia asked.

"I agreed to assist Arthur with his magical training for his help in the woods. He seems to be a quick study so far." Allendria said with pride in her voice.

"Well, isn't he a surprise," Dalia said as she looked Arthur in the eye. "He never mentioned he had any magical training at all when I last spoke to him." She said with a bit of steel in her voice.

"My apologies Dalia. I didn't tell you because I had no idea how to use my magic for anything useful, and honestly, I'm still trying to get a feel for people I can trust here. After what we've been through so far, I don't believe it would be any harm for you to know." Arthur explained.

"How the hell do you have magical training but not know how to use any magic? That seems impossible to learn a skill without actually doing something in said skill." Dalia said in astonishment.

"It was a unique situation that I would not divulge at the moment. Allendria has already helped correct some of my deficiencies, and it shouldn't be long until I can be useful with my magical skills."

As luck would have it, Rowan and Daniel entered the room at that moment, and the conversation halted. All of them took a seat at the bar, and Daniel stepped behind the bar and pulled up a small stool he had back there.

"So, what now?" Daniel asked.

"I need to know what is causing this place the most trouble. The village is starving, but we are slowly working to address that. Other than that, it seems to have absolutely no life. I rarely ever see people out of their homes much less walking through the village doing any activities. I understand lack of food would cause much of it, but it seems to be a much worse problem." Arthur said.

"I can answer most of that." Dalia chimed in. "This place is as you described it. There isn't much life in the people, and much of that's because it has become stagnant. To people unfamiliar with this country, it may be a little hard to understand, but Lord Golgara's stranglehold on the resources restricts everyone. Not only is food almost unheard of, but crafting ingredients and trade goods are just as scarce. People can't work when they have no supplies, they can't make any coin without goods or labor to sell, and in turn, they can't buy more ingredients or food. It's a complete stranglehold on the populace."

"I can't understand the purpose of that, though. With that kind of oversight, no one would ever get anything done. Skills would stagnate, and society would dissolve into nothing. I can't grasp why anyone would believe it's a good idea or even an acceptable one." Arthur said as he shook his head angrily.

"It's how he controls the territory more than anything," Daniel said. "Lord Golgara likes to keep a firm grasp on his resources. He usually leaves just enough resources for people to survive. When the crews came through last time, they took even more than normal. I'm beginning to think they are trying to eradicate this village."

"Why would they try to destroy the village? This place is a small village on the edge of the territory. Surely there isn't anything threatening here." Arthur said.

Everyone looked around for a few moments, and they all finally settled on Daniel. He let out a sigh and began to explain.

"This village is hated because of its name. Alem's Crossing came from the person who established the village. Alem was one of the original descendants that became the house of Firebrand. He was a renowned explorer, and this village was the start of his rise to power and eventual taming of the land and the dragons to earn the Firebrand name. The current king and his lords were all part of the group that betrayed the Firebrands." Daniel explained.

"That makes more sense. At least it gives me a bit of an explanation of the issue. The big problem is that I need to get some buy-in from the villagers on this. So far, they have been of no use to this village. I can't figure out how. We finally have some crafting that will need to be done to prepare. With the limited time we have left, I can't dedicate my time to doing all of it myself, so we need everyone's help. Rowan can work in the forge to refine the iron we found and start making useful items but, with the workload, he could probably use some help. I'm assuming you don't have any apprentices with as empty as I saw your shop when we first met?" Arthur asked as he looked toward Rowan.

"I'm relatively new here, and with the lack of work, I never had the need or the resources to hire apprentices. I can convince some to join me now if we can use the food we have as an enticement." Rowan told him.

"I'm sure we can make that work, but the trick isn't just getting you up and running, we need to get more people. We have hides that need to be cured and start the tanning process. That in itself is a very long process." Arthur said contemplatively.

Daniel gave him an odd look as he tilted his head slightly sideways. "What do you classify as a long time? I mean, sure, a few days is a bit of time, but not that long regarding our preparations."

"Are you telling me you can tan hides here in a few days? Are we talking about full leather tanning without hair? Or are we just talking about tanning for fur use? With fur on, it usually takes about a week where I'm from, but if you want full-on leather similar to what's used on most shoes and clothes, it can take much longer." Arthur said. He also left out the part that during medieval times, it took much longer because they didn't have the technology or the chemicals he had. These people should have been closer to that level of technology being forced to use tanning pools.

"We have someone here who mainly works in tanning and has the facility set up just outside of the village. We could get them to work on the process now and have some leather to work within a few days. I'm sure Rowan would need some as well for some things he'll need to make." Daniel told him.

"That's fantastic news, but I still can't seem to tie all of this together to make the village work. Yes, we can bribe people with food, and I'm sure that would work, but isn't there anything around that generates things like quests. We need to not only provide them with things they need and receive items we need, but I also want to help them improve their skills. That will be more valuable to them than anything else after the food. It will also encourage them to take pride in what we're working for." Arthur stressed to Daniel.

"Well, luckily for you, I may have a solution to that," Dalia told him. "As you may recall, I'm now officially a Lady in residence over this village by birthright. While this may seem somewhat trivial, it gives me a bit of freedom, and one vital thing I can do is install a Mayor."

"That sounds great and all, but I don't see how naming someone as Mayor will help our situation," Arthur told her seriously.

"The title of Mayor may not seem like much, but there's one particular function they can do that makes them invaluable to our cause. Mayors can create work orders for the village." She said with a grin.

"Alright, I'll bite. What are work orders?" Arthur asked.

"Work orders are mini-quests that the Mayor creates. He can post certain jobs that need doing in the village with defined criteria. When a villager accepts the task and completes it, they can turn it into the Mayor and will receive the posted rewards and also some experience that's randomly determined based on the work order itself. For instance, they could post a job saying the village needs ten animal hides tanned. The village will provide the raw hides and would be rewarded three meals at the inn. The work order system will also include a random amount of experience. For instance, it may provide 300 Leatherworking experience for the task. The experience rewarded is always related to some aspect of the work order, though." Dalia explained.

"That's fantastic and exactly what we need. You find someone who would be a good candidate for Mayor, and we'll get this place back on its feet. Once we can get the tasks posted and take a good stock of our inventory, it will allow us to figure out priorities. We'll need to fortify this place, so I'm planning to spend a lot of time working on a wall for it. I'll try to get the wall to surround the village, but I can't guarantee all of it will be big enough. Can anyone tell me what direction the force will probably arrive from if they're coming from Seora? I'll focus more effort on that side of the village."

"They'll probably follow the road to the northeast of here so you could plan to fortify that part first, I guess. I don't see what good it will do, though. If you can't get all of it done, they can easily circle the wall to a less fortified spot to come through." Daniel said.

"I worry about that too, but it serves two purposes. Even a small wall in a different area will provide a delay for them to cross it and give us some time to shoot them with arrows. The second purpose is it helps me grind my earth magic skill a little more. Both could prove very helpful in a fight." Arthur told them.

"So how do we want to proportion food then?" Daniel asked. "I assume you will keep up with random trips to the forest for goods as needed. That deer you brought us can be stretched to feed most of the village for almost a week, but we'll need more. We also can't overlook those that cannot work because of age or illness."

"The real question is, how have you survived this long? I arrived a few days ago and can't even figure out how there's anyone here still alive. You have no food, no commerce, nothing. It defies logic how anyone can survive here." Arthur said questioningly.

"Typically, when the enforcers come through, they leave us with just enough to survive long enough to replant some stuff and barely scrounge by before they return. The first month after they leave is usually very rough, but it gradually gets better until they arrive again. This time they took more than usual and almost wiped us out. We weren't expecting to see them back anytime soon since they were just here a few weeks before you arrived. The group we saw wasn't the same one who came here before, though." Daniel explained.

"If not for the little food Vana had scrounged from the forest, I doubt many would still be alive. I try to make rounds to each house with a little food every few days as we can, but it's been more difficult than normal this time." He continued.

"Well, that explains part of that then. Let's find some assistants for the larger jobs we have. Daniel and Rowan, you two will need some help since you have the biggest jobs. We can reward work with food. Those who are still outside the age range and have no trade can still be useful by doing menial tasks that they're physically capable of around here for their food. We need to make sure there are jobs they'll be capable of doing. Those of proper working age without trades can try to apprentice with anybody who will use them in the village. Daniel, I plan to use your inn as a village kitchen until we get everything running again. Once people can get their food, they can shift back to cooking their meals. For now, we can offer food for apprenticeships and assistance and then move on to goods and services as well once established. With the state I've seen the village in, it shouldn't take much effort at all to get people to work for food." Arthur explained to them all.

Each of them shook their heads in agreement, but he noticed that Rowan was still looking despondent and staring at his feet. He would need to have a word with his friend after this meeting.

"Sounds like the last order of business is for Dalia to decide on and name a mayor, and this will get moving," Arthur chirped.

Dalia perked up at her name and gave him an evil grin. She stared him straight in the eyes and, in a sweet and innocent voice, said, "Oh, but I have decided on a mayor already. I, Dalia Flamekissed, Lady in residence of the village of Alem's Crossing, do at this moment name Arthur as the Mayor."

Arthur only had time to think, *Oh shit*, before he got a notification.

Congratulations, you have been named the Mayor of Alem's Crossing. Would you like to access the Village Control Menu?

"Well, that's a dirty, underhanded move, Dalia. How am I supposed to keep up with village assignments and go on resource hunting missions?" Arthur said dejectedly.

She smiled at him and told him, "I have utter faith in your capabilities, Arthur."

"I guess I'll make it work then. Let's all take a break for the night, and I'll see what I can do with the new village controls." Arthur told them.

All of them nodded in agreement and slowly shuffled out of the inn. Daniel stayed behind the bar, but Arthur looked at him and motioned toward Rowan, who was still seated and then motioned toward the back. Daniel seemed to understand what Arthur meant and walked to the kitchen. Arthur got up, walked over to Rowan, and seated himself next to him.

"What's wrong, Rowan? You look like someone ran over your puppy." Arthur asked the big man. Rowan lifted his head to look at Arthur, and Arthur could see conflicting emotions in the man's face. He looked like he was on the verge of a breakdown, but Arthur wasn't sure why.

"Anything I can help with?" Arthur tried again.

Rowan looked him in the eye and sighed, "I've never killed a man before and can't seem to figure out how to feel about it."

Damn, Arthur thought to himself. He never thought about the consequences of the fight from earlier. Looking at it from Rowan's perspective, the man's feelings were completely understandable. He didn't understand how he would feel if, and honestly when, he'd be forced to kill someone. That would be a hard moment to reconcile.

"I know the man deserved it with every fiber of my being, but it's just hard to process. I keep seeing him die over and over again, and it won't get out of my head. I mean, we killed those goblins earlier today, but they were monsters other than their vague human shape. That bandit was an actual man that we'd see walking the streets. We even talked with him for a while, even though he was utterly detestable about it."

Arthur patted him on his shoulder. "Just remind yourself that you did it for a good cause. He was planning on raping someone for no reason other than he thought he could. We even tried to dissuade them from their course of action with multiple warnings, and they still attacked us. I know it'll be hard, but keep focused on our mission. I'm sure focusing on your smithing work tomorrow, after some sleep tonight, will help you out."

"Not sure I'll be able to get any sleep, but I'm sure focusing on some work will help. Guess I'll head to the back and get some of that ore loaded on the cart, so I can get to work on it in the morning."

"Need any help?" Arthur asked.

"Nah, the physical work will help me focus and hopefully get my mind back on track," Rowan said and looked into Arthur's eyes. "Thank you, though. I appreciate it."

"Anytime Rowan, maybe once we get caught up a bit, we can go on another forest dive for resources," Arthur said with a slight punch to the man's arm.

"I'll hold you to that," Rowan told him with a grin.

They both stood and walked toward the back. Rowan moved to the room where the ore had been stored and started loading it into the cart behind the inn. Arthur turned toward the kitchen area and saw Daniel in there.

"Hey Daniel, thanks for your support in all this. Are you going to need any help getting our food supplies up and going for the moment? I think I'm about to head up to my room and dig through the village control options before I sleep."

"I've got it covered. I'll find a couple of hands in the morning and begin getting them up to speed. As you said, the enticement of food should draw all the help I need. I can only stretch the food so far on what we have. Soups go a long way and all, but still, we'll need more."

"Don't worry about that. I'll spend the next few days getting things here in order with the new village control and maybe do a bit of crafting. Once that's done, I'll head back out to the forest for some more hunting. Probably only about three days until I can get more supplies."

"We should have plenty to last until then. Even with the ramped-up rewards for the work orders. I'll also ensure our young and elderly are taken care of."

"Thank you, Daniel. Do me a favor and try to find any single mothers and fathers first when looking for workers. Also, make it known I'll provide supplies for any who wish to take up a hunting trade with me, so they can learn to supply the village from the forest. I want to know if anyone has any fighting skills in the village for our upcoming issues, too." Arthur told him.

"I'll see what I can do. Goodnight, Arthur." Daniel told him.

"Goodnight, Daniel."

Arthur turned and headed to his room. To his surprise, Allendria was waiting for him by his door.

"Hi, Arthur. Headed to bed?" She asked.

"Hey, Allendria. I am, but I'll need to do a little work with my new position, as the village mayor, first. Once I have the main parts of that sorted out, I'll probably hit the hay." Arthur told her.
Allendria had a contemplative look on her face. She looked like she was trying to make a decision but couldn't decide what that decision should be. The indecisive look on her face was almost cute.

"Were you able to talk to Rowan? He looked distracted during our meeting. I was afraid he may have been injured during the fight and was trying to hide it." She said, worried.

"You're right. I'm not sure injured is the correct term, but it hit Rowan hard mentally. He'd never killed a man before, and the act earlier was warring with his emotions. That was what his issue was. I'm hoping that getting to work in the forge tomorrow will help get his mind back on track. Honestly, I doubt he'll be able to sleep much, and I suspect he'll start working tonight until exhaustion takes him." Arthur told her in a low tone.

Allendria covered her mouth, and he saw tears form in the corners of her eyes. "He's suffering because of me. Had I not been there, it may not have come to a fight, and he wouldn't have been forced to help you. Oh, I'm so sorry, Arthur. I didn't mean to cause this trouble for you. I hope you know that I greatly appreciate what you and Rowan both did for me, though."

"It wasn't your fault Allendria. I don't want you to feel sorry for being a victim of someone else. What we did was the right thing even though it resulted in someone's death. We gave that bandit every chance to stop his actions and then gave every warning not to escalate the issue before we were forced to kill him in defense. I would do it in a heartbeat for you or anyone else, to be honest." Arthur told her as he reached out and held her hand.

She looked down at his hand. "I have been trying to decide what to do to thank you for your heroic actions. I have been wrestling with an idea, but it's almost unheard of and wasn't sure if I should. After hearing your words, though, I'm sure it's the right thing. Tomorrow, I want to bestow two gifts on you. First, I want to train you in the art of Enchantment. I've been trained in it but am not very high level. I can teach you what I know, and maybe we can work on it together?" She said hopefully.

"That sounds amazing, Allendria. I would love to learn a skill from you, but you know you don't have to give me anything, don't you?" He asked her.

"I was sure you'd say that. The second gift is something I shall give, but you must never discuss it with anyone. I don't care what excuse you'd use to explain it away, but you absolutely can't tell anyone I was the one that taught you. I'll give you the greatest gift I can give. I will teach you to unlock Fire Magic." She told him.

"Wait, you can do that? I thought you had to find some rare artifact or something like I had to unlock it, that or find a master level magician to teach you." Arthur said, questioningly with shock on his face.

"Magic can be taught by anyone who's
learned the skill. The problem is that it's
very tightly held. Most magicians only learn
the different elemental magics by enrolling in
a magical school or apprenticing to a
magician. When this happens, not only is it
rare to be accepted, but it also costs a large
sum of money. I'm not overly familiar with
human customs, but I understand it is similar.
Typically, it is unlawful for someone not
registered as a magical teacher to teach
another elemental magic of any kind. Since I'm
not human, I'm not as concerned, but I still
want this secret to remain that at all costs.
It isn't strictly forbidden in my culture, but
it would be highly discouraged." Allendria
explained.

"I'm honored Allendria and can promise
your secret is safe with me. I'll cherish this
gift from you. I'm going to head to my room to
work on this village control panel for a few
minutes before I turn in. I'll see you in the
morning. Goodnight, Allendria."

"Goodnight, Arthur."

Arthur entered his room with a huge smile
and was now looking forward to tomorrow.

Chapter 17

Managing a Village

Arthur closed the door behind him and let out a breath he wasn't aware he was holding. Allendria was breathtakingly beautiful, quite literally. He walked over to his bed and sat down. Taking off his new boots, he relaxed for a moment while he sorted through his menu. He decided it was time to sort through this village interface. With a thought, he brought up his options.

Welcome to the Village Control Panel, Mayor Arthur. Would you like a quick overview of the functions of this menu?

Arthur decided it was time to use a bit of a crutch for once. He was tired of never understanding mechanics. He thought of his answer and decided on YES.

Hello Arthur, you have many options in the Village Control Panel. Keep in mind, some of these options may not be available until the village has gained rank and quality. This village is currently Rank 1 out of 5 and is the quality level of Poor. Advancing the quality increases the experience rewards from work orders in the village and grants the village bonuses to different aspects of the village. These can include crafting speed boosts, crop growth boosts, and even disease resistance bonuses, to name a few. These become available by advancing rank and completing particular objectives that the control panel will designate for you.

Once your village has reached level 5, you have the chance to raise the village to a town and from there another five ranks until it reaches a city. Each rank requires certain milestones and objectives that you will see in the control panel.

Creating work orders can be done by accessing the work order option on the main panel. You are only required to choose the required task and description for parameters. You can select base rewards of materials or goods, but the village work order system assigns all experience.

Do you require any further clarification on the Village Control Panel?

Another option to choose. Arthur chose NO this time. After thinking of his answer, the menu changed, and the Village Control Panel itself appeared.

Alem's Crossing Village Control Panel	
Village Rank: (1/5) Criteria for Rank Advancement: (0/5)	Village Quality: Poor Criteria for Village Quality Improvement: (0/5)
View Criteria for Rank Advancement	View Criteria for Village Quality Improvement
Create Work Orders	View Current Work Orders
Current Active Village Bonuses:	

All in all, it was blissfully straightforward, and with his new context from the help notification, it was easy to discern. He decided the first thing he wanted to do was to view the criteria needed to rank up the village. With a thought, he selected the option, and another menu appeared.

Criteria for Rank Advancement
Current Village Rank: (1/5)
Current Criteria for Rank Advancement: 1) Increase Village Population by 10 People. (0/10) 2) Build 2 Additional Houses. (0/2) 3) Assign 2 Village Roles. (0/2) 4) Increase Village Defenses by 30 Points. (0/30) 5) Establish 1 Official Industry in the Village. (0/1)

Well, that was simple. Clear-cut goals are always the best and easier to manage. Arthur would have to see what would be needed to make these goals happen. The houses would probably be the hardest part. With scarce resources, it would be difficult to do, and on top of that, buildings can take a while to build.

Arthur decided he wanted to look at the quality standards as well. He thought about viewing the criteria for village quality, and the menu changed again.

<table>
<tr><td colspan="1">Criteria for Village Quality Improvement</td></tr>
<tr><td>Current Village Quality: Poor</td></tr>
<tr><td>Current Criteria for Quality Advancement:

1) Completely Repair 4 Houses. (0/4)
2) Complete 15 Work Orders. (0/15)
3) Raise Village Health Rating by 20 Points. (0/20)
4) Build 3 Village Improvement Projects. (0/3)
5) Improve the Quality of 25% of the Village Roads by 1 Quality Level (0/25)</td></tr>
</table>

Another set of straightforward improvements. Most seem relatively easy to do. The village health should be trivial. Some necessary village cleaning and food supply to bring their nutrition level back up should fix that problem. The roads would be a decently easy project, especially if he could get his magic involved.

Arthur decided it was time to work on setting out some work orders. He navigated back to the main menu and then checked the Create Work Order option and, with a thought, it came up.

<table>
<tr><td colspan="2" align="center">Alem's Crossing Work Orders</td></tr>
<tr><td colspan="2">Current Work Orders: (0/15)</td></tr>
<tr><td colspan="2">Current Active Work Orders:</td></tr>
<tr><td colspan="2">

</td></tr>
</table>

It looked like Arthur had fifteen work orders to issue. It was time to sort out what he needed. Knowing what needed to be done and the resources on hand made it more comfortable. Arthur didn't know what professions he had available in the village, so he was going to assign everything he needed. After some work, he filled out the first of his work orders and took a look at them.

Work Order	
Completion Criteria: Provide 5 Tanned Animal Hides (0/5)	Provided Materials: Village will provide necessary raw animal hides. Procure from Mayor. Any other necessary materials can be negotiated for.
Completion Timeline: 5 Days	Rewards: 5 Meal tokens to be used at the Village Inn. 200 Leatherworking Experience. 50 Character Experience.

Well, that wasn't bad at all. The experience that the work order system added wasn't anything to be stingy about. Especially with how low level most people around here were rumored to be. He could see why upgrading the quality would be necessary, though, so the rewards would increase. That would be needed as the citizen's progressed levels. He went ahead and filled out the rest and pulled up his new shortlist of active work orders.

Alem's Crossing Work Orders
Current Work Orders: (0/15)
Current Active Work Orders:

1) 5 Tanned Animal Hides
2) 5 Tanned Animal Hides
3) 5 Iron Ingots
4) 5 Iron Ingots
5) 5 Iron Ingots
6) 5 Iron Ingots
7) 1 Standard Bow
8) 1 Iron Sword
9) 1 Iron Dagger
10) 1 Iron Dagger
11) 15 Arrow Shafts
12) 5 Wood Logs
13) 5 Wood Logs
14) 5 Meals Prepared
15) 5 Meals Prepared

Most were super simple tasks, and he wanted to make sure there was a broad spectrum for people to get a chance to use them. There didn't appear to be a limit to how quickly he could post new ones, so as long as he kept up with it, new ones could keep getting added. Those options should cover enough of a skill range to get plenty of people active.

Daniel's new cooking staff could increase their levels with the meal preparation jobs, Rowan's apprentices, and even Rowan himself could use the metal and weapon orders. He knew they had a tanner that could use the hides for that order. Once they finished some of those, he could shift one of those to a leatherworking order. He hoped he could find someone who was a bowyer, but there was no guarantee. He would love to find someone in the village with the skill to craft him a piece on commission from the yew logs Rowan, and himself had gathered. Altogether, it looked like a good spread of jobs available.

He decided it was time to turn in for the evening. He would have to ask Daniel tomorrow what the plan was for getting the message out that these new orders were up for people to use. He would also have to work with Allendria on unlocking his Fire Magic and then make sure he was continually burning mana for experience while she was teaching him Enchanting. He laid down on his bed. After a few moments, he ditched his shirt and pants and fell asleep.

＊＊＊

Arthur woke up feeling refreshed and ready to hit the ground running. It felt good to have at least some idea of a plan on how to get where they needed to be. Once he had the village up and working, he could redirect all the goodwill toward Lianna to help further his goal here. That should also keep her satisfied with his progress for the time being. He was sure she would eventually pressure him into increasing his pace, so he needed to get ahead of some of it.

Arthur got up and got his clothes back on. It was time to head out and get the morning started. He rounded the corner into the main room and found a handful of people milling around the area. He also noticed a delicious smell coming from the kitchen area. Arthur hadn't seen most of the people in the room before, so he wasn't sure how to take this. Daniel came around the corner and greeted him with a smile.

"A bit of a turn out this morning. It seems you were busy last night."

"What do you mean?" Arthur asked him.

"All the work orders you posted. These people are here to collect the materials offered by your orders to get started." Daniel explained.

"How do they even know about them? I was planning to discuss options on how to spread the word about them this morning."

Daniel laughed. "You wouldn't know this, but when Dalia made you Mayor, it sent a message to all villagers informing them of the change. Any residents of the village can access a version of the village control panel. It only shows them the rank, quality, and available work orders, though. Nothing more."

"Well, that makes it much easier. Care to assist with gathering up materials? Something smells delicious in the back."

"I'm sure I could help with that. My new assistants have much of the cooking under control since the main part is done."

Arthur lowered his voice as he approached Daniel, "Many of these people look a bit hostile or upset. I'm guessing the idea of someone they don't know being made Mayor out of nowhere has something to do with that?"

Daniel nodded his head. "I would assume the same thing myself. I have had little chance to speak to any of them. Their life has been so rough they have lost trust in almost everyone, though."

"Can you do me another favor then? I want to get on their good side so my tasks will get completed in an orderly fashion. I also want to make sure they keep coming back to do more. Can you get me a full round of food served this morning for everyone here? I want to make sure everyone gets a meal before they get to work, and it'll give me a chance to address many of them."

"I'll see it done. Earning some goodwill with the crowd will go a long way for our plans." Daniel said as he walked back toward the kitchen. Arthur was sure he was arranging for the food to be brought out.

Arthur turned to face the crowd of people milling about around the room. They all shuffled from place to place, looking like zombies. Each one was dirty and somewhat emaciated, but they had shown up to work, regardless.

Arthur cleared his throat loudly to get their attention. "Hello all, I know some of you may be a bit uneasy about having someone you've never met as your Mayor. I assure you I have nothing but the best intentions for this place. We're going to get this village back on track. In a show of good faith, I want all of you to find yourself a seat. I'm having a meal brought out for every one of you at no charge. I only ask that you thank our gracious host, Daniel. I would also like to extend one more act of goodwill. If any of you have other family members, please send a message to them to come and receive a free meal as well. It's always better for families to get a chance to eat together."

Arthur noticed looks of shock on almost every face in the room. A few of the people in the crowd were even in tears. They all began to find a seat and get comfortable just as Daniel and his two new assistants started streaming out of the kitchen with bowls of soup for everyone.

Arthur wasn't sure what all Daniel had put in the soup, but it looked delicious. He could see some venison cut into smaller chunks floating around in it and even saw the occasional piece of potato. Arthur himself was also looking forward to it.

He raised his voice once more to address them. "Please take your time and enjoy this warm meal. I'll sit here and eat with you. Once we finish, feel free to approach me with the order you wish to fulfill, and I can ensure you get what you need to get started."

Everyone looked awestruck at his statement. These people were overjoyed to have a meal. Something that was a basic human necessity, all because of a corrupt lord who thought he could do whatever he wanted. Arthur felt his anger starting to bubble up and then quickly reined it in. He didn't want to show those emotions around these people and possibly frighten some of them. A few of them looked frail enough to die from a good scare.

Arthur sat and enjoyed his meal, which tasted as good as it smelled and did a little people watching. He desperately wanted to help these people but knew it would be a gradual process. He had always had a bit of a soft spot for those less fortunate, but this seemed like an odd feeling for him to be so driven to make a change for people he barely knew or had never even met. There wasn't much use dwelling on that sentiment, though.

As everyone finished up their meal, Arthur laid his spoon down, and people slowly began to mill about toward him. The first person approached him after a bit of hesitation.

"Hello, what's your name, and what can I do for you today?" Arthur asked her.

"My name is Corianne. I'm here for the two hide tanning work orders you posted Lord Mayor." She said deferentially.

"Oh no, Corianne, I'm no lord. Please, call me Arthur." Arthur looked over his shoulder and found one of Daniel's assistants.

"Young lady. Could you ask Daniel to bring ten of the animal pelts we have out here for Corianne? I would appreciate it."

She quickly nodded her head and darted toward the back in a hurry. Daniel appeared less than a minute later carrying a bundle of furs.

"Thank you for your help in this matter, Corianne. I plan on having more animal pelts in a few more days so you can look forward to more of these orders in the future." Arthur told her with a smile.

"Oh, thank you, my lord… uh, I mean Arthur."

"Good luck in your task, Lady Corianne," Arthur said as he motioned for her to step to the side, and the next person in line came forward.

The next two people to come forward were a bit of a surprise. One man that looked to be around twenty and a woman who appeared close to the same age approached him. Arthur was correct in his assumption that Rowan wouldn't get much sleep last night, as he had already decided upon these two for his new assistants. The man was named Alex, and the woman's name was Lana. After a bit of discussion, Arthur discovered they were a young married couple, and Rowan had taken both of them into his service.

Their work order was quick to issue. Arthur just needed to approve each of them for two of the requests for ingots. Rowan had the supplies. They just needed to accept the task formally. They told him Rowan would come to find him later to receive the orders for the sword and daggers.

The next person was both a surprise and a delight for him. The village did have someone who was a bowyer. His name was Zeke, and he had the bowyer skill, albeit a somewhat low skill level. Arthur told the man that depending on the work done on the bow and arrows, that he wanted the man to make him a bow out of yew wood he had found. The man eagerly agreed to quickly get the two orders done so he would have the chance at making the yew bow for Arthur.

Daniel brought out the supplies he would need, and Arthur handed the man the pine sap he had gathered, knowing it would be useful to the man in making a resin for glue.

The next to approach him was a man in his late thirties and a younger man in his teens. Arthur was sure this was a father and his son. They both came for the wood cutting orders, and Arthur gave one to each of them.

Arthur was surprised by the next two that came up. It was the two assistants Daniel had hired. Arthur quickly gave the first food order to the young redhead named Paula and the other to the slightly older brunette named Trisha.

With this complete, Arthur was a bit concerned. He still had a handful of people milling about, but no work orders left to give out. He motioned the first person forward.

It was a young woman who appeared to be in her early twenties. She shuffled up to him and looked into his face. She was in as poor shape as the rest of the villagers. She looked dirty, and her clothes were threadbare. Her blonde hair was down past her shoulders but matted and filthy. She had the same gaunt face and sunken cheeks as most of the others in this village. Not only did these people shuffle around like zombies, but he'd be damned if they didn't almost look the part as well.

"Hello, Lord Mayor," the young woman stumbled.

Arthur held up a hand. "Let me stop you right there. I am no lord and want to be called Arthur, please. What is your name, young lady, and what can I assist you with?" He asked her with a sincere smile.

"My apologies, Arthur. My name is Katherine, and I was hoping you would have a position that I might fill for you on your staff? I don't have any trade skills of any kind, but I'm open to learning any of them you deem necessary. I have one particular skill that may be of note for me to obtain a position with you. I have the skill of Scribe. I'm fluent in our language and can read and write as well." She told him matter-of-factly.

Arthur looked astonished for a second. On the one hand, the woman could read and write, which he was sure was uncommon around here. On the other, she also thought Arthur had staff. He thought about it for a moment and decided he would need help with his endeavors. Having someone that could read and write would be essential as the village grew. If he could hire her on now, she could be part of the project from the ground up. Arthur decided on the matter quickly. There was no way he could let a skill like this slip his grasp.

"I accept your proposal and am prepared to offer you a civil service position with the village. Your current duties would be as an administrative assistant to myself and keeping up with any village tasks I deem necessary. As you can imagine, the village doesn't have much to offer in the way of resources, but I'm willing to pledge you two hot meals a day at the inn and access to bathing facilities here. I'll also provide materials needed for you to do your job and will promise that when we have revived a bit of the economy in the village, your position will include pay in coinage that we can negotiate at that time."

Katherine looked like she was about to burst with tears as she shook her head up and down.

"Fantastic, why don't you stay by me while I talk to the last couple of people here and then we can get you sorted out," Arthur said.

She nodded again and moved to his side and a bit behind him. Arthur motioned for the next person to approach. This man appeared to be in his thirties with hard lines in his face. Arthur wasn't sure, but he looked like the textbook definition of a grizzled old soldier with short cut hair and a short beard. He had a scar on his left cheek that stretched down to his jawline. He approached Arthur and came to a halt with a firm stance. *Yep, a military veteran.*

"Good morning Sir, my name is Samson, and I would like to request a position with you for guard service. I have proficiency in swords, spears, shields, and some light proficiency in archery."

Arthur was taken aback for a moment at the man's abruptness but quickly decided he liked the approach.

"What do you expect in return for your service, and what services are you willing to offer for the village?" Arthur asked.

"Well, to be honest, Sir, I expected you to detail those responsibilities, but I'm willing to perform guard service for the village in any capacity needed. I have also heard a rumor of you personally running supply missions into the forest, and would like to join you in those endeavors when possible." Samson summed up for him.

His statement thrilled Arthur. He needed more people to buy into the village itself and work to make it better. This man would also be useful to him on their supply missions, especially since Rowan would probably be busy with the forge for the time being. He and Allendria could do most of the hunting, but an extra person would help things move faster.

"I'd be thrilled to accept your service then. I'll offer you two meals a day at the inn here and a promise to work with you on supplying the gear you will need to do your job. Once the village has recovered somewhat, we can negotiate a salary in coinage to cover your expenses moving forward. The key goal is for us to get the village operational first."

"I'll accept those terms and work toward that goal. I'm sad to say I have little in the way of gear, though. I was forced to sell what little I had to survive this long with my family. I'm afraid I might not be of much use to you yet."

"No worries about that. I'll work with Rowan and at least get you a sword. As you can see, I don't have much in the way of armor myself, but we can remedy that as time goes by. We have some leather production started, and Rowan has a decent amount of ore to work with. I plan on at least getting us some vambraces to help block with and protect our arms a bit. From there, we can start considering other pieces."

Samson was nodding his head along as Arthur spoke and seemed pleased by the answer.

"Why don't you head over to the forge and speak with Rowan about needs for you to do your job. Understand that we won't have much of it at the start, but it's a goal to work toward. I plan on going out on another hunting trip tomorrow so you can join me and my companion Allendria. I assume you have no issue working with a dark elf?" Arthur continued.

"None, sir. I have no issues with anyone willing to pull their weight." He told him.

"Then you're hired. Run over to the forge, and I'll catch up with you later. I already have some things planned for the day, but Rowan will be the one you need to work with the most at the moment."

He saluted, turned on his heel, and took off out the door. Arthur was already starting to like the man and hadn't even got to know him yet. There was one more person in line, and he wanted to get this over with.

The last person approached as Samson stepped out of the inn. This person was a little less than six feet tall with a lithe build. She had long brown hair that went a bit past her shoulders. Her hair wasn't quite as dirty, looking like most of the other villagers, and her clothing was at least serviceable. She walked up to Arthur and smiled.

"Well, it looks like there's some new blood here, and he even conjured a miracle and made himself Mayor. My name is Vana. I was hoping to join you as a ranger on your trips. I've noticed you coming and going from the village, and I saw you return yesterday with Rowan and the cart of goods you scavenged from the woods. I have experience with small blades and bows. I also have herbalism and farming skills that could be of use. I can say, though, that like everyone else, I have nothing essential in the way of gear other than what you see me wearing. The only thing I have is a cheap bow that's barely serviceable. Would you be willing to offer me a spot on your team?" She asked him.

     "Well, Vana, I'm Arthur. I can say I
would take all the help I can get right now.
The others here also tell me you are the only
reason the village hasn't fallen apart yet, so
I would be crazy not to say yes. Would you be
willing to help me defend this village as well
if needed?" Arthur asked her.
     She took on a thoughtful look. "I guess I
can agree to that. Honestly, as bad as things
have gotten, you're probably better off dying
in a fight to defend what you have than slowly
starving to death in a miserable life."
     "Well, that's a frightening way to look
at things, but I can't argue with your logic.
I'd be willing to offer you the standard two
meals a day and agree to get you equipped for
your duties and negotiate pay in coinage once
the village recovers to that ability. Do you
accept these terms?" Arthur asked her.
     "I do."
     "Out of curiosity, do you have any
crafting skills of any kind?"
     "I have some minimal skill in
leatherworking, but that's all. If I had some
skill as a bowyer, I wouldn't be forced to use
the junk I'm using." She told him.

"That's fine. We'll have some leather to work within a few days so that can give us a chance to get some armor made. I have a bowyer working on a bow as we speak, which would solve one problem. I'll acquire a dagger from Rowan once he has finished his orders, so you'll have one to work with on our trips. That'll get you to where you're of use if nothing else. None of us are in a great place for gear, to be honest, but we'll fix that. You can either talk to Rowan to see if he needs help or talk to Daniel to see if he has any needs in terms of herbs for us to find. If we have a priority list of herbs we need to find, it might help us decide what areas to search first."

"I think I'll consult with Daniel and get up to speed with him. I'll catch you later." As she took off toward the back, he saw Allendria make her way toward him from the kitchen. He was sure she was hiding out in the back away from the crowd, trying not to spook anyone. Arthur would have to break her of that.

"Good to see you this morning, Allendria," Arthur told her.

"You looked busy this morning. I guessed you'd be tied up for a while, so I talked to Daniel and helped him in the back. Are you about ready to start your fire magic training? I have a feeling you'll pick up the concept fast, and unlocking it won't take long at all. I think most of our time today will be spent with you working on Enchanting." She explained to him.

"That sounds great. Anywhere specific you want to go for it?" Arthur asked.

"Nowhere specific, I'd prefer we go a distance out of the village though, to prevent any eavesdroppers from interfering. I also don't want you to accidentally catch this place on fire if you let the power get out of control." She said thoughtfully.

"I like how you think. Let me get a quick word in with Daniel, and we'll head out." Arthur turned from her and headed toward the kitchen, looking for Daniel. As soon as he walked in, he saw the two new assistants busy at work while Daniel was hovering over Trisha, watching what she was doing with the food. Arthur waved at Daniel as he turned to see who'd entered the kitchen. Daniel made his way to Arthur, and they both made their way out of the kitchen.

"The food was great, Daniel. I assume the new assistants are working out so far?" Arthur asked him.

"They were old assistants that I was able to hire back. It's been a while, but luckily they both remember the ins and outs of the place. It looks like you had a good crowd this morning. Did you already assign all the work orders?" Daniel asked.

Arthur laughed. "Actually, I did. I'm sorry I was unable to keep one for you, but I'll make sure to do an extra food-related order in the next batch just for you. I gave the only two I had made to your assistants. I wanted to check on how far you think our supplies can go. With the rewards offered by the orders and the few people I hired on, we'll need to keep this kitchen running."

"Wait, hired? What are you referring to by hired? What positions could we have that need to be filled? There isn't much of this place even up and running." Daniel asked, surprised.

"Well, I hired an assistant who will monitor things and document requests when I leave on my hunting trips. I also hired two others who will work as security. A man by the name of Samson who appears to be prior military and the ranger, Vana, I've heard so much about have joined us. They'll be acting as security and also assisting me in our resource gathering trips. Each staff member has been guaranteed two meals a day here."

"That shouldn't be an issue. Especially if that will give you more people to help gather resources. I estimate I can feed about forty people for a week with all the supplies we have stashed so far. Now keep in mind that's nothing fancy, but simple soups and things to keep them alive and healthy. With enough resources, I can move to better meals, but that will require more hunting for you." Daniel told him.

"No worries Daniel, I plan to go on another trip tomorrow for some resource gathering. I have some things to take care of today, so keep on top of things for me while I'm gone. I'll catch up with anything you need when I return."

"Will do."

Arthur turned back to Allendria and motioned it was time for them to leave. They walked through the front door and almost ran headfirst into Rowan as he entered. The burly man looked like he hadn't slept at all with his sweat covered face and bloodshot eyes.

"Oh, sorry, Arthur. Was coming by to pick up those weapon orders from you."

"Sure thing Rowan. If you could get these sorted out by tomorrow, I would appreciate it. I know it isn't much time, but since they are standard iron weapons, I figure you can take care of it. I need them for our new hunters who'll be coming with me."

"I'll see it done, Arthur. I'll get back to work so I can get those done for you."

Rowan waved over his shoulder as he took off back toward the forge. Arthur turned back to Allendria.

"I believe it's finally time for us to go. Would you like to lead the way?"

"I'd be happy to. Off we go." Allendria told him.

Chapter 18

The Mystery of Magic

Allendria darted off at full speed from the inn, and Arthur had to rush to keep up with her. In all honesty, he wasn't fond of the exertion but decided he better get used to it. Arthur had let himself get more out of shape than was good for him. That would require some conditioning to fix. The stats and stamina in this world seemed to work out well for him in maintaining a pace. He could never have survived that long back home.

They quickly made their way out of the village and continued into the surrounding fields. They kept walking about three-quarters of the way toward the forest when Allendria decided it was time to stop. She stopped in between two low hills within easy view of the woods. Arthur decided he trusted her on the space needed for the task.

"Alright, Arthur, I need your full attention for this training, so that means you can't go staring at my ass as usual."

Arthur felt a deep red blush color his cheeks, and his ears got hot with her statement. *Had she noticed him staring at her ass? Surely not.* After a few moments of Arthur's introspection, Allendria let out a big laugh.

"Sorry, I couldn't help it. I wanted to see your reaction, but it appears I was correct. I don't mind if you were looking as long as you keep your hands to yourself. Now on to business."

Arthur felt sheepish after she called him out like that, and then his foolishness only caused her to see the truth in her jest. He decided he'd find a way to get back at her in the future for that. He turned his attention to Allendria to work on his training.

"As we discussed when I was teaching you Earth Magic, you have a specific feeling associated with the magic as it flows through, do you not?"

Arthur nodded his head to her.

"Come on, Arthur, we're adults in a teaching situation. Use your words like a big boy."

Again, Arthur was embarrassed by her statement but also felt oddly good about it. It appeared she was loosening up around him and cracking jokes. She was a little antisocial when they had first met.

"Yes." He replied.

"Better, now let's get started. The feeling of your Earth Magic will be a big difference here. Each realm of magical skill works similarly, but the key difference is the feel of the magic. Theoretically, anyone can learn any magic skill, even without a teacher, if they can find the correct feel and power flow. With someone to assist, it makes this process faster and more likely to succeed. Since you're well aware of the absolute basics of magic now, I will skip over a lot of it, and we'll go straight to unlocking your fire magic skill. Please come over to me and put out your hand, palm up."

Arthur strolled a few steps toward her and cautiously stretched his right hand out. He wasn't sure why she needed it but worried it might be harmful.

"Now, I'm going to place my hand on yours, and I need you to focus."
She placed her hand on his, and Arthur felt a slight warmth spreading into his hand from hers. It wasn't painful but wasn't overly comfortable either.

"Focus, Arthur. Most instructors would let you squirm for a bit and flaunt their talent, but I will push this straight to where we need to go. I want you to focus on this power as it enters your hand. Pay close attention to the feel of the magic as it leaves my hand and enters you. Once you figure out the feel, try to regulate the flow of the magic into your hand to match the same feeling. Once you can control the fire energy entering you, it should unlock your skill for you, and you'll understand how to manipulate and create the flow of power yourself."

Arthur focused on Fire Magic as it entered him. He couldn't quite grasp what she meant by the feel. It just felt like a dull pain. He thought about his Earth Magic and analyzed it first. Earth Magic had a distinct feeling to it. It was the feeling of thick sap flowing over a solid stone and accented with a deep drumbeat. The beat was a steady thrum that never changed pace, and the flow was just as smooth.

Keeping that thought in his mind, he tried again to focus on the fire magic. The flow itself felt like a crackling flame in a fire on a cold winter day mixed with a warm breeze. Arthur wasn't sure how to combine those feelings in himself with power. He focused on the energy as it entered him now. He tried to grasp it with his mind and force it to his will, but this did nothing. The power seemed to flow right past his will.

He took a deep breath and tried again. This time he pictured himself in a leaping tackle to force the power to his will. Instead, it felt like he tackled nothing but missed and stumbled past. He wasn't sure how to do it, and nothing he tried to do was working. He supposed Allendria was paying attention to the struggle on his face because she gave him a bit of a hint.

"Arthur, you need to calm your mind. You can't force an elemental power to your will. You need to influence the power carefully. Instead, try to focus on what you wish it to be and coax it into being that way." Allendria told him calmly.

Arthur nodded and turned his attention
back inward. Instead, he tried to approach it
her way. Trying to hold his will and assert
the necessary feeling wasn't working either.
He thought about it and decided it was an
issue with trying to do too much at once. He
couldn't honestly expect to align the entire
power all at once, perfectly. He focused on
one aspect of this power and slowly molded it.
He focused on the feel of a crackling fire and
pushed his will in the direction of the energy
entering his body, but was careful not to
force it directly into the power stream. He
kept the slow push of will in place and felt
the power slowly shifting.

The power seemed to shift into separate
bands subtly, and he felt one of them morph
into the feeling of the crackling fire he had
pictured. This change gave him hope, and he
wanted to jump up and yell in triumph but knew
he couldn't break his concentration. He
focused on the next feeling of a cold winter
day and felt the bands shift again. To his
disappointment, though, the crackling fire
band turned back to the raw stream while the
second one changed to the aura of a cold
winter day. Well, at least he knew they would
get progressively harder. He had to keep the
original idea firm in his mind and add piece
by piece to shape the power.

He went back to the first idea of the crackling fire, and it quickly solidified one stream, and the cold aura stream went back to normal. He then pictured the crackling fire with the aura of a cold winter day around it. This time two of the streams solidified into place. He then added the warm breeze feeling into the mix, and all three bands of power came into being as he felt them coming from Allendria. He waited like that for a while, and nothing happened. He expected some feeling to let him know he had succeeded, but nothing was happening. He looked closer to the power coming from Allendria and realized that her magic wasn't split into three separate bands that matched the feelings. Hers was all one solid band that contained the three distinct characteristics. That meant he needed to meld his streams of power back together.

He focused on each band and went in the same order. Holding the idea of the fire, he slowly pictured the power of the cold aura wrapping around the power strand of the crackling fire. It resisted shortly and snapped into place. He finally brought the warm breeze band of power into the equation and pictured the energy flowing through the entire scene to create a consistent breeze. After a few moments, it solidified, and he heard a chime in his head.

Congratulations, you have learned Fire Magic for a 100 experience bonus.

"Fantastic job. I don't know of many who ever accomplished that so fast. Usually, it's a slow process over a few days, but I had faith in you. Now that you've unlocked the power, it'll come as naturally as your earth magic and won't require all the in-depth visualizations. I know you didn't realize it, but that tome of earth magic did this same process to you forcefully and made the visualization solidify there to give you the skill. Now you need some spells. I'll be able to teach you one beginner spell of Basic Fire Bolt. That should get you started, and you can use your imagination to find more." Allendria told him. She was smiling at him, and the look on her face warmed his heart.

"Thank you so much. I hope you know how much I truly appreciate this gift. I understand the consequences of what this means to you, and I won't betray your trust or friendship." He told her somberly.

"Thank you. Now on to your new spell. The Basic Fire Bolt spell is relatively weak but is a good distraction and a good fire-starter in a pinch." Allendria said as she winked at him.

She walked him through the Fire Bolt spell. It was similar to what he had done before. He had to visualize the small projectile of fire and picture it shooting away from him. Everything was working well until he tried to cast it. He failed spectacularly, and the little ball of flame popped right in front of him. Not only did it utterly surprise Arthur, but it also did an excellent job of scorching his hands.

You have been hit with 10 HP damage from Fire Backlash.

"Oh!" she exclaimed. "I'm so sorry about that. I wanted you to fail that spell so you could learn a lesson from it, but I completely forgot to instruct you on protecting yourself from your flames. Please forgive me."

Arthur laughed at himself and winced as he felt his hands sting a little from the heat that had blasted them. He was sure he'd end up with a few blisters later, but it wasn't too bad. Better to understand that lesson on a weak spell like this.

"It's alright. I know you wouldn't have done that on purpose. Okay, so how do I protect myself from those flames?" Arthur asked.

"That's a good question," she said in a mock sarcastic teaching voice. She stared at him for a moment as he cocked an eyebrow at her, and then she giggled a bit. "To protect yourself from the flame, you need to coat your body parts in your flame power at the same time. So while you visualize your spell, also visualize a thin barrier of that same power covering your hands. Your hands and lower arms are good enough for these lower spells, but as you get more advanced spells, you'll need to expand that coating and sometimes thicken it depending on the heat." She explained to him.

"Now, on to the other portion of that spell, the failure itself." She continued, "Don't feel bad about it because I have honestly known no one to handle that kind of spell their first time without fail. All the current spells you've done so far have been stationary type spells. They may change the shapes of things, but they never leave contact with your power. With this Fire Bolt, the flame itself leaves you and your ability to influence it. Once it leaves your hand, it becomes its own separate entity. Due to this, you have to do a couple of things different. First and foremost, you must have a distinct picture in your head of where you want it to go. Since it's magic, you can have it fly around things or change its course, but all of that must be determined and set before letting it go. Also, keep in mind, it can slow the spell if you make it change course a lot, which means your target will be long gone before it arrives. Any questions on that so far?" She asked.

"So, let me get this straight, I can make this bolt fly around a tree and strike a target behind it?" He asked.

"Indeed, you can, but keep in mind, you still have to know precisely where it should go, or you'll still miss the target. You can direct it around a tree, but if the enemy doesn't inhabit the target spot you choose, you have wasted a shot. Alternately, you can anticipate an opponent's movement and have the bolt fly directly at them to make them dodge, but swerve to the area they will dodge to hit them. It's difficult to do unless you're familiar with their type of fighting and techniques." She told him.

Arthur nodded. He was sure that knowledge would come in very handy.

"Secondly, you'll need to incorporate an element of time into the spell. Time is the main thing that caused your spell attempt to blow up as soon as you tried to cast it. Your visualization lacked time, so when released, it exploded where it was. To fix that, you need to add time to it. I know this sounds difficult, but it's effortless. You don't have to predict and imagine the future or anything perfectly. You honestly don't even have to picture the correct thing at all. You have to show at least one thing moving for comparison to show the time. For instance, you can cast the spell and imagine yourself dashing to the side as your bolt flies. It simulates the time needed for it to fly. You don't even have to do that action. It's just a reference. The one exception is if you're trying to predict a target, as we discussed before. In that case, you must picture what they'll do and where they're going to be as the bolt flies." She told him matter-of-factly.

"That makes sense. I never thought of the time aspect of it, but without that factor, it would be difficult to judge the missile speed and for it to go anywhere. I'm relieved it doesn't expect me to simulate what will happen though perfectly. That would be almost impossible." Arthur said with a relieved sigh.

"Now try it again. This spell is simple enough that you should have enough mana to attempt it again without running out." She told him.

Arthur checked, and he did indeed have almost three-quarters of his mana left. He followed Allendria's instructions about the protective layer and then cast the spell. This time it worked great and shot off like an arrow. It flew directly at the tall stem of dead grass he had been aiming at and lit it on fire in an instant. He jumped up and cheered at his success as he heard the familiar chime.

Congratulations, you have discovered the Fire Magic Spell: Basic Fire Bolt. You have gained 250 experience in Fire Magic for discovering a known spell.
You have gained 60 experience in Fire Magic for successfully casting Basic Fire Bolt.

Spell: Basic Fire Bolt	
Requirements: Fire Magic Spell Damage: 4-6 Mana Cost: 15MP Cast Time: 2 seconds	Description: Shoots a small bolt of fire at the designated target.
Mastery Level: 1	

Allendria had been right. The spell wasn't very powerful, but with the short cast time and low mana cost, it could be handy as a distraction or to throw someone off guard at the right time.

"Now for you to learn the art of Enchanting. We can walk back toward the village and discuss the basics of it as we go. We will need a place to work in the village to practice this skill. I have a few of the basic items we will need for it, so don't worry about that." She told him.

"So what exactly is Enchanting used for? I imagine from my prior knowledge of the skill it has to do with magically enhancing items."

"That isn't far off from the mark."

He had played enough games in his day to understand the implications of this skill and was excited to learn it.

"Part of the reason I taught you this skill is that only those who have unlocked a magical power can use it. It's the ability to combine an item with a specific arcane script and infuse mana of that power into the item to permanently enhance that item in some way. With you now having two sources of magic, you can make items that utilize both fire and earth magic. You also don't have to know the spell itself to enchant it onto an item; You merely have to use the correct symbols to hold power. After that, you can modify the power in the item to do the desired effect. It isn't uncommon to learn spells while performing Enchanting either. If you successfully imbue an item with an enchantment, there's a chance you'll learn how to do that spell on your own. Conversely, if you already know a spell, it's much faster to enchant and imbue the power."

"You're an absolute lifesaver Allendria. I don't know if I can ever repay you for this." Arthur told her.

"Well, you saved my life, so there's that, and I like the way you treat me. Even among my people, I could never be like I am now. I may think of something later on, though, if I think I need to." She said to him with a wink.

"For Enchanting, is it a new set of letters I have to learn, or is it based on a distinct language?" Arthur asked.

"Oh, it's based on an old language, but I doubt it's one that you're familiar with… well, I say that, but your ability to speak multiple languages without knowing them may be a big benefit to you in this. If that gift works the same for this, you'll be a natural with this skill."

"Let's hope it does. I'm not sure I have the time to learn another language with everything else that's going on now. If it came down to that, I would probably have to postpone working on much of this skill for a while." Arthur told her.

They calmly made their way back to the village with some pleasant conversation about the surrounding landscape and weather. Arthur decided they should swing back by the inn on the way in to check on how things were progressing. When he arrived, he saw a few people standing around and assumed they were there for him.

The first two were Rowan's new apprentices. They were there to turn in their orders for the ingots. He acknowledged their completion and immediately made two more identical orders for them to accept and sent them on their way. He instructed them to take the newly smelted ingots back to Rowan at the forge for immediate use, and they were happy to comply. It surprised him when they asked another question he hadn't considered.

"Sir, are we able to allocate our meals for others to use? I know if we keep up this speed for orders, we will have more than we can reasonably use and wanted to know if I could allow family or friends to cash in on some of my meal tokens?"

"I have no issues with that, but it could be hard to keep up with. We wouldn't want people to steal meal tokens from others, so I think we'll just have to keep a tally book at the inn for tracking meals earned and used. We can allow each person to allocate others to use their tokens. That should keep things straight." Arthur told them seriously.

Both of them smiled at that and took off while saying their thanks. The other two who were milling around in front of the inn were the father and son pair he'd seen that morning, and they had a small cart with the necessary logs on them he had requested. He accepted their order completion and made them again. They both accepted the order again, and Arthur explained that he was implementing a tally system in the inn so they could allow others to use their meal tokens as they wished. They both perked up and smiled at that. He was sure they had other family members they were worried about and were probably trying to figure out how to get meals for them as well. He asked them to drop the logs behind the inn for now, and both of them left with a little more oomph in their step as they went straight back out of the village.

Arthur went inside to check on Daniel. Once inside, he saw Daniel at the counter and walked over.

"How have things been so far?" Arthur asked.

"Honestly, this place has been more alive this morning than I've seen it in months. People are out and about, even some I haven't seen in a while, and as I'm sure you found out, there are some already turning in orders." He told Arthur with a smile.

"Yeah, I swapped out the orders for the guys out front and got them back to work already. Allendria and I are about to work on some crafting. I had an idea run by me outside, though. Do you know where Katherine is?" Arthur asked.

"Katherine! Can you, Paula, and Trisha all come out here real quick?" Daniel yelled toward the back.

Arthur saw Katherine round the corner first and was taken aback by her. She looked like a new woman with some food in her, and she had gotten cleaned up. He assumed she took advantage of the inn cleaning facility he told her she could use.

"Thank you for getting her cleaned up, Daniel. She almost looks like a real person again." Arthur told him with a grin.

"Wasn't hard, to be honest. She was willing to hit the floor running, but since you weren't here, she didn't have a lot to do yet, so she helped my girls for a while in the kitchen after she got cleaned up."

Katherine approached, and as she got close, he saw Trisha and Paula leaving the kitchen and heading his way.

"Hello, Katherine. I'm pleased to see you're ready to work now." Arthur told her.

"Yes, Sir. What can I do for you?" She asked.

"Arthur, Katherine, just Arthur. I need you to set up a log of meal tokens in the inn. You can see what was awarded on the village interface screen under work orders. Keep track of those tokens with this log. The key feature of this is that it allows the villagers to add anyone to the log under their name, who are also allowed to use their meal tokens. This is the best option to keep them working and keep a surplus of tokens from being collected for no reason. It also allows a bit of freedom for them to feel useful and provide for their families and even friends if they feel like it." He told her.

"That sounds like a great idea!" exclaimed Katherine. "I'll get that taken care of right now. Is there anything else you need me to work on?"

"That should be good for now." He told her.

Trisha and Paula stepped forward and turned in their work orders and accepted the new ones he made for them. They made their way back to the kitchen as Daniel shooed them away. Looking around, Arthur saw nothing else that looked like it needed his attention, so he turned to Allendria.

"Ready for that crafting?" he asked.

"Sure, let me grab a few things from my room. We can work on it somewhere outside for now. There isn't much danger in what we'll work on today, but it never hurts to be safe. We can't go putting the village food kitchen in danger." She told him with a laugh. She bounded off upstairs, and Arthur turned to Daniel.

"She is sure livening up quickly. I
thought it might take her a while longer to
come out of her shell, but I'll be damned if
it hasn't pretty much fallen off already."
Arthur told him.

"I'd wager she was probably sheltered
where she was from. People like that seem to
go full circle when finally given the freedom
to do so. It'll probably do her some good too.
She has the potential to be a great woman."
Daniel told him.

Allendria came down the stairs with the
small bag she had retrieved from the cave and
motioned for them to go as she passed him for
the door.

"Later, Daniel," Arthur said as he waved
over his shoulder and followed Allendria out
the door.

She led him through the streets of the
village, and they made their way over to the
smithy. Arthur wasn't sure why they came here,
but he figured he'd trust Allendria. She
hadn't shown him any reason not to… well,
unless you count almost letting him
practically blow himself up. He thought as he
chuckled to himself.

Arthur saw Rowan and waved to him. The
big man was sweating profusely and pounding
away at what Arthur was sure would be the
sword he had an order for. Rowan nodded at him
and kept at his work. He saw Allendria wave at
the big man as well, and he saw a slightly
deeper nod for her. Arthur wasn't sure if he
felt insulted or pleased by that, but ignored
it and moved forward.

"Arthur, I'm sure you want to know why we're here. Honestly, there are two main reasons. First is I'm going to teach you a basic enchantment of fire, although the chance of anything bad happening is extremely low, this place doesn't have much that can catch on fire. The second reason is I have a limited supply of writing ink so that we can use the coal here as a substitute for the process for now. It's perfectly acceptable for lower level enchantments, but anything complicated will need specially blended inks." She told him.

"Are you ready to get started?" She asked.

"Let's do this." He said enthusiastically.

Chapter 19

A Craft Above

"You seem to be at least vaguely familiar with the idea of Enchanting, so hopefully, you'll pick this up quickly. First off, let me draw four symbols and see if your ability to understand languages will apply to this." She grabbed a small chunk of coal from nearby and drew four symbols into the side of a scrap board lying around. She turned it to face him, and he studied it.

It took a while, but just before he was about to give up, the letters shifted into something he could read. He gave it a few more moments, and he could somehow understand what they meant. He looked at Allendria and smiled as he pointed to each of the symbols. "That one is fire, that one is water, that one is air, and that final one is earth."

"Well, I'm kind of jealous, to be honest. It took a lot of studying to remember the symbols I know. I wonder if your power works the other way. Are you able to write these symbols natively for other words now that you have seen these?" she said.

Arthur thought about it for a moment and grabbed the coal from her. Next to her last symbol, he drew one of his own. After he finished, he showed it to Allendria. Her eyes widened when she saw what he wrote.

"Wow, I guess it does work. That's the symbol of power." She told him in astonishment. "Well, this is the perfect skill for you; it would seem. How about we get down to business?"

Allendria pulled out a small knife and asked him to find a small stick about as long as his forearm and the width of his thumb. He found one near a tree by the forge and brought it back to her. She used the knife to smooth off the wood and pull the larger pieces of bark from it.

"We'll do a minor enchantment here. This basic stick has no chance of holding a powerful enchantment. The yew wood you found could hold a decent enchantment, though, and might be useful to you as you progress." She explained to him.

She carefully drew symbols onto the side of the stick in tiny writing with a metal-tipped quill she had pulled out of her bag. When she finished, she turned it for Arthur to see. He could look at these symbols and see what she wrote. He saw the symbol for fire, the symbol that signified power, and finally, a symbol that meant weak.

"So that's all you need? How do you determine the effect it'll have?" Arthur asked.

"That's all we need for this particular spell. More advanced spells require more advanced symbol combinations, and you can make simple spells more powerful by adding additional symbols that complement the intended effect. Keep in mind you don't want to add too much if the source can't hold the necessary power. It would be catastrophic to do that and, at best, will result in the item exploding. At worst, it might do a lot more damage in the explosion. You'll know when you're approaching that point in the next step. It's essential if you feel the power trying to overload the object to cease the enchantment immediately. Don't push the boundaries and try to snap it into place, or you will cause damage." She told him seriously.

"You asked what determined the effect, and it's this next step. If you recall from our walk, I told you that you'd have to visualize the spell and imbue it into the enchantment. That's the step that determines the effect, and it's solely based on your will and the symbols. You can't draw symbols for water powers and try to imbue it with a fire spell. It'll just fail as you try to push your mana into the object. The better your symbols match your will, the more powerful the spell. Some advanced magical items are known to have very in-depth descriptions of their abilities to augment the power."

"For this part, I want you to envision a flame shooting out of the end of the stick for 10 seconds. It shouldn't be more than a foot long at most. Also, remember our discussion on time in spells. This will be a fire-starting wand. Some enchantments are permanent, while others only have charges. This spell will use charges. To make it permanent, you have to include runes to allow the item to replenish power from the surrounding area naturally. This works best if you have something capable of storing magical energy placed in the item itself to tie the power draw into. Now, I want you to picture this spell effect and push your will into the symbols themselves. Push mana into the runes with your will, and once you feel that the enchantment is complete, cut the flow. You'll know by the feeling you get. When it's ready and complete, the runes will permanently burn into the material." She told him.

Arthur focused on the item and pictured the intended effect. He focused on the flame becoming a foot long and lasting roughly ten seconds by using a time passage of him taking five deep and slow breaths in the vision of his effect. The mana started to trickle into the wood. The effect soaked into the wood, and he could feel the spell occupying the stick, but it felt incomplete. He couldn't explain it, but it felt like a sensation of the wood being hungry. He kept pushing mana into the item, and after it infused 20 mana in, the feeling shifted. The thing felt like complete, so he cut the flow and was amazed as he heard a chime and watched the symbols permanently burn themselves into the wood.

Congratulations, you have learned Enchanting for a 100 experience bonus.

Congratulations, you have successfully created Basic Wood Fire-starter. You have gained 50 experience in Enchanting for creating this item.

Item: Basic Wood Fire-starter	**Durability**: 50/50 **Rarity**: Common **Quality**: Good **Weight**: 0.3 kg **Slot**: Main Hand **Traits**: Emits a flame that's one foot long and lasts for 10 seconds. Each use of this item will reduce durability by 1. When the durability runs out, the item will disintegrate. Able to be activated by anyone holding it with the command word "Fira."

Congratulations, you have learned the Fire Magic Spell: Weak Flame. You have gained 250 experience in Fire Magic for discovering a known spell.

Congratulations, you have reached level 2 in Fire Magic. Fire Magic spells now have a 3% increased effect.

Spell: Weak Flame	
Requirements: Fire Magic Spell Damage: 1-2/sec channeled Mana Cost: 1 MP/sec channeled Cast Time: 1 second	Description: Releases a small flame from your hand for the duration channeled. Great for starting fires.
Mastery Level: 1	

This development thrilled Arthur. Not only did he learn a new skill, but he also learned the spell from it, as Allendria said, could happen.

"Awesome, I also learned the weak flame spell from that. What are the limitations of this ability?" Arthur asked.
"I'm glad you could pick it up on the first try. You seem to be a bit of a prodigy here. The limitations will come down to your mana available and the power the item can absorb. That's another reason that casters are the only ones able to use this skill. You need larger mana pools for the better enchantments. Now, you'll be able to use this skill to make new effects. You don't need to know the spell or effect you wish to enchant into the item. You only have to correctly picture the effect and put the minimum necessary symbols to harness that power."

"I can't thank you enough, Allendria. Is there anything else I need to know of importance?" Arthur asked.

"Nothing much. You know the basics, and now it's up to you to advance your skills. Your ability to interpret the symbols naturally turned this from a long process to a speedy one. I'll give you two pieces of advice. The first is always to make the script as in-depth as you can. You can never overdo the script, but if you don't have enough to hold the necessary power, it will cause a failure. The second piece of advice is to have a metal quill tip made for your work. You can get by with shaved pieces of coal for simple things, but as you start doing better enchantments, you'll need it. Even more so when you use the special inks."

"Well, I appreciate the help. Why don't you take the rest of the day to have some time to yourself? I think I'll hang out here at the forge for a while with Rowan. Might help him a bit and pick up another skill, since I have the time." Arthur told her.

"I think I will. I'll see you around Arthur." She said as she walked off.

Arthur turned his attention back to the forge and saw Rowan still working away at his project. He continued to watch the man for a few more moments until he stopped what he was doing. Arthur could see his metal had cooled too much to continue working, and Rowan threw it back into the coals to reheat.

"Mind if I help out, Rowan?" Arthur asked.

"Do you even have any skill in Smithing?" Rowan asked him.

"Technically, no. I understand the process of it and know how it works, though, but I've never done it here before." Arthur told him. He had dabbled in some forging back on Earth. He had a small propane forge and enjoyed making knives and the occasional sword, but since he had never done it on this world, he had no skill in it here.

"How is it you know the process, but don't have the skill? You seem to be stranger every time we talk. I've noticed this with multiple things. You seem to recognize many herbs although you had almost no skill in herbalism, you understand the basics of farming and even knew to ask me about certain things I used in smithing and, yet again, have almost no skill in those either. You tend to have some advanced knowledge of skills without the actual skill in them." Rowan said as he eyed Arthur carefully.

Arthur wasn't sure how to respond to that. He couldn't very well tell him the truth. He decided on what he believed was a probable answer.

"Where I come from, most of us are similar to scholars. We study a lot of different skills and trades, but we mainly learn how they work and read about them. Very rarely do we perform the skill itself. Since we don't do the skill, we don't gain the skill or experience in it, but we are very familiar with how it's done." He told him in a severe tone.

Rowan eyed him for a second and then shook his head. "Well, that would explain it, but I can't understand the good of learning about something without actually performing the skill. Learning advanced techniques is also somewhat worthless without the skill to use them. I can say that, based on my experience, it'll help you with skill points. Skill points in the later trees can allow you to learn some of the advanced techniques, but if you already know them, it'll save you some points."

"I hadn't thought about that, but it'll be nice to save the points for other things," Arthur told him with a cheerful tone.

"Well, get over here. I have a few extra tools around. Grab you a pair of tongs and a hammer from that rack over there." He said as he pointed to his left. Arthur walked over and grabbed the tools as he was instructed.

"Is there anything specific you need me to make?" Arthur asked.

Rowan thought about it for a moment. "Can you make me a pick head? I could use a decent pick, so I don't damage my axe again. You'll probably have to put it to use yourself when you go on your next gathering trip tomorrow."

"Do you have a punch and a drift around here somewhere?" Arthur asked.

Rowan raised an eyebrow at him and, after a few seconds, shook his head in resignation. "They're over by the tool rack where the others were. They're usually lying on the bottom."

Arthur sifted through the tools until he found what he needed. He walked over to a stack of iron bars that had been prepared. There was no way to tell for sure if Rowan had made them or his apprentices. Either way, he grabbed one close to the size he needed and tossed it into the fire with the center of it in the hottest part of the flame.

He let it slowly heat to a bright red that was almost white-hot and pulled it from the fire. He felt the heat pouring from the iron onto him as he brought it to a smaller anvil that Rowan had in the forge. Using the punch, he punched a hole in the center. It took him a few heats to get all the way through as he would hit the metal and flip it back and forth. Eventually, a compressed metal disk popped out, and the hole was complete.

From there, he threw it back in the heat again and let it climb back to temperature. By this time, Arthur was building up a good sweat and was sure he had some coal dust on his face by now. He pulled it back out and used the drift to slowly widen the hole until it got to a diameter he felt was good enough for a decent size handle. The metal flowed smoothly as the point was hammered into it on one side. Once that side was done, he made the other side mirror it, and the pick looked ready to go. He heard the telltale chime he knew to expect.

Congratulations, you have learned Blacksmithing for a 100 experience bonus.
Congratulations, you have successfully created Basic Iron Pick Head. You have gained 75 experience in Blacksmithing for creating this item.

Arthur noticed he wasn't as tired as he usually got working in the forge back home. He could do this work in a lot less time than it would've taken him back on Earth. Not only that, but it didn't require all the tedious grinding work to smooth everything out. The skill in this world seemed to assist in both speed and the outcome of the final product. Other than the sweat, he was feeling fine.

He took the finished pick over to Rowan for him to look it over. Rowan glanced at it and turned it in his hands.

"Well, I'll be damned. Is there nothing you can't do? Are you sure you don't have a magical ability to learn skills as well?" He said while laughing.

Arthur laughed with him. "Not that I know of. It would be nice if I did, though. I'll be honest I expected it to take a lot longer to make that, and I was surprised at how smooth the final product turned out."

"Your skill will determine how nice the item finishes out. Since you made an entry-level item out of one of the softer metals, it turned out fine. Check the quality of the item."

Arthur did as he suggested and looked at the item.

Item: Basic Iron Pick Head	**Durability:** 30/30 **Rarity:** Common **Quality:** Good **Weight:** 1.5 kg **Slot:** Crafting Item

<table><tr><td></td><td>Traits: The head of a pick. Combine with a handle to assemble a Basic Iron Pick.</td></tr></table>

"The item turned out Good quality because of those criteria. If you tried that with steel, you would have been lucky for it to be Common quality and would more than likely have ended up as Poor quality. That also affects how the final item turns out visibly. That's why you need to ensure you level up your skill before attempting things too high above your skill level. Some of the higher metals you wouldn't even be able to move. Had you tried to forge Magesteel? You could have heated it all you wanted and hit it with the largest hammer you could find for hours, and it would still be a perfectly flat bar." Rowan explained.

"I appreciate the advice and explanation on that. I honestly wasn't entirely sure how that all worked. I want to work a little longer, though. That got the blood flowing, and I still have a good amount of time left before I need to head back to the inn. Anything else you need?" Arthur asked him.

"Well, normally, I wouldn't ask for a weapon from someone just starting off but, since you did so well on the pick head, how about you make an iron dagger? I'm sure one of your hunters will need it anyway." Rowan suggested.

"I'll give it a shot," Arthur said enthusiastically.

Arthur walked over and grabbed another of the iron bars. He tossed this bar in the middle of the fire. As he walked away, he wiped off a fresh bead of sweat while it raced for his face. The heat was the only downside to being in here. He turned to walk away from the forge when he froze. Why was he such an idiot? He always hated it when he had read books or watched TV, and people had done idiotic things without thinking about them. Here he was suffering from the heat, and he would bet that the magic he used to shield himself from his fire spells would serve the same purpose to protect him from the heat here.

Giddy with excitement, Arthur practically bounced in place as he waited for the metal to heat back up. He walked over to the tool rack and grabbed the hot cut tool to place in the anvil. A full bar wouldn't be necessary to create a dagger. If he cut it down the middle, he should be able to make two of them at the same time. As soon as the metal was hot enough, he took it out and placed it on the cutting wedge and pounded on the bar with the hammer until it split in two. While it was still hot, he took the cut end of each half and lightly hammered them until they were back in a uniform shape. He tossed one piece into the fire to let it heat up and set the other on the edge of the coals. If he placed both in, the extreme heat from the fuel would burn the second one and destroy the metal while he worked on the first. But if he put the second in the fire as he pulled the first one out, it should correctly time the work so as not to burn the metal.

After a few minutes, he pulled the first bar out of the fire and placed the second one in it. He took it over to the anvil and started working on stretching the bar out to the correct length for the dagger and the tang. He took care to keep his fire shield up and was pleased that the heat was barely noticeable. He was also happy to see that this protective layer didn't seem to drain mana. He could only imagine the draw on it was so low that he natively regenerated the mana faster than was spent. He worked the first piece and watched as the metal stretched out longer. When it had cooled too far to work correctly, he tossed it into the fire and grabbed the other piece. He continued the same process on the second piece until he had to put it back in the heat.

He kept going back and forth with each piece as he started to work the metal into the shape needed. He got the blank to the required length for the blade and worked on putting the point in. He shifted to the back part of the dagger and started hammering down to stretch and thin the tang into a long and skinny stem for the handle to fit on. He didn't see any type of resin in this shop, so he figured that a scale handle wouldn't work, and he would need to do a through-tang construction. Once he got the tang to shape, he flipped it around and worked on putting the bevels into the blades. He then did a bit of touch up hammering to clean up the shoulders of the knives and cleaning up some stray hammer marks. Once he completed, he felt accomplished and looked at his work.

Congratulations, you have successfully created Basic Iron Dagger Blade. You have gained 160 experience in Blacksmithing for creating this item (x2).

Item: Basic Iron Dagger Blade	**Durability**: 35/35 **Rarity**: Common **Quality**: Good **Weight**: 0.6 kg **Slot**: Crafting Item **Traits**: The blade of an unfinished Iron Dagger. Combine with handle components to assemble a Basic Iron Dagger.

Arthur was pleased with the work he'd done, and, as before, he completed this in a fraction of the time he would usually have been able to. Not only that, but the blades were already ready to use and just missing a handle. There was also one other surprise message he hadn't been expecting.

Congratulations, you have learned Alternate Heating, a subskill of Blacksmithing for a 100 experience bonus.
For completing two Basic Iron Dagger Blades simultaneously, you have gained 160 experience in Alternate Heating.

Arthur decided he wanted to finish the blades completely. Finding two small pieces of metal, he did a simple oval-shaped guard for these and punched a hole in them. Two wooden blocks were found that could be used for the handles.

Congratulations, you have successfully created Basic Iron Dagger Guard. You have gained 20 experience in Blacksmithing for creating this item. (x2)

Item: Basic Iron Dagger Guard	**Durability:** 15/15 **Rarity:** Common **Quality:** Good **Weight:** 0.2 kg **Slot:** Crafting Item **Traits:** An iron guard for a dagger.

The wooden blocks were the right length that he needed, but the shapes were blocky and unwieldy. To start, he needed to drill the hole in it. Since he didn't expect to see a drill press anywhere, he walked around the shop until coming across something he had only seen in pictures in history class. He stumbled across a pump drill. It was a solid wood rod with a metal bit on the end that looked slightly like an arrowhead, and a metal disk mounted on the shaft marginally higher but under the crossbar. There was another wooden rod that crossed it to form a plus symbol, and it had a hole in it that the main shaft slid through.

From each end of the cross-piece was a piece of rope that looped up through a hole in the rod's top opposite the bit. The user could spin the cross piece until they got a decent amount of twist on the rope and then press down on the cross-piece. This would cause the center shaft to spin very rapidly, and the metal disk would cause it to rotate until it wrapped back on the pole again in the other direction. From there, the user could press down again for it to spin. Using this tool, he could get both center holes drilled. He searched around the shop until he found a small knife and used it to carve one of the blocks into a handle that would work well and contour for the hand. Once he finished the handle, he heard a chime and checked the notification.

Congratulations, you have learned Woodworking for a 100 experience bonus.

Congratulations, you have successfully created Basic Wood Dagger Handle. You have gained 40 experience in Woodworking for creating this item. (x2)

Item: Basic Wooden Dagger Handle	**Durability:** 20/20 **Rarity:** Common **Quality:** Good **Weight:** 0.3 kg **Slot:** Crafting Item **Traits:** A wooden handle for a dagger.

That was interesting. It seemed some skills would be directly complementing each other, which honestly made sense. Arthur finished shaping the other handle in the same way. He moved on to making a small metal pommel by hammering a small chunk of metal for each dagger. With the hole complete, the assembly continued. He heated the tip of the tang in the forge until it was white-hot, and as soon as he pulled it out, he quickly slid the guard on. The handle followed, and the blade was wedged in between some metal. The end of the tang that was protruding from the pommel was lightly hammered and peened over to hold it in place. Once finished, the end cap smoothed over, and the item was completed.

Congratulations, you have successfully created Basic Iron Dagger. You have gained 200 experience in Blacksmithing for creating this item. Since you created all items in its assembly, you also receive a 20% experience boost of 40 experience.

Item: Basic Iron Dagger	**Attack:** 4-6 **Durability:** 40/40 **Rarity:** Common **Quality:** Good **Weight:** 0.8 kg **Slot:** Main Hand/Off Hand **Traits:** A basic dagger made out of iron.

That was amazing. The experience was nothing to sneeze at, and the bonus was even better. Arthur guessed there was a clear benefit to learning the necessary skills for all parts of the process. He went ahead and finished the second dagger in the same fashion, and as soon as the end smoothed out, showing it was complete, he was awarded another sound and message.

Congratulations, you have progressed to Level 2 in Blacksmithing. You are granted a 3% bonus to forging speed.

    More great news. Arthur had already made
it to level 2. Not that level 2 was anything
special, but it gave him some confidence. He
strolled over to Rowan with a bit of swagger
in his step and handed over the two daggers.
Rowan gave him a lopsided grin.

    "Had to go above and beyond, huh?
Couldn't just do one?" He asked.

    "There wasn't much point in only making
one. One ingot was too big, and since I had to
cut it in half anyway, I figured I might as
well do both. Even picked up the subskill of
Alternate Heating because of it." Arthur said
cheerily.

    "What do you mean, you got a subskill? I
don't even have that subskill in
Blacksmithing!" he said, exasperated.

    "How could you not?" Arthur asked.

    "Well, for one, Smart-ass, I don't know
what it means," Rowan told him.

    "Oh," Arthur said sheepishly. "Sorry
about that. I got it from working both daggers
at the same time."

    "You can't do that. The fire would've
burned the other one and ruined the metal!"
Rowan said to him. It looked like a vein was
going to pop on his head.

"You can. You just can't put the second piece of metal in until you take the first out to work it. While working the first the second heats and when the first is cold, you swap their places. Keep doing that, and you have no issues. The trick is to keep a steady working speed and not take a long break without removing the metal from the fire." Arthur explained to him. He honestly wasn't sure how the idea wasn't common knowledge to a smith like Rowan but, when he thought about it, everyone here was very low on skills since the lords here beat them into submission and kept them on the borderline of worthless.

Rowan took on a speculative look and seemed to think the idea over. "Now that you say that, it makes sense. I can't figure out why I hadn't thought of it before. It looks like it's my turn to pick up that subskill, as well. Either way, the blades you made look good. I'm about to finish up with this sword you have an open work order for, and then I'll do two daggers too. Anything else we need after that?" Rowan asked.

"Actually, can you make a decent size shield? Something for someone of my size to use?" Arthur asked.

Rowan eyed him warily. "Why in the world would you use a shield? I haven't ever seen you wield one before."

"It's not for me. One of the new recruits has skill with one, and I figured he'd be a great asset with that sword and shield on our hunting trips. Especially if we ran into something dangerous that needed some more muscle." Arthur explained.

"I'll see it done. I think I have enough scrap supplies around to rig up a way for him to hold it until we get some of the leather in. Anything you have planned now?" he asked.

Arthur thought about it for a moment and decided he wanted to try one more thing before he left for the day. He gave Rowan a dangerous smile. "There's one more thing I've got to try. It could be dangerous, but who knows. I'll make another dagger, but this time I can't make two at once."

"Please don't do anything stupid, Arthur. I know my workshop here isn't the best, but I still would like it intact." He sighed in resignation.

"I don't think it will cause any harm to the building, but it may just fail spectacularly." He told him in response.

Arthur moved back over to the iron and grabbed another piece. He would start it the same by cutting the bar in half, but after that, things would change. What was planned should work, but he couldn't tell for sure with how different some things were here. Ingenuity was supposedly rewarded here, so he had confidence it would work.

He quickly got the bar cut and properly squared off. He took this process slow, though. He started by layering his fire protection on him and started pushing heat into the bar. The process was excruciatingly slow, but he watched the metal slowly begin to heat. To his surprise, he could hold on to it even as it started turning red. He began to feel some heat with it as the red deepened in color and decided to set it down and grab it with the tongs. When he had the bar firmly in the tongs, he continued with pushing heat toward it. It deepened to a bright red with hints of white, and he decided it was time to hammer.

He took some steady swings at it, and each hit caused the metal to cool a bit as he expected, but he was able to focus more and bring the heat back up. He noticed a bit of his mana drain as he kept working, but it wasn't draining at a terrible rate. He maintained the pace and saw it was moving faster than he expected. With less time wasted putting it back in the fire, the process was moving quick. As he worked, he still kept feeling like he was missing something. Surely this process could be done in a better way.

Shortly after this consideration, he had a "eureka" moment. Allendria had told him that Earth Magic could manipulate the movement of metals as it could dirt, it just couldn't manage the metal itself because of the hardness. With the Fire Magic softening the metal, he should be able to use his Earth Magic to shape the metal itself quickly. He tried to send a tendril of earth magic into the metal as he worked and noticed his heat start to subside. Pulling back the Earth Magic, the heat returned.

Surely this would work. Arthur just needed to figure out how. He approached this the same way he had to learn his new fire magic. The elements had to be intertwined for it to work correctly. With this in mind, he focused on interweaving his Fire and Earth Magic together as he pushed them in the metal. He focused on his will to shape and heat at the same time in a concentrated stream of woven power and was amazed as the metal started to move.

It started at the tip of the metal. Arthur had only been stretching the metal and hadn't begun shaping it yet, but starting from the end, the metal began to compress, and it looked like a kid playing with Play-Doh. The metal started forming and flowing into a perfect tip, and the magic started working backward. There was almost a distinct line in the blade that moved from tip to end. As it passed, the metal turned from a flat piece of iron to a perfectly beveled dagger blade in a few moments as it continued to crawl. When it reached the end, the dagger looked perfect, and he slowly drew the heat out of it and let it quickly dissipate into the air. When he grabbed the finished blank, it was cool to the touch and looked great. He heard the chime that was quickly becoming one of his favorite sounds and looked at what appeared.

Congratulations, you have learned the hidden subskill Arcane Smithing for a 500 experience bonus.

You have gained 50 experience in Earth Magic and Fire Magic for successfully casting Crafting Spell: Arcane Forging.

Item: Basic Mage-crafted Iron Dagger Blade	**Attack:** 4-6 **Durability:** 50/50 **Rarity:** Uncommon **Quality:** Well Crafted **Weight:** 0.6 kg **Slot:** Crafting Item **Traits:** A basic iron dagger created using magical techniques. This blade will have more capacity for absorbing magical power. Combine with handle components to assemble a Basic Mage-crafted Iron Dagger.

Congratulations, you have learned the Crafting Spell: Arcane Forging. You have gained 350 experience in Fire and Earth Magic for discovering a known spell.

Congratulations, you have reached level 4 in Earth Magic. Earth magic spells now have a 9% increased effect.

Spell: Arcane Forging

Requirements: Fire Magic and Earth Magic Mana Cost: 30 MP Cast Time: 5 seconds	Description: Cast a spell to forge metal into the desired shape. The initial cast takes 5 seconds, but the length of time required to complete the item depends on the size of the project. The project will complete faster if already brought to the correct temperature before casting. Special Traits: Using this spell increases the base Rarity and Quality by one rank as long as the item and materials used are within your skill range.
Mastery Level: 1	

That was amazing! This spell would be invaluable to him, and to top it off, Arthur had discovered a hidden smithing subskill. He assumed that it didn't happen very often at all. He was so excited he thought he might burst, so Arthur took off as quick as he could to Rowan. He held the item out and was sure he looked like a giddy child opening a Christmas present. Rowan gave him a look of exasperation and turned to look at the dagger blade. As he studied it, his eyes started to widen.

"How in the blazes did you manage to do this? You're what? Level 2? Maybe level 3? Now you come out here having made an Uncommon item. Not only that, but an Uncommon item that has the Mage-crafted mark. What the hell are you, Arthur?" Rowan said in amazement.

"I combined my magical skills with my new smithing skills. I was rather sure it would work because I had heard of something similar in a book, so I had to try it myself. Successfully combining those skills also unlocked a hidden subskill. I have now learned the subskill of Arcane Smithing." Arthur explained to him.

"You fucking did what?" Rowan yelled.

Chapter 20

The Devil is in the Details

"Umm, I unlocked a hidden subskill..." Arthur said carefully.

"You know what? I'm not sure why I'm even surprised anymore. You must truly be blessed by one of the Gods to have the kind of luck you have in these things." Rowan said in resignation.

"A Goddess, but I agree," Arthur told him seriously.

Rowan eyed him, curiously, "You're serious, aren't you?"

"I told you I had a mission. My Goddess sent me here to help. That's my goal here."

"Well, we must be truly blessed to have the attention. What was the name of your Goddess again?" He asked.

"Her name is Lianna," Arthur told him.

"Thank you, Arthur. So this new skill, how long does it take you to forge with it, and are there any restrictions?" Rowan asked.

"It only takes a few seconds to cast the spell, and the time it takes to finish the entire thing depends on the size of the item. Once I cast the spell, it completed that dagger in roughly two minutes. It costs me thirty mana each time to cast, though, so I can't use it infinitely. Another benefit is the spell will raise the Rarity and Quality level by one rank as long as the materials used are within my skill range." Arthur explained to him.

Rowan's eyes grew wider and wider as Arthur described the spell. When he got to the part where it increased the Rarity and Quality level, he thought Rowan's head would explode. The man looked borderline apoplectic.

"Do you have any idea how special that skill is? That spell could make or break a kingdom, especially once you boost your skills high enough to use better materials. Now that I think of it, you might be more valuable than you know. One of the rarest metals to use is Magesteel, but the method to make it is extremely guarded. I have a feeling it's related to this arcane forging of yours, and once you have the skill to do that, the sky is the limit." He said in awe.

"What's so special about Magesteel?" Arthur asked.

"Magesteel is special because it has an extremely high capacity for magical enhancements. The most advanced and special weapons and armor in this entire world are all made with Magesteel. Other metals are harder than Magesteel, such as Ruinite or Adamantite, but when combined with the magical enhancements and the sheer power it can contain, Magesteel wins hands down." Rowan explained.

"I look forward to getting to that point, and I promise you we can discover it together. Until then, I'm sure I at least need to make it up to steel before I can even consider trying to make it."

"I agree with that. It looks like you need to do plenty of work on your skills. If you can combine this with your new Enchanting skill, it would be a formidable pairing. You can practice on pieces you make as well. That would give a decent starting weapon for many around here. Would you mind sticking around and helping with some more work? I think having a Mage-crafted item for each of our recruits would go a long way toward earning their trust and admiration. I can work on the handle pieces for each if you can make a couple more daggers and even a sword or two. I would also like to see if you could add an enhancement to them with your Enchanting skill." Rowan said.

"I'd love to. Let's get to it, Rowan. Let me make a couple more daggers and a sword in this manner, and while you're working on the handle material, I can focus on creating an enchantment to use. I have a feeling the enchantment must be placed on the blades before they're assembled." Arthur told him.

Arthur went to work and grabbed a couple of iron ingots from the stack. He started them by letting the forge heat them. His Earth Magic separated one bar, and he left the other bar whole for the sword. Casting his spell on each of the small pieces successfully created two more matching dagger blades to the one he had presented to Rowan. After this, he picked up the final bar and cast the spell while picturing the shape of the sword he wanted. He was amazed as he watched that line of power slowly crawl down the metal and change the entire shape of it into what he wanted.

The metal seemed to flow like liquid as it formed the pointed tip and gradually worked its way toward the tang of the blade. The sharp, double edge looked perfect as the spell continued shaping. The tang itself tapered quickly to the needed length. The shoulders where the guard sat were perfectly flat. The weapon itself had a dull sheen to it, but as soon as the spell completed and the finished blade fell into his hands, it had increased its luster. He couldn't help but pull up the stats on the item.

You have gained 150 experience in Earth Magic and Fire Magic for successfully casting Combination Spell: Arcane Forging. (x3)
Congratulations, you have successfully created Basic Mage-crafted Iron Dagger Blade. You have gained 150 experience in Arcane Smithing and Blacksmithing for creating this item. (x2)
Congratulations, you have successfully created Basic Mage-crafted Iron Bastard Sword Blade. You have gained 85 experience in Arcane Smithing and Blacksmithing for creating this item.

| Item:
Basic Mage-crafted
Iron Bastard Sword
Blade | **Attack:** 8-12

Durability: 65/65

Rarity: Uncommon

Quality: Well Crafted

Weight: 1.2 kg

Slot: Crafting Item

Traits: A basic Iron Bastard Sword Blade, created using magical techniques. This blade will have more capacity for absorbing magical power. Combine with handle components to assemble a Basic Mage-crafted Iron Bastard Sword. |

It still wasn't as good as the one he had found, but it was an incredible start for a crafted item when he was such a low skill level. Now it was time for him to incorporate his Enchanting into these pieces. He handed the sword blade over to Rowan and grabbed one of the dagger blades to start.

Arthur moved to the side and found a metal awl that he decided would fit his purposes. Locating a small hammer and a seat allowed him to get to work. His main concern with these blades was that they were iron. Because of this, they wouldn't be nearly as hard as steel and would easily damage faster. The trick would be to find a way to increase the hardness of the blade. He started by trying the symbols for weak, power, and durability. The awl carefully peeled those symbols into the metal. He then scratched the symbols weak, power, and sharp down one side of the blade directly between the center spine and the edge. He copied this symbol set for the other side as well.

He decided that would probably be the best set to start with. Usually, he would only try one since this was his first time with these enchantments, but since Rowan told him the mage-crafted ability would help it hold more power, he decided it would be fine. Both spells should require an Earth base to them.

So far, every time he did any spell that required multiple components or elements, he was forced to do all at the same time, or they would fail. If they were different powers, he also had to weave them together while performing the spell. For this, he decided he would have to attempt all three symbol sets at the same time. He pictured the blade increasing in durability and taking less damage from blows. He also imagined both edges of the blade being perfectly sharp at all times and never dull. While picturing these two things, he directed his attention to all three sets of symbols and started feeding each of them mana simultaneously.

Arthur's mana took a quick nosedive as soon as he started. He had spent enough time scribing the symbols for it, but the mana draw still scared him. Within a few seconds, he had dropped 75 mana. The drain was immense at the start but quickly steadied out as he continued to feed all three of the symbols. He watched as his mana kept falling but felt a feeling of satisfaction from the magic itself. It was an odd feeling, but he assumed it meant the enchantments were almost done. After thirty more seconds, the symbols faded and permanently burned into the metal, and the flow of power ceased abruptly.

Arthur was amazed at the process. For all three of them, it took 150 mana to complete. Arthur assumed that the process would be typical for other attempts with roughly half coming out immediately, and the rest slowly trickling in. He couldn't help but step back and admire his work, though. The blade was now simply amazing for something he had made.

Congratulations, you have successfully enchanted Basic Mage-crafted Iron Dagger Blade for 120 experience in Enchanting.

Item: Enchanted Basic Mage-crafted Iron Dagger Blade	**Attack:** 5-7 **Durability:** 60/60 **Rarity:** Rare **Quality:** Well Crafted **Weight:** 0.6 kg **Slot:** Crafting Item

	Traits: An Enchanted Basic Iron Dagger Blade, created using magical techniques. This blade will have more capacity for absorbing magical power. Combine with handle components to assemble an Enchanted Basic Mage-crafted Iron Dagger. Enchantments: • This blade won't lose attack damage as the durability falls. • This blade loses durability 10% slower.

That was a great success. Arthur was delighted with the results but knew he needed to get to work on the other blades. The hammer and awl quickly scrawled across the metal as the next piece was inscribed. He didn't want sloppy work to cause an issue with his enchanting, so he took his time. It took him a good thirty minutes to put the same symbols in, and by then, he had the mana he needed to enchant it again. Completing the enchantments two more times gave him three identical dagger blades.

Congratulations, you have successfully enchanted Basic Mage-crafted Iron Dagger Blade for 240 experience in Enchanting. (x2)

He walked them over to Rowan to show off his work. He needed to get the sword blade from him anyway so he could finish it. He made it up to Rowan, while he was busy working on a wooden handle and flipped him one of the blades. Rowan looked at it and let out a slow whistle.

"Those are some damn fine blades for the level of their crafting. Most would probably say they are a waste, but I believe there's no such thing as a waste when it comes to making something correct. That would fetch quite a hefty sum even though it's only an iron blade. Fine craftsmanship is almost nonexistent in the human kingdoms anymore with the horrible conditions everyone is subjected to. The only current magical artifacts are those passed down through families or won in war." Rowan told him.

"Any of our people would be honored to use one of these. I'm getting pretty close to finishing the remaining pieces for the blades. I have the guards and pommels for all three daggers and the sword. Just working on the handle pieces to fit it all together. Based on the time it took you to do those other three, I should be done about the same time as you are with that sword."

"I'll do my best to match your timing so we can get these wrapped up. I'm sure I have some work backed up by now for the village at the inn, and I need to get some things together for my hunting trip tomorrow. Also, I need to give you some time to get that shield done I asked for."

Arthur grabbed the sword from the nearby table and walked back over to his working area while Rowan continued working on the handle he had. The runes used on the daggers would have to suffice for this sword. There wasn't time to experiment with something new, and he needed this sword complete without accidentally destroying it. He got the runes in place quickly and finished the enchantment. The sword took a little more mana, though. It took 180 mana to do the three enchantments on the sword. The finished product didn't look bad, though.

Congratulations, you have successfully enchanted Basic Mage-crafted Iron Bastard Sword Blade for 150 experience in Enchanting.
Congratulations, you have reached level 2 in Enchanting. Your enchantments have a 3% decreased mana cost.

Item: Enchanted Basic Mage-crafted Iron Bastard Sword Blade	**Attack:** 9-13
	Durability: 75/75
	Rarity: Rare
	Quality: Well Crafted
	Weight: 1.2 kg
	Slot: Crafting Item

	Traits: An Enchanted Basic Iron Bastard Sword Blade, created using magical techniques. This blade will have more capacity for absorbing magical power. Combine with handle components to assemble an Enchanted Basic Mage-crafted Iron Bastard Sword. Enchantments: • This blade won't lose attack damage as the durability falls. • This blade loses durability 10% slower.

Not bad for half a day's work. He went to check in with Rowan so they could finish the blades up. When he got back over to Rowan, he saw the man was finishing the wooden handles with a thin, semi-clear oil to preserve them. He strolled over to him, and Rowan gazed admiringly at the sword blade.

They worked on the daggers first. Arthur heated the end of the tang on the first while Rowan prepped the handle components. As soon as it was hot enough, Rowan slipped on the guard, followed by the handle and then the pommel. They wedged it in a small wooden vice, and Arthur peened the end over to finish the blade. When done, he looked at his notifications.

Congratulations, you have successfully created Enchanted Basic Mage-crafted Iron Dagger. You have gained 220 experience in Blacksmithing for creating this item.

Congratulations, you have reached level 3 in Blacksmithing. You are granted a 6% bonus to forging speed.

Item: Enchanted Basic Mage-crafted Iron Dagger	**Attack:** 5-7 **Durability:** 60/60 **Rarity:** Rare **Quality:** Well Crafted **Weight:** 1.1 kg **Slot:** Main Hand/Off Hand **Traits:** A dagger made out of iron with magical means and enchanted. Enchantments: • This blade won't lose attack damage as the durability falls. • This blade loses durability 10% slower.

Arthur and Rowan finished up the other two daggers and admired their work.

Congratulations, you have successfully created Enchanted Basic Mage-crafted Iron Dagger. You have gained 440 experience in Blacksmithing for creating this item. (x2)

"I almost forgot the feeling of gaining a level. It's a great sense of accomplishment." Rowan told him.

"Has it been that long? I guess you could also gain experience from helping me finish those?" Arthur asked.

"Work has been scarce in the last few months, I may have completed a handful of items a week, and those were all with garbage scrap. I got experience from helping you finish those blades, but it was only a percentage since you did most of it. It was still enough to push me into the next level when combined with the things I've already completed."

"If you don't mind me asking, what level are you up to?" Arthur asked.

Rowan eyed him warily. "Most people won't answer questions like those. Being too high of a level in anything is a quick way to find yourself having an accident with the control the lords try to keep hold of. I'll tell you, though, that I've made it up to level 8 now. Resources are heavily regulated in the cities, and typically, you're only allowed to make small things that reward little experience such as nails."

"Well, congratulations on the level either way. That should get you another talent point to play with, at least. Hopefully, you can find something good you want to use it on."

"I've had my talent picked out for a while but wasn't sure I would ever see it happen. If we keep up this pace though and stay under the notice long enough, we should be able to get our skills up high, and I'll probably be more skilled than most of the kingdom except for some of the royal court and their retainers." Rowan said.

"Sadly, I think that'll be our only hope. I know that this first attack coming our way won't be the last. If we can kill all of them and prevent them from reporting the problem back, we should at least buy ourselves some time, but eventually, higher powers will notice us, and we'll have to defend what we're building here. I have a feeling we won't be able to hide from Lord Golgara for long before someone notices something odd." Arthur stressed to him.

"Then we need to get to work. Let's get that sword complete." Rowan told him with a nod.

They did the same process with the sword they had for the daggers, and before long, the final hammer blow marked the completion.

Congratulations, you have successfully created Enchanted Basic Mage-crafted Iron Bastard Sword. You have gained 260 experience in Blacksmithing for creating this item.

Item: Enchanted Basic Mage-crafted Iron Bastard Sword	**Attack:** 9-13 **Durability:** 75/75 **Rarity:** Rare **Quality:** Well Crafted

	Weight: 1.8 kg
	Slot: Main Hand/Off Hand
	Traits: A sword made out of iron with magical means and enchanted.
	Enchantments:
	• This blade won't lose attack damage as the durability falls. • This blade loses durability 10% slower.

"Definitely items of beauty. Do you suppose you can help me get the shield crafted too before you head off? I'd hate to pair a sword this nice with a normal shield." Rowan said.

Arthur looked up at the sun and determined he still had enough time to work on the shield with him before he needed to be back at the inn. They both marched over to the forge area, and Arthur picked up an ingot of iron. Rowan wanted to watch the process this time. He didn't get to see the magic last time and couldn't resist getting the chance to observe.

"Any specific shield style you think would work best?" Arthur asked Rowan.

"I admit I'm not very knowledgeable about shields, but I'd say a heater shield would probably suffice. I'll guess you'll need two ingots to make one as large as it needs to be. I know the iron is heavy, but you can't afford to make it too thin, or it will be too weak." Rowan told him.

"I have somewhat of an idea to help with that using my Enchanting. I think it needs to be a little thicker, though. It should help Samson build up his strength slightly one way or another. By the time we can get him a true steel shield, it should feel light as a feather to him." Arthur said happily.
He walked over and grabbed another ingot and threw both into the forge to heat up. He chatted with Rowan for a few minutes until both were hot.

"Alright, Rowan, step back and prepare to be amazed," Arthur told him.

Rowan scoffed at him and stepped back. Arthur used his magic to pick up both pieces and set them against one another. He pictured the shield he wanted in his mind. This would be a great test to make a typical heater shield, but with his magic, it also gave him the chance to make it intricate as well. He made a slightly raised edge on the shield that made the edge a little thicker and more resilient. He also made sure the boss on the front was tapered well and smooth to help deflect blows better. He also pictured small metal rivet pegs sticking out of the back where Rowan would need to attach the enarmes for the hand. This was a design item that would be almost impossible to do without the spell. He wanted to keep rivet holes out of the front, though, so this was the best option. He made the inside of the boss slightly hollow to keep the weight down too. He planned on enchanting it anyway to help. Once he had the idea in his mind, he cast his spell.

The shield worked slightly different from the blades. Instead of just showing a magical line moving on the ingot, both ingots melted together, and the bars started flowing into a larger rectangular shape. Once it got close to the final shield measurements, the familiar line of power began moving from the top to bottom and transformed the hunk of the rectangular metal into the shield Arthur had pictured. The edges thickened and had some delicate scroll patterns etched into them as the power continued through the shield. As the metal kept moving, he heard a gasp from behind him. A smile crept onto his face as he knew that Rowan was watching, and by the sound he had made, he was rather impressed.

Arthur waited patiently as the spell kept moving over the metal. This process was a little slower, but he couldn't complain. It was still infinitely faster than doing it the conventional way. It took around five minutes, but the shield finally finished, and the heat was pulled out. It dropped into Arthur's hands, and the weight startled him for a minute.

You have gained 50 experience in Earth Magic and Fire Magic for successfully casting Combination Spell: Arcane Forging.

Congratulations, you have successfully created Intricate Mage-crafted Iron Heater Shield. You have gained 140 experience in Arcane Smithing and Blacksmithing for creating this item.

Congratulations, you have reached level 4 in Blacksmithing. You are granted a 9% bonus to forging speed.

Item: Intricate Mage-crafted Iron Heater Shield (Unfinished)	**Block:** 10-12 **Durability:** 100/100 **Rarity:** Uncommon **Quality:** Well Crafted **Weight:** 5.0 kg **Slot:** Crafting Item

	Traits: A basic Iron Heater Shield, created using magical techniques. This shield will have more capacity for absorbing magical power. Combine with handle components to assemble an Intricate Mage-crafted Iron Heater Shield.

"Dear sweet Goddess, that's beautiful," Rowan said in awe. Arthur turned and saw the man had watery eyes as if he were on the verge of crying.

"I wholeheartedly agree with you, my friend. I tried to make it both functional and intricate." Arthur told him solemnly.

Rowan looked at him. "You don't understand what you have done here. There has been nothing made with this amount of beauty since before the fall of the Firebrand family. Yeah, I know it's only an iron shield, but the sheer beauty of it makes that irrelevant."

Arthur felt a swell of pride at the man's reaction. "I thank you for that, Rowan. How about we make it even nicer by adding a few enchantments to it?" Arthur asked.

"That sounds like a plan. I'll find some of the leather pieces I have around here and get the enarmes made to strap the arm in. I should be done about the same time you are, and we can fully assemble it. I don't want you only to get a small percentage of the experience after you made it look that good." Rowan told him.

"Wait, I get experience for it being completed even if I'm not actively helping with it?" Arthur asked.

"Yes, you do. It doesn't matter how far away the craft is when it's completed. If you had a hand in making it, you would get at least a portion of the experience. If you left right now, and I finished it, I would get the experience for completing it, and you would get 10% of that experience. If not for that, the unfinished products would never be allowed to leave the shops until complete for any reason. No one would ever want to export their unfinished items so that a better crafter could complete another piece." Rowan explained.

Arthur thought about it and saw an advantage to it. Even if he didn't have time to focus on finishing the items, he could still make a lot with his arcane smithing and just let Rowan and his apprentices finish them up. This would allow him to get a small percent of the experience, and his apprentices would get the full amount to help their skill progress faster. He supposed it could also be used as a reward system for artisans and their apprentices by letting them finish specific projects for the massive amounts of experience they offered.

"I'll get back to my seat and get to work on the enchantment then. You get those straps ready for the inside." Arthur told him.

"While I'm pleased you at least know what they are, can you use the real term for them? Can't sully the craft. They are enarmes." Rowan told him in mock tones.

"Of course, Ole wise one," Arthur said with a mocking bow and a smile.

Arthur walked back over to his spot and got to work. He decided to use the durability enchantment again as before and inscribed it along each side. The boss would be a little different, the symbols for weak, power, and deflect were used instead. Man, he was glad he could naturally translate any word to the symbols. If he didn't have that advantage, it would take him forever to figure out new enchantments. He just hoped this one did what he wanted. He started the mana infusion and pushed in power. As before, it was the quick flood followed by a slow trickling of power. The process completed, and the symbols permanently etched themselves in with fire and faded slightly. Now he was suitably impressed.

Congratulations, you have successfully enchanted Basic Mage-crafted Iron Heater Shield (Unfinished) for 180 experience in Enchanting.

Item: Intricate Mage-crafted Iron Heater Shield (Unfinished)	**Block:** 11-13 **Durability:** 120/120 **Rarity:** Rare **Quality:** Well Crafted **Weight:** 5.0 kg **Slot:** Crafting Item

	Traits: A basic Iron Heater Shield, created using magical techniques. This shield will have more capacity for absorbing magical power. Combine with handle components to assemble a Basic Magecrafted Iron Heater Shield. Enchantments: ● 10% increased chance to parry blows. ● This shield loses durability 10% slower.

Arthur took the finished product over to Rowan. He was holding the leather in his hands and looked ready to attach them. He looked at the back and frowned for a moment before his face brightened.

"Could you heat each of those rivet ends with your Fire Magic? I don't want to tarnish the rest of the beauty of this shield by throwing the entire thing back in the fire to heat them." Rowan asked.

Arthur felt stupid for a moment. Of course, the design looked good, but Rowan was right. You had to throw the entire thing in the fire to heat the pegs. Typically, you would heat the small rivet and put it in through the hole to peen it over. Luckily Rowan saw the problem and immediately thought of a brilliant solution.

"Absolutely," Arthur replied. Rowan stood by as they flipped the shield upside down, and both got ready. Rowan had the leather, and a small hammer prepared to go, so Arthur focused on the first peg and cast his weak flame spell while holding his finger close to the rivet. He had to channel the flame for thirty seconds to heat it enough, but he quickly slipped the leather on and peened it over. Luckily, this spell wasn't too expensive. They had to take a couple of breaks for Arthur's mana to recover while they worked, but they got the rest of the rivets heated and peened on, and the shield was complete.

You have gained 150 experience in Fire Magic for successfully casting Weak Flame. (x5)

Congratulations, you have reached level 3 in Fire Magic. Fire Magic spells now have a 6% increased effect.

Congratulations, you have successfully created Enchanted Intricate Mage-crafted Iron Heater Shield. You have gained 300 experience in Blacksmithing for creating this item.

Item: Intricate Mage-crafted Iron Heater Shield	
	Block: 11-13
	Durability: 120/120
	Rarity: Rare
	Quality: Well Crafted
	Weight: 5.0 kg
	Slot: Off Hand

	Traits: A shield made out of iron with magical means and enchanted. Enchantments: • 10% increased chance to parry blows. • This shield loses durability 10% slower.

"Well, I'll be damned, Arthur. If you hand out these weapons to your hunting group, I have a feeling you'll be their friend for life. I almost feel bad now that I have to go back to making normal items after seeing what you just accomplished. I guess someone needs to make everyday items too. Anything specific you need?" Rowan asked.

Arthur thought for a moment and realized he could do something real quick, and he acknowledged Rowan's completion of the weapon work orders. That would give him a good boost to his skill, and Arthur had the finished products in front of him and could verify them as complete. Rowan was beyond surprised as he looked at Arthur.

"Holy crap, that was an outstanding amount of experience! Not only that but since the items were rare quality, it gave me a large experience bonus!" He exclaimed.

"I'm happy for you, but I'm afraid you have to get back to doing some boring work now. The main weapon requirements for the hunting party are done, but we can wait a while until we worry about arming the rest of the villagers for the attack. Now that I know we can grind through this fairly quickly, we can shift focus. I would like for you to start making nails. This village is falling apart, and nails will be of utmost importance to help us repair some of these places." He said.

Rowan nodded his head in acknowledgment. Arthur created two work orders for a bundle of fifty nails each and assigned them both to Rowan.

"It isn't much, but the free experience is just that free experience. Once your apprentices get to a higher level, I can start giving them better work orders as well, but I'm sure you need them smelting ingots more than anything with all that raw ore we brought in. I'll see if I can't find us some more while out tomorrow." Arthur told him.

"I'll take what I can get. Don't you have work to do? Get on with yourself."

Arthur got up, dusted himself off, and put the tools he had used back in their places. He was raised to clean up after himself and wasn't going to leave a mess for Rowan to pick up. A few slim pieces of coal were slipped into his bag to use for drawing symbols if needed, and he took off back to the inn. There was a bit of life in the village around him as he walked. He saw many faces he had never seen before. There were not a whole lot of people here, but he still hadn't met most of them. Most he at least had seen in a glimpse outside or through a window, but some new faces still popped up.

He reached the front of the inn as the sun was starting to go down. He sure had a busy day that felt like an entire week. Walking into the inn, he saw it full of vibrant life. People were seated around the room, eating. There were smiles everywhere as they ate. The sight of it all brought warmth to his heart. No matter what he thought, he could see they were making a difference, and this was just the start.

Shortly after he entered, the energy picked up, and he could see a handful of people were looking toward him. He knew some of them had items they probably wanted to turn in. Arthur sat at an empty table and waited for the crowd to work their way to him as they finished eating.

The first people to make their way to him were the father and son woodcutting duo. He accepted their order and issued them new ones. He had seen the logs piled up outside and assumed they'd be here.

The next person to approach him was the person he hoped against hope would show up. It was Zeke, and he was holding a bow in one hand and a small bundle of arrows in the other. Arthur had no idea how the man had completed both items in such a short amount of time, but he wouldn't question good luck. He needed another bow so Vana would have a decent weapon to use tomorrow for the hunt. She wouldn't be fond of only using a dagger. The orders for Zeke were completed, and he issued two more requests for bows. He knew they needed many more arrows, but Rowan hadn't had time to make arrowheads yet to fill those orders, so he would have to wait until tomorrow. They also needed to gather some feathers from birds tomorrow for fletching the arrows.

Rowan's apprentices, Alex and Lana, were the next in line, so Arthur completed their four orders for ingots. He hoped they were progressing quickly in their levels. Rowan would need help soon. He saw his hunting team around the area. Samson was sitting at a table in the corner, and Vana was leaning against the bar. He caught a glimpse of Allendria back by the entrance to the kitchen. He waved Vana and Samson over.

"Hey, you two. I want to go on a hunting trip tomorrow. Our primary goal is to find food and animals, but we keep our eyes open for any useful materials. I'll provide each of you with a weapon for the trip, but unfortunately, I have little in the way of armor. You can look at what I'm wearing and see that. Vana, I have a basic bow for you and some arrows. You can go ahead and take them now since I already have them here with me. I'll also provide you with a dagger for close-quarters protection. Samson, I have something a little beefier for you. I also have a sword and shield prepared for you that I'll hand out in the morning. Any questions?" Arthur asked.

Both looked at each other and shrugged. Samson turned to him and asked, "Are we going to be looking anywhere specific? Game animals can be tricky to find just stumbling around, but there's a low-level dungeon out there that's primarily occupied by animals of all different kinds. It would probably be a good location for skins and meat."

"That would be perfect. I only worry about people being injured. We have little in the way of healing abilities." Arthur told them.

Vana spoke up at that, "I have medical field knowledge. I can create a few different things from ingredients found locally in the forest to help heal. It should suffice for anything not overly major, such as hefty bleeding or broken bones."

"Well, I guess you get to play the unofficial healer for now, on top of your ranger duties. It'll just be us three and Allendria going on the trip. If you have any armor at all stashed away, now would be the time to dust it off. I'm sure you won't be disappointed in the weapons I supply you tomorrow, and with any luck, we might find something good in this beast dungeon. Once Rowan has some time, and Corianne has some leather tanned, we can work on getting you two more properly equipped but bear with me until then." Arthur told them.

"Any weapon will be welcome at this point. I miss the feel of a weapon in hand." Samson told him.

"That's the plan then. Meet me back here at first light tomorrow, and we'll get moving. Until then, feel free to do as you wish."

Chapter 21

Finally a Dungeon

Arthur woke up a little before sunrise and stretched. He had a hunt today and needed to get up and get a bit of food. Arthur got himself dressed and took a little time to make sure the smell wafting from him wasn't terrible. Body odor was something he was slowly getting used to, but God did he miss deodorant. Hygiene would be a significant endeavor once this attack was over, and they had succeeded.

He stumbled down the stairs, half-awake, and saw the other three members of his party already eating. Arthur just thought he was up early. It appeared they beat him to the punch. He walked over to the table and saw Daniel standing over by the bar. Daniel saw him, nodded, and headed to the back.

Arthur plopped into an empty chair at the table and looked around. There was a mixture of excitement and some trepidation painted on the faces around him. It was to be expected that dungeon runs were not the safest things to do here, but since they suggested it, he would go along with it. Daniel came from the back with his two apprentices trailing him and set his food down on the table.

    Both girls looked expectantly at him, and
he realized they were there to accept the
completion of their orders. He acknowledged
their order completion and reassigned them new
ones. Since he only gave Rowan two orders this
time instead of three, he created an extra
order of 10 meal preps and gave it to a
surprised looking Daniel.
    "You deserve the chance to benefit from
the experience as well," Arthur told him.
    "Thank you. It'll be good to get a bit of
extra experience to go with the work." Daniel
told him.
    "Anything specific you need me to look
out for?" Arthur asked him.
    "Just the normal food items and herbs. It
would help kick the cooking up a bit once we
get a good set of herbs and spices in stock."
    "I'll keep on the lookout then. The
others suggested we hit up a local beast
dungeon in the forest, so I'm hoping we'll get
a good haul of meat and furs to work with."
Arthur told him.
    "Be careful. Dungeons are a great way to
get some experience but can be very dangerous.
Just stay on your toes."
    "Will do, and thanks for the advice."
    Daniel turned and walked back to the bar
while Arthur finished his meal at the table.
He glanced around and noticed everyone else
looked ready to go and had finished their
meals. Samson had some sturdy looking work
clothing on but hadn't found any armor. The
rest were wearing their regular clothes, so he
had no hope for that. They badly needed some
leather to get some armor together. Arthur
rose from his seat as he looked at each of
them.

"Grab any provisions you may need from Daniel before we leave. Make sure each of you has a water skin and at least a few pieces of dried rations. Vana, feel free to ask for any herbs he may have that you could find useful for your healing. I'll grab my stuff and meet you guys out front." Arthur told them.

They all nodded their agreement. Arthur went upstairs to grab his bag and the few provisions and water skin he had stashed. He also took the chance to throw his bow over his shoulder and toss his arrows into his bag. His sword had been strapped on by instinct when he got dressed, so it wasn't a concern, and he went ahead and attached his dagger to the right side of his belt. Arthur left the room and made his way back downstairs. The common area had cleared out, so he walked straight out the front door and walked into the morning air. The soft breeze felt good on his skin. The weather was rather comfortable right now, but he was sure they'd be sweating good by the end of the day.

He looked around and saw the entire group arrayed outside, nervously shifting from foot to foot. All except for Samson that is. He had the stoic look of a military veteran waiting in ranks for a commander to walk by for an inspection. He didn't stand at full attention or anything, but his rigid posture told Arthur all he needed to know.

"Glad you're all ready. Let's make our way to the blacksmith to pick up your weapons before we get on the road." Arthur said as he led them through the village. They made their way to the blacksmith in no time, and Arthur waved at Rowan as he approached. The man was bent over working on the iron nails he had asked for. It was a slow and tedious process.

"How are you faring this morning?" Arthur
asked him.
Rowan looked up from his work and smiled at
the group. "Pretty well so far. I see the
fearsome hunting party has arrived. I take it
they're here to pick up their weapons?"
"That's the plan," Arthur told him.
"I don't think they'll be disappointed,"
Rowan told him with a wink.
"I took the liberty to clean them up a
bit, early this morning, and oiled them down
for protection." He said as he walked to the
back of the shop and came forward carrying a
bundle. Arthur led the group closer and turned
to address them.
"I want to start by saying that under no
circumstances do these weapons leave your
possession except to sleep. That may sound
harsh, but you will understand in a moment.
First off, I have two daggers to hand out. I'm
giving one to Vana and one to Allendria. I'll
be keeping one for myself to replace the old
dagger I've been wearing. Allendria has her
magic to protect her, and Vana has a bow and
some arrows. I know the bow isn't the best,
but it's what we have for now. Samson, I have
different pieces for you, but I'm saving those
for last." Arthur told them.
He turned to the bundle and grabbed two
of the daggers, and handed one each to Vana
and Allendria. Both of them glanced at them
and started to look up before their faces
froze, and they turned to stare at the
weapons.
"Where in the hell did you find these?
Did you bargain with a demon for your soul?"
Vana asked him in disbelief.

"I know you probably won't believe this, but I made those yesterday right here in the forge," Arthur told her as he replaced the dagger he had on him with the new one. He placed the old one on the table for Rowan to use as needed.

"I wasn't even aware the human kingdoms even had a crafter with the knowledge of mage-crafting anymore," Allendria said out loud. Then her eyes narrowed. "I know some of the prerequisites for this skill myself and know you couldn't have possibly been able to perform this until yesterday. Did you seriously discover the rare art of Arcane Smithing completely on your own and then proceed to make all these in one afternoon?" Allendria asked him in disbelief.

"Actually, yes. I knew how it should work, and it just took some trial and error to get it right. I needed a little experimentation to get it right, and then some work on the enchantments." He told her.

"I also noticed you had done those as well." She said while pointing to the symbols on the blade. "It appears that your special skill we discussed is, indeed, beneficial in your enchanting. I haven't personally seen either of these final symbols myself." She told him.
Arthur grinned at her. "I thought you might notice that. I can say that special skill has been immensely helpful and I think it will be a game-changer for us in the long run. I want to get more enchantments done and see if you can share with me some of the more advanced methods for creating enchantments. I'd be willing to show you any symbols you wish to know and tell you any of the effects I have discovered."

"Consider it a deal." She told him.

"Vana, I hope you understand now why I said these couldn't leave your possession. They're our upper hand right now, and we will need them to succeed with this village." He told her.

"I truly understand, and we will be vigilant. I know these weapons are precious even if they are lower-level materials." She said seriously.

Arthur turned to face Samson. "I can't explain why, but I truly trust you. I think it's a combination of your military training and your naturally outgoing nature. That said, I want to ask you one important question. Will you be the shield for our group?"

Samson faced him and stood straight-backed. "It would be an honor. I'll ensure you all stay as safe as I can."

"I thought you might say that. Please keep in mind your equipment is infinitely more important to keep track of, and it absolutely can't leave this village unless in your hands."

Arthur turned and grabbed the longsword first. He turned and presented the weapon to Samson. He held it with one hand on the handle and the blade laying sideways across his other arm. Samson gingerly took the sword and looked at it with a gleam in his eye. Arthur could see the beaten-down warrior inside of him rising from the ashes.

"If you think that's nice, wait until you see this," Arthur said with a chuckle.

He turned and grabbed the shield by the sides and turned to present it to Samson. Samson looked at the shield, and Arthur saw a look of childlike glee in the man's eyes mixed with a small tear running down one cheek.

"That's breathtaking. Are you sure it's for me to use? It almost looks too good to use." Samson croaked out.

"Its purpose is to protect us, so I'm sure it's for you to use. Put it to good use, and we can call it even." Arthur told him.

Arthur helped Samson slip the shield onto his left arm and watched as he tested the weight and speed of the device as he moved it around.

"Not only is it beautiful, but it isn't near as heavy as I expected for an iron shield. The reinforced edges are a very nice touch, and the detailed scroll-work is perfect. I can't wait to smash something's face in with it." He said with glee.

"I'm glad you approve. Rowan, do you mind if we use your cart again? I'm hoping we can fill it to the top today." Arthur asked.

"Sure, but bring it back in one piece. If you find any good metal, make sure to bring me some. Also, make sure you grab the pick from yesterday. You probably never checked, but I finished it last night. Oh, and take these too." He told him as he tossed Arthur two leather sheaths for the daggers he had given Vana and Allendria and a sheath for Samson's sword.

Arthur was pleased that Rowan had taken the time to make sheaths to keep them from hurting themselves while traveling. He did a quick check and saw the notification he hadn't paid attention to earlier from the work Rowan had completed.

Congratulations, Basic Iron Pick, has been completed. You have gained 15 experience in Blacksmithing for another finishing this item.

"I'll make sure it's on the cart. Thank you for the heads up." Arthur walked over and made sure the pick was on the cart and threw in a few old looking ropes lying near the cart. He thought they might need them if they had a big load that needed to be tied down.

He pushed the cart back to the group as they were each testing their new weapons and getting them secured to get moving. Arthur motioned for them to head out, and they began to leave.

"Samson, do you know where that animal dungeon is located?" Arthur asked.

"I know it's pretty close to where the entrance is but never been to the exact entrance myself. I'm sure once we get close, it won't be hard for us to find it." He told him.

"That's good enough for me. I want you to take the lead on our trip out." Arthur told him.

Samson nodded. Everyone seemed rather quiet as they kept walking out of the village and approached the forest. Arthur noticed it wasn't far off from where he had exited the forest upon his initial arrival that they now entered the woods. They were heading in a southwestern direction and followed Samson diligently.

"Vana, can you get your bow ready for use? If we see any game animals, I want you to take them down. I'm occupied with this cart, or I would do it. If it's edible or has a good hide that we can use, kill it. Samson can focus on getting us where we need to go." Arthur told her.

She nodded her head and pulled the bow off of her shoulder and got an arrow ready on the string. They kept walking through the forest and met little resistance for the first two miles into the woods. Once they passed the two-mile mark, Vana was able to bag a few rabbits as they traveled, and they gladly gutted them and added them to the cart. They would worry about the furs later. They couldn't be tanned for leather, but they could be cured for clothing use.

They kept moving, and the efficiency of the team was excellent. Vana and Samson were naturals out here. Every time Vana fired, Samson instinctively moved to interpose himself between the group and where she had fired, in anticipation of an enemy. Arthur was impressed and quickly realized this man must have been a fantastic warrior at one time. He wouldn't press now, but he had a feeling the man was more skilled than most. After another mile, Samson slowed and held up a hand.

"We are close to the border where the dungeon entrance is. I know it's in this area, but not sure exactly where. We should proceed from here alert and with caution. Enemies could be anywhere near here, and dungeons usually attract powerful monsters and beasts near their entrance." Samson told them.

Arthur stopped with the cart and unslung his bow from his back. He laid the bow and a handful of arrows on the cart in front of him so he could quickly set the cart down and pick them up for use if needed. He picked the cart back up and nodded for Samson to continue. They kept moving again and slowly walked forward. The party tried to stay as quiet as possible, but with the cart, it was difficult.

They had made it another hundred yards
before Vana signaled for them to stop.

"Something's wrong." She whispered just
loud enough for everyone to hear. Arthur sat
the cart down, and they sat in silence for a
moment.

"Shit, it's an ambush," Vana said right
as four giant timberwolves emerged and fanned
out in front of them, and one wolf came
bounding at them from each flank.

"Vana, take the one on our back left.
Allendria, you take the one on the back right.
Samson, try to stop the four up front, and
I'll help take them down with my bow." Arthur
yelled as he had already got an arrow knocked.
Samson took a few quick steps forward and
roared at the top of his lungs. Arthur guessed
the man had some skills for tank effects
because that looked like an area of effect
style taunt skill. He aimed at the wolf on the
far left of Samson and fired. The arrow sunk
deep into the wolf's flank, and it yelped and
stumbled away from Samson temporarily. Arthur
grabbed another shaft, and as he did, he took
a glance and saw Vana had two arrows in her
wolf. The first arrow took the creature in the
front shoulder and looked like it had caused
it to temporarily crash into the ground, while
the second arrow landed in the creature's
neck. Arthur was relatively sure these
creatures would be resilient. He did a quick
scan as he lined up the next shot.

<table>
<tr><td>

Name: Timber Wolf
Level: 7
Type: Beast
Rarity: Common
HP: 159/180
Stamina: 150/150

</td></tr>
</table>

Strength: 4 Agility: 6 Endurance: 6	Experience: N/A
	Skills
	Combat Skills:
	Rend: ? (???/???)
	Slash: ? (???/???)

You have gained 80 experience in Scan for successful use against Timber Wolf (Level 7).

It was apparent his first attack hadn't done as much damage as he had hoped for. He seriously needed to score a mortal wound on this animal to take it out of the fight.

"Samson, can you stun the one on your far left for a moment," Arthur asked.

He knew it was asking for a lot since the man was using his sword and shield to keep the wolves focused on himself and was trying to keep them from doing any damage to him. Arthur got his arrow ready and activated Aim Shot to ensure he got a good hit. Samson grunted and took a quick step to his left and bashed the wolf, right as it tried to snap at him. The blow stunned the creature, and it staggered back. His arrow left the string, and it hit perfectly behind the creature's front shoulder. The creature collapsed to the ground, unmoving. Arthur needed to know how he was doing, so he let his combat notifications flow into him as they happened.

You have dealt 180 damage to Timber Wolf (1) (Level 7) with Aim Shot (Heart Strike) for 25 Stamina.

Timber Wolf (1) (Level 7) has died.

You have gained 125 experience in both Archery and the Subskill Aim shot for killing Timber Wolf (1) (Level 7).

You have gained 150 experience for slaying Timber Wolf (1) (Level 7).

       Perfect, Arthur had dealt a heart strike on it with his aimed shot, so it was instantly killed. Arthur focused on the wolf on Samson's far-right this time. He noticed the two directly in front of Samson had some decent sword wounds on them, so Samson was holding his own. He also saw that Allendria had taken the wolf down she was assigned to, and it appeared to be bleeding out on the ground. Arthur was surprised the wolf wasn't a smoldering pile of fire. It looked like Allendria had hit it with extremely concentrated fire bolts that punched through the hide of the wolf and burned the internal organs instead of igniting the entire wolf on fire. Arthur was pleased with that because he worried that she'd end up ruining anything she killed.

       He put an arrow on the string, took aim, activated Aim Shot again, and let it fly. The arrow punched into the creature's spine near the back legs, and it lost control of its hind legs.

You have dealt 35 damage to Timber Wolf (2) (Level 7) with Simple Iron Arrow (Critical Strike) (Mortal Strike) (Fatal Blow) for 25 Stamina.

You have inflicted Paralyze (Hind End) to Timber Wolf (2) (Level 7).

That was a new one. Arthur guessed severing a spinal connection here would also cripple an animal as usual. While the creature was dragging its hind end, Arthur sent two more arrows at it. The first took it in the throat, and the second hit it directly in the heart.

You have dealt 21 damage to Timber Wolf (2) (Level 7) with Simple Iron Arrow (Critical Strike).
You have dealt 100 damage to Timber Wolf (2) (Level 7) with Simple Iron Arrow (Heart Strike).
Timber Wolf (2) (Level 7) has died.
You have gained 125 experience in both Archery and the Subskill Aim shot for killing Timber Wolf (2) (Level 7).
You have gained 150 experience for slaying Timber Wolf (2) (Level 7).

Arthur shifted focus. That was two he had now taken down. Vana and Allendria had taken out both of the wolves they had been assigned, and Samson had landed a mortal blow on one of the wolves he'd been facing, which left only one standing, and it was looking pretty ragged. Vana had landed a couple of arrows in its side, and Allendria had hit it in the rear with one of her concentrated fire bolts. The thing was limping along, so Samson stepped forward and drove his sword to the hilt through the side of the creature's neck into organs, dropping the wolf to the ground.

They all took a step back and swept their
gaze around their surroundings. All the wolves
were either dead or quickly bleeding out.
Everything else looked clear around them, so
they started checking themselves for any
damage. They were all utterly unscathed except
for Samson. Even he fared well and only had a
few shallow scratches on his arms where claws
had barely made it past the edge of his shield
as he moved it to block. He didn't need any
medical attention, and they had hardly taken
any of his health from him. They gave the
wolves a minute while they checked their gear
so they would finish bleeding out.

*You have gained 900 experience for the
death of Timber Wolf (Level 7) (x4).*
*Congratulations, you have advanced to
level 8. You have 5 available skill points.
Moving kind of slow, aren't you?*

The experience was rather lovely. Each of
the parties pulled out their daggers and got
to work gutting the animals. Wolves were not
the best meat to eat, but when you had a food
shortage, as they did, you used whatever you
could find. The hides would be useful, though.
The skin was thick enough to make a thin
leather. It was nowhere near as good or as
thick as leather from a cow but was usable.
They neatly stacked them on the cart, and he
tied them down with a rope. There was still
plenty more space on the handcart, though, so
he knew they needed to push on. With this
ambush, Arthur was sure the entrance was
nearby.

They continued on their way and, after
ten minutes of aimlessly walking around,
discovered a large cave entrance. It looked
like a sinkhole with a sloped bottom on it. It
wasn't your typical cave entrance in a wall
but was instead directly on the ground. They
approached it cautiously, looking for enemies.
As they got close, a message appeared to each
of them.

*Warning: You are about to enter the
Dungeon of Graceful Beasts. Proceed with
caution and watch the shadows.*

Well, that was overly ominous. At least
it warned them so they wouldn't accidentally
stumble into a dungeon while exploring. Arthur
called them to a brief halt.

"Everyone, take a moment to get a drink
and something quick to snack on before we go
in. Check and make sure your equipment is
ready."

They all nodded in acknowledgment and set
about doing just that. Arthur ate a stick of
dried meat and took a quick drink from his
water-skin. He checked his sword and dagger,
and both looked good.

"Alright, everyone. Once we get inside the entrance, I will leave the cart in the first big clearing we find. We can't afford to lug it through a dungeon. We can bring back anything we find to load it on later. Samson has the lead, and we will cover. Pick your targets carefully. Anything speedy is our primary target. I have faith Samson can hold back some of the slower and bulkier beasts without an issue. Vana, make sure to choose your shots carefully. Allendria, continue as you have been, but if we get in trouble, don't be afraid to unleash hell. I'll take some ruined beast remains over us being dead any day." Arthur told them.

"Let's get this show on the road then," Samson said good-naturedly.

They entered the cave slowly and kept a close watch around them. Arthur knew the warning was there for a reason, so they carefully watched the shadows. He was sure some sleeker predators were hiding in them. A little way in, the tunnel expanded to an open cavern, and he pulled the cart to the side. They grouped up in a semi-loose formation to give himself and Vana room to use their bows. They heard a low growl come from around the corner ahead of them, and they froze. A large cat of some kind crept around the corner to face them as they watched three more follow behind it. The four cats slowly approached the group and had crouched down as if they were stalking prey.

The group was standing there, staring at the cats in awe when one of the felines screeched and stumbled. Vana wasn't as enraptured as the rest and was smart enough to get an arrow off. That one action caused the whole scene to spring into motion. The other three cats took off in bounding leaps for the group while Samson ran to intercept them. Vana took another shot at the cat she had hit initially, and Arthur got his bow up and launched an arrow at one of the other animals charging Samson.
The cat was moving so fast it glanced off its side and just scratched it.

You have dealt 5 damage to Night Stalker (1) (Level 9) with Simple Iron Arrow (Glancing Blow).

"Shit, they're fast! Samson, can you pin them down?" Arthur yelled.
He retook aim, this time activating Aim Shot to slow down time. The arrow flew and took the animal in the rear leg. He had aimed for the heart but didn't judge the speed correctly.

You have dealt 20 damage to Night Stalker (1) (Level 9) with Simple Iron Arrow (Critical Strike).
You have inflicted Paralyze (Rear Left Leg) to Night Stalker (1) (Level 9).

Well, that should at least slow it down a bit, Arthur thought to himself.
"I'm trying to, but have you ever heard the expression about herding cats? Yep, this is worse." Samson responded.

Samson had reached the first one that was charging him and barreled into it shield first. The cat had twisted and avoided some damage before getting hit, but it was still stunned. Samson pivoted and swung at another of the creatures that had veered toward him and caused it to jump back. Vana had turned her original target into a pincushion, and she had already changed focus to another that was attacking Samson. Arthur said, screw it, and went with his sword. He dropped his bow and pulled his sword free. The distance melted away as he closed with the cat. With the damage to its leg slowing it down, he thought he could take it without much trouble.

As he closed the distance with the cat, it swung a paw at him. He took a quick step back, and as soon as the claw passed, he dashed forward and stabbed the sword through the front of the animal's shoulder and into its chest. The cat mewled and fell to the ground.

You have dealt 96 damage to Night Stalker (1) (Level 9) with Steel Longsword of Minor Beastslaying (Critical Strike) (Mortal Strike) (Fatal Blow).

Another one out of the way. Arthur had taken a step backward and pulled his sword free when another of the animals barreled into him from the side. It pinned him to the ground, and its head came down to bite him. His arm rose to protect his face on instinct, and the cat's jaws closed around his forearm.

Night Stalker (2) (Level 9) has dealt 35 HP damage to you with Bite (Sneak Attack) (Critical Strike).

Night Stalker (2) (Level 9) has inflicted Critical Bleed to you.

Son of a bitch that hurt, Arthur thought to himself. He roared in pain at the night stalker as he held it at bay with his arm. He activated Weak Flame and pointed the palm of his free hand at the cat. A gout of fire erupted from his palm right into the animal's face. The cat jumped away quickly with a snarl. The spell had done little damage, but it had scared it off.

You have gained 30 experience in Fire Magic for successfully casting Weak Flame.
You have dealt 3 damage to Night Stalker (2) (Level 9) with Fire Magic: Weak Flame.

Arthur stumbled back to his feet, while the stalker that had taken him down was busy swatting at its face. He leaped at it and swung down as hard as he could. The blade hit right on the cat's neck and sheared into it smoothly. It slowed when it hit the spine but kept pushing through until its head was hanging by a small amount of skin.

Night Stalker (1) (Level 9) has Died.
You have gained 150 experience in Archery, and the Subskill Aim shot for killing Night Stalker (1) (Level 9).
You have gained 240 experience for killing Night Stalker (1) (Level 9).
Congratulations, you have reached level 2 in the Subskill Aim Shot. Increases firing speed and time dilation by 3%.

You have dealt 197 damage to Night Stalker (2) (Level 9) with Steel Longsword of Minor Beastslaying (Decapitating Blow) (Instant Kill)
Night Stalker (2) (Level 9) has Died.
You have gained 150 experience in Swords for killing Night Stalker (2) (Level 9).
You have gained 240 experience for killing Night Stalker (2) (Level 9).

That was a relief. Another cat out of the fight permanently. Arthur looked around to see how the battle was going. Allendria had been surprised by a stalker just as he had, but she had let loose with her fire. It looked somewhat crispy and was lying on the ground, unmoving. Vana had taken another feline out of the fight with her arrows. Arthur was extremely grateful he recruited her for the team. She was holding her own and more. He could only imagine how damned good she'd be once he found her a good bow.

He was about to race to Samson to help him dispatch the last cat when he saw the man slam his shield into the animal and plunge his sword into its ribcage. The beast mewled and fell still. They all stood up, breathing a bit heavy and looked around. Six of the creatures lie around them at different levels of carnage.

"Fucking sneaky ass cats jumping on people," Arthur swore as he examined the damage to his left forearm. He had multiple puncture marks on his arm where the creature's jaws had bit into as he tried to block his face. A couple of them were bleeding pretty good as well. Vana seemed to notice what had happened, and she headed in his direction.

She took a quick look at the wounds and nodded as she began digging in a pouch on her hip. She pulled out a small container with an odd green goop in it. She scooped out a chunk of it and dabbed a small amount on the more minor puncture wounds. When she finished the small ones, she took a piece of cloth and wiped off the blood around the two bigger ones and quickly packed a big chunk of the poultice into each of those.

"For fuck's sake! Can you warn me before you do that?" Arthur yelled.

"Why? So you can bitch about it before I do it instead?" She said with a wry grin on her face.

"Don't worry about it, you baby. The bleeding will stop shortly, and the wound itself will heal pretty quickly. They're mainly superficial wounds except for those two larger ones." She told him.

"That was some fine shooting, by the way. You're truly a force to be reckoned with. I can see how you could help the village stay afloat for now." Arthur told her.

"I appreciate that. It's hard to find a job as a ranger. The last one I worked for kicked me out because the guys I worked with were insecure and resented me for being better than all of them. Men and their insecurities." She said with a huff.

"I assure you, I'm more than happy you're much better than I am. Now, if I can get you a good bow and some better quality arrows, I'm sure you'll shine."

"Hopefully, we can find something before our big confrontation. I'll feel better facing the thugs with some better equipment." She told him.

"We must get better equipment for sure. I'm not worried about it, though. I think the village bowyer will be ready to make another one shortly. I have some yew logs from an earlier scavenging trip and plan to have a few bows made from that. Those should prove far superior to what we're currently using. We can easily find some sturdy wood for arrows, but until we can get a hold of some steel, I think iron arrows are the best we can do." Arthur told her.

"At least you have a plan, and for that, I'm thankful. I need to see to Samson. I saw a few cuts on him I need to inspect. Can we get Rowan to work on a set of armor for him? If nothing else, he needs some greaves and bracers to protect his arms and legs where the shield doesn't always cover." She asked.

"It's one of my top priorities, and if we didn't need the meat so bad, I would have delayed the trip a few days. I decided against it because of our pressing need for food. The man seems to be very skilled with that shield, though."

"Yes, he does." She said as she left to check on him.
Arthur made his way over to Allendria, who was checking herself for injuries. Luckily she looked somewhat unscathed.

"Did that cat get the jump on you as well?" Arthur asked as he approached.

"The bastard almost did." She said as she spat in its direction. "I barely saw it out of the corner of my eye and didn't have time to take a subtle approach. I unleashed a pure stream of flame at it and didn't stop until it ceased moving. Sapped almost all of my mana, though." She told him wearily.

"We can take a break here and gather ourselves. It should give you time to recover a good amount of your mana. I want to get these cats taken care of before we move on." He told her.

They set to work on gutting the creatures. They left the one Allendria had charbroiled alone and focused on the other five instead. After getting those five cleaned and packed onto the cart, they turned around and made their way back to the bend the cats had come from. Arthur was pleased with the experience he gained from the kills, though.

You have gained 960 experience for the death of Night Stalker (Level 9) (x4).

As they continued around the bend, they found another open room that appeared to be empty. The group walked through it slowly, but right before they made it to the next passage, they were ambushed by two more of the night stalkers. Arthur and Vana quickly filled one full of arrows and left it immobile while Samson had smashed the second, and between his sword and Allendria's targeted fire, they took it out as well. He could see why people would brave a dungeon, though. The experience here was a great benefit. Either the creature's higher levels or the fact that it was a dungeon was causing the experience to be higher than expected. He figured it was probably a bit of both.

Night Stalker (1) (Level 10) has Died.
You have gained 150 experience in Archery for killing Night Stalker (1) (Level 10).
You have gained 300 experience for killing Night Stalker (Level 10).

None of them had taken any damage in the confrontation, so they continued forward. Arthur and Samson's wounds had healed up, and both were back to full health from their regeneration. It amazed Arthur at how much nicer it was to heal deep cuts and holes with a bit of poultice in a short amount of time. Back on Earth, it would have taken him some stitches and a few weeks' worth of time to heal.

They made their way through the next tunnel, and as soon as they came to the next opening, they froze. Just like the other caverns, there were a few spots that light filtered in from the ceiling of the cave so they could see passably well. The problem was the creature that sat in the middle of the cave. There was a massive night stalker seated in the middle of the cavern. It had to stand six feet tall at its shoulders, and its teeth were the size of daggers. It also had a beautiful white coat of fur on it.

To make matters worse, there were three other stalkers in the cave with it. Arthur decided now was a good time to do a quick scan of them.

Name: Night Stalker	
Level: 10	
Type: Beast	
Rarity: Common	
HP: 210/210	
Stamina: 180/180	
Strength: 5	**Experience:** N/A
Agility: 8	**Skills**
Endurance: 7	**Combat Skills:**

| | **Rend:** ? (???/???) |
| | **Slash:** ? (???/???) |

You have gained 100 experience in Scan for successful use against Night Stalker (Level 10).

Name: Primal Night Stalker	
Level: 12	
Type: Beast	
Rarity: Boss	
HP: 300/300	
Stamina: 200/200	
Strength: 7 **Agility:** 10 **Endurance:** 8	**Experience:** N/A **Skills** **Combat Skills:** **Rend:** ? (???/???) **Slash:** ? (???/???) **Fierce Blow:** ? (???/???)

You have gained 120 experience in Scan for successful use against Primal Night Stalker (Level 12).

Congratulations, you have reached level 2 in Scan. You can now see the level of their first combat skills. You're slowly working your way up.

"Holy shit, that's the boss," Arthur whispered.

"No, shit? What else would it be?" Samson asked sarcastically.

Chapter 22

A Big Cat to Tame

"Alright, smartass. Now to figure out how to deal with it. You think you can go toe to toe with it while the rest of us take care of those adds?" Arthur asked.

Samson eyed the big cat skeptically. "I think I could hold it off for a bit, but I can't do it with any of the other stalkers on me. I need you three to pull them off while I handle big girl one on one."

"We can see it done, but be careful. Those teeth on that thing are huge, and I'm sure its claws aren't much better."

"Thanks for the pep talk. Do me a favor and don't try it again." Samson told him.

Arthur ignored his comment and turned to Allendria and Vana. "I'll take the one on the left. Vana, you take the middle, and Allendria, you take the one on the right. We need to take them down as quickly as possible to help Samson. As soon as we engage, he will charge the boss and hold it by himself, so we need to take ours out as quickly as possible."

They both nodded in acknowledgment, and they all got in place. They each spread out, and Arthur counted to three in a low whisper. On three, all three of their attacks launched to their respective targets. Arthur was lost in the fight with his cat and didn't pay attention to their attacks. His arrow had hit the cat he aimed at in the hind leg.

You have dealt 12 damage to Night Stalker (1) (Level 10) with Simple Iron Arrow.
You have inflicted Weak Paralyze (Rear Left Leg) to Night Stalker (1) (Level 10).

Damn, I have to get this Archery skill higher. Arthur thought to himself. The stalker took off, running toward him. Luckily, the arrow slowed it a little, but it wasn't much. He barely had the time to get one more bolt off, which stuck in the cat's front shoulder but must have hit the bone because it didn't score a critical hit.

You have dealt 12 damage to Night Stalker (1) (Level 10) with Simple Iron Arrow.

The cat was now too close to mess with his bow, so he dropped it and pulled the sword. He charged at the animal, but right before he reached it, he swung the sword in a horizontal arc. The feline came to a quick halt and jumped backward. The creature stalked around him as they circled each other for a few moments. The cat lunged at him and swiped with a claw. He swung his sword out to intercept the paw and was pleased when the sword bit into its leg.

You have dealt 16 damage to Night Stalker (1) (Level 10) with Steel Longsword of Minor Beastslaying (Deep Cut).

You have inflicted Weak Paralyze (Front Right Leg) and Weak Bleed to Night Stalker (1) (Level 10).

The stalker backed up again and limped a little on the leg. Arthur glanced around since the creature had backed up and noticed that Vana and Allendria seemed to be holding out without much issue. Samson, on the other hand, was getting battered. The boss's blows looked to be hitting hard, and each hit caused him to stumble. Luckily his defense seemed to be holding up. Arthur shifted his focus back to his fight. He needed to hurry and dispatch this animal to help Samson. It was time for him to take a risk.

He charged at the animal and swung in a downward arc toward its head. As expected, it leaped a step to its right to avoid the hit. Arthur had hoped it would go that direction. He pulled the sword out of its swing and stepped in and lunged at the cat point first. The end went straight through its neck and scraped across the bone. The blow was devastating, though, and looked like it had severed its airway.

You have dealt 106 damage to Night Stalker (1) (Level 10) with Steel Longsword of Minor Beastslaying (Critical Hit) (Mortal Blow) (Fatal Blow).

Arthur rushed to his bow now that the smaller cat was out of the fight. He got the bow up and let an arrow fly at the boss. The shaft sunk into its side, but the creature didn't even flinch when it hit.

You have dealt 8 damage to Primal Night Stalker (Level 12) with Simple Iron Arrow.

Well, at that amount of damage, he didn't even have enough arrows to kill it, possibly. He would have to leave ranged damage to Vana and go in with his sword. He took a glance and saw Vana circling her stalker, but she was in a dead sprint as she did and was still putting arrows in it. The thing was ambling, and Arthur was sure it would be down in no time. He took a glance at Allendria and immediately changed his plan. She was struggling and had taken a nasty gash on one of her legs. He switched focus and activated Aim Shot to send an arrow into her stalker and hit it in the heart.

You have dealt 72 damage to Night Stalker (2) (Level 10) with Aim Shot (Heart Strike).
Night Stalker (2) (Level 10) has died.
You have gained 150 experience in Archery and the Subskill Aim Shot for killing Night Stalker (2) (Level 10).
You have gained 300 experience for killing Night Stalker (2) (Level 10).

That should take care of that. Arthur
dropped the bow again, grabbed his sword, and
charged the boss. He approached it from the
side while Samson continued to struggle
against it. He charged straight at the cat and
rammed his sword all the way to the hilt,
directly into the animal's ribcage. Arthur
roared in triumph. That feeling lasted all of
two seconds until the feline swung full force
at him. It caught him off guard, and he took
the full force of the blow directly in his
chest. The powerful attack launched him
backward, and he rolled across the ground.

*You have dealt 92 damage to Primal Night
Stalker (Level 12) with Steel Longsword of
Minor Beastslaying (Critical Hit).*
Night Stalker (1) (Level 10) has died.
*You have gained 150 experience in Archery
and the Subskill Aim Shot for killing Night
Stalker (1) (Level 10).*
*You have gained 300 experience for
killing Night Stalker (1) (Level 10).*
*Primal Night Stalker (Level 12) has dealt
100 HP damage to you with Fierce Blow
(Crushing Blow).*
*Primal Night Stalker (Level 12) has
fractured your ribs. You move 10% slower. The
effect will last for two minutes without
further damage.*
*Primal Night Stalker (Level 12) has
caused you to take a concussion. Spells take
100% more time to cast. The effect will last
30 seconds.*

"Son of a bitch that hurt." Arthur spat as he slowly got back to his feet. The right side of his ribcage ached maddeningly, and he was quite dizzy while trying to get up. Thank God his previous damage had recovered or that would have likely taken him dangerously close to death. He took stock of the battle as he tried to catch his breath. Allendria was launching fire at the boss but was looking drained. Arthur knew she was about out of mana and had a feeling she would be next to useless when she got to that point. Samson had several cuts on his arms and legs, and he even had a cut on his forehead that was bleeding down his right cheek. Arthur had a nagging feeling that Samson was almost out of stamina, and if that happened, he would be in big trouble.

Vana was strafing the boss, sending in arrows as fast as she could. Most of her shots didn't seem to affect the boss much. If she hit a meatier part of the animal, it seemed to stop short and do minimal damage like his shot. He saw two arrows in the beast that had caused bleeding, though. One bolt was in its ribcage and had punched through, causing it to bleed. The second one was in the base of its neck on the bottom side. He took a quick check of the boss with a scan.

<table>
<tr><td colspan="2">Name: Primal Night Stalker</td></tr>
<tr><td colspan="2">Level: 12</td></tr>
<tr><td colspan="2">Type: Beast</td></tr>
<tr><td colspan="2">Rarity: Boss</td></tr>
<tr><td colspan="2">HP: 140/300</td></tr>
<tr><td colspan="2">Stamina: 120/200</td></tr>
<tr><td>Strength: 7</td><td>Experience: N/A</td></tr>
<tr><td>Agility: 10</td><td>Skills</td></tr>
<tr><td>Endurance: 8</td><td>Combat Skills:</td></tr>
</table>

	Rend: 4 (???/???)
	Slash: ? (???/???)
	Fierce Blow: ?
	(???/???)

Night Stalker (1) (Level 10) has died.
You have gained 150 experience in Archery for killing Night Stalker (1) (Level 10).
You have gained 150 experience in Swords for killing Night Stalker (1) (Level 10).
Congratulations, you have reached level 2 in Swords. Swing speed with swords increased by 3%. Stab it with the pointy end!
You have gained 300 experience for killing Night Stalker (1) (Level 10).

It appeared their attacks were taking their toll. They needed to end this quickly before they ran out of mana and stamina. Arthur needed to come up with a plan and fast.

"Samson, you have the strength left for one good attack?" Arthur yelled.

"If we can do it soon! Blocking is taking most of my stamina!" He hollered back at him.

"Allendria and Vana. Can you each give us one good shot to its face? Let me get slightly closer and blast it. We need it distracted more than anything. Samson, when they distract it, you circle to the right, and I'll get to the left. Each of us can take one good downward chop to its neck. With luck, that should be enough damage to take it out." He told him.

"I'm with you," Samson told him.

Arthur started creeping toward the side of the cat again. When he was ten feet away, he yelled to the girls, "Now!" Allendria let loose a massive fireball at the boss's face while Vana let fly an arrow she had been concentrating on. Arthur saw the bolt glow a bit and start spinning as it flew and hit right in the boss's left eye. Arthur charged forward while Samson sidestepped to the opposite side of the cat, and each brought their sword down in a powerful stroke. Their swords both cut into the neck and came to a halt against the animal's spine. The primal stalker collapsed on the ground in a heap and went still.

You have dealt 84 damage to Primal Night Stalker (Level 12) with Steel Longsword of Minor Beastslaying (Critical Hit).
Primal Night Stalker (Level 12) has died.
You have gained 200 experience in Archery for killing Primal Night Stalker (Level 12).
You have gained 200 experience in Swords for killing Primal Night Stalker (Level 12).
You have gained 400 experience for killing Primal Night Stalker (Level 12).

Congratulations, your party has completed the Dungeon of Graceful Beasts. You have all gained a 1500 experience bonus. This was the first time you have completed this dungeon earning you 3 bonus stat points.
Congratulations, you have reached level 9! You now have 13 available skill points.

That was an awesome bonus. To top it off, Arthur had reached level 9. Oddly enough, his pains all disappeared. The ribs were excellent, and nothing hurt anymore. He checked his health, and it was back at full.

"Anyone hurt? Anyone need any help?" Arthur asked.

The party looked around and checked themselves and each other. They all shook their heads.

"I would imagine that big experience boost at the end probably leveled us all up so that would have completely restored our health." Vana finally said.

That was good to know. Leveling up was an instant reset on your health and statuses. They looked around and explored the room for a minute. In the far back of the room was a long treasure chest that sat around five feet long and three-feet-wide. It was a sturdy wood, possibly oak, and it was banded in riveted iron. Arthur approached the chest and carefully lifted it. Inside was a beautiful bow that looked to be made of molten silver and under the bow was a quiver of arrows. Arthur picked up both to check them.

Delicate Silverwood Bow of Accuracy	**Attack:** 16-20 **Durability:** 130/130 **Rarity:** Rare **Quality:** Well Crafted **Weight:** 1.4 kg **Slot:** Main Hand

	Traits: A bow made of delicate Silverwood. Enchantments: ● 10% increased chance to deal a Mortal Blow.
Wildwood Quiver of Speed	**Durability**: 130/130 **Rarity**: Rare **Quality**: Well Crafted **Weight**: 1.0 kg **Slot**: Ammunition **Traits**: A wildwood quiver Enchantments: ● 10% increased firing speed with a bow
Steel Arrow	**Damage Modifier**: +3 **Durability**: 30/30 **Rarity**: Common **Quality**: Well Crafted **Weight**: 0.3 kg **Slot**: Ammunition

	Traits: Steel headed arrow with feather fletching

The haul was amazing. *What are the odds he would get exactly what they needed?* Arthur thought to himself.

"Vana, this is your lucky day. I told you I wanted to find you a good bow, and based on your final skill shot against the boss, I know you have a good base in archery, so I feel comfortable giving you this prize." Arthur told her as he handed the bow and quiver of arrows over to her. She took them reverently at first and then turned back to Arthur.

"I can't take these, Arthur. I know you could use them as well." Vana said as she started to hand them back to him.

Arthur shook his head. "No, you've earned it. You're a far better archer than I am right now and could put it to better use than I. I only ask you to save those steel arrows for an emergency or our big confrontation." Arthur told her.

"Consider it done," Vana told him seriously.

Arthur was about to close the chest when he saw something tucked into one corner. He pulled it out and saw that it was a small, folded piece of paper. He took a step over by himself and opened it.

My Dearest Arthur,

You continue to persevere, and I'm proud of your progress. Your efforts have started to show returns now. I have started to get the occasional prayer from Rowan and Daniel now, so a few people are beginning to come around. I have a feeling this number will continue to grow. Please accept these needed items as a token of my appreciation for your hard work and continue to make me proud, my champion.

Your Goddess,
Lianna

He should have known she would have had a hand in this. She had told him last time she couldn't directly hand him anything, but she could alter what he received from rewards in some locations. Leave it up to her to read his needs and throw him a bone. He determined this was an excellent time to spread the influence again. He held the note up and quickly burned it with a channeled weak flame.

You have gained 30 experience in Fire Magic for successfully casting Weak Flame.

"It seems the Goddess Lianna is the one to thank for those gifts. That was a letter from her congratulating us on our achievement and sending her best wishes with the items. It appears our party is blessed."

Each of the members looked at him with awe in their faces. Arthur explored around some more. This cave would be the perfect spot to check for minerals and ore. He knew it wasn't uncommon for dungeons in games to have hidden treasures and mining spots, so why should this be any different?

    While he went to the closest wall, he noticed the rest of the party had started gutting the cats. He put his hand up to the wall and cast his magical prospecting spell.

You have gained 300 experience in Earth Magic for successfully casting Magical Prospecting (x3).

    His first two attempts yielded nothing as he circled the room. On his third attempt, though, he found something useful but unexpected. He thought about it for a moment and used his spell to extract what was in the stone. He didn't relish the idea of swinging a pick at the wall. He still had mana to spare, anyway. He cast his Transform Stone: Gravel spell, and after some time, his rewards fell out of the wall.

You have gained 150 experience in Earth Magic for successfully casting Transform Stone: Gravel.
You have gained 700 experience in Mining and Magical Mining for finding Sapphire Chips (x35).

Sapphire Chip	**Durability**: 50/50
	Rarity: Uncommon
	Quality: Good
	Weight: 0.1 kg
	Slot: Crafting Item/Magical Reagent

	Traits: A small chip of a sapphire gemstone. It shines with a deep blue hue.

That was a good find. Arthur wasn't sure what he would use them for, but thirty-five pieces of sapphire the size of his thumbnail were sure to come in handy for something. He put them in his bag and kept going around the room. He had enough mana to cast one more prospecting spell, so he moved to the next space and cast it again but found nothing there.

You have gained 100 experience in Earth Magic for successfully casting Magical Prospecting.

Arthur had to kill some time while waiting for his mana to regenerate, so he assessed the skill points he had earned. He now had thirteen points banked, and he wasn't one that believed in saving them. That's just wasted stats that could save his life in a fight. He had already messed up and forgot to assign the first five before they faced the boss. He took a quick look at his current status.

Name: Arthur	
Level: 9	
Age: 26	
Race: Human	
HP: 230/230	
MP: 20/190	
Stamina: 230/230	

Strength: 8
Agility: 8
Intellect: 8
Wisdom: 5
Endurance: 8
Charisma: 5
Luck: 5

Experience: 1190/4600 (13 stat points available)

Skills (75% boost to any skill for level up)
Combat Skills:

Archery: 5 (1365/1900)
 - **Aim Shot:** 2 (275/750)
Block: 1 (180/500)
Dual Wield: 1 (175/500)
Identify: 1 (75/500)
Parry: 1 (100/500)
Scan: 2 (50/750)
Small Blades: 2 (575/750)
Stealth: 1 (370/500)
 - **Detect Hidden:** 1 (50/500)
Swords: 2 (285/750)
Unarmed: 1 (275/500)

Magic:

Earth Magic: 4 (1050/1400)
 - **Earthen Wall** (1)
 - **Magical Prospecting** (1)
 - **Transform Stone: Gravel** (1)
Fire Magic: 3 (120/1000)
 - **Arcane Forging** (1)
 - **Basic Firebolt** (1)
 - **Weak Flame** (1)

Professions:

	Barter: 3 (100/1000)
	 Blacksmithing: 4 (420/1000)
	  - **Alternate Heating**: 1 (160/500)
	  - **Arcane Smithing**: 1 (450/500)
	 Cooking: 2 (400/750)
	 Enchanting: 2 (240/750)
	 Farming: 5 (0/1900)
	 Firemaking: 2 (700/750)
	 Herbalism: 5 (660/1900)
	 Mining: 3 (750/1000)
	  - **Magical Mining** 3 (750/1000)
	 Skinning: 3 (500/1000)
	 Woodworking: 1 (40/500)

Looking at his sheet, Arthur thought it was time for him to specialize in his stats. He was currently spread even and balanced, but now that he had a bit of time under his belt, he needed to figure out what class would be best. A magic-related class would be a must. They had a ranger, a tank, and a caster, so that left him with the melee damage role. He decided he needed to consult with Allendria. She seemed to have a much better knowledge base being from another race of people. He hoped she would have some useful information for him.

"Allendria, can you come here for a moment?" Arthur asked her.
He watched as she approached. She had some amazing curves to her. She had a twinkle in her eye, and it looked like her adrenaline was still running incredibly high.

"Allendria, I could use some advice," Arthur told her as she got close.

"If I can offer any, I'll. What about?" Allendria told him.

"I'm to the point in my levels where I need to focus my stats into a specific fighting style and class, but I'm not familiar with many fighting styles or even classes. I'm leaning toward a melee and caster hybrid fighter, but I don't know if any are available or feasible." He explained to her.

She thought about the situation for a moment, "That would be a good option for you. Especially if we can keep together our current group." She looked to the side toward Vana and Samson, "Those two are both incredible at what they do. Vana has some amazing archery skills, and I can honestly say I haven't seen many people who could have held out as long as Samson did against that boss without a healer. Your situation is a little more complex. I know of a handful of classes that would probably work for you, but since you think a melee caster style is the best, I would suggest you focus your efforts to become a Spell Blade."

"If you think that's best. What's a Spell Blade, and what do they focus on?" Arthur asked.

“A spell blade is a melee combat fighter that focuses on bladed weapons combined with temporary weapon enchantments and combat spells. It’s common for them to wield a sword in the main hand and a dagger in the off-hand. They typically use spells that coat their blades to deal extra damage. For instance, they may coat a blade in the magic of shearing wind to make damaging wounds or coat it in electricity to shock and paralyze those they damage. They can be an absolute nightmare on the battlefield. There was even one who was a legendary figure amongst the Dark Elves. His name was Jarazian Swiftstride. He could harness the magic that would make him move at unseen speeds and slice through people before they even knew he was there.”

“That sounds perfect. Do you know what stats I need to focus on for it, and if there are any skills I need to work on for it?” Arthur asked her.

"Well, classes can be unlocked at level twenty. The process is unique for each person and depends on the class, so I can't help you much with that. What I can tell you is that a spell blade mainly focuses on magical power and speed. They rely on speed and their enhancements to their blades to deal massive amounts of damage. The dual weapon focus is something you must work on. I would suggest the sword and dagger combo since it works well. I would use your stat points to focus primarily on your Intellect and Agility. You can throw the occasional point into strength to help boost your raw blade damage, but most of it will come from the magic effects you imbue your blade with. It's also important to note that your magical enhancements as a Spell Blade will also work with any natural enchantments already on a blade, so they're stackable."

"That sounds perfect," Arthur said and then subconsciously rubbed his chest. "The only downside of melee combat is getting your shit handed to you by a giant cat." He said as he chuckled.

"So I need to work on speed and spells, which should be quite easy. Thank you so much for your help. I know I can always count on you for advice. I truly appreciate it." Arthur told her sincerely.

"Anytime. Even though this was dangerous, it sure was fun. I haven't felt this free in forever."

"Stick with me, and I'm sure we'll see much more."

"I look forward to it." She said with a wink.

Arthur turned his attention back to his stats. He followed what Allendria said. Completely ignoring the advice she had given him would be utter foolishness. With that in mind, he allocated six points into Intellect, four points into Agility, and three points into Wisdom. That should help improve his magical ability as well. He chose to also use his 75% boost for swords to help get him a little more skill. It was enough to get him to level three in swords.

Congratulations, you have reached level 3 in Swords. Swing speed with swords increased by 6%. Is this thing sharp?

His stat sheet looked much better, and he was more comfortable with his magic now. His larger mana pool would vastly help with his enchanting and spells he would need to cast for the village. Between the added mana and his regen, he could already cast more spells looking for ore, and now he had a very respectable regen rate of seventeen per minute. He was highly sure most mages would envy a regen rate that high.

He returned to where he had previously stopped and continued to sweep the room. Another three casts of prospecting later, and he discovered something that made him feel better for the village itself. He went ahead and used his Transform Stone: Gravel spell and looked at his reward.

Copper Ore	**Durability:** 30/30
	Rarity: Common

	Quality: Good **Weight:** 3.0 kg **Slot:** Crafting Item/Currency **Traits:** A chunk of copper ore. Can be used for crafting. Also serves as currency if minted into coins.

You have gained 300 experience in Earth Magic for successfully casting Magical Prospecting (x3).

You have gained 150 experience in Earth Magic for successfully casting Transform Stone: Gravel.

Congratulations, you have reached level 5 in Earth Magic. Increases the effect of your earth magic spells by 12%. Dig in that dirt!

You have gained 600 experience in Mining and Magical Mining for finding Copper Ore (x12)

Congratulations, you have reached level 4 in Mining. You have a 9% increased chance to find rare materials while mining. Just keep swinging, just keep swinging.

Congratulations, you have reached level 4 in Magical Mining. Increases the chance that items found will be a higher rarity by 9%. This should be against the law, lazy man!

"Samson! Can you come here a minute?" Arthur called over his shoulder. These bigger chunks of copper had a bit of heft to them, and they'd need to plan how they were getting this stuff out.

"What's up, Arthur?" Samson asked.

"Would you mind going back to the entrance and grabbing our cart? We don't want to have to carry all these out the entrance." Arthur said as he motioned toward the chunks of copper. "We also need to get those cats loaded up on it. I'm not sure we'll be able to fit much more on it today. We'll need to head back once we wrap up in here. It'll already be packed tremendously high, and I think the workload for getting these things skinned and boned out will certainly be bad this afternoon."

Samson nodded to him, "Of course, I'll run to go get it real quick. It's not that far away, and the cats are all gutted now."

He took off up the path at a quick jog. Arthur noticed he left the shield behind but took his sword just in case. Smart man.

Arthur cast another prospect spell while he waited. He had regenerated enough mana from the time he started this second round to add one additional prospecting spell but had no luck with it.

You have gained 100 experience in Earth Magic for successfully casting Magical Prospecting.

He walked over to chat with Vana and Allendria, who were standing by the boss cat. Vana was lovingly admiring her new bow while Allendria was chuckling about something.

"Everything good to go over here?" Arthur asked.

"Everything's perfectly fine," Allendria said with a smile. "Where did Samson run off to?"

"I asked him to run up and grab the cart, so we could get this stuff loaded. I didn't relish the idea of carrying it all back to the cave entrance. The damn cart is already going to look like something in a Dr. Seuss cartoon piled up high and tied down tight to keep the load from swaying around." Arthur chuckled to himself.

"Who's this, Dr. Seuss?" Vana asked.

"He is an author from where I come from," Arthur told them.

They seemed to shrug off that statement. Vana looked at the boss and then back at him.

"That hide should make a nice outfit."

"I plan on laying claim to a bunch of it to make me some armor and clothing. It's stunning, I'll admit." Arthur told her.

"I don't have any objection to it. Hopefully, we can put some of this plan of yours to work in the next few days. I want to get my hands on some armor. If nothing else, some sturdier clothing would be preferable." She told him.

"Don't worry about it. With the haul we've had today, we'll be spending the next few days doing nothing but work around the village. I need to get a lot of crafting done to prepare for the upcoming fight with Lord Golgara's men. Additionally, I need to get to work on the earthen wall around the village. I also have plans for some improvements to the buildings around the village to help the citizenry itself. I would also like to get a sawmill running so we can get lumber for building repairs." Arthur explained.

"Well, if nothing else, you sure do dream big. Regardless, I hope you can make it all happen. I look forward to living in a place that feels safe and prosperous." Vana said wistfully.

"It isn't just me who'll make it happen. I'm counting on you guys to help me just as much. There are plenty of things that need to be done around the village. I saw some life back in it yesterday for the first time since I had arrived and am hoping it'll get more and more lively." Arthur told them.

Samson came around the corner, pushing the cart, and they all got busy loading everything. It took all four of them to get the boss up on the cart. Arthur and Samson had to lift the cat's head and front shoulders and set it on the cart while Vana and Allendria took the rear end. They tucked the copper ore under the assorted cats and in between some of their bodies. Arthur had regenerated another 200 mana in the time it took them to load the cats, so he did a few more prospecting spells. He went to where he had previously stopped and continued to work his way around. This time it took four spells until he found something useful. His Transform Stone: Gravel spell extracted these latest contents.

You have gained 400 experience in Earth Magic for successfully casting Magical Prospecting (x4).

Congratulations, you have unlocked Mastery level 2 for Magical Prospecting. The mana cost for this spell has decreased by 5.

You have gained 150 experience in Earth Magic for successfully casting Transform Stone: Gravel.

*You have gained 350 experience in Mining
and Magical Mining for finding Raw Iron Ore
(x14).*

They also got those chunks of ore loaded
on the cart, and Arthur noticed that two of
the fourteen were exquisite quality. It
appeared his skill bonus came into play with
that a bit. He guessed that would help
increase the final product of items made with
it.

The cart completely loaded and strapped
down. It was heavy enough that Arthur and
Samson were having to take turns pushing it.
The strain of the weight was severe with that
much on it. I would kill for a good truck
right now to throw it all in. Arthur thought
to himself.

Vana took the lead and kept an eye out
for dangers. Arthur made sure she also kept
her eye out for any herbs or spices and was
pleased when she found some more wild
potatoes, carrots, radishes, and even some
garlic. Arthur halted her before she pulled
any of them up and used his new Germination
ability. Since he had thrown the point in the
talent for Cultivation, he could use it on
wild plants too. He used the skill each time
they found one of them and came out with a
bundle of seeds for each plant.

*You have gained 1600 total experience in
Farming for successfully casting Germination
(x8).*

You have gained 45 Potato Seeds.
You have gained 33 Garlic Seeds.
You have gained 42 Carrot Seeds.
You have gained 24 Radish Seeds.

Luckily, they found them far enough apart for his mana to have regenerated. They made their way out of the forest and back onto the smoother track of the road. It wasn't a very well-maintained road by any means, but it was better than weaving through the forest underbrush. Arthur and Samson were practically dead on their feet by the time they returned to the inn. Taking their turns with the cart had worn them out.

They parked the cart behind the inn and walked inside. The place was packed full for the middle of the afternoon. Arthur found Daniel and walked up to him.

"Holy shit. What the hell happened to you?" Daniel exclaimed.

"Oh, you know, just killed a bunch of night stalker cats and their boss cat. Then hauled all of their massive asses back to the village. We have them all loaded on the cart in the back. We also found more iron ore and even scrounged up some copper ore. I think I can use my magic to melt them into coins that match local currency. That should help get the monetary system back on track in the village. If nothing else, it'll help get it started. I also found a handful of vegetables for you, and I have some pouches of seeds we can use for planting."

"Well, I'll be damned if you're not a miracle worker. Give me a second, and I'll come to help you guys out." Daniel told him.

"Thank you. I'll meet you out there. We'll get the cats laid out in the back and get the vegetables brought in for you. I'll have the ore put back on the cart so that I can take it over to Rowan."

Arthur walked out the back, and they started laying the cats and the wolves out along the back wall. They took the vegetables and seeds collected inside the inn and placed them in the kitchen for Daniel to sort and then went back outside and got to work skinning. Arthur asked Vana to start with the primal cat. She had a higher Skinning skill than him, and he wanted that hide in the best shape possible. The other three started skinning the rest of the animals.

It took them two hours to finish up the skinning, and that was with Daniel coming to join them and bringing two other people who were in the inn to assist. Arthur assumed Daniel had promised them some food if they helped in the skinning.

Once all the skins had been laid out, salted, and rolled back up, they stacked them in the storage room in the inn. They had stacked the animal carcasses on the cart to keep them off the ground. They took them three at a time inside, and all got to work cutting the meat off of them. They stacked all the meat on one of the far counters in the kitchen. Arthur felt terrible for Daniel because he and his apprentices would have a lot of meat to cure and a lot of blood to clean up.

They finally got the meat off of the animals and got all of the remnants loaded back on the cart. Arthur and Allendria helped Daniel start salting down the meat and cutting some of it into smaller bits for stews while Vana and Samson took the carcasses out to the edge of the forest to dump.

When they returned with the cart, Arthur excused himself and loaded the cart back up with the ore they had found. He took the cart over to Rowan and saw the man still working hard. It looked like the man had shifted from iron nails to iron arrowheads. He wasn't about to question him, though.

He was a blacksmith by trade and knew what the village needed more than he did. Arthur stopped the cart and waved to Rowan. He started unloading the raw iron ore into the shop where Rowan had stacked the metal last time. There was still a little left from their previous trip, but his apprentices must have been working hard because most of them were gone, and the stack of iron ingots had grown.

He had just finished unloading the last chunk of iron when Rowan finished what he had been working on and approached him. Arthur showed him the copper ore on the cart.

"Do me a favor and set this somewhere safe, will you? I plan on using my magic to try to mold this into some copper currency to help get the village up and running a little faster. I don't think it'll be of much use for crafting anytime soon, so I think that's the best use for now." Arthur told him.

"I agree. I have a safe spot in the back of one of the rooms here that I can store it in. It will keep anyone from messing with it until you can get around to it." He told him.

"I appreciate it. How did things go here today?" Arthur asked.

"It went pretty smoothly. I was able to make around five hundred iron nails, so I shifted my work to do some iron arrowheads as well. I knew we would need them eventually." Rowan said.

"I appreciate the forethought there. That gives me an idea, though. Can you bring all of those nails out real quick? I'm guessing you have them in some kind of bucket?" Arthur asked.

"Yeah, just a second." Rowan walked into the shop and brought out a bucket full of iron nails. Arthur smiled and hoped this was going to work. He accepted the completion for both of the orders of nails he had assigned to Rowan already and immediately recreated the order and reassigned them to him. As soon as that happened, he accepted it again and repeated this three more times until he had assigned ten of these work orders to Rowan and acknowledged all ten for completion.

Rowan's eyes bulged slightly as he was sure the man was just sent a mini flood of experience for this. Arthur was thrilled because it meant that the items could keep getting turned in as quickly as they were assigned. So long as the same things had not been redeemed, of course. This should work for anyone. Some people could immensely benefit from this — the tanner and Daniel for example. Daniel would be quite harder since the food had to be accepted for completion before him handing it out for someone to eat, but they could give all the hides to the tanner, and when they brought them back, he could keep reassigning work orders as they were handed in until he accepted them all. That would prevent them from having to wait so long between turn-ins and work being completed. Arthur just needed to put out the word to the people.

Arthur put the cart back where Rowan usually kept it and bid Rowan farewell. It was getting late in the evening from all of their travels today, and he was exhausted. Entering the inn led him into the evening crowd. He couldn't be sure, but he thought half the village must be in here eating. It was always a plus to see everyone together. A few people came up to him and handed in some work orders, so he reassigned them to new ones. He didn't have time to mess with anything else because he was dead tired. He walked to the back and took a quick bath in the old washtub. He cheated and used a bit of his weak flame to warm the water.

You have gained 30 experience in Fire Magic for successfully casting Weak Flame.

He got himself as clean as he could with
a quick scrub and made his way to his room.
His shirt and boots came off before he passed
smooth out on his bed.

Chapter 23

A Wall to Build

Arthur woke up the next morning, feeling great. He made his way downstairs and saw the inn was once again crowded with people. The crowd was full of energy as he made his way through visiting with people. Corianne's presence in the room was a relief. He walked up to her to discuss the hide situation.

"Hello, Corianne. How are you today?" Arthur asked.

"I'm doing good. I should have your first set of skins ready today." She told him.

"That's fabulous news. As a matter of fact, I wanted to ask you about your process. If you did a lot of skins at once, would it slow you down any, or is a lot of your work only wait time?"

"I can do a lot all at once. Each one requires a bit of prep time before it can undergo the tanning process, but all in all, it would take about the same time for a whole group." She explained.

"Even better. I found out yesterday that I can rapidly assign and accept work orders for completed work all at one time. For instance, if I wanted to hand over a large bundle of furs to you and have you tan them all at the same time I can create multiple small work orders and you can hand them in as I accept them, or I can just assign one work order for all of them. As long as the skins have never been turned in for a work order, I can accept them as payment. I want to give you all of our hides so you can get all of them going at once. I have one special hide that might take a bit longer, but it's for me." Arthur told her.

"I can agree with that. I want to build up a large influx since the time won't take me any longer. What do you have for me to work with?" Corianne asked.

"I have six Timber Wolf furs, eight Night Stalker hides, and a Primal Night Stalker hide. The Primal is for me. I also have an assortment of smaller hides. I can give them all to you after you finish up your meal here."

"That's a lot of hides to take care of, but I look forward to the challenge." She told him.

"I look forward to getting the ones you need to turn in today. We're going to get to work on some fur clothing and leather armor." He told her.
He waved to her as he walked away from the table. Arthur decided now was a good time to address everyone in the room. He went to the bar and turned to face the crowd.

"Can I have everyone's attention, please?" Arthur yelled.

Everyone around started to quiet down. Arthur took a quick scan of all of them and continued.

"Ladies and Gentlemen, I appreciate all of your hard work to help bring this village back to life. We still need a lot of resources but are quickly working on getting what we need. I know many of you have been doing work orders already. I want to explain something about them. You can stockpile items to turn in. I can create custom work orders for you to turn in for larger amounts of the items, or I can keep assigning the same order over and over and accepting them as you hand them to me. The only stipulation is that the items can't have been turned in for any other work order. I also encourage people that have trade goods of other kinds to approach me about it. If it's something I think will benefit the village, I have no problem creating a work order on the spot so you can turn it in. Everyone keep up the good work and don't hesitate to approach me if you have any questions."

Arthur waved everyone back to their food and went off in search of Daniel. He found the man in the back tending to a big pot of boiling stew. Both of his apprentices were scurrying around gathering items and cutting up vegetables and meat to add to the food.

"That was a rather rousing speech." Daniel joked.

"I do try. How are things going for you?" Arthur asked.

"I'm busier now than I've been in months. I'm not sure whether I should thank you or curse you." He told him.

"I'm sure it's probably a bit of both. Need any help with anything here? I think I'll focus on getting the wall started outside the village today. I increased my mana pool a decent amount since I leveled up twice yesterday, so I plan on putting it to good use." Arthur told him.

"That sounds far more important than anything I could ask you to do around here. Good luck with that. Do you have a few minutes, though?" Daniel asked.

"Of course, what do you need?"

"I heard your speech, and I have a large pot of stew here that's ready to serve. Could you get us the experience for it?"

"Sure, let me get the original work orders for your apprentices turned in first."

He had both of the apprentices serve up their meals and accepted theirs.

"How about I assign one work order for the whole pot and give it to you? Then the next one I assign to one of the girls and so on. It's easier than one meal at a time and would give you large batches of experience." Arthur explained.

"That sounds perfect."

"How many servings of soup do you think are in that pot?" Arthur asked.

Daniel eyed it for a moment and told him, "I think there are around fifty in there."

Arthur thought about it and created a work order for a cauldron of stew with fifty servings in it. He assigned it to Daniel and then accepted its completion. Daniels's eyes widened a bit, and a smile crept on his face.

"I'll be damned if that wasn't a good amount of experience. Thank you. That even helped me get a level."

"Glad I could help. Let me know when the next fresh pot is ready and which girl will be getting it. I have to head out and get to work."

Arthur made his way back through the inn and out the front door. Allendria was waiting for him outside the front of the building. She approached him and waved.

"What's the plan for the day?"

"I plan on getting to work on the defenses today. You're free to do whatever you want. I don't think you have earth magic, so I doubt you can help." Arthur told her.

"Do you mind if I tag along, anyway? I have nothing that needs to be done here, and although the village is coming back from the edge of death, they're still not very warm to me yet." She explained.

"I would never turn down your company Allendria. I just don't want you to feel as if I'm bossing you around. I still want you to do things you want to do. I might need your help and advice from time to time."

"I truly appreciate it. This is what I would like to do, though, so let's go. We have a long day ahead of us… well, at least you do." She said with a chuckle.

Arthur didn't want to continue that conversation because he knew, in the end, she would still win the quip war. They both strutted down the road that led them northeast out of the village. That was the general direction the bandits were suspected of coming down, so he wanted to start his work there. He would need to start on each side of the road and see if there was any way he could make some kind of gatehouse. He wasn't sure he could accomplish it, but if he could at least get the sides up, they might use some wood and stones to make a makeshift top.

They made their way about two hundred yards out of the village and decided it was far enough to start the wall. Arthur was hoping they could grow this village into something truly remarkable, so he wanted to make sure they had enough room to expand inside the walls. Although he wasn't sure, this was the best plan. Starting closer to the village would help finish the wall a little faster. They could always build another wall further out in the future, but he wanted to do it right the first time.

He determined that he wanted the walls to be six feet tall. He genuinely wanted them ten feet or higher, but he knew that the walls would not be strong enough, structurally, made of dirt at that height. He would have to wait for the ability to work with stone. He created the bottom section of the walls by using three earthen wall spells side by side. He needed the base wider to hold the weight as the structure got taller. Due to this, he added another layer to the base for strength.

He was now looking at a section of the wall that was three feet deep, two-feet-tall, and three-feet-wide. Arthur thought it was a rather respectable-looking base. He finished this section by doing two layers, two spells deep, and topping it off with one-layer of Earthen Wall. This would give him a piece of wall that's base was three foot deep, and it slimmed to one foot wide at the top. It wasn't a perfect wall, but it would be a way to delay people. The best part is he could always easily add layers on the back in a step fashion to increase its strength, and once he was able to use stone, he could stack stone in the same manner and even leave the original dirt wall inside for solidity. He decided to hold off on worrying about his talent points.

This first section of the wall ended up costing him 240 mana total. That was for one three-foot part. At that pace, he would never finish this wall. It took him about ten minutes to get it all laid out, so he had already regenerated around 170 mana. This would be a slow process. He laid a base for a more significant part of the wall and started laying out where the wall would go. He determined he would do a single spell and link them together to form a short foot tall section. Once he had the wall laid out for a distance, he could regenerate some mana and lay another layer beside it until he finished each piece of the wall. He was able to get nine more Earthen Wall spells cast in an unbroken line away from his original finished piece. It was a twenty-seven-foot span along the field that was only a foot tall and a foot deep, but it gave him a sense of accomplishment.

You have gained 540 experience in Earth Magic for successfully casting Earthen Wall (x9).
Congratulations, you have reached level 6 in Earth Magic. Increases the effect of your earth magic spells by 15%. Not tired of this skill yet?
Congratulations, you have unlocked Mastery Level 2 for Earthen Wall. The mana cost for this spell has decreased by 5.

That was more welcome news. Arthur wasn't entirely sure what affected the mastery level of a spell but was sure it had something to do with the number of times he'd used it. He wouldn't complain about the spell cost being reduced because it would help him cast even more spells.

He looked around the area and admired some of his surroundings. The place itself seemed quite barren with yellow grasses everywhere. He hoped this was the dry season, and this place was in the dead of summer. It would be nice to see it lush and green. He turned to Allendria, who'd been watching him and admired her. She was looking toward the forest to the south of them. The sun on her face perfectly reflected in her eyes. Her hair was stunning as the dull grey shimmered in the sun.

"Allendria," Arthur called to her.

She turned to look at him. "Yes, Arthur?"

"I hope you don't mind me asking, but would you tell me a bit more about yourself? I know you're only here to repay a debt and settle an agreement between us, but I would still like to know you better. It's also a pleasant way to pass the time while I wait for my mana to regenerate." Arthur said.

"Oh, so now I'm just a way to kill time for you, huh? Is that all you see in me? Is all I'm good at throwing fireballs and wasting downtime?" She said to him with heat in her voice.

Arthur stumbled for a second and stuttered out his first few words, "No… of course not… I didn't mean to upset you, Allendria I just truly wanted to chat." He blurted. She looked at him for a moment with a fierce look on her face, and then a huge smile slowly crept onto her face, and she burst out laughing.

"I'm sorry, Arthur. I couldn't help but do that. It was too good a chance to pass up. Of course, you can ask me anything you want."

"Remind me never to upset you truly. Your mock anger was bad enough. I just wanted to know why you were in the forest alone when we found you, and once you were saved, why didn't you want to return home?"

She looked disturbed for a moment and let out a sigh. "I suppose it won't hurt to tell you some of the stories, at least. My uncle is a cruel man. The Dark Elves have been going through some very rough political infighting recently, and it has caused much stress on our people. My uncle has been trying to influence this to favor him pitting him directly against my father and I. I fled because my uncle had all but secured his victory, and I knew it would spell bad tidings for me. I don't wish to go back to how things are there now."

"Is there anything I can do to help? I know I have little to offer in this small village, but I'll help if I can." Arthur told her honestly.

"I appreciate the thought Arthur, but you're correct in saying it isn't much you could offer. Right now, you're doing exactly what I need from you. You are giving me a place to be with a purpose. I have needed this more than anything." She told him.

Arthur decided he would go for broke here and take a shot. Taking a step toward her, he reached out and tucked a stray section of her hair behind her delicate left ear and whispered to her, "If you ever need a knight in shining armor, I'll be there for you."

The idea of going in for a kiss was dismissed. Arthur didn't want things to go wrong if it wasn't received well, so instead, he reached down, grabbed her hand, and placed a gentle kiss on the back of it.

Her skin turned a color shade Arthur wasn't sure was possible in what he could only assume was a blush. The purple color of her skin marked with a flush of red turned her an almost magenta color. She lowered her eyes and told him, "Thank you, Arthur. I might take you up on that offer one day."

The feel of her hand in his made his heart soar, and he didn't want that feeling to end. Instead of making a fatal mistake, he started to walk around the area slowly, but he kept her hand in his as they walked.

He pointed out different locations and his ideas for different places and what he wanted to do with the village. They had been walking around for a while when, surprisingly, he realized he was back to full mana again. He hadn't even realized it because the time had flown by with Allendria.

They made their way back to the area he had started, and he turned to her and asked her to give him a moment, and they would resume their trip. He started laying the single line on the other side of the road with his current mana, so he set about walking the meandering path the wall would take while he cast his spells. With the time it took him, he could get a full twenty-two earthen wall spells off before he was out of mana again.

You have gained 1320 experience in Earth Magic for successfully casting Earthen Wall (x22).

Arthur was thrilled about the idea of accessing talent points for his Earth Magic now that he had even more of them, but when he turned and looked at Allendria, her smile made all thoughts of that fly out the window. He decided that he could wait because he wasn't going to lose the chance to spend time with this beauty alone. She already had her hand out toward him as he approached her, so he took it quickly, and they resumed their casual stroll.

They talked about little things here and there. Arthur learned a few details about the Dark Elves, most of it revolving around their aggressive and magical nature. Allendria had a younger sister, and her mother had died a few years before. Arthur told her about being an orphan but being adopted by a kind family who treated him like their flesh and blood son. He spoke about some of his adventures as a kid but was careful to avoid anything that might give away the fact he wasn't from this world.

Quicker than he expected, he was back to full mana again. They went back to the wall he had worked on last time and connected a second row to the first one to make the wall two-foot deep now. He did this for another full twenty casts of the spell.

You have gained 1200 experience in Earth Magic for successfully casting Earthen Wall (x20).
Congratulations, you have reached level 7 in Earth Magic. Increases the effect of your earth magic spells by 18%. What is your obsession with dirt?

They once again resumed their trek and went right back into their conversation. Arthur was feeling on top of the world, getting to spend his day with the enchanting beauty. He almost felt bad that it would eventually come to an end, but he resolved to make the most of it while he had it. With his incredible regeneration rate, he could recover his entire mana pool in about twenty minutes. They spent another half-hour visiting and then went back to the wall once more. He did the final row for the foundation of this part of the wall. He walked through for another twenty casts of Earthen Wall, and the bottom layer was complete. It was three foot deep, one foot tall, and sixty-feet long. It was a remarkable feat for an hour worth of work. He was admiring the job when he checked the experience and an idea dawned on him.

You have gained 1200 experience in Earth Magic for successfully casting Earthen Wall (x20).

There was no reason that he couldn't also benefit from the work order system. He was sure it rarely happened in larger cities. They probably hired someone to work in an administrative position to do this work and didn't expect them ever to do any of the work themselves. He should be able to make work orders for himself and turn them in just as he had for the others. He could take advantage of the loophole he discovered yesterday as well and turn in items he had already completed. He had two open slots in work orders since he hadn't reassigned the cooking orders for Daniel's group. He made one work order for himself to test it out real quick.

Work Order	
Completion Criteria: Complete a foundation layer for 5 sections of the wall around the village. The part must measure a minimum of three-foot deep, one foot tall, and three-foot-wide.	Provided Materials: Materials to be provided by a person fulfilling the order.
Completion Timeline: 5 Days	Rewards: 1 Meal token to be used at the Village Inn. 500 Earth Magic Experience. 300 Character Experience.

As before, he had only filled out the criteria and the base reward of one token. He had hoped the rewards would be higher for the experience if the requirements and rewards were different. He was not disappointed. With the compensation being set so low, it allowed the system to compensate with higher than typical experience rewards. That order was accepted as well as three others just like it.

Congratulations, you have completed the Work Order: Wall Base for Alem's Crossing for the following rewards: 4 Meal Tokens, 2000 Earth Magic Experience, and 1200 Character Experience. (x4).
Congratulations, you have reached level 8 in Earth Magic. Increases the effect of your earth magic spells by 21%. You still here?

Wow, what a rush. That was an insane amount of experience for such a short amount of time. This should give him a fantastic chance to get ahead of things in the limited time they had left. He also decided it was time to check on the skill tree for Earth Magic. He could ignore something that could give him a considerable boost.

You have 8 unused Talent points.

Talent	Description
Tier 1	
Earthen Will (0/5)	Increases effectiveness of Earth Magic spells by 5%

Talent	Description
Solid Foundations (0/5)	*Strengthens the spell Earthen Wall and allows it to hold 15% more weight per point before becoming unstable.*
Earthen Focus (0/5)	*Decreases the resistance of Earth Magic when using a material not touching the earth by 15%*

Well, there wasn't much thought needed behind this decision for him. One option seemed tailored for exactly what he was doing. He dropped two points in Solid Foundations and then checked to see what Tier 2 options came up for him.

You have 6 unused Talent Points.

Talent	**Description**
Tier 2	
Hard as Stone (0/1)	*This ability will temporarily increase the hardness of your skin for one minute. You gain the following buffs from it:* *• 15% decreased damage taken by physical attacks* *• 15% increased strength* *• Edged weapons are 40% less likely to penetrate your skin.*

	Cost: 50 Mana Cooldown: 3 Hours
Earth Commune (0/1)	*Enter a meditative state and become one with the Earth increasing your health and mana regen by 100%. You may enter and leave this state at any time, but once used, there is a 1-hour cooldown before it can be used again.*
(Hidden Ability) Transform Earth: Stone (0/1) *This ability will only become available if you have the following prerequisites:* • *Earth Magic > Level 5* • *Fire Magic > Level 2* • *Have learned at least one combination spell*	*This will teach you the combination spell Transform Earth: Stone. This spell will turn a desired section of earth measuring one foot deep by one foot wide, by one foot tall to solid stone.* *Cost: 40 Mana*

"Fuck Yea!" Arthur exclaimed as he saw the Tier 2 options. Who would have guessed there were hidden talents that didn't show up without specific criteria met? Allendria heard Arthur and came over to investigate.

"What happened?" She asked.

"I discovered a hidden talent in my Earth Magic skill tree, and it also happened to show me how an earth mage can transform the dirt into stone." He told her with glee.

"I didn't even know there were hidden talents. What do you mean by a hidden talent?" Allendria asked.

"Well, one of my second tier skills has a label stating hidden skill and the requirements you need to have for it to show." He said.

"Well, that would explain why few people find it. Having a wide range of magics can be difficult to obtain, and I only know a handful of people who would've discovered combination magic. I can only guess at that because it's so tightly guarded. I can't be sure that's what they have learned. Secrets like that tend to stay with a master once they discover it, and it isn't uncommon for them to never teach it." She told him.

"That sounds like a complete waste of knowledge. Is there no repository of spell knowledge people can use to learn these things?" Arthur asked.

"There are a handful of magical schools around, but they teach nothing but the bare basic spells in each element. None of them teach advanced spells or techniques. That's something you can only learn by apprenticing yourself to a powerful master and hoping he will be generous enough to pass down any knowledge."

"That seems like another thing to add to my list. I must set up some kind of magical school here eventually and make sure we teach the students everything we can collectively learn. If we can discover some of these secrets and get them out, it'll be amazing what can be accomplished in this world." Arthur said with resolve.

Arthur saw a flash of what looked like admiration in Allendria's eyes.

"What?" he asked her as she looked at him.

She shook her head slightly. "Nothing, you just remind me a bit of my father. He has felt the same as you do but has never been able to put the ideas into action. The people who rely on the old ways of thinking always block him when they can. That's the reason he and his brother had their original split and what caused the separate factions." She said sadly.

"Well, we can do it the right way here," Arthur said with cheer. Allendria nodded her head at that and went silent for a bit. She appeared lost in thought, so he decided it was time to assign some points. He knew for a fact the spell to transform into stone was one choice he would make, but there were still five more points since the talent tree had been ignored since level five. He took the Hard as Stone skill and also put two more points into Solid Foundations in addition to learning Transform Earth: Stone. He held on to the last 2 points for now.

Transform Earth: Stone

Requirements: Fire Magic and Earth Magic Mana Cost: 40 MP Cast Time: 10 seconds	Description: Transforms a wall of earth into stone that's 1'x1'x3'.
Mastery Level: 1	

Arthur wanted to give the spell a shot. He had recovered his mana again and went back to the section closest to the wall to cast the spell three more times to transform the first section of the wall foundation into stone.

You have gained 240 experience in Earth Magic and Fire Magic for successfully casting Combination Spell: Transform Earth: Stone. (x3)

Arthur walked around the section to admire his work. The part was now one substantial chunk of stone around three-feet-deep, one foot tall, and three-feet-wide. Arthur was thrilled with this piece. If he could get the wall made of stone instead, it would be infinitely better. With the ability to use stone, it should allow the chance to build a proper gatehouse with a few intelligent applications. He experimented with this idea. If he knew the way to make an earthen wall and also knew the way to turn it into stone, there should be no reason he couldn't do both things at the same time.

He cast the Transform Earth: Stone spell one more time on the piece of foundation next to him, but this time he paid very close attention to exactly how the spell functioned. His magic allowed him to know how to do the elements of the spell instinctively, but he wanted to see the change so he could incorporate it into his new spell. The granular structure shifted as he watched the spell complete, and it gave him an idea of how to adjust his spell to match.

You have gained 80 experience in Earth Magic and Fire Magic for successfully casting Combination Spell: Transform Earth: Stone.

"I think I can save myself some time and speed up this whole process. I'll discover the spell to make a stone wall instead of these earthen ones." Arthur told her.

"I think that would be a good investment. I'm sure the spell will be more costly, but it will still cost less than doing the whole thing in dirt and then transforming it all into stone. You might not get as far with the stone wall as you would with dirt, but it'll be much sturdier." Allendria said.

"I'll take that chance. I need a few minutes to recover my mana. I want to make sure I'm full mana before I attempt this new spell." Arthur said. She nodded, and they sat on the ground and just relaxed until his mana had recovered.

He got back to his feet and got to work. He concentrated on the first section he had turned to stone, and this time increased the size he would use as a standard. He started by raising an area of dirt on top of the existing section of stone. He wasn't quite sure how that worked, but he wasn't going to question it.

He stretched his base size of this and kept moving it to be broader. His eyes continuously scanned his mana amount. He didn't want to use more than a third of it for the dirt work because he knew the transformation took a bit more mana. When he started nearing his mana threshold, he smoothed the edges of his work and cut in the corners.

He had made a section of dirt that was two-feet-deep, two-feet-high, and eight-feet-long. This was drastically better, and before he let go of the spell, he started weaving fire magic into it and forcing the change he knew it needed. Starting at the bottom, the dirt began to change to stone slowly, and the magic kept moving upward and out further from the corner he started on. As the transformation crawled up the rock, Arthur got distracted by watching Allendria. Before he could fix the error, his mana dropped out, and the spell failed.

Arthur brought in a big breath and let out a heavy sigh.

"I got distracted and failed the spell." He told Allendria dejectedly.

"Do you think you had enough mana to complete it otherwise? If so, we can wait a while longer, and you can complete it." She told him with a smile.

"I'm sure I could have done it. Just need to focus better."

"Let's just give it some time, and you can try again," she told him in a soothing tone.

They waited for about twenty minutes, and he attempted it again in the same manner. This time he maintained his focus and received a welcome notification.

Congratulations, you have discovered the Combination Spell: Raise Stone Wall. You have gained 250 experience in Earth Magic and Fire Magic for discovering a known spell.

You have gained 90 experience in Earth Magic and Fire Magic for successfully casting Combination Spell: Raise Stone Wall.

Raise Stone Wall	
Requirements: Fire Magic and Earth Magic Mana Cost: 50 MP Cast Time: 10 seconds	Description: Creates a 2' x 2' x 8' wall of stone from the ground.
Mastery Level: 1	

These combination spells would be an excellent way for him to level two skills at once. This would also save him some time and effort. Being able to spend 50 mana to get all the work done at once would be a great advantage. It took him 120 mana just to cast the spells to raise an earthen wall, and that was only six feet long instead of the new eight-foot he just unlocked.

    This spell was invaluable since it would
also cost an additional 240 mana to transform
that small section to stone. Arthur was
immensely thankful that Allendria had told him
that the base size of a spell is equal to the
extent you discovered the magic. His much
larger mana pool and higher intellect also
helped him achieve this larger base size.
    "Well, we are in business." He told
Allendria.
    "That was pretty impressive." She told
him. "I was watching the whole thing, so I
knew you had discovered it. Hopefully, the
mana cost of this new spell is much more cost-
effective than your old way of doing things."
    "Infinitely so. I can only cast around
seven of these before I'm out of mana, but
that'll span sixty-three feet of length and be
slightly over two-foot-tall and two-foot-deep
when you add in my bonuses. I also plan to
make a gatehouse here. I'm going to do it
first. I want to see how this new skill works.
I think the stone melding will work overhead
as long as I focus on keeping the dirt in
place until it transforms. The trick will be
spanning the distance."
    Arthur walked back to where the road was.
He went to the side; he had already been
working with the stone on and figured he could
get started here. Discovering this new spell
could be cast directly over areas that already
had an earthen wall present, enabled him to
save time converting the old sections. He
decided he would have to make the wall deeper,
too. Three-feet was a bare minimum for an
earthen wall and honestly would only barely
deter someone from entering.

Now that he could make stone, he needed the wall to be a minimum of four feet deep. He could always add to it later. He cast one more spell on the base to add a one-foot section to stretch it to four feet wide. It also lifted it to two-feet-high. He then cast the same spell on the other side to give him an even chunk of stone that was four-feet-deep, two-feet-tall, and nine-feet-long.

He then cast the spell four more times to keep the wall four-feet-deep and eight-feet-wide, but it also raised it to six-feet-high.

It was now time for him to regenerate his mana once again. He walked around with Allendria, and they discussed the need for the gatehouse. Arthur wanted it to be at least ten feet high for the entryway, which meant he would have to raise the walls to twelve feet so he could have at least a two-foot thick top on the doorway.

He supposed he could leave the top open, but why bother? They chatted away the time, and Arthur walked back to his current section. He cast the spell six more times and watched the wall shift from six-feet-tall to a towering twelve-feet-tall.

He was happy with this part of the wall and decided that it was time to work on the other side of the road. They had to kill more time until he regained his mana and then returned to the wall. He did the same thing as last time and cast the spell six times to get it halfway done, and then he waited for the regen and cast another six times.

You have gained 2160 experience in Earth Magic and Fire Magic for successfully casting Combination Spell: Raise Stone Wall (x24).

The wall was looking fantastic on each side of the road now. Granted, it didn't span very far away, but Arthur would make the rest of the wall only six feet tall as he went around the village. That would let him do roughly nine-feet of the wall every half hour or so. He at least hoped he could get this side of the village surrounded before the gang showed up. He also used the two talent points he had saved. Reflecting, he didn't think holding onto them was a good idea.

He hadn't unlocked the third tier yet, so he still had the same options to choose from in his Earth Magic. He dumped one point into Solid Foundations bringing it to 5/5, and the bonus jumped to 75%. He also put one point into Earthen Will. He then looked at the Fire Talent tree.

You have 2 unused Talent Points.

Talent	Description
Tier 1	
Furious Fire (0/5)	Increases effectiveness of Fire Magic spells by 5%

Superheating (0/3)	Decreases the base mana cost of Arcane Forging spell by 5 mana per rank.
Flame Blade (0/1)	Ability that creates a blade of pure fire that's two-foot-long for 30 seconds. The blade deals damage based on Intellect. (Base damage = 0.75 x Intellect) Cost: 25 Mana Cooldown: 2 Hours

There were some good options in there, and he seriously considered getting the Flame Blade, if for no other reason than he wanted to be a Sith Lord with a red lightsaber. He chose the option that would probably be best for the village and decided to put a point in Superheating.

You have 1 unused Talent Point.

Talent	Description
Tier 2	
Power of Flame (0/6)	You gain a deeper knowledge of the Flame. This ability decreases the required mana for your fire spells by 5%. For every two ranks, you also gain 1 Intellect.

Fan the Flames (0/5)	*This ability increases damage done by your offensive fire spells by 5% per rank.*

Arthur liked the new options but spent the second point in Superheating as well. That would be the most beneficial in the short term. He was also sure that this wall would get him numerous skill points by the time he finished it. He knew he would burn mana like crazy for the next few weeks.

His mana had returned yet again, so he wanted to give the gate a top. The trick would be how he would do it. The span across the road was left at a respectable sixteen feet to make sure any large carts could get through without issues. His spell would only cover eight feet of it at a time, and he knew the stone would snap off at the wall if he tried to let it hang free.

He decided he would have to cast the first spell and then use his raw earth power to support the weight while he proceeded with the second spell and fused it solidly between the two. He cast the first spell, and as soon as it completed, he pushed out his will to hold the edge of the stone.

While he burned raw mana holding the stone in place, he started the next cast and stretched the piece from the other side and fused them in the center. He then did the same thing to the backside and ended up with a top part of the gate that was sixteen-feet across and a little over two-feet-high. It covered the full four-foot width of the wall as well.

He was rather pleased with how it looked. It was a smooth dark gray stone and was somewhat intimidating. If they could get some wooden doors made for it and installed, they'd be set.

You have gained 360 experience in Earth Magic and Fire Magic for successfully casting Combination Spell: Raise Stone Wall (x4).

Arthur gave himself another boost, and this time set a work order to create a stone gatehouse for the village. He made the dimensions match what he had already created and finished the order. Once again, he listed himself as the supplier of the materials and only one token as the reward. The rewards were astounding.

Congratulations, you have completed the Work Order: Stone Gatehouse for Alem's Crossing for the following rewards: 1 Meal Token, 1500 Earth Magic Experience, 1500 Fire Magic Experience, and 750 Character Experience.
Congratulations, you have reached level 9 in Earth Magic. Increases the effect of your earth magic spells by 24%. Beautiful looking stones you have.
Congratulations, you have reached level 6 in Fire Magic. Fire Magic spells now have a 15% increased effect. Doubt thou the stars are fire?

That was an incredible reward. Arthur supposed it was a lot of magic, though. It meant he couldn't turn in the wall sections on either side of the road that made up the gatehouse, and its large dimensions were probably a significant factor for the immense rewards. With the gatehouse in place, he decided just to spend time with Allendria and keep casting spells as possible.

They spent the next four hours chatting and casting spells as needed. After Arthur finished casting all the spells and completed all the sections, he created one work order to encompass them all. He performed eight sets of these spells resulting in a wall that was eighty-feet-long. His Earth Magic bonus didn't seem like much with each spell, but when you added a bunch of them together, the inches you gained with each spell added up quickly.

You have gained 4320 experience in Earth Magic and Fire Magic for successfully casting Combination Spell: Raise Stone Wall (x48).

Congratulations, you have reached levels 7 and 8 in Fire Magic. Fire Magic spells now have a 21% increased effect. Life is the fire that burns.

Congratulations, you have reached level 10 in Earth Magic. Increases the effect of your earth magic spells by 27%. Can't even dig for shiny metals? Spice it up a bit?

Congratulations, you have unlocked Mastery Level 2 for Raise Stone Wall. The mana cost for this spell has decreased by 10.

Congratulations, you have completed the Work Order: Stone Wall for Alem's Crossing for the following rewards: 1 Meal Token, 1800 Earth Magic Experience, 1800 Fire Magic Experience, and 900 Character Experience.

Eighty-feet wasn't a very long span, but it looked impressive with a wall that was six feet of solid, seamless stone. If nothing else, he was sure it would intimidate the shit out of the enemies they expected.

The sheer amount of experience he gained from keeping his work order criteria at large dimensions while keeping rewards low was a great way for him to boost his skills. He would have to let Daniel and Rowan know about it. They may wish to sacrifice token rewards for more significant skill experience too.

"I appreciate you spending the day with me today. I know it was probably very boring, but it was good to have someone to visit with." Arthur told Allendria.

"I didn't mind at all, Arthur. It was nice to have a day to just to walk and talk. Having some time with no real worries is nice." She told him.

They joined hands and made their way back to the village. It was already the middle of the afternoon, but Arthur knew he still had plenty to do. As they walked toward Alem's Crossing, he glanced over at Allendria's smiling face and determined he wasn't worried about whatever needed to be done. This had been one of the best days he'd ever had.

Chapter 24

The Toil of a Village

Arthur and Allendria returned to the village and were greeted by a hustle of activity. The whole place seemed to be alive. Arthur stopped at the edge as they approached. This village would need to work toward increasing its quality and level. To do that, they had some items on their list to accomplish. Arthur decided now was a good time to do some work.

The road situation would be the easiest to improve. Now that Arthur understood the magic behind transforming stone, he could make a fantastic road in the village.

He initially thought about making a solid stone road through the village as they walked, but decided against it. If it were solid stone, there'd be a good chance it would end up wearing smooth and become slippery. Instead, he made the road in a cobblestone style. He could use his magic to create larger pieces of stone and put finely ground gravel, bonded together, in between them to form a functional and elegant road.

He told Allendria to hold up for a second because he was going to try a new spell. He poured his focus into his Earth Magic and used it to follow a section of the road in front of them. To anyone looking, it appeared as though a wave of fresh gravel and dirt was sweeping away from Arthur and smoothing into a perfectly flat road that was slightly taller than the surrounding ground.

When he reached what he thought was the maximum distance possible, he weaved his fire magic into the power. A wave of Fire Magic rolled over the earth and started transforming it into the stone pattern envisioned. It reminded him of when he was using his Arcane Smithing. When he started, it was just a rough dirt and gravel road that was slightly elevated, but as soon as the wave of magic passed by, it turned into the perfect cobblestone pattern. He let the power fade as the spell completed and sagged a bit. He looked up with pride in his vision as he received a new spell.

Congratulations, you have discovered the Combination Spell: Raise Cobblestone Street. You have gained 250 experience in Earth Magic and Fire Magic for discovering a known spell.
You have gained 80 experience in Earth Magic and Fire Magic for successfully casting Combination Spell: Raise Cobblestone Street.

Raise Cobblestone Street	
Requirements: Fire Magic and Earth Magic Mana Cost: 40 MP Cast Time: 10 seconds	Description: Creates a slightly elevated stretch of road that's 30′ x 4″ x 10′.
Mastery Level: 1	

The spell was pretty nice for the distance he made it cover. With the magic that included that much space, he could fix the roads in the village without too much trouble. He was drained of mana from discovering that new spell, but he could put it to good use before long. Rowan would be ideal for him to bounce some ideas off of, though.

With that thought in mind, he and Allendria made their way toward the blacksmith. They were pleased to see people out in the streets and even received some smiles and waves. The changes had been slow coming, but they were finally starting to show. They had done little more than get them some food so far, and they had already turned things around. Arthur couldn't wait to see how they reacted when he started making improvements.

As they approached the blacksmith, Arthur was surprised to see Daniel talking to Rowan at the shop. This worked in Arthur's favor since he also needed to discuss plans with Daniel. The problem was so many areas of the village needed his attention that it was almost impossible to keep up with. He approached the two men with a friendly wave.

"Hey guys, what's going on up here?" he asked.

"Oh, just talking to Rowan about where to focus our attention on the village," Daniel told him.

"Then I arrived just in time. I also wanted to discuss the same thing. I've been out working on the wall this morning. I'm happy to report we now have a twelve-foot tall stone gatehouse and about eighty-feet of the stone wall that's six feet tall." Arthur told them.

"Wait, stone? How did you manage a stone wall? Not only that, but it sure is a large amount of work for just over half a day." Daniel said.

"I gained some levels in Earth Magic and discovered a talent that taught me how to transform them into stone. I was able to use this new knowledge to discover a new spell to do it all at once." Arthur told them.

"Damn, man, what are you going to do next? Tame a unicorn or something?" Daniel said with a laugh.

"Are there any around? I might give it a shot." Arthur said with a smile.

Daniel shook his head. "We're trying to come up with some major priorities for what we needed before our upcoming confrontation. We know the basic necessity of food but, with what you guys brought in yesterday, we are pretty set on it for a while. This village only has about seventy-five people total in it, and with what you guys brought back, I could stretch what we have to feed the entire village for around two weeks."

"That's good to know that we're safe on food for the moment. I don't want you to skimp on the food, though. Cook and serve only good portions of food. That's the biggest benefit we can offer the village now. It should also help with one of our village upgrade criteria for increasing the health of the village. I just discovered a spell earlier to create good roads and already did one small part of the road. When I get time, I'll go through the village, converting the main roadways to this better version. That should meet the criteria for that on the village upgrade list." Arthur said.

"So do we want to focus on village upgrades, or do we need to focus on combat?" Daniel asked, confused.

"I have been considering that option myself. I honestly believe our best option is to do both. Now before you start telling me why we can't, I want to stress that it's because of the people we have. I know good and well, most of the villagers will not take any role in defense of this village. Most of them have no skills to do so. I honestly believe that Rowan, Samson, Vana, Allendria, and myself can probably hold back whatever they decide to bring, but just in case, I want to make sure most of the men in the village at least have basic proficiency with bows. We should be able to take a few of them into the woods for a bit of archery work." Arthur explained.

"The village itself will need to be advanced as quickly as we can, and that means repairs and improvements. I hope to work on some of those items myself as I get time. The blacksmith shop here will play a large part in all of this. We will need many items for repairs and improvements. I plan on trying to spend a decent amount of my time here, helping you forge and enchant items as necessary. We'll eventually have to focus on getting a sawmill up and running. I would like us to get a gate made for the gatehouse I just erected. We should be able to find the wood in the forest nearby and can use thin iron bars to band the door for strength and make hinges. I'm sure I'll need to go on a couple more hunting parties to mine more ore as time goes on, but we have a good stock of materials at the moment." Arthur said.

"I have those nails I completed, and I had already thought of some of those issues myself," Rowan told him. "I also made a couple of saw blades for hand saws and another basic mining pick."

"All useful items that should help with our supply. I also need to experiment with my magic a bit and figure out the best way to melt that copper and get it into proper coinage. Would anyone happen to have a copper coin stashed away? I need to see one to know what I need to make them look like." Arthur asked.

"I have one you can use as a pattern when you get to it," Rowan told him.

"Great. Another serious issue I would like to address is hygiene. This village's residents seem to all be filthy. I know most of it's because of their circumstances, but it needs to be fixed. I've never even noticed, but where does the village's water come from?" Arthur asked.

"There are a few wells scattered through the village. We drop our buckets down and fill them up there." Daniel told him.

"So when I take a bath at your inn, someone had to lug the water there, in individual buckets?"

"Of course, how else would it all get there? We don't completely change the water that often, though, because of it."

Arthur blanched at that statement. That meant he had been washing in dirty bathwater a few times. After hearing that news, work on a bathhouse quickly jumped to the top of the list for tomorrow. He even knew how to make the place rather efficient and clean with a few of the sapphire chips he'd found and a bit of clever enchanting.

"I'll work on getting a functional bathhouse tomorrow then as my main priority. That should help improve everyone greatly. Can we find a few people who can use the saws Rowan made to cut the wood we have been harvesting into lumber? I know it hasn't had enough time to dry and cure, but it should get us one step closer. I'm positive I can use my fire magic to do a quick cure on the wood and get it usable." Arthur told them.

"I'll see who I can find. Our resident father and son team of woodcutters have been busy. They have a few more loads ready for you to turn in. We have a few people who want to take advantage of the multiple turn-ins you mentioned." Daniel told him.

"I also discovered something else interesting with the system today while working. For one, I could accept and turn in work orders myself, but that isn't very surprising. The best thing I found out was that if you decrease the rewards gained and word it, so the materials are to be supplied by you, it'll increase the amount of experience you gain proportionately. If you guys decide you want to forgo some of the smaller rewards and get more skill and experience, then let me know. When you want to turn in items, I can customize the order to fit your needs. Hell, I have gained multiple levels in Earth Magic and Fire Magic today alone." Arthur explained.

Rowan's eyes lit up at that. "I might just take you up on that offer." He told Arthur.

"I want to make sure we have a bit of armor to protect us, so I'll be focusing on that this afternoon. I also plan on forging something I'll need for the bathhouse tomorrow. How are we doing in terms of weaponry, Rowan?" Arthur asked.

"Honestly, I haven't made much in the way of weaponry except for a few daggers. There aren't a lot of other fighters currently, so not much that needs to be done."

Arthur thought about that for a second. "I guess that means I have time to work on a set of armor for Samson. I need to get all of us some metal bracers at a minimum, and I would like for Samson to be decked out in a good set of protective gear. He took quite a beating from that boss last time, but he held his ground. Not only that, but he held it with pretty much no armor of any kind. I can't wait to see the man with real armor. Vana was also absolutely amazing, and she got herself a new bow and quiver at the dungeon. She'll be a real force to be reckoned with. Corianne said she expected to have the first shipment of leather to me today and I convinced her to do the rest of the hides we have all at once and turn them in via work order together. This will give us a larger supply quickly for the rest of us." He said.

"That's a good plan. You can make the armor a lot faster than I with your Arcane Smithing, and knowing you; I'm sure you'll want to put some enchantments on them. I can handle some of the more simple items like the arrowheads for now. You get your bathhouse piece made and work on getting that armor together." Rowan told him.

"Daniel, do me a favor and work with Katherine on ideas to help get our village quality and level improved. Also, please make a priority list of what buildings need improvements and repairs."

"Sounds like a plan. I'll head back to the inn and get started. The girls have the cooking and meal preparation well in hand right now." Daniel said as he took off toward the inn.

"I will start working on my items. Do you need anything before I get started?" Arthur asked Rowan.

"No, I'm good for now. Do me a favor and check in with me before you head back over to the inn, though. I want to turn in some of the things I've made for work orders."

"Consider it done," Arthur said as he walked over to the spare anvil in the place. The first thing he wanted to work on was an idea he had for the bathhouse. Since they didn't have any kind of water system, this thing would have to be filled by hand, and, with the size he was planning to make it, he was not about to keep changing out the water. They would never stop carrying water back and forth. Instead, he created a filtration system.

He didn't have Water Magic, so he couldn't just make a water pump with enchanting. Instead, he used iron and made a long tube about three feet in diameter and eight-foot-long. Each section of this tube would have a specific purpose. As water flowed into it, the first part of the tunnel would heat that water up to kill any bacteria in it. As it rushed to the next section, it would have some of the heat drawn from it to make it a comfortable temperature for bathing, and the final section of tubing would use earth magic to infuse the water with minerals to nourish the skin.

The sapphire chips should be able to hold a sufficient amount of power for these enchantments. He thought he might be able to put in some enchanting that would allow the sorcery to draw and store energy on its own, but he could always supplement the magic in the filter on his own if it ever ran low.

He grabbed a few of the iron ingots and tossed them in the fire. When they got hot, he pulled them out and suspended them with his magic as he pictured the long, slender tunnel he was going to make. He also gave the entire thing a bit of an arc. He planned on embedding it near the bottom under a protective layer of stone to prevent people from messing with it and accidentally hurting themselves.

He imagined the shape he wanted and cast the spell. The metal flowed out into a long and thin sheet and then started to fold and roll into a tunnel shape. Once the ends fused, the entire tube bent itself into the arc he wanted, and he pulled the excess heat out and set the tunnel to the side.

He had created the control spots on each one where the gems would be embedded and where he would do his enchanting. The project could wait until tomorrow. It was time to work on some armor. Iron wasn't the best option, but it was what they had, so he went with it.

Arthur started with the bracers first. They would be rather easy to do, and he needed to make a set of them for each of his party members. They'd work well for a quick block or two if things came down to close combat. Since he would be switching to a more melee-oriented role, he needed some. A sturdy pair of bracers may have saved him from a lot of damage and pain during his fight when the cat jumped him and bit into his arm.

He grabbed two iron ingots and got them
up to heat. He split each of them in half.
Bracers were somewhat thin metal and only had
to wrap around a forearm, so half of an ingot
would be more than enough for each. He
wouldn't be able to finish them until he got
some leather to line them, but he could get
the casings made and ensure the studs were on
them.

Since it didn't cost him anything extra,
he would make these a little more intricate
like he had with Samson's Shield. There was no
reason his team couldn't look fancy. He
designed the bracers with the slightly thicker
edges embossed with the intricate scroll-work
patterns, the same way he had the shield. He
cast the spell and looked at the first
example.

*You have gained 50 experience in Earth
Magic and Fire Magic for successfully casting
Crafting Spell: Arcane Forging.*

*Congratulations, you have successfully
created Intricate Mage-crafted Iron Bracer
(Unfinished). You have gained 80 experience in
Arcane Smithing and Blacksmithing for creating
this item.*

*Congratulations, you have reached level 2
in Arcane Smithing. Increases the stats on
items created using this ability by 2%. You
kids and your fancy skills.*

Intricate Mage-crafted Iron Bracer (Unfinished)	**Armor:** 20
	Block: 6-10
	Durability: 75/75
	Rarity: Uncommon

	Quality: Well Crafted **Weight**: 0.8 kg **Slot**: Crafting Item **Traits**: An Intricate Iron Bracer, created using magical techniques. This armor will have more capacity for absorbing magical power. Combine with lining and straps to create Intricate Mage-crafted Iron Bracer.

The piece was pretty lovely. It looked like Arthur finally found something that would give an armor rating as well. He assumed the shield didn't have an armor rating because it didn't natively protect anything. It would only block if it were moved into the correct place. Armor, on the other hand, would dampen any damage that made it to the piece. He cast his forging spell three more times to make the last of them. Arthur hid experience notifications for now and only saw level gains.

Those pieces were done and just needed a little enchanting attention. Arthur couldn't think of anything he and the girls might wear in terms of metal armor. He planned on trying to stay more flexible. For his armor, iron banded studs would be incorporated into leather armor for the mixture of flexibility and durability. He considered the possibility of making metal greaves for himself but thought they might get in the way. He was sure he would regret that later on, but hopefully, before too long, he would gain the skill to use a better metal such as steel. That would reduce the weight while making the piece stronger.

He focused on making Samson what he needed. He made plate gauntlets next, but he didn't want to make the bulky garbage he'd seen on the Internet. They barely had flexibility in the hands, and those that did were only because it was just a solid metal plate mounted on the back of leather gloves. He determined that he would make a fully flexible version of it complete with interlocking scale pieces.

He had seen some examples of it before, on the Internet, when he had searched around. Most of them were the glove style with metal scales that would bend down over the fingers as they closed. This design would have fully enclosed fingers. He would make small cylindrical sections that connected on the sides and would allow the next piece to bend up and down. This would extend all the way to the fingers that would be capped off.

The substantial portion on the back of the hand and the palms could be more significant, although he would have to contour the palm a bit to help grip the weapon in the gauntlet. It might take some getting used to, but he thought it might be the best bet. He could also make the entire thing quickly, and Samson could slide a glove on his hand before putting it on. The arm portion of it would have to go far enough past the wrist to overlap with the bracers, but he was confident that wouldn't be a problem.

He threw an ingot in the fire, and, as soon as it was ready, he pictured the gauntlet in detail with its intricate connections. He cast the spell and watched the metal flatten, wrap-around, and mold to the different pieces. Once the basic structure was the right shape, the familiar line of power took over and started defining the features. When it finished, he examined the final result.

Intricate Mage-crafted Articulating Iron Gauntlet (Unfinished)	**Armor:** 25
	Attack: 5-8
	Durability: 80/80
	Rarity: Uncommon
	Quality: Well Crafted
	Weight: 0.8 kg
	Slot: Crafting Item

	Traits: An Intricate Articulating Iron Gauntlet, created using magical techniques. This armor will have more capacity for absorbing magical power. Combine with a glove to create Intricate Mage-crafted Articulating Iron Gauntlet.

He was sure doing more complicated and intricate items meant he would get higher experience gains. That gauntlet he just made would have taken an ordinary smith a very long time if they were even able to do it. He made another but made sure he pictured it on the other hand. Wouldn't help to have two right-handed gauntlets.

Congratulations, you have reached level 3 in Arcane Smithing. Increases the stats on items created using this ability by 4%. A man's worth is measured by the size of his mana pool.

Arthur then considered what to make next. After some deliberation, he made a set of greaves. Greaves would be a better alternative to a full set of armored pants for now. He would also create some sabatons to ensure they fit well together, and the armor plating overlapped correctly. The next few minutes were spent picturing how he wanted the sabatons and the greaves to look. The design wouldn't have the ordinarily smooth front seen in many examples. He was more of a fan of the fantasy style ones. He decided the greaves would have the slightly raised edges and a raised middle ridge to give it the look of two fuller grooves running along the front.

For the sabatons, he used a standard iron shell, but he modified it, so the boot had a solid bottom and front, and the back piece was removable. He wanted Samson to be able to put his foot in the boot and then put the backplate on and latch it on to the side. Arthur even figured he could build the latch directly onto the metal with his skill. He used a standard toggle style latch with a few metal studs on the other piece to help draw the parts together. This would allow it to be adjusted to multiple sizes.

For the greaves, he made a flexible knee cover with overlapping metal plates to allow it to bend but only to cover the front of the knee. He also determined the shin cover could include only the front as well, and he could use leather straps to cinch them in place. He made sure that all of his pieces had the necessary rivet holes to connect the lining and straps. The ingot was heated, and the spell was cast.

Intricate Mage-crafted Iron Greave (Unfinished)	**Armor:** 20
	Durability: 80/80
	Rarity: Uncommon
	Quality: Well Crafted
	Weight: 1.0 kg
	Slot: Crafting Item
	Traits: An Intricate Iron Greave, created using magical techniques. This armor will have more capacity for absorbing magical power. Combine with lining to create Intricate Mage-crafted Iron Greave.

The result was pleasing, so a matching
one was made for the other leg. The sabaton
design was next. After ensuring the ingots
were in the fire and ready, Arthur pictured
what he wanted. He split the first ingot but,
instead of doing it in half, he only took a
third of the metal off to make the back shell,
and the rest would make the front. Both pieces
were still transformed with a single spell. He
had to create both parts at the same time to
make the entire unfinished sabaton. Mainly
because he had to make sure the latches and
the back lined up correctly. His spell
completed, and he held both pieces in his
hand. The fit of the parts was almost perfect.

Intricate Mage-crafted Iron Sabaton (Unfinished)	**Armor:** 25
	Durability: 75/75
	Rarity: Uncommon
	Quality: Well Crafted
	Weight: 1.2 kg
	Slot: Crafting Item
	Traits: An Intricate Iron Sabaton, created using magical techniques. This armor will have more capacity for absorbing magical power. Combine with lining to create Intricate Mage-crafted Iron Sabaton.

    This suit of armor was turning out to be
absolutely incredible. Arthur hoped Samson
truly enjoyed it. It would look even better
once he got the needed leather and did the
enchanting. He went ahead and created the
other sabaton.

    *Congratulations, you have reached level 4
in Arcane Smithing. Increases the stats on
items created using this ability by 6%. Try to
work up a little more sweat in the forge.*

    Now that he had both done, he checked to
see what goodies came in the Smithing talents
for him. He pulled up the talent tree.

    You have 2 unused Talent Points.

Talent	**Description**
Tier 1	
In the Flame (0/5)	*Allows greater control of the flame while smithing. This gives you a 2% chance per talent to increase the rarity level by one.*
Weight Reduction (0/5)	*Decreases the weight of finished materials by 5% per talent.*
Material Savings (0/5)	*Every item you create uses 5% less metal per talent.*

The options were not terrible. Any of the options were viable, but Arthur chose to put one point in Weight Reduction first. Since, currently, all they had to use was iron, it would help trim some weight of the items. He looked at the next tier of options.

You have 1 unused Talent Point.

Talent	Description
Tier 2	
Weapons of War (0/5)	Weapons you create have 5% increased attack and durability.
Power of Defense (0/5)	Armor you create has 5% increased armor and durability.

Well, there wasn't anything groundbreaking, but all of those talents would be beneficial in the long run. Arthur put his second skill point in Power of Defense. It would help a bit in the armor he was making. There were still a few pieces left to do. He moved on and figured he needed three more things, and Samson would be set. The set was missing a breastplate, the pauldrons, and a helmet.

The breastplate and pauldrons would be combined into one piece for this set of armor. He would attach layered plates of metal on the shoulders to fold down over the shoulders for protection. And for the breastplate, he would make it in two pieces like he did the sabatons. He'd have the front and back latch together using multiple clasps, and it would be relatively quick and easy to get on.

He threw three ingots in the fire. He
would need one for the front, one for the
back, and one for the shoulder plates on both
sides. He designed the front piece to wrap
over the shoulders so the shoulder plates
could be permanently mounted to it. The back
plate would enclose him.

Arthur pushed his will in and lifted all
three pieces, and he cast his spell and
watched two of the ingots stretch out and form
the front and back plates. Some intricate
scroll-work and the raised edge was added
around the arms and the bottom. The third
ingot split in half, and then each half
flattened and formed solid sheets. From there,
they divided into the smaller plates that
curved themselves to match the contour of a
shoulder. They fused where needed and attached
to the front part of the breastplate. All the
pieces combined and completed, and they fell
into his waiting hands. Arthur wasn't
expecting the weight of it but braced himself
before he dropped it. He looked at the stats
on the item.

Intricate Mage-crafted Iron Breastplate (Unfinished)	**Armor:** 55 **Durability:** 120/120 **Rarity:** Uncommon **Quality:** Well Crafted **Weight:** 5.0 kg **Slot:** Crafting Item

	Traits: An Intricate Iron Breastplate, created using magical techniques. This armor will have more capacity for absorbing magical power. Combine with lining to create Intricate Mage-crafted Iron Breastplate.

With that done, it was time for him to make the last piece he planned on outfitting Samson with. He was going to make a helm. He decided the best design would be to make a barbute style faceplate. He made the opening in a Y shape and decided to make the raised edge with scroll-work on it for the added flair. It would also match the style of the rest of the suit. Knowing what he wanted, he heated an iron ingot and cast his spell.

Congratulations, you have unlocked Mastery Level 2 for Crafting Spell: Arcane Forging. The mana cost for this spell has decreased by 5.

Congratulations, you have reached level 6 in Blacksmithing. You are granted a 15% bonus to forging speed. It's all about that molten metal.

Intricate Mage-crafted Iron Barbute (Unfinished)	**Armor:** 30 **Durability:** 75/75 **Rarity:** Uncommon **Quality:** Well Crafted

	Weight: 3.0 kg **Slot:** Crafting Item **Traits:** An Intricate Iron Barbute, created using magical techniques. This armor will have more capacity for absorbing magical power. Combine with lining to create Intricate Mage-crafted Iron Barbute.

Arthur now had his Earth Magic to level ten and was quite honestly eager to get back to his talent tree. He pulled up his Earth Magic talent tree and had a bit of a surprise. The Tier 3 options were now listed and he took a quick glance at them.

You have 4 unused Talent Points.

Talent	Description
Tier 3	
Advanced Stonework (0/10)	Increases the size of your Raise Stone Wall spell by 4 feet in length per talent.
Earthen Projectiles (0/1)	Teaches you the spell for Earthen Spikes. This spell allows you to learn the secrets of pulling earth from the ground and launching spikes of earth at your targets.

	Cost: 35 Mana
Power of Prospecting (0/10)	Modifies your Magical Prospecting spell to scan an area 20 foot wide and 30 yards deep for minerals and ore. Each point after the first increases this size by 5 feet and 10 yards, respectively.

The talents showed a lot of promise, but Advanced Stonework was the one that was getting all of his points. The talent points had been ignored at levels 9 and 10, so he had 4 points to use. He was pleased to see Tier 3 talents available now and assumed it unlocked at level 10. The Advanced Stonework would make his spell more effective every time, and now each time he cast the magic, it would stretch thirty-two feet with his bonus instead of 10 for the same cost.

He needed to get the enchanting done on each of the pieces. He used the same enchantments he used on the shield on the bracers. Once again, he used the durability enchant on the rest of the pieces, but he changed it up a bit.

For the sabatons, he added a rune set for weak, power, and speed. For the gauntlets, he tried a different rune set by using weak, power, and grip. On the helm, he used a rune set for weak, power, vision — the chest piece he used another two enchantments in addition to the durability enchantment. The first was a rune set of weak, power, and strength. The second additional rune set was weak, power, and defense. Finally, on the greaves, he used a rune set of weak, power, and armor.

He set to work and got all the pieces inscribed with the necessary symbols and then began enchanting each one. He hid the experiences on these.

Enchanted Intricate Mage-crafted Iron Bracer (Unfinished)	**Armor:** 25 **Block:** 7-11 **Durability:** 75/75 **Rarity:** Rare **Quality:** Well Crafted **Weight:** 0.8 kg **Slot:** Crafting Item **Traits:** An Intricate Iron Bracer, created using magical techniques. This armor will have more capacity for absorbing magical power. Combine with lining and straps to create Intricate Mage-crafted Iron Bracer. Enchantments: ● 10% increased chance to parry blows. ● This bracer loses durability 10% slower.

Enchanted Intricate Mage-crafted Articulating Iron Gauntlet (Unfinished)	**Armor:** 30 **Attack:** 5-8 **Durability:** 90/90 **Rarity:** Rare **Quality:** Well Crafted **Weight:** 0.8 kg **Slot:** Crafting Item **Traits:** An Intricate Articulating Iron Gauntlet, created using magical techniques. This armor will have more capacity for absorbing magical power. Combine with a glove to create Intricate Mage-crafted Articulating Iron Gauntlet. Enchantments: ● 10% decreased chance of being disarmed. ● This gauntlet loses durability 10% slower.

Congratulations, you have reached level 3 in Enchanting. Your enchantments have a 6% decreased mana cost. Just pour mana into it, sure that's always a good idea.

Enchanted Intricate Mage-crafted Iron Greave (Unfinished)	**Armor:** 35 **Durability:** 80/80 **Rarity:** Uncommon **Quality:** Well Crafted **Weight:** 1.0 kg **Slot:** Crafting Item **Traits:** An Intricate Iron Greave, created using magical techniques. This armor will have more capacity for absorbing magical power. Combine with lining to create Intricate Mage-crafted Iron Greave. Enchantments: • This greave loses durability 10% slower.
Enchanted Intricate Mage-crafted Iron Sabaton (Unfinished)	**Armor:** 30 **Durability:** 80/80 **Rarity:** Rare **Quality:** Well Crafted **Weight:** 1.2 kg

	Slot: Crafting Item **Traits:** An Intricate Iron Sabaton, created using magical techniques. This armor will have more capacity for absorbing magical power. Combine with lining to create Intricate Mage-crafted Iron Sabaton. Enchantments: ● 10% increased movement speed. ● This sabaton loses durability 10% slower.
Enchanted Intricate Mage-crafted Iron Breastplate (Unfinished)	**Armor:** 75 **Durability:** 135/135 **Rarity:** Rare **Quality:** Well Crafted **Weight:** 5.0 kg **Slot:** Crafting Item

	Traits: An Intricate Iron Breastplate, created using magical techniques. This armor will have more capacity for absorbing magical power. Combine with lining to create Intricate Mage-crafted Iron Breastplate. Enchantments: ● Adds +1 Strength to the wearer. ● This breastplate loses durability 10% slower.

Enchanted Intricate Mage-crafted Iron Barbute (Unfinished)	**Armor**: 30 **Durability**: 85/85 **Rarity**: Rare **Quality**: Well Crafted **Weight**: 3.0 kg **Slot**: Crafting Item

	Traits: An Intricate Iron Barbute, created using magical techniques. This armor will have more capacity for absorbing magical power. Combine with lining to create Intricate Mage-crafted Iron Barbute. Enchantments: ● 10% decreased chance of being blinded. ● This helmet loses durability 10% slower.

The armor set would be quite a masterpiece. At least Arthur thought it'd be. Once some of the leather was finished, these pieces could be completed. He wanted to complete the parts himself to get the bonus experience. The previous items he made had great bonus experience when he finished them, and these had higher experience on the base pieces, so he was sure the bonus would be even higher.

He reflected on the day at his hidden experience gains. He saw he had gained 2,370 experience in Arcane Smithing and Blacksmithing, 795 experience in Earth and Fire Magic, and 1,210 experience in Enchanting.

It was getting late by this point, so he stashed the pieces away in the shop, cleaned up his work area, and walked over to Rowan.

     "I finished up the gear set for Samson.
It just needs leather for it to be complete. I
hope when I get to the inn that Corianne has
the first set of leather there for the
delivery. I'm about to head back for the
night, though. I'm exhausted. I plan on
focusing on a bathhouse tomorrow, but I'll
attempt to finish the armor too."
     "Sounds good, I'll see you tomorrow
then," Rowan told him.
     Arthur headed back to the inn. No one
interrupted him on his trek back, and when he
entered the place, it was pretty crowded.
Corianne approached him to turn in the first
set of leather, and he was more than happy to
accept that order. As an afterthought, he
asked her if she had any thread to use with
the leather. She told him she had a large
spool of it she could part with. It was just a
standard linen thread and nothing overly
special, but it was what she had. They worked
out a deal so Arthur could create a work order
for it, and she would turn it in by the
morning. She agreed and left the inn. He took
the leather in question to Daniel and asked
him to put it in one of the storage locations.
He would need to use some of it tomorrow.
     He made a quick trip over to the bath and
grimaced as he remembered what he had found
out about it. Despite this, the coal dust and
dirt buildup he had on him needed to be washed
off, so he took a quick bath. He made his way
up to his room and once again collapsed into a
deep sleep.

Chapter 25

A Matter of Hygiene

Arthur woke up the next morning with a slight headache, and some of his muscles protested as he got dressed. As he stumbled down the stairs in his half-asleep state, he bumped into Daniel at the bottom.

"Good Morning, Arthur," Daniel greeted him.

"Good morning, Daniel. Anything special happening this morning?" He asked.

"No, just busy trying to keep people fed."

"I'll take whatever you're serving this morning then."

Arthur found an empty seat and sat down. Daniel brought out some food and a mug of water. The water was getting old, and it wouldn't be long before he would need to find something else to take its place. He was sure if he could secure a type of alcohol for the village, the spirits of the villagers would improve.

The food was excellent as usual, and Arthur made his way back to the kitchen. Daniel told him that Paula was to receive the work order for the current large pot of stew, so he turned in her work order for her. She looked rather pleased when she saw the rewards.

"Hey Daniel, I'll be spending most of today working on a proper bathhouse. Is there any place in the village that would be a good spot for this? I want to keep it somewhat close to the inn, so it's easy for guests of the village to get to." Arthur asked.

"That sounds like a great idea but not sure how you will keep it clean. I'll trust you on it, though. As far as I know, the spot of land directly southeast of this inn would work well. There isn't anyone that owns the claim to it for any reason."

"I'll make it happen then. I've got a lot of work to do this morning, so I'll see you around. I'll check back when I finish with the bathhouse." Arthur told him as he left out of the inn.

As Arthur made his way out of the inn, a handful of people stopped him. The father and son team of woodcutters had four work orders of wood to turn in, so he assigned and accepted two work orders for each of them. Both of Rowan's apprentices were there, and each of them had six work orders worth of ingots to turn. He assigned and accepted all of their orders, and they left with smiles on their faces.

Zeke made it to him next and had two more bows and three bundles of arrows. Arthur created orders for each of those items and accepted their completions. Corianne was there as well so she could get a reward for the spool of linen thread she told him about. He recognized that, and she moved on. Finally, he was surprised when Katherine approached.

"Good morning, Katherine. How are you doing?" Arthur asked her.

"I'm doing well, Arthur. Would you be willing to do a work order for me?" She asked sheepishly.

"I'm more than willing to issue work orders for anything useful no matter who provides it," Arthur told her.

"Well, I have skill with weaving cloth and have a bit of raw flax that I can spin into linen, and have some spare linen I have already made."

"That's great. How did you end up learning that skill?" Arthur asked.

"It goes along with my scribe skill. I need to know the art of cloth to make paper. I use a method to make paper from linen." She explained.

"That's impressive. I wasn't aware the skills could go together like that. I'm familiar with a method of making it with wood but hadn't learned the method with linen." Arthur told her.

He asked her about the amount of linen she had and what she thought she could still make and made the necessary work orders for her. She walked away happy, and he continued on his way out the door. Arthur made his way toward the designated spot that Daniel had told him about and surveyed the area.

It was plenty big and easily accessible. The first thing to do would be to level the land. He knew he'd be burning a lot of mana today because he'd have to make a bunch of new spells. The best part was, these spells could help him with repairs and building structures in the village.

He focused his magic and pictured the landscape being flat around him. What he needed were scalable spells. Making spells for each size he needed wasn't feasible. A scalable form of magic was what was needed. He wasn't sure how to do it, but he decided he'd do it by completing the stage in multiple phases.

With that in mind, he pictured a smaller area around him in a square shape and pushed the power to level it quickly. Before he let the power go, he made the space larger and pushed the power again. He waited one more time because he still had plenty of mana left and made the size a lot larger. The energy flowed one final time, and he let the power dissipate. He received the notice he was hoping to get.

Congratulations, you have discovered the Earth Magic Spell: Flatten Earth. You have gained 250 experience in Earth Magic for discovering a known spell.

Spell: Flatten Earth	
Requirements: Earth Magic Mana Cost: 10-50 MP Cast Time: 2-5 seconds	Description: Levels a stretch of earth. The size affected by this spell ranges from a 6' square to a 24' square depending on the amount of mana used.
Mastery Level: 1	

The spell was cast one more time at max cost to make a foundation that was 48 feet by 24 feet. Arthur needed it bare earth for now because he planned to dig the bathing area into the ground.

The village didn't need a place this large, but he didn't want to have to rebuild this thing in a few months because of the increased population. He sincerely hoped to make this village grand. Since most of his mana was used developing the spell and casting the second one, he needed to kill some time to regain it.

He took some time to look at a few of the nearby houses. Checking the buildings for their level of disrepair allowed him to see the true scope of the work needing to be done. He determined that these buildings have to be replaced by sturdier stone buildings. They could salvage the current premises for their wood and use the better pieces to make solid wood floors. This would lead to a comfortable walking surface and a solid structure that was very sturdy.

When his mana was back, he walked back to his construction site. He wanted roughly three-quarters of the building to be the bathing area giving a solid landing surface to get out and dry off. It was time for him to discover another spell. He needed magic to dig down and remove the dirt. The best way would be to make the earth melt back into itself, for lack of a better description. Since this one also needed to be scalable, the same approach was used as discovering the last one.

He started by making a hole that was a five-foot square and two-foot deep. Once that one was finished, he expanded it and pushed again. One more time at what he thought would be the maximum size he needed and the spell snapped into place.

Congratulations, you have discovered the Earth Magic Spell: Excavate. You have gained 250 experience in Earth Magic for discovering a known spell.

Spell: Excavate	
Requirements: Earth Magic Mana Cost: 10-50 MP Cast Time: 2-5 seconds	Description: Removes the dirt in a specified area. The size affected by this spell ranges from a 5′ square to a 15′ square and up to 4′ deep depending on the amount of mana used.
Mastery Level: 1	

His original spell had cleared a small area, so he ended up having to cast the spell a few more times once his mana was back. The final dimensions of the bathing hole ended up being a large rectangle that was thirty-two feet long, eighteen feet wide, and started at two feet deep and gradually deepened to four feet deep.

He didn't want the entire thing to be too deep. There would be kids that would need to bathe, and he didn't want them drowning because it was over their heads. He also knew four feet was plenty deep for a grown adult to get washed up.

The next step for him would be to transform the bottom and the sides of the whole area into solid stone. He thought about using his Transform Earth: Stone spell to change it all, but the size affected by that spell was so small it wasn't practical. His Raise Stone Wall spell was now so large, due to his talent increase, that it wouldn't work as well. So, he needed to create magic designed primarily for building walls, and it was the perfect chance for him to make a scalable one.

He started on one wall of the excavated area and focused on his magic. He would have to go through the motions as if he was going to raise the earth and then convert it to stone even though he only needed the conversion. This spell would do him no good if he had to pull up the dirt first and hold it in place while casting the second spell. It was essential for it to be all one spell like he did with his Stone Wall spell.

He envisioned an area that was a four-foot square and one-foot wide. He changed the thickness of the spell as he made the area larger to ensure the wall could be up to two feet thick. This would allow him to build thicker walls for the ground floor and thinner walls for additional stories if he ever needed to make taller buildings. When he had transformed the initial size, he increased it two more times before he finished the spell.

Congratulations, you have discovered the Combination Spell: Stone Building Wall. You have gained 250 experience in Earth Magic and Fire Magic for discovering a known spell.

Stone Building Wall	
Requirements: Fire Magic and Earth Magic Mana Cost: 15-60 MP Cast Time: 10 seconds	Description: Creates a stone wall of variable size. The size of the wall can range from 4' square and 1' thick to 12' square and 2' thick.
Mastery Level: 1	

    This spell would significantly speed up his construction efforts. He waited again for his mana to recover. It took three spell casts on each long wall to cover the full distance and twice on each end wall for a total of ten spells. He could build an empire overnight if not for the problem of his mana. He quickly discovered this spell could be turned flat and cast as a foundation as well and could cover the entire bottom of the excavated area in another six spell casts. Some of those casts cost more or less mana than others based on the size he had to stretch it to.

    He could adjust the wall to any size he wanted if the dimensions didn't surpass the maximum for the measurements. For instance, he could make a stone wall that was twelve-feet long, one-foot wide, and three-feet-high, but he couldn't stretch the twelve-foot length any farther even though he hadn't used as much stone in other directions.

Congratulations, you have reached level 11 in Earth Magic. Increases the effect of your earth magic spells by 30%. Moving pretty fast. Keep it up.

This did not deter him at all. With the bathing area completed, he raised a smaller section on the shallow edge of the bathing area to act as a step.

Congratulations, you have reached level 9 in Fire Magic. Fire Magic spells now have a 24% increased effect. Count on warmth to keep you alive.

When he stepped back out onto the flat earth above the bathing area, he set to work, making the solid landing stone for the rest of the building. There was a three-foot section on each side of the bathing area and only a two-foot part in the back, which left his landing as a fourteen-foot long section of stone that was twenty-four feet wide. He could do the back corner sections in an L shape with his spell so that he could complete the entire landing surface in eight casts.

While waiting for mana, he determined he would make the walls the full twelve-foot high just for flair. He wanted the building to look grand and imposing. It would be the first high-class building in the village, after all. It took him twelve spell casts of his spell to raise a twelve-foot tall wall that was two-foot thick around the entire outside of the building, and he fused it to the outside edge of the foundation to make them all solid and immovable.

He was debating on what to do about a roof when he decided to leave the bathing area open to the sky. It would give people a pleasant view of the stars if it were nighttime, and when it rained, it would help replace the water in the bathing area with fresh water. He would have to make small drain holes in the stone bathing area so the water would leak through the stone and into the dirt if it were overfilled, but that was simple.

He could just use raw mana and cut those in as he walked around. He made a circuit of the place and cut in small drain holes around the top edge of the entire bathing area and even cut a handful into the landing area as well.

While he didn't want to put anything over the bathing area, he did decide he wanted to put a roof over the landing side of the building. This would be another flex of his raw mana. He pulled up dirt and transformed it to stone as it flowed in a gradual arch over the foundation side of the building. It created a beautiful half dome cover on that side of the building. The doorways he had added into the walls when he had cast the spells on the front were tall arched doorways. There were two of those doorways in the front of the building.

Arthur took a good look around the building and was quite impressed. He stood in a building of solid stone that was rather massive in scale, and he had created it all from barren land in half a day. A few finishing touches were considered, and he cast a few more stone wall spells to add some benches along the walls of the landing.

He also raised some vertical walls near the edge of the bathing area that were two-foot thick at the base but only one-foot thick at the top, which made a natural shelf for people to place towels and soaps on.

The building itself was ready to go except for two main things. The first was it needed the filter system Arthur planned on putting in, and the second was it required a metric shit-ton of water.

Arthur made his way over to the blacksmith shop and grabbed his tube he planned on using for a water filtration system. The sapphire chips were still in their pouch inside his bag. He also grabbed the awl and the small hammer he would need for his enchantment. He let Rowan know he was borrowing the two tools for a bit and headed back to the bathhouse.

When he returned to the bathhouse, he started planning the filter. There were a handful of people wandering around the area and gawking at the large building from the outside. No one had tried to come into the building yet, so he didn't have anyone in his way as he began working. The thing that worried him was that this was going to be a lot more complicated. There would have to be one set of symbols that would do the primary function, one set to set a delay, and the final part of drawing in latent power to keep the spell powered longer without him having to recharge it personally. He also had to hope the sapphire gem would work like he thought it would.

He embedded one small chip into the metal spot on each section he had planned to use and began working on the script. For the first section, he started with moderate, power, and heat. He then put in the second section that comprised of weak, power, and delay, but he added two other symbols to it that meant ten and minutes. He hoped that the part would cause the ability only to activate every 10 minutes.

The final set of symbols was to help keep the magic recharged. He used the symbols for weak, power, mana, and draw. The hope was that this would gradually draw in small amounts of mana from the surrounding area. He considered making it a moderate level power but worried it might start pulling out mana from the people bathing while they were in the pool. It may do that now, but he wasn't concerned about a small draw.

He did the same enchantments on all three sections for the mana draw and the delay, but the primary enchantment was different for the other two parts. The middle section used moderate, power, and regulate. The idea for this was to bring the water temperature back to a comfortably warm level. The final part was weak, power, and rejuvenate. This section would be used to restore minerals to the water that had destroyed out by the heat. The liquid couldn't be allowed to get stale and lose its nutrients.

He was slightly worried since he hadn't used a moderate power enchantment before, but he'd try it anyway. He pushed power into the first set of runes, and he immediately dropped 120 mana. *Damn*, that surprised the hell out of Arthur. He was both scared and happy at the same time. The initial power drain frightened him, but he realized that the spell took half of the mana cost upfront and then spread the rest out, so he should be fine. He kept pushing and finished the enchantment.

Congratulations, you have reached level 4 in Enchanting. Your enchantments have a 9% decreased mana cost. Making something useful for once?

Iron Bathhouse Filter First Stage	**Durability:** 75/75 **Rarity:** Uncommon **Quality:** Well Crafted **Weight:** 4.0 kg **Traits:** A tube of iron enchanted to heat up items that enter it to a heat hot enough to purify. This is the first of 3 stages in this item. **Charges:** 60/60 **Regeneration Rate:** 1 charge per hour

The item appeared to be correct as he looked at it. The charges disturbed him, though, because he had hoped that with the sapphire, it could store more power than that. He knew it couldn't regenerate enough mana on its own to stay charged, and he'd have to charge it from time to time, but he didn't think it would run out so quickly. A closer look at it determined why. It wasn't using the gem at all.

There would be a quick fix to this, but he had to inscribe a symbol directly onto the gem. The trick here would be to use a thin solution of coal and water to draw the runes and let the magic burn it in. The sapphire was too hard for any of his tools to engrave.

Arthur wrote the symbols for power and storage on the gem and then pushed his mana into it. The power sucked out of him in a rush, and by the time the spell finished, he had used 120 mana. The symbols burned into the gem, and the whole enchantment flared to life.

Iron Bathhouse Filter First Stage (Sapphire Storage)	**Durability**: 75/75 **Rarity**: Uncommon **Quality**: Well Crafted **Weight**: 4.0 kg **Traits**: A tube of iron enchanted to heat up items that enter it to a heat hot enough to purify. This is the first of 3 stages in this item.

<table>
<tr><td></td><td>Charges: 1000/1000

Regeneration Rate: 3 charges per hour</td></tr>
</table>

That was much more like it. The gem seemed to be the key to the storage, but it had to have its function defined. He was pleased that not only did it significantly increase the number of charges, but it also increased the rate at which they naturally recharged. That would be much more manageable.

The same process was used to do the other two sections. Arthur thought about inscribing the gem at the same time but thought it might drain too much mana and cause the enchantment to fail. They were completed in two separate steps to play it safe.

Now completed, the filter was ready to be installed. He laid it along the back wall and covered the device in a small stone bench using raw mana to protect people from touching it. This gave the back section of the bath a slightly elevated arc seat in it for people to sit on while bathing. He covered each end of the tunnel with a stone grate to prevent anyone from getting into the filter and getting harmed.

The only thing left to do was to get water into the building. Arthur considered trying to make an earthen ramp to the closest well but decided it would be a waste of time. Daniel should be able to find some of the village people to fill the bathhouse up for use. He just didn't have time for something so tedious right now when his time and mana could be spent doing much more important things. This would be an excellent job for some people without the skills to earn some food. He reflected back on the work for the morning and saw he had gained 1,260 experience in Enchanting, 3,600 experience in Fire Magic, and 4,000 experience in Earth Magic. The ground flowed by quickly as he made his way back to the inn. As usual, he found the man in the kitchen.

"How are you doing, Daniel?"

"Doing fine. I'm just trying to get some meal prep done. You finished up already?" He asked.

"Yeah, there's a brand new, beautiful stone bathhouse that's almost ready for use. The whole place is complete and ready to go; it just needs to be filled with water. Do you think you can find some people around here who'd like to earn some food by doing some labor? There are other things I need to work on instead of hauling water." Arthur said.

"Damn, that was fast. I'll get some people on it now. That should be a big help to the village." Daniel said.

"I have faith my enchantments will work, so it should stay quite warm and clean all the time without anyone having to interfere too much."

"That's even better. Maintaining a small tub here and trying to keep it clean and warm is burdensome, so having a place for the entire village will be fantastic. I shouldn't have any trouble at all finding someone to work on it." Daniel told him.

"Do you need anything here before I head over to see Rowan? I plan on finishing up some other things I was working on yesterday."

"Everything's fine here. There may be a few work orders left, but nothing that can't be seen to later today."

"Alright, I'll see you later," Arthur said as he turned. He headed to the storage room and grabbed some of the leather that Corianne had brought him yesterday. The central area of the inn came into view, and he waved at Paula while passing her. Passing through the front door, his path led him straight to the blacksmith shop.

Upon arriving, he saw Rowan hard at work as usual. It looked like he was working on a farming tool, but it was early on, so he couldn't tell exactly what it was. He made his way to his small spot in the shop, where he tended to work and set the leather down. He walked back into the small storage space and pulled out the pieces he made yesterday. He needed to get them finished so everyone would have some essential protection, and so Samson would be an absolute nightmare to deal with.

There wasn't a sewing needle to be seen anywhere, so he found a small scrap of iron lying around and picked it up. It was big enough to make a few, so he pictured the design he wanted. He used a modern style design but kept the eye larger so the thicker thread could fit through it.

Picturing the pattern in his head, he
made visual representations of multiple
needles within this one small chunk of iron.
Six of them should suffice for this chunk of
metal. He then tossed it in the forge for a
few moments to heat up, pulled it out with his
earth magic, and cast his forging spell. He
watched the line of power pass through the
block as the metal flowed, and six perfectly
formed sewing needles fell into his palm.

Mage-crafted Iron Sewing Needle	**Durability:** 50/50 **Rarity:** Uncommon **Quality:** Well Crafted **Weight:** 0.1 kg **Slot:** Crafting Item **Traits:** A sewing needle, created with magic, and made of iron. • 10% increased speed while sewing.

Being able to make things this small gave
him hope for much more intricate things in the
future. The big hurdle now was being held back
by iron. Once he advanced enough, he could
devote some time to working on a method of
refining the metal into steel before they used
it. He knew the process behind it but was sure
it would take trial and error to get it right.

It was time for him to complete the pieces he started yesterday. He began with the bracers. Making a leather liner for these pieces was quick. He cut a piece of the leather slightly larger than the metal with the correct rivet holes. He completed the first one rather quickly. Mainly because he used a little brute force magic to get it done. The leather was to shape, and he sewed a top and bottom strap onto it quickly. At this point, he figured out it was missing clasps to hold them. Another small piece of iron was found and tossed into the forge. The beauty of being able to create it all with magic meant he could make real buckle style clasps. He used the metal to make a bunch of heel bar-style clasps that were very common on belts from earth. Then grabbed another hunk of metal to make the small metal pins in the center that inserted through the holes in the leather to secure it. He used his magic to heat the end of the metal pins and wrap them around the bottom bar of the buckle, and they were good to go. He sewed one of these with a short leather strap to the other side of the bracer lining and put it into the metal casing. He also used some more targeted Fire Magic to heat the metal rivet studs and used raw Earth Magic to put force on the rivet end and flatten it over.

Congratulations, you have successfully created Mage-crafted Iron Heel Bar Buckle (Unfinished). You have gained 100 experience in Arcane Smithing and Blacksmithing for creating this item (x20).

Congratulations, you have successfully created Mage-crafted Iron Buckle Prong. You have gained 20 experience in Arcane Smithing and Blacksmithing for creating this item (x20).

Congratulations, you have learned Leatherworking for a 100 experience bonus.

Enchanted Intricate Mage-crafted Iron Bracer	**Armor:** 25
	Block: 7-11
	Durability: 75/75
	Rarity: Rare
	Quality: Well Crafted
	Weight: 0.8 kg
	Slot: Forearm
	Traits: An Intricate Iron Bracer, created using magical techniques, and enchanted with special magical power. This armor will have more capacity for absorbing magical power.
	Enchantments:
	• 10% increased chance to parry blows. • This bracer loses durability 10% slower.

It looked just as he pictured it. He grabbed the remaining three of them and finished the lining for all and completed them in turn.

Congratulations, you have reached level 6 in Blacksmithing. You are granted a 15% bonus to your forging speed. On your way to being a dwarf, are ye?

Immediately after the satisfaction of finishing these bracers, he realized he was an idiot. Only four were made because there were only four of them in the party. The dilemma was that each person needed two. He kicked himself for a moment and then ducked his head and got to work. Four more shells were quickly made, enchanted, and then assembled with linings. It took him a reasonable amount of time, but he managed to get it all finished.

Arthur was excited to get that much experience in such a short time. That gave him another two points to play with for his Blacksmithing talent tree. He put two more points in Weight Reduction. He wanted to make sure he could keep Samson well geared. The tank could make or break a whole team and had to be kept alive. Since they didn't have a proper healer, as he would define one in a game, he decided this was even more important.

He wished the bonuses were retroactive, but they weren't. That would be too easy. It just meant Samson's next set of armor would be even more amazing. He had honestly thought his Blacksmithing bonus was a complete waste of time since he used a spell instead of making the items the usual way, but the speed increase seemed to also apply to the Arcane Forging magic. The bracers he made were finished quicker than yesterday. He pulled out the rest of the pieces and got to work.
The next thing he completed was the glove liners for the gauntlets. He finished those and tested fitting them into the gauntlets. He kept from attaching them so Samson could put the gloves on separate and then insert them into the gauntlets on need. It would make arming himself a bit faster, and if one were damaged, he could get it off fairly quickly.

Congratulations, you have reached level 2 in Leatherworking. You are granted a 3% bonus to crafting speed.
Congratulations, you have reached level 7 in Blacksmithing. You are granted an 18% bonus to forging speed. One day you might make it to steel.

Enchanted Intricate Mage-crafted Articulating Iron Gauntlet	**Armor:** 30
	Attack: 5-8
	Durability: 90/90
	Rarity: Rare
	Quality: Well Crafted
	Weight: 0.8 kg

	Slot: Hands **Traits:** An Intricate Articulating Iron Gauntlet, created using magical techniques, and enchanted with special magical power. This armor will have more capacity for absorbing magical power. Enchantments: • 10% decreased chance of being disarmed. • This gauntlet loses durability 10% slower.

So far, everything was coming out just as intended, so he got to work finishing up the rest of the items.

Enchanted Intricate Mage-crafted Iron Greave	**Armor:** 35 **Durability:** 80/80 **Rarity:** Uncommon **Quality:** Well Crafted **Weight:** 1.0 kg **Slot:** Legs

	Traits: An Intricate Iron Greave, created using magical techniques, and enchanted with special magical power. This armor will have more capacity for absorbing magical power. Enchantments: ● This greave loses durability 10% slower.
Enchanted Intricate Mage-crafted Iron Sabaton	**Armor**: 30 **Durability**: 80/80 **Rarity**: Rare **Quality**: Well Crafted **Weight**: 1.2 kg **Slot**: Feet **Traits**: An Intricate Iron Sabaton, created using magical techniques, and enchanted with special magical power. This armor will have more capacity for absorbing magical power. Enchantments:

	<ul><li>10% increased movement speed.</li><li>This sabaton loses durability 10% slower.</li></ul>

Congratulations, you have reached level 3 in Leatherworking. You are granted a 6% bonus to crafting speed. You like animal skin as well, huh?

Enchanted Intricate Mage-crafted Iron Breastplate	**Armor:** 75 **Durability:** 135/135 **Rarity:** Rare **Quality:** Well Crafted **Weight:** 5.0 kg **Slot:** Chest **Traits:** An Intricate Iron Breastplate, created using magical techniques, and enchanted with special magical power. This armor will have more capacity for absorbing magical power. Enchantments: <ul><li>Adds +1 Strength to wearer.</li><li>This breastplate loses</li></ul>

	durability 10% slower.

Congratulations, you have reached level 8 in Blacksmithing. You are granted a 21% bonus to forging speed.

Enchanted Intricate Mage-crafted Iron Barbute	**Armor:** 30 **Durability:** 85/85 **Rarity:** Rare **Quality:** Well Crafted **Weight:** 3.0 kg **Slot:** Head **Traits:** An Intricate Iron Barbute, created using magical techniques, and enchanted with special magical power. This armor will have more capacity for absorbing magical power. Enchantments: • 10% decreased chance to be blinded. • This helmet loses durability 10% slower.

Once the last piece was complete, Arthur heard an odd sound he had never heard before, followed by another notification. Needless to say, he was extremely pleased with it.

Congratulations, you have successfully crafted a full set of high-quality gear. Due to the Rarity and the Quality of the set, it has been granted Set Bonuses. Your Mage-crafted Iron Armor Set has the following bonuses:

2 pieces - Increase base armor of all parts by 5
4 pieces - Increase HP of the wearer by 40.
6 pieces - Unlock Ability - Indomitable Will - This ability allows the user to fight through any pain and removes all movement and disorienting debuffs for 30 seconds. Cooldown: 6 hours.

That was the most badass thing he had seen since he got here if he was being honest. He was sure that Samson would cry when he saw it. Arthur was so excited he had to take it to Rowan to show it to him immediately. The armor was quickly set down on a table near the man.

"Rowan, I don't know what you're working on, but you have to stop for a moment and inspect this armor I just made," Arthur said excitedly.

Rowan eyed him curiously, and he set the chunk of metal he was working on near the edge of the forge so it wouldn't get too hot and burn and then set his hammer down. Wiping his brow with the back of his arm, he walked over to the armor. As soon as his eyes took in the first piece, he stumbled for a moment. He froze in place and stared at the breastplate for a while. Taking two more steps, he reverently reached out to pick it up.

"Arthur, dear Goddess, what have you done?" Rowan said in awe.

"I was surprised myself. I wasn't even aware you could make an armor set, but it was a happy accident when the last piece completed. I'm rather pleased with how the items turned out." Arthur said happily.

"You don't understand Arthur," Rowan said as he shook his head. "This set of armor only has a handful of others, that I know of, in the entire kingdom that can rival it. It would be a set of armor the personal guard of the king would wear, if not the king himself. The only reason the king may not is that it's iron and not steel, but that would be the only reason, and it would be for petty reasons."

"It had to be done. I can't lose Samson to the dangers here, and we'll need the whole group to get through this. It would help if we had a proper magical healer, but I haven't seen any here. Until then, our best chance is keeping him alive and protected."

Rowan chuckled. "Well, this should do it. I dare say he may be able to take out the entire group coming after us by himself, depending on how many they bring."

"I truly hope so. It would save me a lot
of headaches. I have to plan and prepare for
the worst, though. I plan on using the next
couple of days to focus entirely on the wall.
I can use my downtime waiting on mana to do a
little leatherworking while I'm walking
around. This way, I'm still productive most of
the day. I might not be back by the forge for
a few days. I also found out earlier that I
can make multiple items at one time with my
magical forging. For instance, I made a bunch
of sewing needles at the same time. I can
probably do it for arrowheads, too, because I
know how much of a pain they can be. Before
the big fight, I'll be sure to make plenty, so
don't worry about that."

"That's good to hear. Arrowheads and
nails tend to be overly tedious wastes of
time. I'd rather use my time working on
farming tools, foresting axes, and the like.
That's what I've been focusing on lately since
you've got industry running a bit." Rowan told
him.

"Perfect, you keep focusing on that. I'm
going to wrap this set of armor up and take it
back to the inn. I imagine Samson will be
there this evening and I want to present it to
him in front of everyone at dinner. He's going
to be the shining example for this village to
look up to. I want them to feel confident in
their safety." Arthur told him.

"That sounds like a good plan, Arthur.
I'll try to swing by in a little bit."

Arthur nodded at him and grabbed a piece of canvas from the shop. He wrapped it around the armor and trudged back to the inn. While he walked, he checked on his progress this afternoon and was pleased to see he had got 350 experience in Earth and Fire Magic, 560 experience in Arcane Smithing, 6,420 experience in Blacksmithing, 1,480 experience in Leatherworking, and 320 experience in Enchanting. There was a large crowd at the inn, which would do wonders for his plan. He took the bundle straight to the kitchen to keep it from being noticed too much. He waved Daniel over to him when he saw him tending a pot of food.

"Daniel, I plan on making a bit of a surprise announcement tonight. I'll be naming Samson Captain of the Guard of the village and presenting him with a new set of armor. I know he's technically the only guard right now, but I'm hoping it'll be a good morale boost for the village."

Daniel smiled. "That's a great idea. It should help calm the nerves of the village people. Do you plan on telling them about the peril yet?"

"Actually, yes. I plan on announcing that before naming Samson to his position. I'm hoping his new position will give them confidence, and I plan to have him make his appearance in his new set of armor I just finished. I'm sure you'll be impressed." Arthur said as he pointed to the bundle on the table.

"It sounds great to me. What do you need from me?" Daniel asked.

"Nothing right now. I just wanted to make sure you knew what was coming. On second thought, can you send a message to Dalia requesting her presence here? I want to make sure she is here for the announcement so she can show her support."

Daniel nodded in acknowledgment. "I'll make it happen."

"I need to go find the man of the hour then. I assume he's around the inn somewhere? I didn't get a good look around the place."

"He should be out there, somewhere."

"I'll be right back then."

Arthur made his way back into the central area and looked around. It took him a few seconds, but he spotted Samson in the back corner. Oddly enough, he was sitting with Vana as well. Arthur strolled over to them.

"Hi Samson, how are you this evening?" Arthur asked.

"I'm doing well, yourself?" He asked.

"I'm doing alright. I'm here to talk to you about something very important." Arthur said as he sat next to him and lowered his voice. "I plan on announcing the upcoming confrontation shortly. I need your help in this, though."

"What can I do to help?"

Arthur chuckled. "Well, I need you to stand next to me and look pretty. That being said, I have a bit of a surprise for you, well technically two of them. I have something I need you to wear, which is one surprise, and the second surprise is part of the announcement, and I need you to go along with it."

Samson eyed him, skeptically, "That sounds overly cryptic. I guess I can play along."

"My good man, do me a favor and grab your shield and bring it to the kitchen. Try to keep it covered if you can. Vana, you are welcome to come back with us if you want to." Arthur said.

"I'll sit here and enjoy the show. Thank you very much. The last thing I want is you trying to drag me into something sneaky as well." She said with a laugh.

"Fair enough," Arthur said. He walked toward the back and stopped before going into the kitchen. He turned and faced the crowd.

"Can I have your attention, please?" Arthur called over the crowd. He gave everyone a little bit to quiet down. "I have an announcement to make. Can we please try to gather everyone possible in here in the next half hour? I want to address as many as possible. Thank you, and I'll speak to you soon." Arthur said as a few people started leaving through the doors to gather others.

Arthur made his way to the kitchen area, and Samson arrived just a couple minutes after him. He was holding his shield, but it was wrapped up in a towel. He made his way in and looked around expectantly. Arthur looked his way and gestured for him to come closer.

"Thank you for coming, Samson. I know it was rather vague, but I honestly wanted to see how dedicated you might be. It was plenty enough since you came with almost no questions asked. I promised you a surprise, though, and quite honestly, I'm just as excited for you to get it as I'm sure you will be once you see it."

Arthur walked to the table he had laid the armor bundle on. He carefully removed each piece and laid them out to make it look like a person who was lying on the table. He motioned Samson over and gestured to the armor.

"I told you I needed you to protect us, and you were the first one to come forward to volunteer. I was going to let you hear the news when I announced it, but I think you should know ahead of time. This armor is now yours, and I'm naming you, Captain of the Guard. I hope for you to protect the entire village and not just our group." Arthur told him seriously.

Samson slowly approached the table. He reverently ran his hands over each piece of armor, and Arthur noticed he was getting misty-eyed.

"I don't know if I'm worthy of wearing this," he said softly.

"I saw your performance fighting that boss. There's no man I know that would do this suit of armor more justice. You stood your ground wearing rags and still prevailed longer than anyone I know could have." Arthur told him solemnly.

Arthur noticed his sword was also bundled with his shield he had brought down, and it pleased him that Samson had come prepared without being asked.

"Let's get you dressed. I want you to enter when I motion to you. I'll make the announcement of the danger first, and then I'm bringing you in and naming you to your new position. The people here need a beacon of hope. You'll be that man."

Samson turned to Arthur. "I won't let you down," he said with nothing but seriousness and came to attention and offered a crisp salute.

Arthur and Daniel helped get the man buckled into his new armor, and Arthur was beyond impressed. The man looked like an impenetrable wall. Not only that, but the scroll-work on the set seemed to blend well, making a very pleasing pattern to the eye when all assembled.

"I'll be damned if you weren't right." Daniel told him, "That's breathtaking."

"Time to get this show on the road," Arthur said as he made his way out front. Everyone but Samson joined him out there.

"Ladies and Gentlemen!" Arthur waited a few moments for everyone to quiet down. Everyone appeared to be in the room. He saw Vana and Allendria in the corner, and Rowan and Dalia were off to his left by the bar. The room was pretty packed and looked like almost all the village was here.

"I have some news I would like to announce. Most of you probably don't know this, but the village is under threat of attack. Some of the Lord's goons are expected to attack our village in approximately three weeks."

A bunch of murmuring and worried looks spread throughout the inn.

"I want to make sure everyone understands that we're working on this problem. I won't mince words for this. We're done folding to Lord Golgara's tyranny. We will not let his thugs run through the place and steal anything and everything they want. I assure you that in the next few weeks you'll see vast improvements within the village and its defenses. I'll personally stand and fight for this village."

"Are you trying to get us all killed?" One old lady screamed from the back.

"He's going to be the death of us all!" Shouted another random villager.
Arthur let the crowd rumble for a little bit as they all voiced almost identical opinions. He held up his hands to address them.

"I understand your trepidations, but Lord Golgara has been trying to kill you all anyway, just passively. This village was barely hanging on when I first came here, so would you rather sit by as you rot away and die, or at least attempt to stand up for yourselves and make a change?"

Arthur gestured back behind him for Samson to enter. As he was walking in, Arthur announced him.

"As Lord Mayor of the village, I have named Samson as Captain of the Guard to protect us during these tough times."
Samson entered the room, and as people saw him, the room became deathly quiet. The man was a tower of iron with the beautiful scroll-work on his armor. He was holding his shield by his side and had his sword tied to his belt. Arthur could see the awe in everyone's face while looking at the armor.

"I'm currently working toward arming the village against this threat, and we'll welcome anyone here who wishes to take up arms and defend it. If you have any combat skills, it's a bonus, but if you have none, we'll work on training you in archery to defend the walls I'm building."

Arthur paused in his speech to let it all sink in. While he was waiting, he saw Dalia walk toward him and nod his way. He nodded back at her, and she stood beside him.

"I also have an announcement to be made. Some of you may not know, but I have been named the local noble of the village. This was why I was able to assign Arthur as the village mayor. With this same power, I would like to make one more announcement."

She turned and gestured for Samson to come to her. She held out her hand, and he looked at her, confused for a moment, and then realized she wanted his sword. He handed it to her, and she gestured for him to kneel.

"I, Dalia Flamekissed, do hereby name Samson a knight of Alem's Crossing and confirm his position as Knight-Captain of the Guard." The crowd started cheering wildly, and Arthur smiled at Dalia. She nodded at him with a sly grin of her own and handed the man's sword back to him. She resumed her spot by the bar.

"Please have faith in us and keep up the good work. We will turn this village around over the next few weeks. We have the Goddess Lianna looking over us. She sent me here to help you, and I'll do all in my power to ensure this village thrives. Please have a good evening, and feel free to ask me questions anytime."

Arthur waved at everyone and walked back to the kitchen. Daniel and Dalia joined him back there.

"Well, that didn't go too bad. I think Samson suitably calmed their nerves." Arthur said as Samson walked in.

"Congratulations, Sir Samson," Arthur said with a slight bow.

"Thank you, Lord Mayor." He said to Arthur. He turned to Dalia and bowed to her. "Thank you as well, My Lady."

"It was my pleasure, Samson. I can say, in that armor, you look the part." Dalia said.

"Well, it's been a long day, so I'm off to bed," Arthur told them. Turning toward the stairs and waving goodnight, he made it up to his room and fell into bed. While lying in bed, preparing to fall asleep, a village notification sprung into his view. He was thrilled but decided he would deal with that in the morning. He rolled over and fell asleep.

Chapter 26

A New Village

Congratulations! Alem's Crossing has successfully created Magical Stone Bathhouse. The village receives the following exclusive bonuses for this feat: Health of all villagers increased by 500, bathing in this magical bathhouse increases all of your experience gains by 10% for 24 hours.

Arthur was thrilled with that outcome. He never expected the bathhouse would turn out as a unique building of that quality. Not only that, but it had a special bonus for an experience boost. The best part is that the experience boost would naturally influence the villagers to keep their hygiene up.

He rolled out of bed to get the morning started. He wouldn't get anything accomplished sitting around. Upon reaching the central room, he spotted Daniel. He gestured for the man to send some food over, and he nodded in acknowledgment. Arthur went and sat at an empty table to get ready to eat.

Allendria came over and sat next to him, and soon after, Vana followed.

"So I take it you're the reason for the commotion this morning?" Vana asked.

"What commotion?"

"The tizzy everyone's in because of our new magical bathhouse. A handful of people have already used it this morning and have nothing but praise for it." She answered.

"Oh yeah, that was me. I built it yesterday and put the enchantments in it. Daniel had some people filling it with water. They must have finished it last night when the notification went out." Arthur explained.

"Well, I can promise I'll be using it. Does it keep itself clean and warm?" Allendria asked.

"It sure does. The enchantments stay functional for a good amount of time before needing to be manually recharged, but that isn't that big of an issue." He told her.

"I'll definitely be trying it then. That bonus it gives is supposed to be nice." She said.

"Yeah, it is a ten percent bonus to all experience for twenty-four hours…" Arthur said, slightly confused. He then remembered that Allendria wasn't officially a member of the village, so she didn't see the exact notification everyone else in the village had.

"I need to make a trip to it this morning before I get started with work. Planning on spending the day working on the wall, and I'm not one to turn down some free experience." He told them.

Allendria smiled at him, coyly, "Need any company?"

Arthur grinned at her sardonically. "In the bathhouse or at the wall?"
She turned a furious shade of red and lowered her face so he couldn't see her.

"I'd honestly go for either but just need to clarify with you," Arthur said with a chuckle.

    It took her a bit, but she finally
recovered enough to answer. "The wall you
fool. We can discuss the other option on a
later day."
Arthur was kind of surprised by that answer
but wasn't going to press his luck.
    "As I told you before, I'd never turn
down your company out there while I'm working,
but I do worry that there are many other
things you could be doing." He told her.
    "I was hoping you would consider doing
something for me." She said to him, shyly.
    "Anything. What can I do?" He questioned.
    "I know it isn't common, as we've
discussed before, but I was hoping you'd be
willing to teach me Earth Magic. That way, I
could assist you with the walls after some
skill grinding. It would give both of us a bit
of something to burn mana on. My fire magic is
hard to train without a target, and I don't
have many crafts that can use it." She told
him shyly.
    Arthur felt like an idiot. It would be
easy to show her the pattern and give her a
chance to learn it as well. The fact he hadn't
thought of it before was causing him to kick
himself. Hell, he should have offered it to
others as well if he truly wished to make this
a better place. He told himself he didn't want
to hoard knowledge like so many others in this
world, yet he hadn't considered offering the
gift.
    "I would be honored to, my lady." He said
in a mock formal tone.

He reached out and grabbed her hand. A slow trickle of power flowed from his hand into hers so she could see the pattern to learn it. Taking it a step further, he separated it into the three separate strands for her so she could focus on them individually. He hoped this would help her learn faster. They sat there, holding hands while he waited on his food to arrive.

"Take all the time you need. It gives me a good excuse to sit here and hold your hand all I want." Arthur told her with a sheepish grin.

"Hard to concentrate when you make remarks like that. Wait until I figure it out, and then you can make all the jokes you want." She told him.

Arthur smiled at Allendria, who returned it with a grin as they sat and waited. Daniel came out a couple of minutes later with food for all of them. He gave Arthur an odd look when he saw Allendria slightly hunched over holding his hand but then shook his head and walked off. Arthur sat there and ate one-handed while he let Allendria work it out. She spoke to him again right before he had finished his food.

"Alright, I have the three patterns down. Can you show me the order they blend slowly? It should make this quick."

Arthur thought about it for a moment and remembered that when he learned Fire Magic, it only worked when he put the right threads in the proper order and the correct place within that stream of power. He searched his knowledge from the tome and found the exact composition of the power strands and focused on slowly weaving them together. It didn't take Allendria long at all to finish the skill after he showed how the last element fit in.

"Perfect!" she said in triumph. "Now I need to practice with it. I want to come out with you to practice using it myself. Do you mind?"

"Nope, finish your meal, and we'll head out."

Allendria scarfed her meal down real fast, and it frankly surprised Arthur. It wasn't precisely ladylike, but it amused him to see her so giddy. They got up and made their way over to the bar. They made a quick stop by the storage room first. He wanted to grab the leather stored there to work on while he was waiting for his mana to regenerate. From there, they traveled toward the front door. Arthur saw Katherine as he was leaving and got an idea.

"Katherine, I'm naming you the official Assistant Mayor for the village. This should give you the authority to accept and issue work orders on behalf of the village. This way, even when I'm gone, people can still take care of business. Try to issue and accept work orders as they come in instead of anticipating the needs and publishing them ahead of time. Also, feel free to offer retroactive ones like we've been doing."

"Go check with the ladies in the back. I'm sure Daniel knows whose turn it is for the meal turn in. I'll be working on the village wall if you need me." Arthur told her quickly as he continued walking toward the door. She sputtered for a few minutes as if she was going to respond, and he walked out the front door. He had a feeling she would yell at him for that later, but he didn't care.

Arthur decided now was a good time to work on the streets as he was making the trip, anyway. He cast his Raise Cobblestone Street spell seven times from the entrance of the inn toward the eastern exit of the village they were taking. The new street stretched a respectable seventy feet, but they still had a ways to go to finish this portion of the road. Getting everything inside the immediate boundaries of the current buildings and then expanding that to where the walls would be was his plan for the streets. He would do a little here and there as needed.

They made it back to the wall he had started, and he took an appraising look at it. This should move a lot faster today. His new talents would be a boon to him here. With his mastery at level 2 for the spell, it would only cost him forty mana each, and he could cast it eight times before he had to wait on mana regen. Every three casts, he could make a wall that was six foot tall, two-foot-wide, and almost thirty foot long when you counted his level bonus. So nearly sixty foot of wall completed every thirty minutes with an additional 2/3 of the next section.

He chatted with Allendria until all of his mana was returned from the streets he worked on, and once ready, he started his pattern. He would cast all eight spells and then would work on Leatherworking. Allendria was also using her time well. She taught herself the Earth Wall spell, albeit hers was a more significant base size than his. She also taught herself a spell to level the ground too. She used these back and forth so she could raise the wall and then flatten it. It gave her an excellent way to work on her earth magic experience without destroying the terrain. Arthur completed the first set of spells, and they sat to work on Leatherworking.

They got back up half an hour later and cast another eight spells and sat back down to visit while he worked on the current piece he was busy with. They kept this process up, and he managed to make a few pieces of leather as well that he was moderately happy with.

Congratulations, you have reached level 10 in Fire Magic. Fire Magic spells now have a 27% increased effect.

Congratulations, you have successfully created Basic Leather Breeches (Unfinished).

He dumped the two points he had sitting in Earth Magic into Advanced Stonework to push his wall sections another eight feet each cast. He was getting bad about not addressing the talents as he leveled up. With his bonus, the wall now stretched a little over 40 feet per cast. Since he only had one foundation cast done in the latest section, he went ahead and burned the first of his next ones, turning that section to this new length to keep things even and then continued with his casting.

Congratulations, you have reached level 12 in Earth Magic. Earth Magic spells now have a 33% increased effect. You might need therapy playing with all this dirt.
Congratulations, you have successfully created Basic Leather Vest (Unfinished).
Congratulations, you have reached level 11 in Fire Magic. Fire Magic spells now have a 27% increased effect.

Arthur thought to check the Fire Magic Talents now that he had reached level 11. He wanted to see what Tier 3 options there were. He also realized he hadn't used any points since level 5, so he would have a lot to work with.

You have 12 unused Talent Points.

Talent	Description
Tier 3	
Molten Fury (0/10)	*Increases the power of combination spells between Earth and Fire Elements by 3% per point.*

Flame Efficiency (0/10)	All enchantments with the fire element cost 3% less mana per point.
(Hidden Ability) Summon Crimson Whelp (0/1) This ability will only become available if you have the following prerequisites: • Hidden	Allows you to summon a small crimson dragonling to become your familiar. Your familiar will be summoned as a level 5 creature and can level up and learn skills. Familiars stay until the summoner dismisses them, or they are killed. If your familiar is destroyed, it can be re-summoned after a 6-hour cooldown. Cost: 150MP

Well, there was no way in hell Arthur would pass up on the Hidden Ability to summon a companion, so that was down to 11 points left. He decided this would be a good time to dump all 6 points into Power of Flame. Not only did this decrease the mana cost of all his fire spells by 30%, but it also gave him 3 Intellect, which was another 60 mana max.

This gave him 5 points left, so he put all 5 in Molten Fury. That would further increase the size of his wall. That 15% would bring each section of the wall up to around 45 feet of length. With all those points spent, he got back to work.

Congratulations, you have successfully created Basic Leather Glove (Unfinished) (x2).

That added up to almost eight hours' worth of time, so Arthur decided that was enough work on the wall for the day. The wall now stretched from the eastern road to the west over 700 feet. It was a rather impressive feat if he had to say so himself. The experience was also pretty amazing. A devilish smile crept on his face as he created a work order for 700 feet worth of stone wall. The reward did not disappoint him.

Congratulations, you have completed the Work Order: Stone Wall (700 FT) for Alem's Crossing for the following rewards: 1 Meal Token, 2200 Earth Magic Experience, 2200 Fire Magic Experience, and 1250 Character Experience.
Congratulations, you have reached level 13 in Earth Magic. Increases the effect of your earth magic spells by 36%. Still a fan of the stone I see.
Congratulations, you have reached level 10! You now have 5 available skill points.

Arthur was immensely happy to see level 10. It had felt like ages since he had increased his character level. His skills had been getting most of his attention lately, so he quickly checked his status sheet.

Name: Arthur
Level: 10
Age: 26
Race: Human
HP: 230/230
MP: 400/400

Stamina: 230/230	
Strength: 8 **Agility:** 12 **Intellect:** 17 **Wisdom:** 8 **Endurance:** 8 **Charisma:** 5 **Luck:** 5	**Experience:** 40/6000 (5 stat points available) **Skills** (25% boost to any skill for level up) **Combat Skills:** **Archery:** 5 (1365/1900) 　- **Aim Shot:** 2 (275/750) **Block:** 1 (180/500) **Dual Wield:** 1 (175/500) **Identify:** 1 (75/500) **Parry:** 1 (100/500) **Scan:** 2 (50/750) **Small Blades:** 2 (575/750) **Stealth:** 1 (370/500) 　- **Detect Hidden:** 1 (50/500) **Swords:** 2 (285/750) **Unarmed:** 1 (275/500) **Magic:** **Earth Magic:** 13 (535/8500) 　- **Earthen Wall** (2) 　- **Excavate** (1) 　- **Flatten Earth** (1) 　- **Magical Prospecting** (2) 　- **Raise Stone Wall** (1) 　- **Stone Building Wall** (1) 　- **Transform Earth: Stone** (1)

- Transform Stone:
Gravel (1)
Fire Magic: 11
(5305/7200)
    - **Arcane Forging** (2)
    - **Basic Firebolt** (1)
    - **Weak Flame** (1)

Professions:

Barter: 3 (100/1000)
Blacksmithing: 8
(410/3800)
    - **Alternate Heating:**
1 (160/500)
    - **Arcane Smithing:** 4
(1330/1400)
Cooking: 2 (400/750)
Enchanting: 4
(1340/1400)
Farming: 5 (0/1900)
Firemaking: 2 (700/750)
Herbalism: 5 (660/1900)
Leatherworking: 3
(750/1000)
Mining: 4 (700/1400)
    - **Magical Mining** 4
(700/1400)
Skinning: 3 (800/1000)
Woodworking: 1 (40/500)

Arthur thought if he had to start melee fighting, he would drop 3 points into Endurance for some extra health and Stamina. Since his luck stat was so low, he pushed it up to 7 with the final 2 points. This made him feel a little better about his balance as far as stats go. Agility could be the primary focus for his next level. He figured he could try to balance one level for melee stats and then one for casting and go back and forth like that, but it would be situational at best. Those priorities could always shift as time went by.

The two talent points in Earth Magic went into Advanced Stonework again, giving himself another eight-feet of wall per cast, not counting bonuses. He then decided he needed to summon his new companion.

"Allendria, want to come watch?" He asked.

"That depends on what your foolish ass decides to try." She said with a smile.

"I'm going to summon a companion. I had a hidden fire talent to summon one, and I used the point for it." He said excitedly.

She jumped up from where she was sitting and came to him.

"This should be fun," she giggled.

Arthur threw out his arms and activated his spell. The power of fire building in the center of his chest was palpable, and before he knew it, a small portal of fire appeared directly in front of his chest in between his hands. The portal expanded ever so slightly, and then a ball of red flew out of it in a rush. The portal snapped shut, and the magic around them dissipated.

Arthur looked toward the ball of red that had flown out and saw it appear to uncurl. There was a small red dragon that was only about three feet long with tiny wings that stared at him. The scales on the dragon were odd, though. Every scale on it started as a deep red color and gradually faded to almost deep orange. The elongated snout was filled with small teeth that looked dangerous. The two fangs on top and bottom that would be considered canines on other animals were half again as long as the rest of the teeth. The dragon also had eyes that looked like swirling molten magma.

Greetings, Arthur.

"Who said that," Arthur asked as he looked around.

I said that you fool.

The masculine voice caused Arthur to shift his focus to the dragon. It was able to communicate with him.

Hello, then, Arthur thought back at the creature.

Good, you are not a complete simpleton; I was worried about that, the little dragon huffed.

What is your name, young one? Arthur asked it.

I'm known as Balair and don't address me as, young one. I'm almost 300 years old.

How can you be 300 years old and still be so tiny? Arthur thought, amusedly.

What the hell did you call me meat sack? I'll burn you alive! I'm mighty in stature in every aspect, the dragon said with a devilish look in his eyes.

My apologies Balair, but your stature doesn't seem to match your esteemed age is what I meant to say.

The little dragon gave him a condescending look. *You're an idiot, after all. How do you know nothing about dragons? You mustn't even know you… the dragon stared at him for a moment and then shook his head. I hope you figure it out before a grim fate meets you.*

Anyway, what's to eat around here?

Arthur smiled at the little guy. Guess food was a universal language. *We have some food at the inn. How about we go check it out?*

Arthur turned to head toward the inn, and Allendria gave him a questioning glance.

"Sorry Allendria, are you ready to return to the inn for the evening? The crimson dragon here is hungry." Arthur said with a chuckle.

"So you can speak to him?" She asked.

"Of course, he's my familiar." He said carefully.

"I understand that, but most people can't communicate with words with a familiar. They can get a general idea of what they want or need but can't speak to them until they're higher level with additional skills. I have only heard of a handful of dragons being able to be used as familiars, and they're supposed to be the most difficult to get to that point." She said as she narrowed her eyes.

"Where are you from again?" She asked him.

"Nowhere close to here, I can promise you that."

"We shall see," she said cryptically as they walked back to the inn.

    While on their way back, they took their
time so Arthur would be back at full mana by
the time they reached the central part of the
village. Balair leisurely wandered all over
the place, investigating everything like a
cat. When they made it to the original piece
of the cobblestone road, he had made the day
prior; he used his full mana pool to stretch
the street out by casting the spell nine more
times.

    Why are you doing this, Arthur? Balair
asked him.

    *I'm working to improve this village as my
Goddess Lianna commands.*

    *I guess I can see the benefits of
improving your lair. Carry on.*

    Arthur gave the little creature a
sidelong glance and ignored the strange thing.
They continued back to the inn, and as soon as
they entered, Arthur heard a few cries of
alarm. He swept his gaze around him, quickly
looking for a threat but saw nothing. He
glanced at the panicked faces and saw they
were staring at Balair, and a few were even
pointing at him.

    "Don't worry, fellow villagers. He is my
familiar and won't harm any of you." Arthur
told them.

    *I probably won't harm any of them, but
I'll be damned if that girl in the back corner
doesn't look like she wants some of my pure
sexiness.* He heard Balair say.

    *What is wrong with you? You're very odd
for a dragon.* Arthur replied.

    *Really? How many dragons have you
known?* Balair said with a toothy smile.

You know what, that's irrelevant. Arthur said in a huff as he walked to an empty table and sat down. He could admit it was comical watching the little dragon try to climb its way onto the chair, and once it finally got itself on top, it was a never-ending balancing act for it to sit there with its tail and wings giving it balance problems.

Daniel came out and paused for a moment. He then shook his head and made his way to Arthur. Arthur wasn't sure anything could truly surprise the man anymore.

"What fresh new hell is this, Arthur?" he asked.

"Evening Daniel, meet my new familiar Balair. Balair, this is the village innkeeper and our gracious cook, Daniel." Arthur explained.

Daniel bowed his head just a touch to the dragon, and to his surprise, the dragon dipped his head just a bit as well.

"Can we get some food? We are all rather starving." Arthur asked.

"Of course. Does the dragonling need anything special?" Daniel asked.

I like him, and I can eat whatever you are eating.

"Nope, just bring him a helping of the same dinner."

"I'll be right out with it."

Daniel took off back to the kitchen.

"Son of a bitch!" Arthur exclaimed.

"What is it, Arthur?" Allendria asked in a panic as her eyes looked all over the inn.

"Oh, sorry, didn't mean to startle you. I just realized my dumb ass worked all day and forgot to get the experience buff from the bathhouse first. Oh well, I'll go by before I go to bed. I prefer evening baths anyway. I don't enjoy going to bed dirty unless it's for the right reasons." He said with a wink her way.

To her credit, she didn't blush nearly as deeply as she had in the past. It looked like she was getting used to his quips. Daniel returned with three heaping bowls of stew and laid them down for each. Balair eyed him for about half a second before he started noisily scarfing it down.

Little Dragon, will you stop all that damn messy noise? There's no excuse for that kind of behavior.

Call me little, one more time, and see if I don't light your pants on fire. Balair thought to him as he had his snout in the bowl, and his eyes stared at him over the rim in a reserved fury.

Arthur averted his face and dropped it and began eating. He noticed that Balair had slowed down his eating a bit and wasn't making quite as big of a mess. Arthur was a little over halfway done when Allendria scooted close to him.

"You want to get wet with me?" she asked him in a sultry voice.

Arthur snorted and choked as stew went up his nose, and his eyes started to burn. He had a mini coughing fit, and during the event, he noticed that Balair seemed to be chuckling at him. Was it even possible for a dragon to chuckle? After he finally got over his coughing fit, he turned to look at Allendria. She had a look of pure mirth on her face and looked like she was about to explode in raucous laughter.

"That was a cruel joke," he said to her softly.

"Who said it was a joke?" she asked him.

Arthur sprang to his feet, grabbed her hand, and dashed off out the door, straight toward the bathhouse. To hell with the remaining food. He could eat another day. He was not about to pass up this opportunity.

They made it to the bathhouse, and he saw pure awe in her face as they entered the large archway. There were only a couple of people present in the bathhouse, and they looked to be in a state of pure bliss. Arthur quickly dropped out of his clothes and gradually walked into the warm water. The bath felt like absolute heaven, and his stress seemed to melt away. He had almost given in to the pure bliss when he looked and saw Allendria's clothes fall to the ground.

Arthur was quite sure his heart doubled in speed. She was stunning. Her flawless skin looked as smooth as silk, and her exceptional grace let her walk into the bath at a leisurely pace. Arthur heard a noise and spun to look away real quick, only to notice the two other guys, who were currently bathing, looking like they were about to drown. He assumed Allendria's beauty had shocked them so utterly they lost all concentration and went under the water sputtering.

She made her way to him, and he reached out to grab her hand.

"What made you change your mind?" Arthur asked.

"I never changed my mind. I just hadn't had the time to make up my mind." She told him finally.

"Well, either way, I'm glad you did." He told her. They both made their way to a bench on the shallow side and used the soap bar, lying on one of the stands near the water's edge, to scrub up. Arthur helped Allendria wash her hair and gently caressed her shoulders and neck as he massaged her scalp. She finally melted in his arms and relaxed. They got washed up and finally decided it was time to get out.

Congratulations, the special effect of the Magical Bathhouse has granted you 10% increased experience for the next 24 hours.

Too bad, he missed out on a ton of experience today from that. They made their way back to the inn and up the stairs. When they got to his room, they both froze at the door.

"Care to join me?"

She looked conflicted for a moment, but she finally answered, "I'm not ready for that yet. Give me time?"

"Anything for you." He said. Arthur leaned in and gave her a tender kiss, and they parted ways. Heat flushed up through her neck as she turned with a smile and walked to her room.

Arthur made it to his room and fell into bed. He laid there for a while until he heard scraping and banging noises on his door. Confused, he got up and opened it, and Balair butted his way in the door and damn near knocked Arthur over as he smashed into the side of his leg.

Thanks for ditching me asshat! I guess chasing an ass like that, I can't blame you, though. Balair sent to him with a huff.

Arthur smiled to himself as he pictured the ass in question, then shook his head and laid back in bed. Not five seconds after he had laid down again, he was damn near crushed as a weight landed square on his stomach and knocked his breath out. Balair had jumped onto the bed and fell directly on Arthur. He struggled to take in air for a while.

Next time don't jump on me dickhead. Arthur told him.

Don't abandon me for a piece of ass without at least saying something. He huffed.

They both settled into the bed, and Balair curled up along Arthur's legs. Arthur noticed his experience gains for the evening were extensive. He had gained 520 Leatherworking experience and a whopping 11,000 experience in Earth and Fire Magic. He let a small smile slip onto his face as he felt the comforting warmth on his leg and fell asleep.

Chapter 27

A Sudden Arrival

Arthur felt an odd warmth on his face and woke up having trouble breathing. He panicked and jumped up as the warmth on his head fell to the bed.

Why the fuck were you sleeping on my face. You're worse than a damned cat!

I'll sleep wherever I damn well, please. You should be honored that I even grace your presence.

I could always dismiss your annoying ass. Arthur said with a sardonic smile.

I could always breathe fire on you the next time you summon me. Balair replied with a devilish grin.

They both eyed each other for a moment before Arthur gave up. He threw on some clothes and motioned for Balair to join him. They mosied their way downstairs and found some food.

Arthur found Allendria already seated at a table and kissed her on the cheek as he approached and sat. They all sat there in silence as Daniel brought out the food, and all three of them ate their breakfast.

"It looks like another boring day ahead of us today. Balair, I have no problem with you doing whatever you like as long as you don't harm or overly annoy anyone in the village." He told the little dragon.

I'll tag along with you until I get bored and then decide from there.

Arthur relayed his message to Allendria, and they took off to work on the wall.

***

The following five days followed much of the same pattern for the group. They would wake up, get something to eat, and head off to work. Arthur spent four of those days primarily working on the wall and, in turn, worked on his Leatherworking. Corianne had come through and turned in a large order of leathers. She was astounded at the work order reward in terms of experience. She looked on the verge of tears when he completed the quest for her.

He spent seven hours the first two days working on the wall and Leatherworking and netting him substantial gains in his experience, especially since he remembered to bathe every evening for the buff.

You have gained 12,600 experience in Earth Magic and Fire Magic for successfully casting Combination Spell: Raise Stone Wall (x126)

Congratulations, you have reached level 14 in Earth Magic. This increases the effect of your earth magic spells by 39%. What a rush.

Congratulations, you have reached levels 12 and 13 in Fire Magic. Fire Magic spells now have a 36% increased effect. Tell Balair, Hi!

Congratulations, you have unlocked Mastery Level 3 for Combination Spell: Raise Stone Wall. The mana cost for this spell has decreased by an additional 10.

You have gained a total of 760 Leatherworking experience.

Congratulations, you have successfully created Basic Leather Vest (Unfinished), Basic Leather Bag (Unfinished), Basic Leather Cowl (Unfinished), and Basic Leather Boots (Unfinished).

Congratulations, you have reached level 4 in Leatherworking. You are granted a 9% bonus to crafting speed. Tan that hide!

Congratulations, you have completed the Work Order: Stone Wall (900FT) for Alem's Crossing for the following rewards: 1 Meal Token, 2400 Earth Magic Experience, 2400 Fire Magic Experience, and 1000 Character Experience.

Arthur dumped his two new talent points in Earth Magic into Advanced Stonework to max it out at 10/10. This added another 8-foot base length to his wall. He also used all 4 points from his Fire Magic in Molten Fury to bring the combination spell bonus up higher. This brought each section of the wall spell up to a little over 77 feet. With the decreased mana cost, he could now cast more the next two days.

You have gained 16,800 experience in Earth Magic and Fire Magic for successfully casting Combination Spell: Raise Stone Wall (x168).

Congratulations, you have reached levels 15 and 16 in Earth Magic. Increases the effect of your earth magic spells by 45%. Looking good, green thumb.

Congratulations, for reaching level 15 in Earth Magic, you have been granted 1500 bonus character experience.

Congratulations, you have reached levels 14 and 15 in Fire Magic. Fire Magic spells now have a 39% increased effect. Burn baby burn!

Congratulations, for reaching level 15 in Fire Magic, you have been granted 1500 bonus character experience.

You have gained a total of 410 experience in Leatherworking.

Congratulations, you have successfully created Basic Leather Lining for Bracer, Basic Leather Boots (Unfinished), and Basic Leather Gloves (Unfinished).

Congratulations, you have completed the Work Order: Stone Wall (2150 FT) for Alem's Crossing for the following rewards: 1 Meal Token, 4800 Earth Magic Experience, 4800 Fire Magic Experience, and 2000 Character Experience.

After that second day of work, he checked his talent tree for Earth Magic again and saw Tier 4 was now available. There were some good options.

You have 6 unused Talent Points.

Talent	Description
Tier 4	
Summon Stone Golem (0/1)	*Teaches you the spell Earth Magic: Summon Stone Golem. This spell allows you to summon a stone golem to work and fight for you for a duration of five minutes.* *Mana Cost: 150MP* *Cooldown: 24 Hours*

Power of the World (0/10)	*This grants you a deeper knowledge of Earth Magic. Earth Magic spells cost 3% less mana to cast per skill point, and for every two skill points, you permanently gain 1 Intellect.*
Earthen Assistants (0/10)	*This ability allows you to summon earth elementals to assist you in your endeavors for 8 hours. These elementals are adept at many things, including foundation work, clearing and preparing fields, and even digging ditches. Each point allocated allows you to summon one additional elemental.* *Cost: 50 Mana*

Tier 4 in his talent tree was looking amazing. He wished he could buy all the talents in this tier but would have to allocate wisely. He chose Summon Stone Golem, so that left him 5 points. He also put 4 points into Power of the World to give him an additional 2 Intellect points. Then he used 1 point for Earthen Assistants so he could have himself a worker drone for the earth element.

His third day was just as productive.

You have gained 18,200 experience in Earth Magic and Fire Magic for successfully casting Combination Spell: Raise Stone Wall (x182).

Congratulations, you have reached level 16 in Fire Magic. Fire Magic spells now have a 42% increased effect. It's getting hot in here.

You have gained a total of 720 Leatherworking experience.

Congratulations, you have successfully created Basic Leather Boots (Unfinished), and Basic Leather Gloves (Unfinished).

Congratulations, you have reached level 5 in Leatherworking. You are granted a 12% bonus to crafting speed. Do we need more cowbell?

Congratulations, you have completed the Work Order: Stone Wall (2450 FT) for Alem's Crossing for the following rewards: 1 Meal Token, 5000 Earth Magic Experience, 5000 Fire Magic Experience, and 2100 Character Experience.

Congratulations, you have reached level 17 in Earth Magic. Earth Magic spells now have a 48% increased effect.

Congratulations, you have reached level 11! You now have 5 available skill points.

Arthur had now made over a mile of the stone wall around the village. By rough estimates, he could finish the wall in two days. That included making the three other gatehouses. Granted, he would then have to start from the original gatehouse and work his way around, doubling the width of the wall and then make a second trip to raise the height to the full 12 feet. The inside of the second tier would only need to be elevated a few feet instead of the entire 6 feet so that defenders could take cover behind the walls and fire arrows. He would keep expanding them as needed.

He invested his two new Earth Magic points into Power of the World to gain that additional one Intellect. His intellect was up to a respectable twenty points, so he spent his five skill points from leveling on other stats. He put three points into agility and two points into endurance. He wanted the speed, more health, and stamina. He then checked out his new leatherworking skill tree.

You have 2 unused Talent Points.

Talent	Description
Tier 1	
Solid Materials (0/5)	*You have a 3% increased chance for anything you create with leatherworking to raise a quality level per point.*

Scavenger (0/5)	*Makes you more efficient with your materials. You use 3% less material per skill point.*
Nature Provides (0/1)	*Teaches you how to process animal hides and carcasses into useful materials.*

Arthur wasn't upset with these options. He naturally chose Nature Provides with his first point and pulled up the menu again to see the Tier 2 options.

You have 1 unused Talent Point.

Talent	**Description**
Tier 2	
Eye for Rarity (0/10)	*Each skill point gives you a 3% chance to increase the rarity of items made with leatherworking.*
Scavenging (0/5)	*The first level of this skill allows you to break down leather items into usable components. Every skill point after unlocking it grants you 5% more material than you would otherwise receive.*

Another good set of options. He went with
putting a point in Eye for Rarity. He needed
to have the chance to make better gear for
himself, and if he couldn't use a magical
crafting technique like his Arcane Forging,
then this would have to do. He then pulled up
his fire talent tree for Tier 4 now that is
was unlocked.

You have 4 unused Talent Points.

Talent	*Description*
Tier 4	
Power of Light (0/10)	*Each point in this skill deepens your knowledge of Fire Magic and how it relates to Light Magic. You are required to have all 10 of these points to unlock light magic.*
Flame Shield (0/5)	*The first point in this talent unlocks the spell Fire Shield. Every point after the first increases its effectiveness by 5%.* *Fire Shield* *Summon a disc of fire that protects you from 40 ranged damage.* *Cost: 25MP* *Cooldown: 2 minutes*

Familiar Growth (0/10)	*Your familiar is a creature of fire. Each point in this ability will increase his size by 5%, attack by 3%, and Armor by 3%.*

The options here were harder to choose. In the end, Arthur settled on using all 4 points in Furious Fire. He wanted the increased spell power for his fire spells.

On the 4th day, they changed things up a bit. Instead of him grinding away on the walls and his mana, he got the party together, and the four of them, with the assistance of Balair, of course, headed out for some hunting and resource gathering. Rowan had tasked him with finding more metal. A task he wholeheartedly agreed with.

They went looking in the cave where they had recovered Allendria's things. He knew they had found ore there before and was sure there was more. With his increased spell bonuses, he was sure more would make itself known. They hunted through the day as they traveled. Arthur was able to kill two deer with his bow as well as three rabbits.

You have gained 260 experience in Archery for killing Deer (Level 10) (x2).
You have gained 200 experience for killing Deer (Level 10) (x2).
You have gained 180 experience in Archery for killing Rabbit (Level 9) (x3).
You have gained 150 experience for killing Rabbit (Level 9) (x3).

    While they were walking the forest,
Balair managed to kill five Rabbits of his own
and four squirrels.

    *You have gained 50 experience for your
familiar killing Rabbit (Level 9) (x5).*
    *You have gained 40 experience for your
familiar killing Squirrel (Level 9) (x4).*

    Had Arthur known Balair would be good at
hunting and not just an ass most of the time,
he might have invested some points in the fire
tree to strengthen him. Vana found an open
field full of herbs and wild plants. Arthur
took the chance to cultivate seeds from many
of them.

    *You have gained a total of 4400 Farming
experience for assorted plants.*
    You have gained 45 Jalapeño Seeds.
    You have gained 55 Tomato Seeds.
    You have gained 42 Carrot Seeds.
    You have gained 65 Onion Seeds.
    You have gained 34 Garlic Seeds.
    You have gained 26 Rosemary Seeds.
    You have gained 20 Peppermint Seeds.
    You have gained 35 Yellow Squash Seeds.
    *Congratulations, you have reached levels
6 and 7 in Farming. You now have a chance for
up to 30% increased yield from plants. Gather
those seeds and get them in the ground.*

Since Arthur got a significant boost from the spell, he let Vana harvest them all to increase her skill. Since she was the one that found and identified them, she also got the herbalism experience for it. The seeds would help them get a kick start when added to what he had already given Daniel. He knew those were already planted and being cared for.

They made it back to the cavern they'd found Allendria's items in, and Arthur made a sweep of the place. He started on areas he hadn't checked last time and quickly found a decent quantity of ore.

You have gained 770 experience in Earth Magic for successfully casting Magical Prospecting (x7).

You have gained 3630 experience in Earth Magic for successfully casting Transform Stone: Gravel (x22).

You have gained 4625 experience in Mining and Magical Mining for finding Raw Iron Ore (x65), Silver Ore (x15), and Raw Copper Ore (x30).

Congratulations, you have reached levels 5 and 6 in Mining. You have a 15% increased chance to find rare materials while Mining. I notice a pattern with stone here. Obsessed much?

Congratulations, you have reached levels 5 and 6 in Magical Mining. Increases the chance that items found will be a higher rarity by 15%. I think you got gravel in your boots.

They had little resistance until they exited the cave and started making their way back with their haul.

Arthur, we have company headed our way. Balair sent to him.

Before he could say anything, Vana called a halt.

"We have company coming," Arthur said.

Vana nodded, and the rest of them got their gear ready. Arthur had put the cart down so he could get his weapons ready. He decided to use his bow for this. To his surprise, a band of twelve Goblins came barreling into the clearing they had stopped in. Arthur did a quick scan of them to see what they were up against.

Name: Goblin	
Level: 12	
Type: Creature (Sentient)	
Rarity: Common	
HP: 180/180	
Stamina: 150/150	
Strength: 5	Experience: N/A
Agility: 8	Skills
Intellect: 1	Combat Skills:
Wisdom: 1	
Endurance: 3	Cunning Strike: 4
Charisma: 1	(???/???)
Luck: 2	

You have gained 1500 experience in Scan for use on Goblin (1) (Level 12) (x12).

Congratulations, you have reached level 3 in Scan. You can now see the level of their second combat skills. Peeping on things, huh?

Before he could even get an arrow up to fire it, he spotted two massive creatures emerge from the trees behind the goblins. They looked like much taller and far more muscled versions of goblins. Their faces looked more human and not quite as scary, but they had small tusks jutting from the corners of their mouths. They both wore crude leather armor and wielded rusty metal axes. He scanned them too.

Name: Orc	
Level: 14	
Type: Creature (Sentient)	
Rarity: Common	
HP: 240/240	
Stamina: 180/180	
Strength: 10	Experience: N/A
Agility: 6	Skills
Intellect: 3	Combat Skills:
Wisdom: 2	
Endurance: 6	Overpowering Blow: 5
Charisma: 1	(???/???)
Luck: 2	War Cry: 4 (???/???)

You have gained 300 experience in Scan for use on Orc (1) (Level 14) (x2).

Congratulations, you have reached level 4 in Scan. You can now see the level of their third combat skill. You naughty boy.

Arthur felt pride as his group sprang into action. They didn't miss a beat, and he watched Samson run full speed into the group of goblins at the front. It was frightening to watch because as soon as he hit the two in the front, for lack of a better description, they exploded. Limbs went flying as if a steel battering ram hit them. That new armor was paying dividends already. Samson quickly resorted to slashing with his sword and bashing with his shield. Arthur took aim, activated Aim Shot, and hit one goblin in the eye, and it fell dead. He ignored experience gains and would look them over later.

You have dealt 180 damage to Goblin (1) (Level 12) with Aim Shot (Brain Rupture).
Goblin (1) (Level 12) has Died.
Congratulations, you have progressed to Level 6 in Archery. You are granted a 15% bonus to accuracy. Aim down the shaft.

Arthur decided now would be an excellent time to work on his dual wield fighting style. His bow fell to the ground, and he pulled out his sword and dagger. The sword stayed in his right hand, and he turned the dagger around, so it was facing downward in his left hand. That would be used for backhanded stabs and quick parries.

He took off in a sprint toward the fight and saw five of the goblins peeling off toward the girls. Samson had managed to kill or maim the others but was facing both of the orcs, toe to toe.

Arthur took off toward the group that was rushing the girls. Vana took one down quickly with an arrow, and Allendria dropped one with a lance of fire straight into its heart. Arthur came in with a hard overhand blow on the goblin at the edge, and the creature never saw him coming. The blade went straight through its head as blood fountained up and out.

You have dealt 160 damage to Goblin (2) (Level 12) with Steel Longsword of Minor Beastslaying (Critical Strike) (Mortal Blow) (Instant Kill)
Goblin (2) (Level 12) has Died.

Arthur quickly stepped around the dead goblin and drove the dagger in his off-hand directly into the next goblin's rib cage. It squealed, and Arthur ripped the blade backward and out of the back of its ribs. The creature dropped, unmoving.

You have dealt 120 damage to Goblin (2) (Level 12) with Enchanted Basic Mage-crafted Iron Dagger (Critical Strike) (Mortal Blow) (Fatal Blow).

Arthur turned to face the last one and saw it coming with an overhand blow of its own that was aimed right for his shoulder. Before the blade landed, an arrow and a lance of fire both slammed into its side at the same time, sending it to the ground motionless. Arthur looked over and gave the girls a grateful glance.

He took off toward Samson and saw the man holding his own against the orcs, but he couldn't seem to land a solid hit on them. Arthur came in from the side and once again stabbed one of them with a dagger in the ribs. Arthur didn't even see the backhand that followed and sent him stumbling.

You have dealt 35 damage to Orc (1) (Level 14) with Enchanted Basic Mage-crafted Iron Dagger (Critical Strike).
Orc (1) (Level 14) has dealt 40 HP damage to you with Melee.
Orc (1) (Level 14) has inflicted disorientation. You are dazed for 3 seconds.

The orc had turned to strike at him when it was stunned and received an arrow in the chest for its trouble. Instead of falling, as Arthur expected, the beast roared and seemed to grow in size and muscle for a moment.

Its eyes took on a reddish hue, and it swung at Arthur with fury. He had been given enough time to recover a little from the daze, so he stepped to the side and used his dagger to push the blade farther off balance. His sword came down and landed a grave blow to the Orc's left leg.

Goblin (3) (Level 12) has Died.
Congratulations, you have reached level 3 in Small Blades. Swing speed with Small Blades increased by 6%. That's some sneaky work.
You have successfully Parried Melee attack from Orc (1) (Level 14) for 5 Stamina.
Your successful parry has caused Orc (1) (Level 14) to become unbalanced.

You have dealt 48 damage to Orc (1) (Level 14) with Steel Longsword of Minor Beastslaying (Critical Strike).

The skills were helpful and all, but he didn't have time to deal with it. Arthur jumped backward as the orc swung its axe at him, and it received another arrow for its effort. The bolt went into its neck and was quickly followed by a lance of fire that burned into its face. The Orc fell and stopped moving.

Arthur didn't have time to wait and dashed for the last Orc that Samson was still holding off. Samson saw him coming directly behind the Orc, nodded to him, and then leaped backward. Arthur came in behind the orc and plunged the dagger and the sword directly through the Orc's back. The sword punched all the way through its chest. It slumped to the ground as blood started to leak from its mouth.

Arthur did a quick check and saw everything was dead. Samson had been a nightmare on the field when it came to holding steady. He was sure there wasn't anything that man couldn't go toe to toe with. Arthur saw the last of the alerts roll in.

You have gained 820 total experience in Swords for the fight.

Congratulations, you have reached level 3 in Swords. Swing speed with swords increased by 6%. 'Tis but a flesh wound.

You have gained 820 total experience in Small Blades for the fight.

You have gained 600 total experience in Dual Wield for the fight.

Congratulations, you have reached level 2 in Dual Wield. Accuracy penalty with off-hand weapons decreased by 3%. You can use both hands at the same time?

You have gained 4300 total experience for the fight.

You have gained 220 total experience in Archery and the Subskill Aim Shot for the fight.

You have gained 300 total experience in Parry for the fight.

That fight was a complete surprise, but it had worked out well. The group was impressive. Samson was earning every bit of that armor Arthur had thrown at him. He looked, and the man was still at 90% health even after all of that fighting and holding them both solo. He only had a few scrapes on him that were shallow and didn't require attention.

Arthur had only lost a bit of health from that one backhand, but it would return quickly as they traveled. He hadn't noticed it at first, but he saw another small icon flashing as well. The image appeared as a curled up dragon in the corner of his vision. Pressing it showed him something that surprised him.

Congratulations, your familiar, Balair, has advanced to level 6.

That was good news. Arthur forgot Balair
could level up. He talked to Vana and
Allendria as they scoured the battlefield for
useful items and the goblins and orc's few
serviceable pieces of armor and weapons to
load onto the cart. They told him Balair had
swooped down and clawed at one orc to distract
it from Samson a few times, and the little
dragon had also got its teeth into the skull
of a goblin that Samson had as well. Arthur
felt good knowing the little guy was useful.

They were starting to make their way back
when they spooked a pack of boars. Arthur was
able to take down two while Vana knocked down
three. Allendria even got off a shot of fire
and took down one. All in all, it was a
productive trip.

*You have gained 400 total experience in
Archery for the fight*

*You have gained 1350 total experience for
the fight.*

*Congratulations, you have reached level
12! You now have 5 available skill points. You
might just get to a high enough level to
survive.*

Once they made it back to the inn, Arthur
stuck around to help get everything skinned
and quartered out for Daniel.

*You have gained 750 total experience in
Skinning.*

*Congratulations, you have progressed to
Level 4 in Skinning. You have a 6% chance for
any furs you skin to be 1 level higher quality
than your skill would typically allow. You
find out where the balls are yet?*

He even got lucky, and one of the Boar furs was bumped up to good quality. Once finished, they loaded the carcasses onto the cart, and he and Allendria took them out to get rid of them. Arthur let Allendria do the honors of burning the corpses, and they made their way back toward the inn.

They loaded up all the ore and took it over to Rowan. He was impressed with what they had found, and they quickly stashed the copper and silver away.

Allendria and Arthur had their evening bath and their evening dinner, and they turned in for the night.

On the fifth day, Arthur went back to his stonework. With his new enhancements, he got all the walls done and two of the three remaining gatehouses. There was only one gatehouse left, and it was the one on the western side of the village opposite where they expected the attack. He left himself time in the day because he wanted to catch up on some work in the forge.

You have gained 16,800 experience in Earth Magic and Fire Magic for successfully casting Combination Spell: Raise Stone Wall (x168).

Congratulations, you have reached level 17 in Fire Magic. Increases the effect of your fire magic spells by 48%. It's getting hotter, going to keep those clothes on?

You have gained 1080 total experience in Leatherworking.

Congratulations, you have successfully created Basic Leather Boots (Unfinished), Basic Leather Gloves (Unfinished), and Basic Leather Cowl (Unfinished).

He used the two points from Fire Magic and put both into Familiar Growth. He thought Balair should receive a reward for his performance the day before. The little dragon looked up at him when he selected the points and nodded to him. He then curled up and went back to sleep.

For his five stat points, he put one into Agility, two into Wisdom, and two into Endurance. His last couple of fights had been brutal, and one hit had done significant damage. He felt the dire need for better health. It would also help when he finished the leather pieces he had been working on. That was part of his goal for the last part of the day. He needed to enchant them all so he could finish them.

Arthur made his way to the blacksmith. He seemed to work better there. This was an excellent time to focus on the leather armor that needed to be finished. He went about getting the leather items enchanted. He put enchantments for Agility and Durability on the vest and pants, Durability and speed on the boots, Durability and accuracy on the gloves, and Durability and Constitution on the cowl. He also made the metal stud bands for the leather to help increase the defense.

Congratulations, you have successfully created Mage-crafted Iron Studded Bands. You have gained 500 experience in Arcane Smithing and Blacksmithing for creating this item (x10).

Congratulations, you have reached level 5 in Arcane Smithing. Increases the stats on items created using this ability by 8%. Still taking the easy route, I see.

You have gained 2235 total experience in Enchanting.
Congratulations, you have reached levels 5 and 6 in Enchanting. Your enchantments have a 15% decreased mana cost. Add stats, man!

Arthur put the studs on the vest and breeches and finished all the pieces.

You have gained 3275 total experience in Leatherworking.

Congratulations, you have reached levels 6 and 7 in Leatherworking. You are granted an 18% bonus to crafting speed. Figure out that stitching yet?

Item: Enchanted Basic Studded Leather Vest	**Armor:** 15 **Durability:** 50/50 **Rarity:** Uncommon **Quality:** Good **Weight:** 1.6 kg **Slot:** Chest

	Traits: A Basic Studded Leather Vest created using magical techniques and enchanted with special magical power. This armor will have more capacity for absorbing magical power. Enchantments: • Grants wearer +1 Agility • This vest loses durability 10% slower.
Item: Enchanted Basic Studded Leather Breeches	**Armor:** 15 **Durability:** 50/50 **Rarity:** Uncommon **Quality:** Good **Weight:** 1.4 kg **Slot:** Legs **Traits:** Basic Studded Leather Breeches, created using magical techniques and enchanted with special magical power. This armor will have more capacity for absorbing magical power. Enchantments:

	• Grants wearer +1 Agility • These pants lose durability 10% slower.

Item: Enchanted Basic Leather Glove	**Armor:** 5 **Durability:** 35/35 **Rarity:** Uncommon **Quality:** Good **Weight:** 0.8 kg **Slot:** Hands **Traits:** A Basic Leather Glove created using magical techniques and enchanted with special magical power. This armor will have more capacity for absorbing magical power. Enchantments: • Increases chance to hit by 5%. • This glove loses durability 10% slower.

Item: Enchanted Basic Leather Boot	**Armor:** 5 **Durability:** 35/35

	Rarity: Uncommon
	Quality: Good
	Weight: 1.5 kg
	Slot: Feet
	Traits: A Basic Leather Boot created using magical techniques and enchanted with special magical power. This armor will have more capacity for absorbing magical power.
	Enchantments:
	• Increases movement speed by 10%. • This boot loses durability 10% slower.

Item: Enchanted Basic Leather Cowl	**Armor**: 5
	Durability: 35/35
	Rarity: Uncommon
	Quality: Good
	Weight: 1.0 kg
	Slot: Head

	Traits: A Basic Leather Cowl created using magical techniques and enchanted with special magical power. This armor will have more capacity for absorbing magical power. Enchantments: • Increases maximum stamina by 20 points. • This cowl loses durability 10% slower.

Arthur was happy with the armor. It would give him and the girls all at least a bit of protection. It also had a few stats built-in, which made it better. He put all 4 points in Eye of Rarity for his leatherworking. He then pulled up his new skill tree for Arcane Smithing.

You have 2 unused Talent Points.

Talent	Description
Tier 1	
Eye for Quality (0/5)	*Each point increases the chance of the quality of the items you create, increasing by one by 5%.*
Unlock Steel (0/1)	*Teaches you the secrets of forging steel with magic.*

Granular Structure (0/5)	*Each point increases the amount of armor on items you create by 4%.*

There was no question about it. Arthur may not have steel yet, but he wanted the knowledge for it. He used that point and checked again.

You have 1 unused Talent Point.

Talent	Description
Tier 2	
Material Savings (0/10)	*Each point decreases the material needed to make items by 3%.*
Will of the Many (0/5)	*Each point increases the amount of items made when forging multiple items at once by 10%.*

Arthur took Will of the Many for his second point. He wanted it because he would be making arrowheads. He then pulled up his new Enchanting talents.

You have 2 unused Talent Points.

Talent	Description
Tier 1	
Mana Conservation (0/10)	*Each point decreases the mana needed to complete an enchantment by 3%.*
Powered Enchantments (0/1)	*Teaches you how to use gems to latently power enchantments.*

Power of Symbols (0/5)	*Each point teaches you how to use an additional rune in your enchanting symbol structures.*

He went ahead and picked up Powered Enchantments. He had succeeded in this already, but he was sure there were better ways to do it, and there was probably much more that could be done with the skill. He looked at the new talents.

You have 1 unused Talent Point.

Talent	**Description**
Tier 2	
Charge Up (0/10)	*Each point increases the base amount of charges on enchanted items by 20.*
Secrets of Mana Cycling (0/5)	*After investing all 5 points, this will teach you the secret of naturally recharging your enchantments using latent mana.*

There were some good options. Arthur would have to work on Secrets of Mana Cycling, but he settled on Power of Symbols. Being able to use 4 symbols in an enchantment properly should help him create more powerful enchantments.

When Arthur finished the leather, he
turned his attention to the forge. The first
thing he needed to deal with was the silver
and copper. It was time to create a new spell.
Rowan had a silver and copper coin he could
use as a reference. He pulled out the silver
and the copper ore and found two small
chests.

The first part would be melting them down
and separating the metal from the chunks of
impurities. Once Arthur managed that, he
should be able to use his Arcane Forging spell
to make the coins. So to start, he had to
develop magic for melting the metal. A fire
shield surrounded a chunk of the copper ore.
He then raised the temperature in the
protection until the metal started to flow.

Weaving his Earth Magic into the spell,
he could pull the impurities away from the
ore. Once they were separated, he held the
melted metal with his earth magic and let the
contaminants fall out of the protection.

While it was still hot, and he was
holding it aloft with magic, he pictured the
copper coin and pictured as many coins as
possible with this amount of metal. He started
the forging spell and watched the metal flow
into the thickness of the coins, and then the
line of power flowed over the metal, and the
coins started appearing. The chunk of ore
turned out 30 copper coins, and he also
received a spell.

*Congratulations, you have learned the
Crafting Spell: Arcane Furnace. You have
gained 350 experience in Fire and Earth Magic
for discovering a known spell.*

Spell: Arcane Furnace

Requirements: Fire Magic and Earth Magic Mana Cost: 30 MP Cast Time: 5 seconds	Description: Cast a spell to melt metal and remove impurities. The initial cast takes 5 seconds, but the length of time required to complete the item depends on the amount of metal and impurities to sort. Special Traits: Using this spell increases the base Quality by one rank as long as the item and materials used are within your skill range.
Mastery Level: 1	

Mage-crafted Copper Coin	**Durability:** 15/15 **Rarity:** Uncommon **Quality:** Well crafted **Weight:** 0.1 kg **Traits:** A standard copper coin of currency. This coin was made using magic means and can accept more magical power.

Well, his idea worked fine. The problem was he doubted common currency in the world was mage-crafted. He stuck with the coins he had made, anyway. The mage-crafted currency would allow him to enchant them easier and would help prevent fraud in the future. He melted the rest of the copper as well as silver.

You have gained 2950 total experience in Earth and Fire Magic.
Congratulations, you have reached level 18 in Earth Magic. Earth Magic spells now have a 51% increased effect. Quickly becoming a master of Earth, I see.
You have gained 2450 total experience in Arcane Smithing and Blacksmithing.
Congratulations, you have reached level 6 in Arcane Smithing. Increases the stats on items created using this ability by 10%. Meh, whatever.

Mage-crafted Silver Coin	**Durability:** 15/15
	Rarity: Uncommon
	Quality: Well crafted
	Weight: 0.2 kg
	Traits: A standard silver coin of currency. This coin was made using magic means and can accept more magical power.

He now had 1,260 copper coins and 300 silver coins to work with. That could allow him to start handing out some coppers as rewards for orders. They needed to get an idea of fair trade value. He wouldn't rely on other cities for prices because he knew they were all in horrible shape, and the costs would be all wrong. The leaders of the village would need to set fair prices. He also put the 2 points from his Arcane Smithing level into Will of the Many.

Arthur had another idea he had to try out as well. He wanted to make a stack of arrowheads, but he had a new design to try. Hopefully, it wouldn't be a failure. He grabbed a chunk of iron and tossed it in the fire. While it was heating up, he pictured the design. He was changing the design of the arrows and was also doing an additional step.

The act of engraving the symbols for his enchanting took a long time. Being able to do it on loads of arrowheads would take forever. Since his spell replicated what he pictured, he would try to forge them with his arcane forging with the symbols already engraved on them. This would mean he had to dump mana into them to activate the enchantments.

Arthur pictured the new design with the forged symbols and lifted the metal out of the fire. He cast his arcane forging spell and watched the metal flow somewhat flat, and then the line of power carved out the arrowheads. To his pleasure, the arrowheads appeared how he had pictured them, and the symbols seemed to be correct. These would be lethal.

He went ahead and imbued them with his
mana, and to his surprise, the mana was pulled
into all of them at once. It looked like batch
created items would also complete enchantments
together. This would save him a ton of time
having to enchant each one individually. The
magic finished, and he was pleased with his
new arrowheads.

Enchanted Mage-crafted Serrated Iron Arrowheads	**Damage Modifier:** +1
	Durability: 40/40
	Rarity: Rare
	Quality: Well Crafted
	Weight: 0.2 kg
	Slot: Crafting item
	Traits: Iron Arrowheads, created using magical techniques and enchanted with special magical power. The serrated edge on these causes the target to bleed for an additional 4 HP per bleed effect. If the arrow is removed, this doubles to 8 HP per bleed effect until healed.
	Enchantments:
	● This arrowhead ignores

	up to 10 points of armor.

    These would be perfect. Arthur spent some time making more of these. He made ten more sets of them so they would have 165 sitting in reserve.

    You have gained 550 total experience in Earth and Fire Magic.
    You have gained 1650 total experience in Arcane Smithing and Blacksmithing.
    Congratulations, you have reached level 7 in Arcane Smithing. Increases the stats on items created using this ability by 12%. I like your train of thought.
    Congratulations, you have progressed to Level 9 in Blacksmithing. You are granted a 24% bonus to forging speed. Swing away.
    Congratulations, you have successfully enchanted Mage-crafted Serrated Iron Arrowheads (x15). You have gained 3300 experience in Enchanting (x10).
    Congratulations, you have reached level 7 in Enchanting. Your enchantments have an 18% decreased mana cost. Try some clothing for once.

    He put all 4 points into Charge Up for his Enchanting levels. Charged items would be a significant focus now that he had the storage secrets unlocked, as well. He should be able to create some beneficial things for the village. The arrowheads were taken over to Rowan to show them off.
    Rowan looked at them and whistled appreciatively. His eyebrows rose as he saw the details on the item.

"Those are some damn nasty things, aren't
they?"

"They are, but they're exclusively for
our fight."

"Should give us an advantage for sure,"
Rowan said.

"Either way, I'm off to the inn, I got
the coins completed so I'll take them with me.
We'll have to discuss fair prices soon so we
can start using them as rewards. I'll take the
arrowheads too. I'm hoping Zeke has the orders
done for feathered arrow shafts. If so, I'll
have him get these completed." Arthur told
him.

"Goodnight then, Arthur," Rowan said with
a wave.

Arthur cleaned up his area in the shop,
grabbed the two boxes of coins, and walked to
the inn. He kept the arrowheads in his bag so
he wouldn't have to worry about them. Once
inside the inn, he handed the chests to
Daniel, who opened them and eyed the contents.
Daniel looked surprised. Arthur was certain it
was the uncommon quality of the coins, but he
only nodded and took them to stash.

Arthur was pleased to see Zeke there, and
the man had been working overtime. There were
more than enough shafts, and Arthur completed
his work orders. He then presented the man
with the arrowheads and asked him to complete
the arrows. He stressed the importance of
getting them back to him and keeping it quiet.
The man was more than happy to oblige.

Zeke also surprised Arthur by handing him a beautiful yew bow. The middle was carved into the vague shape he had seen from compound bows back on earth, but the ends of the arms sloped backward like a recurve style bow. It was beautifully crafted and looked fantastic. He submitted the work order for Zeke and accepted the item. Arthur was glad to now have himself a good bow since Vana got the dungeon one.

Carved Yew Bow	**Attack:** 12-16
	Durability: 75/75
	Rarity: Uncommon
	Quality: Well Crafted
	Weight: 1.8 kg
	Slot: Main Hand
	Traits: A bow made of wood from a yew tree.

The only thing that could have made it better was if Arthur had stopped him to enchant it before the man finished it. Oh well, it would suit his purposes. The day was long, and he settled into bed with Balair and fell asleep. The dragon had been worthless all day just sleeping anyway, so Arthur was surprised he was still going to sleep now. He dozed off to sleep.

Chapter 28

Fight for the Village

The morning of the sixth day started similar to the last five. Arthur got himself up, threw Balair off of him, and got dressed. He made his way downstairs and kissed Allendria on the cheek. They had been spending time with each other more often now. She had been working on her Earth Magic alongside him every day when he worked on the wall. She had even made it high enough where Arthur could teach her the spell Raise Stone Wall. Her base size wasn't as big as his, but she was quickly progressing.

They were eating their food at the table when the father and son woodcutting duo burst into the inn in a rush. The father looked around the room frantically and finally spotted Arthur. He headed straight to him as fast as he could and stopped at Arthur's table.

"My Lord Mayor, we have spotted trouble outside the village." He said partially out of breath.

"Calm down, good man. Arthur is just fine. What have you seen?" Arthur asked.

"We were out early this morning, harvesting wood from the forest edge to the east of the village when we saw a large group of travelers headed down the road. We only waited until they were close enough for us to make them out barely, but it looks like the attacking force you were expecting is getting here early."

"What?" Arthur exclaimed as he jumped up from his chair. "How many were there?"

"It was hard to get an accurate count. We left before they got too close so we could get here and give warning. There looked to be at least twenty."

"Damn. Alright, I need to get moving this morning. I have to get the last few preparations made and gather anyone who wants to help."

The lumberjack stepped forward and held his hand out to Arthur. "I'm with you, Arthur. I have at least a basic comprehension of a bow, and I'm willing to help."

Arthur took his hand and shook it. He learned the man's name was James, and his son was named Jack. James followed him and left Jack in the inn's safety. They made their way to the back, where he found Daniel.

"Daniel looks like our time's up for preparations. James just spotted the attack group making their way from the eastern road where we thought they might approach from."

"Damn, they must have run across a group of them traveling the countryside and returned quicker than we thought. Numbers?"

"Can't be certain, but we're expecting at least twenty." Daniel looked pale for a moment but then shook it off. He hadn't seen Arthur's gang in action but knew they were an incredible group.

"I'll start gathering all the villagers here. You grab what weapons you think we'll need and get them here for the fight. We may have a few more volunteers shortly." Daniel told him.

"I'll make it happen." Arthur turned and dashed off to the blacksmith. He found Rowan working diligently on some iron. Rowan saw the look on his face and the speed in which he approached and quickly stopped what he was doing.

"What's wrong, Arthur?"

"The attacking force is early. They've just been spotted to the east. We still have a little time before they get here, so we're preparing. It might be time for you to dust off your axe. I wish I had time to make you some proper armor, but I wasn't expecting them here yet." Arthur told him.

"I'll be fine. I made myself some basic greaves, sabatons, and bracers. I also have an old chest piece that didn't turn out how I wanted, but it's better than nothing." He told him.

Arthur thought about it real quick. He decided to go ahead with his idea. "Let me see that chest piece. I might be able to fix it up quickly."

Rowan walked into the shop and pulled out an old and worn looking chest piece of iron. It looked like it had seen better days, and it was not the best quality to start with. Arthur focused on his magical gifts and grabbed a small chunk of spare iron lying around. Instead of thinking of the process as he did for his forging skill, he pictured the extra iron he had melding into the breastplate and filling in the bad dings and cracks. This should smooth out the design and even out the width of all of it as it should have been. He used his power of fire to bring the metals up to heat and then used his earth magic to smooth it out. He focused more flame on the extra chunk of metal until it was almost molten and used his earth magic to guide it to fix the cracks and dents. After it was finished, Arthur was pleased that the magic had only taken him about half of his total mana, and to his surprise, he got a new skill for it.

Congratulations, you have learned Arcane Repair for a 100 experience bonus.
Congratulations, you have learned the Crafting Spell: Arcane Repair (Metal). You have gained 350 experience in Fire and Earth Magic for discovering a known spell.
You have gained 110 experience in Earth Magic and Fire Magic for successfully casting Arcane Repair.

Spell: Arcane Repair (Metal)

Requirements: Fire Magic and Earth Magic Mana Cost: 40 MP Cast Time: 5 seconds	Description: This spell allows you to repair damaged metal objects. The severity of the damage will determine any additional materials that need to be added during the process. Special Traits: Using this spell increases the quality of the item by 1 level. This bonus won't stack with subsequent uses of this spell on the same item.
Mastery Level: 1	

Rowan looked at the item in wonder. The original chest piece had been poor quality and looked like hammered shit. The repaired version of it was back to one good solid breastplate that had even thicknesses and none of the nasty-looking hammer marks or dents. It also increased to a Fair quality rating.

"Damn, Arthur, you will put me out of business if you keep that kind of work going," Rowan told him.

Arthur thought about that statement for a moment. "I'll tell you what Rowan, you have been a good friend to me and have helped me plenty. Once we finish up this fight for the village, I'll train you in Earth and Fire Magic and then teach you to become an Arcane Smith like myself. It would be good to have someone other than just myself doing this. There's never enough time in the day."

Rowan looked immensely pleased. "I could never repay you for that, Arthur. Not only would you be teaching me, not one, but two magic skills, something that's quite unheard of, but you would also teach me a hidden art. I don't know if I can accept that." He said humbly.

"Anything for a friend Rowan. We'll make it happen one way or another. Let's get this gear to the inn and start getting everyone ready."

They loaded up the cart with all the different pieces of gear that had been made. Rowan had been working nonstop to make things for today, and Arthur had a few spare blades lying around from items he swapped out or made in his early blacksmithing. When all was said and done, they could fully armor two additional people with iron armor, not counting Rowan's armor he would personally wear.

As they made it back to the inn, they saw a crowd of people gathered there. They pushed their cart through to the inn, and he went searching for Daniel.

"Daniel, where are you?" Arthur called over the crowd.

"Over here, Arthur." He heard Daniel call from his right. He made it to the man to assess the situation.

"Any more news?"

"James just came back in and he said it looks like they are about an hour from the wall now. They don't appear to be pushing themselves real fast. I bet they think they will just walk through the village, destroying everything. They haven't made it to where they can see the wall and gatehouse yet. Not sure how much good they will do, though since they're short, and the gatehouse has no gate yet." He said grimly.

"I think that'll work out best for us. I don't want the bandits circling to another entrance or spreading out too far along the wall. With the gatehouse open, I know those idiots will probably try to charge their way through it. I plan on having Samson in the doorway to show them the folly of their ways. I'm hoping we can get a few archers to volunteer and pick off anyone who tries to jump the wall while we hold the gate." Arthur told him.

"That sounds like a good plan. I have had two people already offer their skills. James said he had a bit of skill with the bow, and Zeke offered to help too. I'm assuming the bowyer knows how to use a bow since he offered." Daniel told him.

"Good, grab the two spare bows we have from work orders and give them to those two along with a couple of bundles of iron arrows for each. I'll ask if we have anyone else to volunteer to take up the armor and a blade. I don't want them fighting at the wall, but I do want them guarding the inn, and I want people taking shelter here in case anyone sneaks past us and tries to cause trouble."

"I'll go get the bows and arrows, you find the people," Daniel said as he raced toward the back.

Arthur turned to face the crowd and climbed up on top of a chair to get a little height.

"Everyone, please be calm for a moment and hear me out!" He called over the crowd.

Everyone slowly stopped their frantic talking and looked to him.

"I understand everyone's worries. The people I warned you about have shown up much quicker than we initially expected, but don't be worried, I have faith that the group of people I've been fighting with can hold them off. Two of your villagers, Woodsman James and Bowyer Zeke, have volunteered to take up a bow in defense of the village, and I can't thank them enough."

"My group plans on holding the gatehouse closest to their approach, and I'll rely on those two to keep the walls clear if anyone tries to climb over them. That being said, I would like to find two volunteers who would be willing to don armor and stand guard at the inn to protect the villagers that take shelter here. I would also like for people to gather their families and get them here at the inn."

Arthur looked around expectantly. There was a palpable silence that stretched on before a gruff voice in the back called out, "I'll stand guard." Arthur swung his view to the man in question, but he wasn't someone that Arthur recognized. He was a burly man with dark black hair. His eyes were dark as well, but he looked like he was built to fight.

"What is your name, good man? I don't believe I have seen you around before." Arthur asked.

"I'm Toren, Lord Mayor. I don't have many skills, so you haven't seen me doing work orders. I want to take this chance to make myself useful, though." Toren said.

"Well, come over here with us, and as soon as we finish here, we'll get you geared up," Arthur told him. "Anyone else?"

This time a younger man came forward and called out to him. "I will, Lord Mayor!" he said with a fire in his eyes. The young man couldn't have been much over sixteen, but Arthur knew that in a medieval society such as this, the young man was more than welcome to fight. He wasn't overly comfortable with it, but, in all honesty, they were just guards. He didn't expect them to fight.

"What is your name, brave young lad?" Arthur called to him.

"My name is Noah."

"Well, Noah, come to us so we can get you ready. Everyone else, gather together, and take shelter. We will get our armor and weapons ready and soon be heading out to stop this force."

The people wore nervous looks still, but they weren't in quite as much of a panic as before. Some wandered their way into the inn and found a seat while others dashed back out to their homes. He assumed they were gathering their families to return. Arthur and Daniel found Rowan, and they walked out to the cart loaded with weapons. Zeke came up to him as they were grabbing the gear and handed him a bundle. It was the arrows he asked him to make last night with the new arrowheads he had made attached to them. Arthur clapped the man on the shoulder.

"Fantastic work Zeke and not a moment too soon. These will be useful."

Zeke just nodded in approval. Arthur gave the man a dozen of them and told him to make the shots count. He turned and gave a score to James as well, who'd made his way over to the group.

"James, these are special arrows. Use them for the leaders or if someone is in trouble and needs help quick, otherwise use your normal arrows." Arthur told him.

"Understood Arthur." He said.

"Good Man."

Arthur took the rest of the arrows and handed them to Vana. She got a devilish gleam in her eyes as she read the description.

"These will do perfectly." She said to him with a grin.

"Well, I know you'll be able to put them to good use. When we wrap this up, I'll try some more designs I think you might like." He told her, matching her smile.

"I look forward to it."

They got Toren and Noah geared up in the iron armor they had and gave each of them a standard iron sword with an iron dagger to put on their waist. Arthur hoped they wouldn't need them, but he wouldn't leave them unprepared.

Vana and Allendria had gathered around him, so he thought it was time to present them with their armor. He handed out a set of the leather armor he had made and enchanted to each of them. They each looked on their armor with appreciation.

"Thank you, Arthur. Feels a little better having some protection." Vana told him.

Allendria walked up and kissed him on the cheek. "Thank you, as well." She told him in a husky voice.

They ran back inside and set about getting their armor on. Upon walking out of the inn, Arthur, Allendria, and Vana spotted Samson, James, and Zeke and gathered them all together.

"I appreciate your help," Arthur said as he looked to Zeke and James.

"We'll proceed to the gatehouse that covers the road they're traveling. Once we arrive, I want Zeke and James to keep a slight distance. I want you to be close enough to cover the wall with your bows but at enough of a range to escape if needed. Try to stay the max distance you are accurate at. Your main job is to shoot anyone who tries to climb it. Vana will assist when she can."

"Samson, I need you to be my gate door. Use that armor well and sit in the doorway to block them as much as possible. I'll be covering your back and helping fill gaps as needed. Allendria, you're the support for everyone. Take shots when you can and disable enemies. If anyone gets through us or over the walls, they're yours. Any questions?" No one said anything. Arthur wanted to take Rowan with him, but he couldn't afford to lose the man and his skill. He would be better keeping their two volunteers calm guarding the inn.

They took off at a brisk walk toward the wall. The group didn't want to run and tire themselves out for no reason, and they still had some time, anyway. They reached the wall and got to their positions. Arthur burned some raw mana and created a small hump in front of the gatehouse entrance and a slight dip right behind it. It wasn't overly noticeable, but it would trip some of them up. It would also give Samson a spot to hold them a little easier. While they were getting set, there was a surprise prompt that popped up. Arthur noticed that everyone had the same surprised look on their faces.

Defend Alem's Crossing	
Requirements: Level 12 Rewards: 25000 experience, 7500 skill experience to allocate as you choose, unknown rewards also possible.	Description: The village is under attack. Rally your friends and defend the village. Go forth protectors of righteousness and end the threat.
Do you accept this quest? Yes/No	

They all quickly accepted YES with excitement. The group spotted the bandits as they finally came within view. The bandits stopped, and it was clear they couldn't make heads or tails of what they were seeing. The stone wall had thrown them for a loop.

There was some barely audible yelling for a couple of minutes, and then they moved forward. When they were within a hundred yards of the gatehouse, Arthur called to them.

"Stop where you are by the authority of the Mayor of Alem's Crossing!" he yelled at the group.

They came to a quick halt and started looking around. Arthur could tell they were muttering between themselves about what they had heard, but they were too far away to hear anything. One man started to make his way forward. He was quickly followed by two others, trailing slightly behind him. It didn't take long for Arthur to realize that the man coming toward them was the leader of the group they confronted. Arthur never caught the man's name. The two directly behind him were Xavier and Alex. Alex was still missing his right hand from where Arthur had removed it with his sword. They continued toward Arthur and Samson at the gatehouse and stopped when they were roughly thirty-five yards away.

"What the hell do you think you are doing, and where did this wall come from?" The leader said with a sneer.

"I'm here telling your rabble to leave my village. You have no formal reason to be here and look like a group of bandits. This wall is none of your concern. If you come to this village with hostility, you'll be forcefully removed." Arthur told him in a grim tone.

"Oh, it's your village now?"

"As a matter of fact, it is. I'm the mayor of this village and, as such, have the authority to tell you to fuck off." He told the man.

The man chuckled to himself. "You sure do have some balls. I guess I should be polite and introduce myself since I never did the last time we met. I'm Lazaru, leader of this band of merry men." He said as he gestured at the group.

"I don't foresee us having any problem getting past your handful of defenders with what we brought, and when I do, we will burn this village to the ground. I look forward to killing all the residents as a reminder to those who decide to stand against us. Naturally, we will take our time with the women first, but in the end, all will be shown the same fate." He said with an evil grin.

Arthur's rage was building at the callous attitude this man had for people. "You're welcome to try, but I can promise you that you won't leave the fight alive this time, no matter how many worthless thugs you have brought."

"Well, you were certainly interesting for the small amount of time I knew you." Lazaru turned and looked at the people with him. He made a waving gesture with his hand, and the group rushed for the gate. He stayed behind with his two companions as the rest of the group rushed them.

Most of the group looked to be wearing barely serviceable clothes and were holding either shitty looking clubs or somewhat rusty daggers. None of them were wearing quality weapons of any kind. They ran at them at full speed with murder in their eyes, and Arthur took a few steps behind Samson. He had a feeling this would be a fierce clash. He pulled his sword and dagger up to their ready positions and waited for the crash. Samson stood resolute with his right leg braced backward slightly while bracing his shield with his left shoulder and holding his sword down by his side. The man was braced to accept the charge.

The enemy covered the distance quickly, but it wasn't long before Arthur saw an arrow zip past him at incredible speed and slam into one of the charging enemy's throat. He grabbed his neck, dropped his weapon, and collapsed while sputtering blood. The rest of the group kept running, and a few of them even ran directly over their fallen comrade. Before the group made it to Samson, another shot had sped through and taken one in the chest. Vana was sure making good use of every chance she got.

The group made it to Samson, and the loud crash that followed made Arthur visibly cringe. The guy in the lead had tried to swing his weapon, but the sheer speed at which they ran caused the rest of the group to push him right into Samson's shield, and it crushed him on the spot. He fell in a heap of broken bones. The rest around him had quickly slowed and were trying to get in swinging blows. A few of the idiots even managed to hit their allies. It was apparent they didn't have a lot of training and weren't used to fighting in a bottleneck like this. There were around thirty of the raiders who'd assaulted the place, and most had stalled in their charge. Luckily, none of them seemed to be smart enough to use a bow, so it was all poorly trained melee fighters.

The raiders had spread out slightly as they waited at the bottleneck. They couldn't get over three people in the gap at a time, or they wouldn't have room to swing properly. The rest looked on in eager anticipation. Samson was making spectacular use of his sword and shield as he would bash one to stun them and use that chance to swipe at another. After the initial clash, Arthur stepped up beside him and started fighting one of them on his side.

The man hadn't been paying attention and was swinging an overhand blow at Samson when Arthur stepped in under the man's arm and buried his dagger into the man's chest. Arthur quickly stepped back, even with Samson, to keep either of them from being attacked from the side. Seeing the man go down, shifted some of the attention to him, and he had two people clamoring to hit him with their daggers. Arthur wasn't overly skilled in melee combat, but was using their swings against them and parrying their swings toward their nearest allies hoping to make them hurt one another. During one swing, he was able to get a firm push on the redirect and caused the man to stumble into the other fighter facing him and stab him in the leg. During the second man's shock, Arthur took advantage of the opportunity and lunged forward to impale the man on his sword. He pulled out the sword and spun to slash the other man in his neck. Both fell to the ground, unmoving and bleeding profusely.

You have dealt 140 damage to Bandit (1) (Level 12) with Enchanted Basic Mage-crafted Iron Dagger (Critical Strike) (Mortal Blow) (Fatal Blow).
You have dealt 160 damage to Bandit (2) (Level 12) with Steel Longsword of Minor Beastslaying (Critical Strike) (Mortal Blow) (Fatal Blow).
You have dealt 140 damage to Bandit (3) (Level 12) with Enchanted Basic Mage-crafted Iron Dagger (Critical Strike) (Mortal Blow) (Fatal Blow).

Arthur didn't even have a chance to catch his breath before two more people took their place. One of them swung at him, and he blocked it with his sword. The other person facing him swung toward his head with manic glee on his face. Before Arthur had a chance to react, an arrow went right through the man's eye, and he collapsed to the ground twitching. Arthur used that moment to drive his dagger into the ribs of the man he had blocked. He stumbled backward and fell into the crowd behind him.

You have dealt 140 damage to Bandit (4) (Level 12) with Enchanted Basic Mage-crafted Iron Dagger (Critical Strike) (Mortal Blow) (Fatal Blow).

"Arthur, we have trouble!" Allendria yelled.

"What is it?" He yelled back.

"Too many bandits have gotten over the wall. They are making their way toward your back." She told him.

"On your back, Samson." He called to his friend. He spun around and put his back to Samson. Arthur worked to hold off the people that were trying to swarm them from the rear. Some of the others who'd made it over were trying to rush their ranged defenders as well.

Arthur held his ground to protect Samson's back as the man dealt with the people still trying to push in the gate. He was taking wild swings and bashes with his shield trying to plug the entire gap, and he moved side to side. He wasn't doing a lot of permanent damage, but he was doing an excellent job of stalling them.

Three people rushed Arthur together and started swinging. Arthur was able to push one blade out of the way with his dagger and block another blow with his sword, but the third hit made it through. He was able to deflect it slightly with a bracer, and the blade caught him in the side. If not for his armor, it would have done tremendous damage, but he had slowed it enough for it not to be terrible.

Bandit (7) (Level 12) has dealt 60 HP damage to you with Rusty Iron Dagger.

The bandit who'd hit him was struck from behind with fire and stumbled forward. Arthur took that chance to put a dagger in his heart.

You have dealt 220 damage to Bandit (7) (Level 12) with Enchanted Basic Mage-crafted Iron Dagger (Heart Strike).
Bandit (7) (Level 12) has Died.
Congratulations, you have learned Light Armor for a 100 experience bonus.
Congratulations, you have progressed to Level 4 in Small Blades. Your attack speed has increased by 8%. Think you could have used a larger blade.

Arthur's attack had left him open, and the bandit on his side scored a slash to his thigh.

Bandit (8) (Level 12) has dealt 40 HP damage to you with Rusty Iron Dagger.

Arthur leaped backward to get himself some space. He couldn't go too far back, or he'd run into Samson. His eyes fixed on both of the enemies in front of him. He took a quick look and saw some of the club-wielding bandits rushing Zeke and James. Vana was running and shooting her bow at the same time, trying to keep the distance. She was trying to assist the other two, but she couldn't while she was being pursued.

Allendria was standing to the side, dodging attacks and sending in occasional sprays of fire at people to get them to back up. He saw her score a hit and burn through one bandit assaulting her with her concentrated flame, but she still had two others on her. He couldn't see the number of people behind him that Samson was squaring off with, but based on what he was hearing, there were probably at least eight of them on the other side of the iron wall now known as Samson.

The situation was looking grim, and he didn't know what they could do. He had lost a little less than half his health already, and they still had numerous people to fight off. He took a glance around at the villagers and his friends with a sigh of despair as he turned his attention back to the two he was facing off against.

Chapter 29

Miraculous Finish

Arthur intercepted a swing from one of the two men in front of him and pushed the blade back, trying to knock him off balance. The man recovered faster than expected, and Arthur had to quickly block an attack coming from the guy on his side.

He needed to find an opening quick, or this would turn ugly. He couldn't figure out what to do. It was about this time that his mind finally caught up to something that he felt stupid for not remembering. One of his biggest problems had been learning to blend magic into his fighting, and that was just what he needed. He quickly let out a Basic Fire Bolt directly into the face of the bandit on his right. The cast time didn't affect his fighting. It was merely a delay. He had to wait before the spell happened after he willed it to activate. The stunned look on the bandit's face and the face of the one standing next to him told the story. They were both so surprised by the attack that they stood there with jaws hanging open. Arthur took that chance to lunge a blade at each of them. The one on his left received the dagger into his abdomen, and the one on the right took his sword directly to his heart.

You have dealt 15 damage to Bandit (6) (Level 12) with Basic Fire Bolt.

You have dealt 140 damage to Bandit (6) (Level 12) with Enchanted Basic Mage-crafted Iron Dagger (Critical Strike) (Mortal Blow) (Fatal Blow).

You have dealt 160 damage to Bandit (7) (Level 12) with Steel Longsword of Minor Beastslaying (Heart Strike).

Bandit (7) (Level 12) has Died.

Congratulations, you have reached level 4 in Swords. Swing speed with swords increased by 9%. Kind of behind on these skills.

Congratulations, you have reached level 3 in Dual Wield. Accuracy penalty with off-hand weapons decreased by 6%. Ambidextrous as well?

Congratulations, you have reached level 2 in Block. Successful blocks grant you a 3% chance to stumble the opponent. Oh, you almost had it, you gotta be quicker than that.

Bandit (2) (Level 12) has Died.

Congratulations, you have reached level 2 in Parry. Increased success chance with parry by 3%. Push back!

Bandit (3) (Level 12) has Died.

Congratulations, you have reached levels 2 and 3 in Light Armor. Movement speed increased by 6% when wearing Light Armor. Something is better than nothing.

It looked like some of the original bandits were dying due to hemorrhaging since no one had attended to them. Arthur thought it was time to change things up a bit and adjust tactics. He pulled a small wall up in front of two of the bandits who were chasing Vana. Both of them ran into the short wall and fell to the ground on their faces. She took that chance to place an arrow in each one of their backs and kept moving. He then sent a Basic Fire Bolt at one of the two people after James. James was using his bow to block the club blows as they flew at him, but he was slightly beaten up and having trouble moving quickly enough to keep up with them.

That slowed down many of the problems out in the field. The enemy was still clamoring over the walls, but not very many were left. It looked like they were finally getting to the end of the group. Arthur turned to look at Samson. The man was barely holding on anymore. He didn't look like he had taken a lot of damage, although his armor was a little banged up. More than anything, he just looked like he was out of Stamina. Arthur determined it was time for him to get a break.

He came up to Samson's side and poured raw mana into his Fire Magic and sent a ball of fire at the group, trying to beat Samson into submission. The group all jumped backward and tried to dash out of the way.

"Samson, step back quickly!" Arthur yelled at him.

As soon as he had given some room, Arthur cast his Raise Stone Wall spell, and the wall started coming up in front of the gatehouse. The group outside stood there and watched as it kept climbing and closed off the gatehouse.

"Catch your breath real quick and get back into the fight. It won't take those guys long to hop the wall, and then we'll be fighting them in the open field. We all need to regroup." Arthur told him.

Samson nodded at him, looking exhausted. He stood still for a moment, taking a few large breaths before he turned and surveyed the field of battle. He was a military veteran and saw the field of action as the mess it indeed was. Zeke had been knocked to the ground and appeared to be unconscious. He didn't look like his life was in danger, though. James could barely walk anymore because one of his legs was in bad shape, but he was still holding off strikes of one other person. The man that Arthur had hit in the back with the Basic Fire Bolt had turned and headed for Arthur. Vana was still running around, trying to stay out of range. Now and then, she would stop and quickly fire and then take off again while she grabbed another arrow and made ready. He saw plenty of people down and bleeding with arrows sticking out of them. He also saw eight more people climbing the walls on both sides of the gatehouse.

Now they had lost the little advantage they had with the short wall and were down one person with another almost useless. Arthur decided it was time to get James out of this fight. He sent a bolt of fire at the man that was still attacking James. The man stumbled, and Arthur rushed in his direction. He ignored the man that had headed for him earlier and needed to get to James first. He wished he had his bow, but instead, he had to close the distance on foot. It took him a few seconds to rush the range. The man had recovered from his stumble and was back to harassing James, sensing he was the less dangerous prey right now. Since the man was focused on James, it was easy for Arthur to come at him from the side and plunge his sword through the man's ribs. His dagger came around to hit the man in the chest.

You have dealt 15 damage to Bandit (8) (Level 12) with Basic Fire Bolt.

You have dealt 120 damage to Bandit (8) (Level 12) with Enchanted Basic Mage-crafted Iron Dagger (Critical Strike) (Mortal Blow) (Fatal Blow).

You have dealt 90 damage to Bandit (8) (Level 12) with Steel Longsword of Minor Beastslaying (Critical Strike) (Mortal Blow) (Fatal Blow).

Bandit (8) (Level 12) has Died.

Congratulations, you have reached level 5 in Small Blades. Swing speed with Small Blades increased by 12%. Trying to be an assassin now?

Congratulations, you have reached level 4 in Dual Wield. Accuracy penalty with off-hand weapons decreased by 9%.

Bandit (1) (Level 12) has Died.

Congratulations, you have reached level 4 in Light Armor. Movement speed increased by 9% when wearing Light Armor. Try adding some flair to your leather next time.

Congratulations, you have reached level 5 in Swords. Swing speed with swords increased by 12%. Surely you can do better than that?

Bandit (5) (Level 12) has Died.

Bandit (6) (Level 12) has Died.

Congratulations, you have reached level 3 in Parry. Increased success chance with parry by 6%. Bounce those blades.

"James! Get yourself away from here. This fight is over for you. We can handle it from here."

James gave Arthur a weary nod and shambled away as quickly as he could. Arthur ran over to Allendria to assist her. She was holding two people off, but she had some cuts and scrapes on her upper arms and one on her side. She was looking weary from the action as well. He came up behind one of them and rammed his sword into their back.

You have dealt 90 damage to Bandit (9) (Level 12) with Steel Longsword of Minor Beastslaying (Critical Strike) (Mortal Blow) (Fatal Blow).

Bandit (9) (Level 12) has Died.

Arthur turned to the other man assaulting Allendria and channeled his Weak Flame spell into his face. They stumbled and shrieked in surprise. Allendria took that chance to bury her dagger in the man's throat. He slumped forward, unmoving. She looked at him breathing hard for a moment.

"Look out!" She yelled in a rush. Arthur turned the direction she was looking as she sent a blast of fire over his shoulder. The man that had been pursuing him since he took off to help James stumbled and was trying to brush fire off of his face when Arthur dashed in and stabbed him with his dagger in the heart.

You have dealt 120 damage to Bandit (11) (Level 12) with Enchanted Basic Mage-crafted Iron Dagger (Heart Strike).
Bandit (11) (Level 12) has Died.
Congratulations, you have reached level 5 in Light Armor. Movement speed increased by 12% when wearing Light Armor. Try padding the armor a bit?

"Thanks," Arthur told her while gasping for breath. He took a quick look around the field and saw that Samson and Vana had made their way to each other. James had managed to get a good distance away, and everyone was ignoring him as he continued to flee. Samson and Vana were back to back, fighting off four others, and six more were closing in. He looked to Allendria and motioned toward the group.

"Let's go help our friends." He yelled as he dashed toward them.

He closed the distance and thought it was time to stop holding back. He cast Fire Bolts at both of the bandits attacking Vana. She was in more danger than Samson. She didn't have the protection Samson did. The bolts stumbled both the bandits and Arthur had closed the distance enough for an overhead chop at one of them. His sword dug into the man's shoulder and sheared through his collarbone. Arthur quickly followed with a dagger thrust to the back. At the same time, Vana leaped at the other surprised attacker and stabbed him with her dagger, and he fell to the ground writhing.

You have dealt 15 damage to Bandit (12) (Level 12) with Basic Fire Bolt.
You have dealt 15 damage to Bandit (13) (Level 12) with Basic Fire Bolt.
You have dealt 130 damage to Bandit (12) (Level 12) with Steel Longsword of Minor Beastslaying (Critical Strike) (Mortal Blow).
You have dealt 80 damage to Bandit (12) (Level 12) with Enchanted Basic Magecrafted Iron Dagger (Critical Strike) (Mortal Blow) (Fatal Blow).
Bandit (12) (Level 12) has Died.
Congratulations, you have reached level 6 in Small Blades. Swing speed with Small Blades increased by 15%. Trying to power level a little combat, I see.
Congratulations, you have reached level 5 in Dual Wield. Accuracy penalty with off-hand weapons decreased by 12%. Unlock those talents!

There were only eight of them left now,
that he could see, and luckily only a couple
of them had blades while the rest had clubs.
His group was exhausted, though. Samson had
dings and cuts all over his armor and was
bleeding a little on his upper arms and legs.
He cut down one of the two people he had been
holding off, and the other got a hit on his
helmet that caused him to stumble sideways and
fall to a knee. Arthur and Allendria both sent
a blast of fire at the man who had hit Samson
and forced him backward.

*You have dealt 15 damage to Bandit (14)
(Level 12) with Basic Fire Bolt.*

Arthur swung his sword at the bandit
while Samson tried to regain his feet. The man
parried his attack and tried to counterattack.
Arthur was tired and running out of energy. He
dodged most of the damage but still took the
hit to his left arm. His dagger fell from his
grip, and the limb felt somewhat numb.

*Bandit (14) (Level 12) has dealt 40 HP
damage to you with Rusty Iron Dagger.*
*Bandit (14) (Level 12) has inflicted
Paralyze (Left Arm) on you. This will last 2
minutes unless an additional injury occurs.*

Arthur didn't let the damage deter him.
He gritted his teeth against the pain and
swung right back with his sword. The sideways
arc cut deep into the man's neck and nearly
decapitated him.

*You have dealt 195 damage to Bandit (14)
(Level 12) with Steel Longsword of Minor
Beastslaying (Decapitating Blow).*

Bandit (14) (Level 12) has Died.
Congratulations, you have reached level 6 in Swords. Swing speed with swords increased by 15%. Nice decapitation!

Arthur still couldn't feel his left arm. There were still six more headed their way, and they had almost arrived. Samson had regained his footing and was ready to hold his ground. Vana looked on the verge of collapse due to some blood loss and exhaustion. Allendria didn't look much better. Arthur stepped up beside Samson to hold the charge. When the remaining six closed on them, he cast another Fire Bolt at the closest to him. The spell startled the man and caused him to run blindly at Arthur, giving Arthur the chance to run him through with his sword.

You have dealt 195 damage to Bandit (14) (Level 12) with Steel Longsword of Minor Beastslaying (Critical Strike) (Mortal Blow) (Fatal Blow).

The remaining five fanned out a bit, and three of them came for Arthur while two faced off with Samson. Arthur parried a blow from the first on him and blocked the second swing. The third man came in with a high swing, and Arthur got his sword up to prevent part of the damage but wasn't fast enough to stop it all. The club the man was wielding slammed into Arthur's left shoulder with enough force to cause him to stumble.

Bandit (14) (Level 12) has dealt 30 HP damage to you with Wooden Club.
Your Paralyze (Left Arm) has been extended by 2 minutes.

The man started to advance on Arthur, but a dagger punched through his side as Vana jumped up beside him to assist. This gave Arthur the short time he needed to recover from his hit. He did a quick check on his essential stats.

HP: 120/290
Mana: 220/480
Stamina 100/290

He couldn't let anything significant through, or it could be the end of him. He dodged the next swing coming for him and parried the following one. The feeling was returning in his left arm now, but it still wouldn't respond well. He retaliated with his sword to the man on his left, but the man caught his blade in a block. Vana took that chance to bury her dagger into the man who was trying to swing at Arthur while his sword was blocked. He fell to the ground holding his side.

Arthur pushed with his strength and forced the man who'd blocked his blade backward. He stumbled, and Arthur used that chance to swing across his body and slice into the man's stomach. The bandit dropped his weapon and clutched at his stomach, trying to hold it together, and Arthur swung in a reverse motion and caught the man in the neck. He fell to the ground dead.

You have dealt 110 damage to Bandit (15) (Level 12) with Steel Longsword of Minor Beastslaying (Critical Strike) (Mortal Blow) (Fatal Blow).

*You have dealt 100 damage to Bandit
(15)(Level 12) with Steel Longsword of Minor
Beastslaying (Critical Strike) (Mortal Blow)
(Fatal Blow).*
Bandit (15) (Level 12) has Died.

As the last person who Arthur was facing
fell, Samson took out one of the two on him,
and Allendria came around his side with a
burst of fire into the other's face, followed
by a dagger to his chest. Samson slumped his
shoulders with the exhaustion plain to see in
his eyes as Arthur looked to him.

Before Arthur could react, a war hammer
came from behind Samson and slammed into the
back of his head. He went down hard and wasn't
moving. Stunned, Arthur took a quick look
behind them. The three main problems were
there waiting for him. Alex was standing there
holding the war hammer while Xavier was
standing next to him blades in each hand.
Slightly behind them was Lazaru with a plain-
looking iron sword in his hand and a devilish
smile on his face.

"Well, you put up one hell of a fight,
but I'm sure you can't hold us off now,"
Lazaru said.

"We shall see about that," Arthur said as
he plastered a false smile on his face. He
needed to buy a few moments. This close combat
fighting was taking a toll on him. He needed
to get some distance on them and knew how. It
was time to channel a little of his inner
Elric.

For absolutely no reason, other than to make him smile, he clapped his hands together and then knelt to place his right hand on the ground. He quickly pulled his Earth Magic to him and caused the dirt under him to swirl into a rod as he pulled it out of the land. He kept pulling the rod up and transforming the entire thing to a dense stone as he did. He kept rising, and when it reached about chest high, he caused the bottom to pull out in a full blade shape to make a Stone Spear.

Congratulations, you have discovered the Combination Spell: Summon: Stone Spear. You have gained 250 experience in Earth Magic and Fire Magic for discovering a known spell.

Summon: Stone Spear	
Requirements: Fire Magic and Earth Magic Mana Cost: 40 MP Cast Time: 4 seconds	Description: Calls forth a spear of stone from the ground for combat. This spear's damage is based on the user's Earth Magic level multiplied by 1.2.
Mastery Level: 1	

The three people facing him stood there with looks of wonder on their faces.

"You ready to try your luck?" Arthur asked with a sly grin.

"Get the bastard. Don't let his fancy tricks scare you." Lazaru bellowed.

Alex and Xavier rushed the three remaining people. Alex made his way for Arthur and swung the war hammer at him. Arthur knew he couldn't block that weapon and would need to dodge. Arthur dodged out of the way, but Alex's speed was faster and clipped him on his side. He stumbled and gasped as he felt the pain in his ribs.

Alex (Level 15) has dealt 40 HP damage to you with Iron War Hammer (Glancing Blow).

Shit! Arthur thought. If that had been a substantial hit, he was sure he'd be dead or disabled. He spun the shaft of his spear and swung the blunt end toward Alex's head. The man quickly jumped back out of range and tried to close in. Arthur expected this, so he promptly twisted the staff in his hands and swung back the other direction. Alex tried to jump back, but the blade of the spear cut into his chest and caused blood to trickle down the front of his shirt slowly.

You have dealt 40 damage to Alex (Level 15) with Stone Spear (Minor Bleed).

Alex slowed his approach and took his time feeling for a weakness. He calmly walked back and forth, trying to get an opening. Arthur heard a yell and watched Vana go down. She had a deep cut on her ribs and had fallen holding onto her side and unable to get up. Arthur didn't have any time to waste. Allendria was facing off against Xavier, and she was already exhausted. He decided to trip up Alex a bit, quite literally.

Since Alex was stalking back and forth, he waited, and right before he changed direction, Arthur silently conjured a short earth wall in his reverse path. When Alex turned and headed back, his boot caught the wall, and he stumbled to a knee. Arthur used that chance to stab forward with his spear and stabbed the man high in his left shoulder.

You have dealt 130 damage to Alex (Level 15) with Stone Spear (Critical Strike).

Arthur quickly pulled the spear out and stabbed it into Alex's chest. The man crumpled to the ground.

You have dealt 130 damage to Alex (Level 15) with Stone Spear (Critical Strike) (Mortal Blow) (Fatal Blow).

Arthur turned and darted the short distance to Allendria. Xavier ducked one of her strikes and hit her in the head with the hilt of one of his daggers. She fell to the ground and couldn't seem to get back up. She looked a little dazed and unsteady as she tried to make her way up onto an arm.

Xavier had turned in time to see him approach, but Arthur had already committed to the strike. He plunged his spear into the man's side, but the momentum of Xavier's arm caused his dagger to go into Arthur's left leg simultaneously.

You have dealt 125 damage to Xavier (Level 15) with Stone Spear (Critical Strike) (Mortal Blow) (Fatal Blow).

*Xavier (Level 15) has dealt 30 HP damage
to you with Iron Dagger (Crippled Left Leg)
(Minor Bleed).*

Arthur fell to the ground in pain, and
his vision was flaring red. He was down to
only 50 HP, but Xavier had gone still. At
least Allendria would be safe.

"Well, well, well, what a shame. The
valiant party falls, and all are on the
ground. It looks like I get the pleasure of
the dark elf's company all to myself, after
all. Don't worry I'll also make sure your
ranger friend gets her share of attention too.
I will take my time with both of them, and
then I'll kill them both off. Can't let people
that powerful live to oppose us again." Lazaru
said with a smile on his face.

Arthur looked up at the man with disgust
in his face. People like him should be wiped
clear off from the face of this planet. If he
had his way, that would be the case, and he
wouldn't feel a single bit of remorse.

"I'm impressed you managed to stand up to
us and get to this point. The people you took
out were borderline useless, but that's what
happens in this line of business. We always
have a steady supply of these disposable
people, though. I'll finish you off, take your
nice weapons and armor, and travel to Seora
and pick up some more hands to come back and
kill all the villagers. Without all of you
here to help, they'll be easy to deal with."

Arthur was furious at this point. If nothing else, he was now sure that Lord Golgara and every one of his enforcers needed to die. Lazaru started slowly walking over toward Allendria as his eyes roamed all over her in a predatory manner. This only served to infuriate him more. Arthur was able to grind his teeth together and slowly force himself up. It was a slow process, but he made it to his feet, although he wasn't very steady on them.

"I'm not going to give you that chance. I'll protect my friends and the people of this village." Arthur told him vehemently.

Lazaru kept walking toward Allendria and didn't even change pace.

"Ha, how do you plan on doing that? You can barely stand up. I think a stiff breeze might finish you off. I might just take her in front of you, though. It would be interesting to see the look of defeat in your eyes. Do you think she will cry? It would be ni…"

Arthur's fury had been building higher as the man spoke. He couldn't understand what was happening, but he felt an immense heat flush through him. Out of instinct, he raised his hand with his palm facing Lazaru.

"DRAGONFIRE!" he screamed out in rage.

A searing, white-hot, flame burst from his palm and slammed into Lazaru. The man's mouth opened to scream, but the fire melted him away. Arthur could only see his silhouette as the man was burned to ashes in front of his eyes.

"Burn you bastard," Arthur muttered to himself.

Chapter 30

Revelations

Arthur slumped to the ground, exhausted. Lazaru was a smoldering pile of ash with a few bits here and there that hadn't completely burned. Arthur wasn't sure what had happened.

Alex (Level 15) has died.

Congratulations, you have learned Spears for a 100 experience bonus.

Congratulations, you have reached level 13! You now have 5 available skill points. Looking good, champ.

Xavier (Level 15) has died.

Congratulations, you have reached level 2 in Spears. Strikes with two-handed weapons deal 3% more damage. I liked the flair of that summoning. Stop stealing moves, though.

You have dealt 500 damage to Lazaru (Level 16) with Dragonfire.

Lazaru (Level 16) has died.

Congratulations, you have reached level 6 in Light Armor. Movement speed increased by 15% when wearing Light Armor. The bastard deserved that.

Congratulations, you have learned the Bloodline Ability: Dragonfire for a 500 experience bonus.

You have gained 5600 total experience in Light Armor for the fight.

You have gained 4550 total experience in Swords for the fight.
You have gained 3850 total experience in Small Blades for the fight.
You have gained 3850 total experience in Dual Wield for the fight.
You have gained 920 total experience in Fire Magic for the fight.
You have gained 240 total experience in Earth Magic for the fight.
You have gained 700 total experience in Block for the fight.
You have gained 1400 total experience in Parry for the fight.
You have gained 700 total experience in Spears for the fight.
You have gained 13850 total experience for the fight.

Bloodline Ability: Dragonfire	
Requirements: Fire Magic, House of Firebrand Spell Damage: 500 HP Cast Time: Instant	Description: Summon pure Dragonfire to deal with your enemies. Only useable once a day and only useable by a member of the Firebrand Family.
Mastery Level: 1	

Arthur heard trumpets blaring in his head.

Defend Alem's Crossing

Requirements: Level 12 Rewards: 25000 experience, 7500 skill experience to allocate as you choose, unknown rewards also possible.	Description: The village is under attack. Rally your friends and defend the village. Go forth protectors of righteousness and end the threat.
You have successfully fulfilled the required objectives. Do you wish to complete this quest now? Yes/No	

Arthur couldn't hit YES fast enough on that prompt. He had already healed and was back on his feet from when Alex had finally bled out. Now he felt a rush of experience flow over him.

Congratulations, you have reached level 14! You now have 10 available skill points. Is that what you call teamwork?

Congratulations, you have reached level 15! You now have 15 available skill points. Hey, where is your worthless pet?

You have 7500 unallocated skill experience to use at any time. Do you wish to use any now? Yes/No

Arthur heard the cheering of a large crowd in his head.

Congratulations, you have been blessed by the Goddess Lianna for fulfilling this quest and have gained the title of Righteous Defender.

Title: Righteous Defender

Arthur couldn't believe it. He had earned a title and three levels to go with it, not to mention the experience for skills. He told himself he would wait on it but was sure that experience would go toward combat skills. He had no problem gaining experience in crafting skills or magical skills. The combat arts were what was holding him back. There were also talents to look at now that he had leveled many skills in the fight.

Arthur went and knelt by Allendria's side. She was shaking and trying to regain control of herself. He grabbed her shoulder.

"It's okay, Allendria. You're safe now. I saw the hit you took and knew it shook you up. Accept the defense quest, and everything will be good."

Arthur sat there watching her for a few moments as she slowly regained composure and then suddenly went perfectly still and sat up straight to look at him. She had a slightly scared look in her eyes, but she smiled at him and wrapped her arms around him, anyway. He kissed her on the cheek and held her tightly.

Looking around, he saw Vana stand up, good as new, shortly followed by Samson.

"Dear maker, a title…" He said in awe.

"Holy shit! That's amazing." Vana exclaimed.

Vana took off to Zeke and started slowly trying to bring the man back to consciousness so he could accept the quest and restore his health as well.

"Woo Hoo!" said James as he came sprinting back. "A title and some well-earned levels. I'll be damned if that wasn't as intense as hell. I thank you for bailing me out there at the end, Arthur. I was almost done for had you not showed up when you did."

"We watch out for each other, James. That's how we roll." Arthur told him with a smile.

I'm also pleased you survived intact. Balair told him mentally.

"Where the fuck were you, you useless damn dragon!" Arthur yelled as he looked around.

You honestly didn't expect me to fight people twice my level, did you? I know I'm a dragonling and all, but there are limits for me too. You had it covered, and I had faith you would awaken. He told him cryptically.

"What the hell do you mean, awaken?" Arthur asked.

"Um… Arthur, your hair changed color…" Allendria said slowly as she looked at him.

"That's not possible. How would my hair change color?" He asked.

"I'm guessing it's because of who you are. It would be a family trait, although you're supposed to be dead." Allendria said to him in disbelief.

"Allendria, nothing you're saying is making any sense," Arthur said, exasperated.

"Arthur, your hair has turned a purple color. There's only one family in all of this world who has distinct hair that was that color, and they were all killed 100 years ago. King Tristan Firebrand, Queen Violet Firebrand, and their infant son Arturian Firebrand."

Our current king led a coup against them and hunted them down. When he finally trapped them, he killed them before they could find help. It was said he murdered Tristan first because he stayed back to buy time for Violet to summon a gate to escape through. She was trying to flee with young Arturian. The story goes that he killed her and the child before she could complete the gate. With you being here, though, she must have cast the gate and sent you through to safety before she was killed." She told him.

Arthur sat down on the ground for a moment. There was no way that could be right. That was far too long ago. He would have already grown old and died by now if that was true. He couldn't possibly be this Arturian Firebrand.

Lianna, is this true? He whispered in his mind.

I'm sorry you found out this way, Arthur, but yes, it is. I told you coming here would be the chance for you to discover what happened to your parents. Allendria speaks the truth, but you were sent through the gate before they got to your mother. Out of fear, the current king lied to hold his power after he overthrew your parents. Your parents had the power of dimensional magic and were able to escape, but he kept finding them, and they couldn't figure out how. She told him solemnly.

This is possible because time doesn't always flow normally with dimensions. When your mother crossed dimensions with her spell, it was hasty and not well planned out. It was an emergency decision, and when it happened, it sent you as an infant many years into the future in the dimension you lived in on Earth. When I brought you back, I did it in a stable gate, and there was no time distortion. You are Arturian Firebrand, true born prince of this land and rightful king. I would be careful about letting that information spread too quickly, or it might bring more trouble than you can handle in a short time. I'm so very proud of you, my champion. You have done much to help this village and bring these people out of their squalor. It's time you start expanding your village and preparing defenses. This is just the beginning of your struggle. I wish you the best; she said as her voice faded from his mind.

"I'm Arturian Firebrand," Arthur whispered to himself. "That's why I never knew my real parents and why John and Eve could never give me any details about them. They honestly didn't know."

He looked up to Allendria with tears in his eyes.

"What did my parents do to deserve this?" he demanded.

Allendria sighed and looked sad. "They did nothing wrong, Arthur. When your parents ruled this country, it flourished. There were amicable relationships with most of the races. Armed conflict was also something they prevented much of. They were betrayed for greed and malice. King Wailyn and some of their court betrayed them. Almost no one knew what happened until after your parents were dead, and Wailyn had already assumed control of the capital. Some cities held out against him, and many other races turned their backs on him, that's why the Dark Elves no longer have relations with humans."

Arthur thought about this for a moment and looked to Balair, who'd come down and landed near him.

"You knew all of this, you little shit, and you didn't tell me?"

He made a sighing noise in Arthur's mind. *I did not know what happened to your family, but I knew you were a Firebrand. Only a member of the Firebrand family could have summoned one of my kind because of your bloodline. You have the power of dragons in your blood. I assumed you would find out when you needed to know.*

Arthur grunted at him. "What fine timing this is. I don't even know what to do with this information."

"I'd suggest you keep it quiet as long as you can. The hair will set off some alarms, but most out there will probably not remember that. You could say it was a problem with some errant magic during the fight. The time of your parents was so long ago most of the people still alive wouldn't remember much of them." Allendria told him.

"Fine," he said as he waved it away, "it doesn't change any of my goals, anyway. I'm still the same person I've always been. I guess all of you turned in your quest and got your titles?" He asked as he looked around.

They all beamed with pride and nodded at him.

"To think a Goddess herself blessed me. She is the one you have been doing this work for correct?" Samson asked.

"The very same one," Arthur told him with a nod.

Samson fell to his knees and looked up to the sky.

"Goddess Lianna. I want to become a paladin on your behalf, sworn to the service of Arturian Firebrand, the rightful king of Dravincia!" he yelled to the sky.

They all looked around nervously for a moment until a golden light enveloped Samson.

"Oh my dear Samson, I could never deny the request from one as valiant and stalwart as you. I name you Paladin and Grandmaster of the Order of Aduro on the world of Dravincia. Go forth and serve well, my brave soul."

As she finished speaking, the light that had surrounded him faded. He stood up in a daze. Everyone around was staring at each other with dumbfounded looks.

Arthur was the first to shake away the confusion. "Congratulations, Paladin Samson. She couldn't have picked a better person for the job." Arthur told him seriously.

"I thank you for bringing life and a purpose back to me, Arthur. Now it's time we fix the wrongs that have been done here." He said.

"You're ever so correct in that. We have a bit of time before we're on the radar again, or at least I hope, and it should allow us a chance to fortify and build. I want this place turned into a proper village. No more run-down and collapsing buildings. Hopefully, word will make it to surrounding villages, and we can have some of the villagers come to join us here for safety. We finally have some crops planted and are still foraging for more. With some magic, we can truly turn this place around. That being said, I have a lot of skill points and experience to allocate." Arthur said with a laugh.

All the others joined him in the laughter. He looked at Balair and noticed that the dragon had gained levels as well. The little freeloader had jumped to level 10 with the quest Arthur turned in. Hopefully, that would get him to be a bit more useful, but Arthur doubted it. They walked back to the village and were chatting like old friends. Zeke had gotten back on his feet and after accepting the quest, was as good as new. All of them walked into the village with bloody and cut up clothing but looking as healthy as can be.

When they got close to the inn, people started streaming out of it and cheering for them. They all waved at the attention but kept walking. Leveling may have restored all of their stamina and health, but they were still mentally tired from the fight. They made it inside, and Daniel and Dalia approached.

Arthur smiled at them both. "The day is won. The entire group has been killed, and the village is safe."

The crowd broke out into cheering and clapping. Arthur held up his hands for them to calm down.

"The Goddess Lianna blessed the fight and handed us titles for the defense of the village. The biggest news, though, is that Goddess Lianna has named Samson as a Paladin and Grandmaster of the new Order of Aduro!"

The cheering was even louder this time around, and Samson looked around shyly at all the attention. Arthur let the crowd carry on for a while with their enthusiasm. When it finally died down, he spoke up again.

"We have come far in this village, but the road still has a ways to go. Now is the time to get the battlefield cleaned up and get the village back to work. There are big plans in progress. That being said, my first order of business is to visit our great bathhouse to wash the filth off of me." Arthur said to a mixture of cheers and chuckles.

He made his way to Daniel and Dalia and hugged them both.

"We did it!" He told them both.

"We sure did," Daniel said with a smile.

"Thank the Goddess," Dalia said.

"Thank the Goddess, indeed," Arthur told her.

Arthur made his way up the stairs and stripped off most of his combat armor. He kept his bag on him but carried the armor pieces back downstairs. If left upstairs, it would make his room smell like rotten blood, and it needed to be cleaned. He made it downstairs and set it by the washroom and let Daniel know. Daniel just nodded and said he'd have someone take care of it.

Allendria made her way downstairs at this time, as well. He grabbed her hand, and they rushed off to the bathhouse. They both soaked in the water and let its warmth relax their stress away. After an hour of sitting in the warm water, they decided it was again time to hit the ground running.

They dried off and got dressed in some extra clothes they had brought. They walked out to the wall and helped people as they were cleaning up the mess. The bandits were being stripped of anything that could be used. The cloth from their clothing could be repurposed, and none of them had much gear. It was no wonder many of them were so easy to kill. The occasional iron dagger would pop up, and of course, Lazaru had the iron sword he had used, but mostly everything they found needed to be melted and reforged into something useful.

Arthur took the time while doing the mind-numbing work of cleaning up the bodies to work on his stats. He looked at his current status.

Name: Arthur Firebrand	
Level: 15	
Age: 26	
Race: Human	
HP: 290/290	
MP: 480/480	
Stamina: 290/290	
Strength: 8	**Experience:** 12580/15000 (25 stat points available)
Agility: 16	
Intellect: 20	
Wisdom: 10	**Skills** (125% boost to any skill for level up)
Endurance: 14	**Combat Skills:**
Charisma: 5	
Luck: 7	**Archery:** 6 (525/1900)

	- Aim Shot: 2 (495/750)
	Block: 2 (380/750)
	Dual Wield: 5 (975/1900)
	Identify: 1 (75/500)
	Light Armor: 6 (300/2500)
	Parry: 3 (550/750)
	Scan: 4 (100/1400)
	Small Blades: 6 (795/2500)
	Spears: 2 (200/750)
	Stealth: 1 (370/500)
	  - Detect Hidden: 1 (50/500)
	Swords: 6 (605/2500)
	Unarmed: 1 (275/500)
	
	Magic:
	
	Earth Magic: 18 (3525/38000)
	  - Earthen Wall (2)
	  - Excavate (1)
	  - Flatten Earth (1)
	  - Magical Prospecting (2)
	  - Raise Stone Wall (1)
	  - Stone Building Wall (1)
	  - Transform Earth: Stone (1)
	  - Transform Stone: Gravel (1)
	Fire Magic: 17 (17945/30000)
	  - Arcane Forging (2)

	- **Arcane Furnace** (1)
	- **Basic Firebolt** (1)
	- **Weak Flame** (1)
	
	Professions:
	
	Barter: 3 (100/1000)
	Blacksmithing: 9 (1210/4600)
	  - **Alternate Heating:** 1 (160/500)
	  - **Arcane Smithing:** 7 (130/2500)
	Cooking: 2 (400/750)
	Enchanting: 7 (1075/3200)
	Farming: 7 (0/3200)
	Firemaking: 2 (700/750)
	Herbalism: 5 (660/1900)
	Leatherworking: 7 (195/3200)
	Mining: 6 (2400/2500)
	  - **Magical Mining** 6 (2025/2500)
	Skinning: 4 (175/1400)
	Woodworking: 1 (40/500)

He was somewhat surprised to see his name
had changed to add in his surname. There was
no way to tell if that were something others
could see or not, though. It was time to round
out his stats a bit. He put four points into
Strength to give his attacks a little extra
damage and added four into Agility for a speed
boost. He put three points into Intellect for
the added mana and two into Wisdom. His mana
regen rate was already formidable, but a
little more never hurt. That and it also gave
him a slight boost to his mana pool. Six
points went into Endurance to provide him with
a larger health pool and he decided he wanted
to put four into Charisma. He was hoping he
could do more of this diplomatically instead
of having to always fight over everything.
Finally, he dropped two in Luck to make it up
to nine.

The skill percentage boost could wait for
now. There was also 7,500 experience to play
with for skills. He also had four combat
skills he needed to dig through the talent
trees for. The talent trees would be the first
order of business. He brought up his new
talent tree for Dual Wield.

You have 2 unused Talent Points.

Talent	Description
Tier 1	
Off Hand Power (0/5)	Increases damage of your off-hand weapon by 5% per point.
Deflection (0/5)	Increases your chance to successfully parry by 5% per point.

Arm Strength (0/5)	Increases damage of your main hand weapon by 5% per point.

All of those were pretty straightforward. Arthur went with Deflection for his first choice and then pulled up the tree again to see the second-tier options.

You have 1 unused Talent Point.

Talent	Description
Tier 2	
Off Hand Coordination (0/1)	Allows you to use an off-hand, full-size, one-handed weapon without additional penalties to off-hand speed or accuracy.
Main Hand Dexterity (0/10)	Increases swing speed with main hand weapon by 3% per point.

Arthur decided he would put another in Deflection. He was more worried about survivability than anything else. He next checked his talent tree for Light Armor.

You have 4 unused Talent Points.

Talent	Description
Tier 1	
Reinforced Armor (0/5)	While wearing at least 4 pieces of Light Armor, increases the base armor of all pieces of Light Armor worn by 3% per piece.

Flexible Stitching (0/5)	*While wearing at least 4 pieces of Light Armor, increases your speed by 3% per point.*
Proper Care (0/5)	*Wearing at least 4 pieces of Light Armor increases the durability by 3% per point.*

He weighed the options and thought all of them had merit. He put a point in Reinforced Armor and checked it again.

You have 3 unused Talent Points.

Talent	**Description**
Tier 2	
Leather Repair (0/1)	*An ability that allows you to close any cuts or holes in light armor leather pieces and restores 15% of its durability.* *Cooldown: 24 Hours*
Armor Modification (0/3)	*Each point in this skill grants you a special ability as follows:* • *1 point – Allows you to add additional leather pieces to your armor to increase its base defense rating.*

	- *2 points - Allows you to add small metal bands to any light armor you have to increase its base defense rating.* - *3 points - Allows you to add beveled metal bands to add block rating to light armor pieces you have.*
Leather Armor Expertise (0/10)	*While wearing at least 4 pieces of Light Armor, increases the base armor and durability of all Light Armor worn by 3% per point.*

It was nice having the boosts to armor stats, and the second tier boosted not only the armor rating but also the durability. That being said, Arthur decided he wanted the Leather Repair ability. He needed a quick way to patch up his armor after a day of fighting. The other two points went into Armor Modification. He looked down and saw the cuts he had in his leather from the fight and knew the skill would come in very handy. He also activated the ability and watched the leather pieces of his armor all meld back together. He noticed the durability had returned on his armor pieces too. He then pulled up his Small Blades talents.

You have 4 unused Talent points.

Talent	Description
Tier 1	
Bleeding Strikes (0/5)	Wounds caused by Small Blades will deal 4% additional bleed damage per point.
Blurring Speed (0/5)	Attack speed with Small Blades increases by 3% per point.
Riposte (0/1)	If any of your attacks are parried, you are able to activate this skill for a guaranteed hit with your Small Blade. Cooldown: 45 seconds

Arthur didn't hesitate and chose Riposte. A guaranteed hit on a target to get past their defense was great. He looked at the tier 2 options.

You have 3 unused Talent Points.

Talent	Description
Tier 2	
Twist (0/10)	Each point causes wounds inflicted by Small Blades to deal 3% additional damage.
Blade Weaver (0/10)	Increases your chance to parry blows with Small Blades by 2% per point.

He decided to put all three points into
Blade Weaver. They were all decent options,
but he typically used his dagger for parrying
while blocking with his sword. There was only
one new talent tree to look through, so he
pulled up his tree for swords.

You have 4 unused Talent Points.

Talent	Description
Tier 1	
Powerful Strikes (0/5)	Increases base damage of swords you use by 1 point per talent point.
Blade Forms (0/5)	Each point increases your swing speed with swords by 2%.
Passata Sotto (0/1)	A melee ability that allows you to avoid an incoming strike by ducking down low and then counter-attacking with an upward angled thrust. Cost: 10 Stamina

Arthur wouldn't turn down another melee
ability, so he put the first point in Passata
Sotto. He then pulled up Tier 2 talents as
well.

You have 3 unused Talent Points.

Talent	Description
Tier 2	

Heavy Guard (0/10)	Each point increases your chance to successfully block attacks by 2%. More points also allow you to block stronger attacks.
Deflection (0/10)	Increases your chance to parry blows with Swords by 2% per point.

The final three points went into Heavy Guard to complement his style well. He would worry about his bonus points at a later time, though. There wasn't anything he just had to have.

His group and many of the villagers worked into the afternoon to clear the field of bodies. They got the bodies stripped of useful items and all piled up in one location outside the walls. They had planned on burying them all but decided against it. Instead, Arthur and Allendria would use their Fire Magic to incinerate the bodies to avoid a lot of extra work. It would take them more than a day to dig the holes and bury all the bandits, but they could turn them to ashes in much less time. Arthur would have to learn a new fire spell for this, though, and he was sure it would cost all his mana to pull it off on a fire this big.

After everyone else had cleared away, he stepped up next to Allendria for this spell.

"You need to focus on refining your magic into a hotter form. You can't just pour out fire magic until you run out of mana. Instead, concentrate and circulate the mana in front of your hands until the temperature of the spell reaches the right height. From there, push the fire outward from you, and the circulation will keep the fire hot."

Arthur nodded at her explanation. He wasn't about to second guess her when it came to fire magic.

"Alright, let's do this."

Arthur put his hands up and focused on his Fire Magic and started to swirl his magic to build the heat as Allendria had told him. He could feel the heat rising in front of his hands and had to instinctually increase the power he channeled to protect himself from the heat. When it reached the right temperature, he pushed forward on the mana and poured the magic through the swirl. He pictured it like a heater from Earth with a heating coil that pushed air through it to warm it. This was the same principle but all with rapidly heating magical currents instead of metal coils.

The fire flew forward and started rapidly eating away at the corpses. The sight of it threatened to make Arthur hurl. He had to fight his impulse and push onward with the flame. Allendria added her fire to the mix when she had seen he had a grasp of it. Arthur watched as his mana steadily dove. He couldn't figure out how Allendria had learned this spell in the first place. She had a smaller mana pool than he did but somehow could still figure this one out. Arthur could only guess she had learned a more modest version and strengthened it with talents.

They let the flames continue to pour, and when Arthur was down to 60 mana, his fire ended, and a message appeared.

Congratulations, you have discovered the Fire Magic Spell: Blazing Inferno. You have gained 250 experience in Fire Magic for discovering a known spell.
You have gained 120 experience in Fire Magic for successfully casting Blazing Inferno.

Blazing Inferno	
Requirements: Fire Magic Mana Cost: 80 MP Cast Time: 4 seconds	Description: Summons white-hot flame to burn everything directly in front of the caster. The damage of this spell is based on the distance from the caster. *This spell can be used to incinerate corpses and infected organic matter. Base damage: 120HP
Mastery Level: 1	

That was a nice amount of damage but a high mana cost. Arthur might need to practice it to increase mastery. It might make the spell more cost-effective. They left a pile of ashes as they traveled back into the walls of the village. Arthur and Allendria, once again, went to the bathhouse together. They needed to clean the dirt and ash from them after working on getting the bodies removed.

They both stripped and walked into the bathhouse water. They quickly scrubbed off and relaxed in each other's arms. Arthur was idly playing with her hair when she looked directly into his eyes.

"I've made my decision. I think I'm ready now," she said to him.

"Ready for what? Were we supposed to be doing something I forgot about?"

She smiled at him seductively. "Oh, I think you know what I'm talking about."

Arthur remembered their conversation from the night in the inn, and his breath caught in his throat. He put on a smile, and they got out of the bath and threw on their clothes. They made their way back to the inn and up to Arthur's room. She entered behind him, and he quickly closed the door and bolted it shut. He rushed to her and started kissing her passionately. He ran his hands up her back and into her hair. He lightly pulled back on her hair while continuing his kisses down to her neck. He came back up and nibbled on her ear and heard her moan.

Both of them started pulling clothing off of each other as quickly as their hands could get it off and fell into bed naked together. They spent the entire night exploring every inch of each other and fell asleep drained, but pleased.

                          ✳ ✳ ✳

     The following morning dawned as usual,
but they stayed in bed together for a little
longer. The late-night activities had worn
them out, and they didn't feel like messing
with the typical day-to-day business. They
cuddled up together and laid there in peace.
     That peace was utterly shattered with
cries of alarm. They could hear screams from
outside the inn and could hear panicked
running throughout the bottom floor. They both
jumped out of bed and quickly dressed. They
threw weapons over their shoulders as they
went rushing downstairs. Arthur saw people
running every direction and stopped someone.
     "What is going on?" he asked.
     "We're not sure. Some big creature was
seen flying around the village."
     Arthur nodded to this and took off
outside. He needed to see this for himself. He
made his way through the crowd and started to
look around the sky. It didn't take him long
to spot the large shadow that was circling the
village. Rushing through the group, brought
him to Vana and Samson, standing together
arguing about it.
     "I'm telling you it's a long, scaled
creature with wings. Its appearance seems to
match the legends of the dragons," Vana said
heatedly.
     "Dragons haven't been seen since the
demise of the Firebrands. What makes you think
any of them would still be around or alive,"
Samson retorted.

"They were supposed to be long-lived creatures. There's no reason one couldn't be alive today. They just disappeared before. There's no record of them being hunted and killed off, so they may have just left. If I had to guess, it's here because of Arthur," Vana told him.

Arthur chose that moment to enter the conversation.

"Vana, what is that thing up there?" he asked, already fearing he knew the answer.

"I'm fairly certain it's a dragon," she told him.

"Are you sure?"

Allendria spoke up before Vana could answer. "That's indeed a dragon and a very odd colored one. There was only one I remember being told about that was that particular color. Violet scales were only mentioned by my father one time, and he told me she was one of the younger dragons. You should go talk to her, Arthur."

"What?" he screeched. "You expect me to go talk to a dragon? Are you out of your mind?" He asked her.

"Well, of course. The dragons were friends of your family. Did you think the Firebrand name was just a coincidence?"

"Fine. How am I supposed to do that?" Arthur asked in a resigned tone.

"I'd say go out to the wall alone and let her come to you," Allendria told him.

"I'll give it a shot, but if she kills me, I'm coming back to haunt you for life," he told her in mock seriousness.

Arthur made his way out of the village
and walked to the wall on the eastern edge.
The dragon spotted him by himself and swooped
down low. She made a quick pass over his head
and then banked and came back toward him. She
came to rest in front of him about eighty
yards away. Arthur gulped as he saw the size
of this creature.

She was the size of a school bus with a
broad nose and rows of razor-sharp teeth. She
had two massive horns that were twisted and
around six feet long. She had two spiked
protrusions from the side of her head that
extended backward and had the same membrane in
between them that was between the bones of her
wings. Her wingspan was impressive and looked
to be around sixty feet. Each wing had two
spiked bones that came from the main wing
bones and stuck out the bottom. She had one
more spike that extended to the end of her
wing.

She had four legs, with the front two
being slightly smaller. Her front legs looked
more like human arms and had claws with five
large nails on them. Her hind legs were built
much thicker and resembled the jointed rear
legs of a lion. Her tail extended out forty
feet and was only slightly shorter than her
body, but it had a ridge of spikes down the
back of it. The sight made Arthur think of the
pictures of a stegosaurus he had seen back on
Earth. This creature exuded power, and its
focus was on Arthur.

Arthur sucked it up and slowly made his
way toward the dragon. She shifted back and
forth on her legs as he approached. When he
got within twenty yards, she lowered her head,
so her eyes were even with his, and it felt
like she stared directly into his soul. Her
eyes were a bright purple that seemed to match
well with the darker purple of her scales.
When he got within ten feet of her, he
stopped.

"Hello, Dragon. Can I have your name? I
prefer to call you by name if possible," he
said nervously.

She looked at him and cocked her head to
the side a bit. After a few uncomfortable
moments, where Arthur was sure he'd be eaten,
she finally answered. Her voice was a melodic
sound with a feminine quality.

"Young Arturian, I guess you don't
remember me. My name is Calfuray, and we were
once soul bonded to each other before you
disappeared a hundred years ago," She told him
in a sad tone.

Epilogue

Confrontation

"You Bitch!" a harsh voice rang out across the white space. Lianna had been relaxing in a chair in her white abyss while reveling the progress of her champion on Dravincia. He had been progressing well, and it looked like her gamble of returning a lost son of the loved Firebrand family would pay dividends. She turned to face the voice.

"I don't recall inviting you in here, Bell," Lianna said sweetly.

"Don't you dare call me that! Who the hell do you think you are? Do you think you could put a champion on one of my worlds and get away with it without me finding out?"

Lianna knew that Isabell hated being called by Bell, and that was precisely why she had done it. They had been bitter rivals for eons.

"Of course, I knew you would find out. I'm not sure what you plan to do about it. My champion is formidable, and I have high hopes he will return the world to my control. Dravincia will be mine again, dear sister." She spat out, the last as a curse.

"Ha, you honestly think your plans will work? I'm not sure where you found a person dumb enough to accept you as a Goddess on this mission, but I feel sorry for them. Once my representatives take care of him, I can go back to forgetting you ever existed." Isabell told her derisively.

Lianna was pleased with this. It looked like Isabell hadn't discovered who her champion was but only that she had one. She couldn't wait to see the fear in the woman's eyes when she found out the truth. Her representative had been responsible for the coup that killed Arthur's parents. This world had been under Lianna's control for hundreds of years before that. She wasn't about to tell her his identity, though. She wanted to make sure Arthur had all the time he could get to prepare. If Isabell found out who her champion was, she would send absolutely everything she had, and he couldn't hope to hold out this early.

"We shall see. You won this war last time, but I have high hopes for my current champion. He is resourceful and seems to know how to fight better than some of the bottom feeders you call followers."

"You watch your tone with me."

"Ha, what do you think you are going to do? There isn't anything you can do to me. We are Gods, and we can't harm each other directly." Lianna said.

"Oh, I know, but you have other worlds I could go for next. I have been content to leave our rivalry alone after I took Dravincia, but it appears I need to resume my work." She said with a sinister grin.

"You can try, dear sister. I've beaten you plenty of times in the past and will do so again."

"Prepare yourself then, sister. It's time for us to go to war, and your champion on Dravincia is doomed." Isabell said with an evil smile.

End Notes

Thank you for reading The Dimensional Wars, Book 1: Dravincia. It was a pleasure to write this book, and I hope you enjoyed it. I have high hopes for this series with a lot of twists and turns to come.

As always, if you enjoyed the book, please leave a review on whatever site you prefer. Reviews are a fantastic way to help support my books and feel free to spread the word yourself.

This is a work of fiction. Names, characters, places, and events are either the products of the Author's imagination or used in a fictitious manner. Any resemblance to actual persons, living or dead, is purely coincidental.

If you are looking for more book recommendations, or if you feel like chatting about books you have already read. Go to the LitRPG Books group on FaceBook.

If you want to see updates on The Dimensional Wars or if you have any questions, comments, or corrections you wish to share with me let me know on The Dimensional Wars FaceBook page.

To learn more about LitRPG, talk to authors including myself, and just have an awesome time, please join the LitRPG Group.

If you want updated news about releases please subscribe to my mailing list by emailing me at thedimensionalwars@gmail.com.

Final Character Stats

Name: Arthur Firebrand
Level: 15
Age: 26
Race: Human
HP: 410/410
MP: 560/560
Stamina: 410/410

Strength: 12
Agility: 20
Intellect: 23
Wisdom: 12
Endurance: 20
Charisma: 9
Luck: 9

Experience: 12580/15000 (0 stat points available)

Skills (125% boost to any skill for level up)
Combat Skills:

Archery: 6 (525/1900)
  - **Aim Shot:** 2 (495/750)
Block: 2 (380/750)
Dual Wield: 5 (975/1900)
Identify: 1 (75/500)
Light Armor: 6 (300/2500)
Parry: 3 (550/750)
Scan: 4 (100/1400)
Small Blades: 6 (795/2500)
Spears: 2 (200/750)
Stealth: 1 (370/500)
  - **Detect Hidden:** 1 (50/500)
Swords: 6 (605/2500)
Unarmed: 1 (275/500)

Magic:

Earth Magic: 18 (3525/38000)
  - Earthen Wall (2)
  - Excavate (1)
  - Flatten Earth (1)
  - Magical Prospecting (2)
  - Raise Stone Wall (3)
  - Stone Building Wall (1)
  - Transform Earth: Stone (1)
  - Transform Stone: Gravel (1)
Fire Magic: 17 (18315/30000)
  - Arcane Forging (2)
  - Arcane Furnace (1)
  - Basic Firebolt (1)
  - Weak Flame (1)

Professions:

Barter: 3 (100/1000)
Blacksmithing: 9 (1210/4600)
  - Alternate Heating: 1 (160/500)
  - Arcane Smithing: 7 (130/2500)
Cooking: 2 (400/750)
Enchanting: 7 (1075/3200)
Farming: 7 (0/3200)
Firemaking: 2 (700/750)
Herbalism: 5 (660/1900)
Leatherworking: 7 (195/3200)

	Mining: 6 (2400/2500) **- Magical Mining** 6 (2025/2500) **Skinning:** 4 (175/1400) **Woodworking:** 1 (40/500)